UNITED STATES OF JAPAN

"*United States of Japan* is a powerful book, unsettling at times – surreal and hypnotic. There's a bit of Philip K Dick in here, and *Wind-Up Bird Chronicle*, but Peter Tieryas is his own voice, a talented author, somebody to keep an eye on for sure. I loved his last book, *Bald New World*, and I loved this one, too."
  Richard Thomas, author of Breaker *and* Disintegration

"Mind-twisting and fiercely imaginative; Tieryas fuses classic sci-fi tradition with his own powerful vision."
  Jay Posey, author of the Legends of the Duskwalker series

"A tense and intriguing read, a blend of alt history and cyberpunk and thriller. I mean, 1988 California where San Diego is a razed landscape home to American rebels, and Japanese mechas patrol the coast? Heck yes!"
  Beth Cato, author of The Clockwork Dagger

"If you took the world building of Philip K Dick, and added in the gritty reality and humor of Haruki Murakami, with a touch of Aldous Huxley (of course), you would get *Bald New World*. An emerging voice... leading to a devastating conclusion."
  Buzzfeed

"Gorgeous language choices... a deceptively deep story."
  Publishers Weekly reviewing Bald New World

D0995913

PETER TIERYAS

UNITED STATES OF JAPAN

ANGRY
ROBOT

ANGRY ROBOT
An imprint of Watkins Media Ltd

Lace Market House,
54-56 High Pavement,
Nottingham,
NG1 1HW
UK

angryrobotbooks.com
twitter.com/angryrobotbooks
Meet your mecha

An Angry Robot paperback original 2016
1

A catalogue record for this book is available from the British Library.

ISBN 978 0 85766 532 4
EBook ISBN 978 0 85766 534 8

Set in Meridien and Agency by Epub Services.
Printed and bound in the UK by 4edge Limited.

Dedicated to the two Phils who changed my life:
  Phil K Dick, for firing the imagination of my youth.
  And Phil Jourdan, for believing in me.

War Relocation Authority Center #051
July 1, 1948
8:15am

The death of the United States of America began with a series of signatures. Twenty year-old Ruth Ishimura had no idea, imprisoned hundreds of mile away in a prison camp for Americans of Japanese descent. The camp was made up of dilapidated barracks, poorly constructed guard posts, and a barbed fence that surrounded the perimeter. Almost everything was covered in coats of dust and Ruth found it hard to breathe. She shared her room with eleven other women and two of them were comforting one of her roommates, Kimiko.

"They always send him back," her companions told her.

Kimiko was frayed, her eyes swollen from tears, throat congested with phlegm and dirt. "Last time, they beat Bernard so hard, he couldn't walk for a month." Bernard's only sin was that eight years ago his work took him to Japan for a month. Despite being completely loyal to America, he was under suspicion.

Ruth's cot was a mess, music sheets scattered over the army blankets. Two of the strings on her violin were broken and the third looked brittle enough to snap at any moment. Her instrument was lying next to faded music sheets from Strauss and Vivaldi. The table, the chairs, even the shelves were built from broken boxes, disassembled crates, and any spare parts they could find. The wood floors were dirty, even though they were swept every morning, and there were gaps she had to be careful not to trip on. The oil stove reeked of overuse and she wished they had something warmer for the freezing nights. She glanced over at Kimiko, who was crying even harder. "This is the first time they've kept him overnight," she said. "They always, always send him back."

Ruth could see the grim expression on both the women next to Kimiko. An overnight stay usually meant the worst. Ruth sneezed, feeling something stuck in her throat. She pounded her rib cages with the flat end of her fist, hoping her breath would clear. It was early in the morning and already getting hot – weather extremes were normal in this part of the desert. Her neck was covered in sweat and she looked over at the picture of a younger Kimiko, a comely lady who had grown up as heiress to what had once been a fortune.

"Ruth! Ruth!" Outside the barracks, her fiancé, Ezekiel Song, rushed towards the room. "All the guards are gone!" he exclaimed, as he entered.

Ruth rubbed the dust off Ezekiel's hair and asked, "What are you talking about?"

"The Americans are gone. No one's seen them all morning. Some of the elders are saying they saw them driving away."

Kimiko looked up. "The Americans are gone?"

Ezekiel gleamed. "Looks like it."

"Why?"

"I think they were scared away."

"Then it's really happening?" Kimiko asked, hope surging in her voice.

Ezekiel shrugged. "I don't know for sure. But I heard the Emperor demanded we all be freed."

"Why would he care about us?"

"Because we're all Japanese," Ruth suggested.

"I'm only half Japanese," Ezekiel replied. His other half was Chinese and he had a scrawny frame and bent shoulders that made him look shorter than he was. Ezekiel had a tanned complexion from his days working in the fields, his skin dried like a prune in sunlight. He was stout, a boyish charm hidden behind his curly black hair that formed a cowlick. "All the elders said we're American."

"Not anymore," Ruth said, aware even those with a sixteenth of Japanese blood in them had been sent to the Japanese-American prison camps independent of actual citizenship. She was thin like most of the other children, with noodly limbs and chapped lips. She had fair skin, although her hair was a disheveled mess that tangled into twisted knots. In contrast to Ezekiel, Ruth stood with poise and determination, refusing to let the dust unnerve her.

"What's wrong?" Ezekiel asked Kimiko.

"Bernard's been gone all night," Kimiko replied.

"Have you checked Wrath Rock?"

"We're not allowed."

"Guards aren't there anymore. We can go check now."

The five of them made their way out of the small room onto the prison grounds. There were hundreds of barracks equidistant to one another, arranged into dreary, desolate blocks. A sign read War Relocation Authority Center 51, which someone had crossed out and marked in substitution, *Wrath 51*. Most of the barrack walls were covered with tarred paper that was peeling away, brittle strips that had worn down from the fickle climate. They'd been layered over multiple times to buttress and strengthen the exterior, but their attempts at thickening the skin had only weakened the overall facade. There was the remains of a school, a baseball diamond, what might have passed as a shop, and the semblance of a community, though most of those were either abandoned or in ruins. It was a prison city with a veil of endless dirt and a scorching sun that imposed its will through an exhaustive haze of suppression.

As the group made their way to Wrath Rock, a crowd gathered around the guard tower in the north-west corner. "Go see what's happening," one of Kimiko's companions said.

Ezekiel and Ruth looked to Kimiko, who ignored the crowd and sprinted towards Wrath Rock without them.

The two approached the guard tower that several of the men had begun to investigate. Both the *Issei* and *Nissei* watched raptly, shouting instructions, asking questions every step of the way. Ruth did not recognize most of them; there were the elderly Issei who had been the first to immigrate to America, then the younger Nissei who were born in the States. Everyone was there, from the man with three moles on his pig nose to a lady who was wearing broken glasses, and the twins whose faces had diverged in the wrinkles formed from the way they reacted to the bitterness of their experiences. Suffering was an unbiased craftsman, molding flesh on bone, dark recesses dipping into pores of unmitigated tribulation. Most of the prisoners had only a few changes of clothing, keeping what they were wearing as clean as they could manage. Knit bindings prevented them from falling apart, subtly woven in to minimize inconsistencies in the fabric. The shoes were harder to mask as they were worn down, unable to be replaced, sandals and callused feet being common. There were many teens gathered, curious as to what all the noise was about.

"Make sure the Americans aren't hiding in a compartment."

"They could just be on break."

"Did they take their rations?"

"What about their weapons?"

The ones who searched came back after a few minutes and confirmed that the American soldiers had evacuated their posts, taking their weapons with them.

The commotion that followed mainly revolved around the question of what to do next.

"Go back home! What else should we do?" one of the younger men posed.

But the older ones were reluctant. "Go back to what? We don't even know what's going on or where we are."

"What if there's still fighting out there?"

"We'll be shot before we get anywhere."

"What if the Americans are just testing us?"

"Testing us for what? They're gone."

Ezekiel looked at Ruth and asked, "What do you want to do?"

"If this is true and they are letting us go... My parents never would have believed it."

It'd been several years since the soldiers came to her school class and ordered them to go outside and stand in line. She had thought it was for a field trip or something short because they only let her take one suitcase of her belongings. She cried so much when she discovered it was going to be their final day in San Jose and she hadn't brought any of her favorite books.

There were gasps and urgent exclamations as people pointed south. Ruth looked where the fingers were aiming. A small column of dust presaged a tiny jeep driving their way.

"Which flag is it?" one of the younger men asked.

Eyes went sharply to the side of the jeep, the dust cloud covering the markings.

"It's American."

"No, you *baka*. It's a big red circle."

"Are you blind? That's definitely American."

With the jeep getting closer, time seemed to stretch. What was only a few meters seemed like kilometers, and some even thought it might be a mirage, taunting them with the illusion of succor. The sun pounded them with its heat and their clothes were getting drenched from sweat and expectation.

Every breeze meant Ruth's lungs became a miasma of breathlessness, but she refused to leave.

"Do you see the flag yet?" someone asked.

"Not yet," another replied.

"What's wrong with your eyes?"

"What's wrong with *yours?*"

A minute later, it was close enough to espy the markings.

"It's someone from the Imperial Japanese Army."

The jeep came to a stop and a staunch young man stepped out. He was almost six feet tall and wore the brown uniform of a Japanese imperial soldier along with a *sennibari*, a red sash with a thousand stitches to bring good luck. The prisoners surrounded him and asked, "What's going on out there?"

Before answering them, he bowed to them. With tears bracing against his brows, he said, "You probably don't recognize me. My name is Sato Fukasaku and I'm a corporal in the IJA. You knew me as Steven when I escaped the camp four years ago and joined the Japanese army. I bring good news."

Ruth, like most of the others in the group, was incredulous. The Fukasaku boy was an emaciated fourteen year-old boy who was barely five feet tall when he disappeared. Other boys refused to let him play baseball because he was so small and struck out every time he was at bat.

"What's happened out there?" one of the women asked.

He looked at them with a giddy grin that belied his soldierly presence and stated, "We've won."

"Won what?"

"The American government surrendered this morning," he said. "This is no longer the United States of America, but the United States of Japan. Some rebels are on the run and they're trying to make a stand in Los Angeles, but it won't last long. Not after yesterday."

"What happened yesterday?"

"The Emperor unleashed a secret weapon to make the

Americans realize they have no chance. Buses are on the way and they should be here soon to take you to safety. You're all to be freed and provided new homes. The Emperor personally asked that you be taken care of. There are over two hundred thousand of us imprisoned throughout the camps who will now be given new opportunities in the USJ. Long live the Emperor!" he yelled.

The Issei instinctively yelled back, "Long live the Emperor," while the Nissei, having been born in the States, didn't know they were expected to yell correspondingly.

Fukasaku shouted again, *"Tenno Heika Banzai!"* which was Japanese for "long live the Emperor."

This time, everyone followed in unison: *"Banzai!"*

Ruth yelled too, surprised that, for the first time in her life, she felt something like awe swell up in her.

A military truck pulled in behind them.

"To celebrate the good news, we've brought food and *sake*," Fukasaku stated.

Then Ruth saw something she'd never seen before. Coming out of the driver's side was a woman in full Imperial uniform. She was ethnically mixed as she had blue eyes with her choppy black hair. Fukasaku saluted her and said, "Welcome, lieutenant."

She waved off his gesture, looked to the crowd with empathetic eyes, and said, "On behalf of the Empire, I honor all of you for your sacrifice and suffering." She bowed low and kept the stance, signifying her deep feeling. She spoke with a perfect English accent so she must have been Nissei. Ruth realized she wasn't the only one surprised by the female officer. The prisoners were staring at her, never having seen a male soldier salute a female superior. Ruth's eyes went to the *shin gunto*, the army sword that was a form of badge for any officer. "My name is Masuyo Yoshida. I grew up in San Francisco, like many of you, where I had a western identity as Erica Blake. My mother was a brave Japanese woman who taught me the importance of our culture. Like you, I was imprisoned, falsely accused of espionage, and separated from my family. The IJA rescued me and gave me a new Japanese name and identity to cast off my false Western one. We were never accepted as Americans, and it was our folly to seek it. I am now a lieutenant in the Imperial Japanese Army and you are all citizens of the Empire. All of you will be given new identities as well. We should celebrate!"

From the back of the truck, four soldiers carted out barrels of alcohol.

"Someone go get the cups."

It wasn't long before everyone was cheering the Emperor and asking Steven/Sato details about the war. Some of the elders took Lieutenant Yoshida on a tour of the prison grounds. Ezekiel's face was flushed red from the alcohol and he said to Ruth, "We both should join the army."

"What will you do? I can do more pushups than you can," she teased him.

"I'll get into shape." He flexed his muscles.

"It looks like a little mouse," she said, feeling the small bump on his arm. "Did you notice they both have the new Nambu Type 18 semi-automatic pistols?"

"I didn't even see their guns."

"The Type 18 is supposed to fix the weaker striker recoil springs and make them much stronger. The older model had 8mm cartridges and–"

Suddenly, there was screaming. Everyone turned around. There were multiple voices wailing from the direction of Wrath Rock. In the shock of all that had transpired, Ruth realized she had forgotten about Kimiko.

Wrath Rock was the only building with three floors in the complex, housing the soldiers as well as a special interrogation center. It was made of red bricks, a big rectangular building with two wings jutting from its sides. Disturbing howls often emanated from the building in the middle of the night, and depending on the angle and strength of the moonlight, it glowed like a crimson stone oozing blood rays. Everyone approaching the building did their best to suppress shudders. The American flag was still waving high above the Rock.

A dozen prisoners had been carried out, emaciated, bloodied, and bruised.

"What happened here?" Corporal Fukasaku asked.

A man wearing only a loincloth with half his hair ripped out shouted, "They killed my brothers and accused me of collaborating with the Empire. I wish I had!" He tried to spit on the ground, but his mouth was too dry to form anything. His scalp was covered with gashes, and his wide nostrils and bulging eyes made him resemble a chimpanzee. He was pulsing with anger and he yelled, "I'm an American and they treated me worse than their dogs."

The corporal replied, "The Emperor has come to save all of you. He has taken revenge on the Americans for all of us."

From the front door, Kimiko emerged, holding a body in her arms.

Ruth gasped. It was Bernard, but his legs were missing, only bandaged stumps in their place. Kimiko's face was wan and there was a shocked stillness in her eyes as though they'd been frozen. Ruth looked at Bernard to see if he was breathing, but she couldn't tell.

"Poor Kimiko," Ruth heard someone say. "Their family was so wealthy and now they've taken everything from her."

"The rich had it the hardest."

Many agreed with deploring nods.

"Sister..." Corporal Fukasaku began.

But, before he could continue, Kimiko demanded in rage, "Why didn't the Emperor save him? Why couldn't he have rescued us just a day earlier?"

"I am very sorry for your loss. Please keep in mind that it wasn't the Emperor who killed your friend, but the Americans. I assure you, the Emperor has taken revenge a hundredfold for what has happened to all of you here."

"I don't care about revenge. He's dead. HE'S DEAD!" she yelled. "If the Emperor was so almighty, why couldn't he have sent you a day earlier?"

"Calm yourself. I know you're upset, but speaking against the Emperor is forbidden."

"Fuck the Emperor. Fuck you. Fuck all Americans."

"I will only ask you once, and that's because I know you're not in a proper mental state. Do not speak against the Emperor or–"

"Or what? He'll take his revenge? I shit on him and the whol–"

Corporal Fukasaku raised his Nambu Type 18 semi-automatic pistol, pointed at her head, and fired. Her head exploded, brain and blood spraying the ground. She fell over, arms interlaced with her dead boyfriend.

"No one is allowed to speak against the Emperor," the corporal stated. He holstered his pistol, stepped around Kimiko's dead body, and went to reassure the other survivors that everything was going to be OK.

Everyone was too stunned to speak. Ezekiel was shaking. Ruth put her arm around him and asked, "Do you still want to be a soldier?" It was as much for herself as it was for him.

She looked back at Kimiko's body and did her best to hold back tears.

"You have to be strong," she said to Ezekiel, as she placed his hands on her belly. "For little Beniko, be strong."

South of San Jose
July 2, 1948
12:13pm

Ruth and Ezekiel were in one of the hundreds of buses driving south towards Los Angeles on the I-99. She looked at Ezekiel and recalled how their courtship had started over arguments about politics and religion. Those arguments turned into long diatribes about the nature of God and existence. Soon, they were fighting in each other's arms. Not long after that, they became lovers. She wondered if the feeling of imminent doom had fused them more tightly together.

Outside, Ruth saw a mountain of smoke that resembled a sea with its own waves within it. Streams of black were being written in a calligraphy of destruction, *kanji* painting lines of woe into the air that, like most suffering, indifferently blended into the rest. The warbling and the heat distortion made the horizon appear to be melting into the ground.

"The Germans have overrun the entire east coast," a man up front with a radio shouted, relaying news updates as he heard them. "Rommel is in Manhattan. The Fuhrer is supposed to arrive within the week. They've imprisoned Mayor La Guardia because he refuses to surrender, but someone else has accepted surrender terms in his place."

"What about San Jose?"

"No word."

The mayor of Los Angeles, Fletcher Bowron, spoke on the radio, assuring Americans, "This is a temporary transitional period. Don't resist the Japanese soldiers and you won't be harmed."

"I hope my uncle's OK," Ezekiel said to her. "He owns one of the biggest clothing factories in Los Angeles and he'll let us work there until we can get something on our own."

"I've only been to LA once and we took streetcars everywhere. Do you know what you're going to change your name to?"

"Why do I have to change my name?"

"Didn't you hear the lieutenant last night? All of us will get Japanese names," Ruth stated.

"I like Ezekiel Song."

"You can keep your western name as a nickname, but you'll get to adopt a formal name too."

"I'll become Ishimura," Ezekiel said.

"Really?"

"If that's OK with you."

"Of course. Are you being serious?"

"Yeah. Unless you were thinking of changing yours?"

She smiled. "I guess that doesn't make sense. What about your first name?"

"Any suggestions?"

"What about Naoki?"

"What's that mean?"

"Docile tree."

"No, thanks. What are you changing your name to?"

"We're still on you. The... Why are we stopping?"

Outside, the buses were stuck in a long line of vehicles. Ahead of them was a huge camp with multiple marquee tents, all massive, bustling with soldiers and civilians. Surrounding them were military transports, tanks, and enormous air balloons. Several fighter planes flew past them. As far as they could see, traffic was at a standstill. The driver got a message on his radio and reported to everyone, "There's some fighting going on south of here, so we've been advised to break here for the night. They're going to set up tents and cots."

Ruth was happy for the chance to stretch her legs and they quickly made their way off the bus. She gestured at the tents and said, "Race you?"

"Is that OK?" Ezekiel asked, looking down at her belly.

"Exercise is good for the body," she said, and bolted before he could begin.

Everyone was getting out of their buses so they couldn't run fast even if they wanted to. They focused on avoiding obstacles like families, impatient adults, and bewildered spectators wondering what was going on, intimidated by the fighter planes zipping by above.

"Look at all those balloons!" Ruth shouted to Ezekiel. There were hundreds of them on the other side of the camp, arrayed in long lines, half of them deflated, others ready to soar. "They're so pretty. Wonder what they're for."

"Don't try to distract me!" Ezekiel yelled back, as he caught up and then sped past her.

That caused several men who saw Ruth behind Ezekiel to say in jovial ribbing, "He should be chasing you!"

A throng of young boys got in Ezekiel's way so that Ruth regained the lead.

"You both should be running away from the fighting!" one man jokingly shouted.

Ruth beat him to the tents. Immediately, the fetid smell of the wounded bombarded her. A fat man and a little boy were running around in circles yelling, "Gorilla, gorilla, gorilla, gorilla, gorilla!"

Ezekiel arrived, mystified by the weird serenade of gorillas. Doctors were busily tending to the injured. The soldiers weren't the traditional ones she'd seen in the past with conservative haircuts and uniforms. Instead, they dyed their hair in a variety of colors, including purple, orange, and green, some with flat tops and others with spiky hair that looked like it took hours to compose. They weren't all Japanese and the soldiers came from a variety of ethnicities, caring for the wounded of which there seemed to be thousands. Inside the tent it was much darker, and it took a minute for their pupils to acclimate. As the black pits within their irises expanded, more of the terror seeped in. Subconsciously, both of their hands found each other's. There were Asians, even more Caucasians, African-Americans, and people of Latino heritage. Many of them had their flesh stripped away, so it was impossible to tell who was of what race. Muscles, burnt skin, and askew limbs were prevalent. They were coated with soot, ash people who looked like they were going to crumble. The odor of shit, vomit, and fire intensified their sense of repulsion. A woman was holding a charred baby in her arms, refusing to let go. Multiple people cried out for missing family members. A young girl had most of her hair burned off and her left eye hanging where her nose should have been. Seared flesh made people look like wax figures that had been disfigured by four thousand degrees of heat. Ruth wondered why there were buckets filled with rusted nails until she realized it wasn't oxidation but blood that stained them. Three of the men lying down had planks and metal pipes sticking out of them. Bodies were being carted in by soldiers and civilians.

"W-what happened here?" Ruth inquired.

"They set off a super weapon," a patient stated. "Most of San Jose was destroyed."

"San Jose!" Ruth exclaimed. "H-how?"

"I was on the outskirts of the city when I saw an explosion that looked like a mushroom," another offered.

"It was more like a bonsai tree made of black clouds that

kept on growing. I've never seen anything like it."

"There was a flash and, after that, I couldn't see anything."

"Yeah, that flash."

"It was quiet right before."

"Everything was on fire and there was an earthquake that didn't stop. Then the black rain came."

"Black rain?" Ezekiel asked.

"I thought it was oil," a woman with a burnt face stated.

"My dog's fur fell out and I could see his jaw through his melted skin."

"There were corpses everywhere and the black rain didn't stop for an hour."

"It was some new weapon the Japs built."

"It wasn't just a weapon!" a man with a soot mask for a face shouted. His left arm was missing and bandages covered his entire body. "I saw a man taller than a building with red eyes right before the explosion."

"You're crazy," someone said, and a few others chimed in.

"I'm not! I saw it right before the explosion and I knew something bad was going to happen."

"You've lost your mind, fool! There's no such thing as a man that big."

"I saw it too," another voice stated. "It made the whole ground shake and I saw it spit fire into the sky."

"What was it?"

"Haven't you heard the Jap Emperor has supernatural powers? That's what all of this is. He destroyed San Jose with his powers. We have no chance against something like that."

"The Japs warned us. They told everyone to evacuate San Jose, Sausalito, and Sacramento, or the Emperor would rain down fire from heaven. But we laughed at them, thought they were just blowing smoke up our asses."

"Why didn't our God protect us?"

No one could answer that and the silence was even more unnerving than the ubiquitous wailing that had been there a moment before.

Ruth was trembling. Ezekiel put his arm around her and rubbed the side of her shoulder.

"What are you two doing in here?" a doctor snapped. "Get out of here right now!"

They were escorted out by a nurse.

"I've heard the Emperor is a god," Ruth said as they stepped outside, and her hand went to the cross around her neck. "Maybe he can do all these things? I mean, is there any other explanation?"

Eight blond men and women with swastika armbands walked by, speaking with a Japanese officer. They were using their cameras to record the victims, asking questions in German, none of which either could understand. Their excitement was only matched by the inquisitiveness apparent in their vociferous tone.

"I have no idea," Ezekiel answered her. Both were terrified by the notion of a walking god who could destroy a city. "Let's get back to the bus," he weakly suggested.

Los Angeles
July 4, 1948
10:23am

Tanks marked with the rising sun of the Japanese flag were rolling down the streets of Los Angeles. Hundreds of bombers soared through the air like a cloud of locusts, led by a fleet of the deadly high-altitude Mansyu Ki-99s. The city reeked of smoke, explosives, and corpses as families wept for their lost ones. Buildings were on fire, houses continued to crumble, and the streets had been decimated into fields of debris. The skyline was a fissured gradient of conflicted red, forlorn gray, and dissipated azure. The temperature was warm with light winds to calm tempers. The only traces of animal life were stray dogs and legions of ants busily scurrying to salvage their homes. There were sporadic bursts of gunfire and the constant hum of fighter plane engines, but it was the silence from the American army that overwhelmingly resounded in the anxious gasps of incredulity. *Had they really lost?*

Ezekiel and Ruth raptly watched the battalions of Japanese soldiers marching through the city. They all blended into one another, most in their teens, tenaciously clutching their rifles. Despite their disciplined gait, their pride was unmistakable.

Their boots were synchronized into a victorious stomp.

The two, along with thousands of other prisoners, had been given special seating in the military parade celebrating the Japanese victory. Above their section was a sign that read: *"Liberating our Fellow Asians and Freeing the World from Western Tyranny."*

Thousands of American prisoners were paraded through the streets, all chained. Taunts and hisses hurled their way. Ezekiel looked over at Ruth and noticed her cross necklace was missing.

Just the day before, he'd been shocked when they'd arrived at his uncle's factory. The main building was a bomb crater and all that was left was the ashen remains of a burned frame. An old Chinese man sat next to the ruins, talking to himself. He had wisps of white hair on either side of his head and his frown formed ripples of skin along his neck, flesh crevasses unwinding in mourning.

"What happened here?"

The old man looked up at him. "Japanese bombers destroyed every factory on the block."

"Do you know where Henry Song is?"

"Why?" he asked, tensing, his eyes going to Ruth. "Who are you?"

"I'm his nephew."

The old man stared at Ezekiel's face. "Henry was one of the few survivors. Most everyone died in the fire or were shot."

"Shot for what?" Ruth asked.

"For resisting."

"You used to work here?" Ezekiel wanted to know.

He shook his head. "My wife."

"Do you want to come with us?"

"I have nowhere to go."

"But–"

"Go away," he said, then began rambling to himself again.

They left him there and Ezekiel said, "It's only a few miles to my uncle's house."

Almost every house they saw had some type of damage. There were whole streets where houses had burned down, fields of embers that were tattered echoes for the community that had once been there. Stacks of smoke formed colonnades along the major streets. Roads were obliterated, buildings exposed their innards, and the cars that normally flowed through the city had nowhere to go. The Americans they saw were in a daze, faces devoid of emotion, a hollowness that made them appear to be ghosts in costume. They saw Ruth and Ezekiel walking past, but gave no reaction, their spirits crushed by the specter of a carmine Helios above. A blond woman walked up to them with a sketch of a man. She was barefooted and her shirt was torn, blood forming a scarf around her neck and shoulders. "Have you seen my husband?" she inquired.

Ezekiel and Ruth looked at the picture. It was so primitive and bare, it could have been anyone. "I'm sorry," Ruth said, getting close to try to comfort her.

But the woman shrieked, "Don't touch me!" Her face became feral and she crouched, hands curved defensively into a claw-like configuration. "Stay away from me!" she demanded, and her eyes were distant, her memory entrenched in some horrible past neither Ezekiel nor Ruth could see.

A mile of wreckage later, they came to a security point. A group of Japanese soldiers had barricaded the entire street. Two tanks were on the other side. There were several dozen dogs that were unusually fat. A lieutenant pointed a sword at Ezekiel and barked at him in Japanese. He had swarthy skin, hadn't shaved in days, and his uniform had splotches of dried bloodstains on the sleeves. Ezekiel answered, "I don't speak Japanese well, but we're–"

The lieutenant placed his sword at Ezekiel's neck, about to chop it off if he was unsatisfied by the answer. The soldier was restrained by another officer, a captain, who ordered, "Cut it out."

"I was going to," the lieutenant answered, in heavily

accented English.

The captain ignored the sarcasm and looked at the two. "Can't you see she's Japanese? What are you doing here?"

"We're here for the celebration tomorrow," Ruth answered, and explained where they'd just come from, showing the stamped clearance papers authorizing their liberation from the prison camp. "We were going to go see his uncle."

"Where's your uncle?"

"Just a few blocks from here."

"Go see your uncle and return here when you're done. I'll have you escorted back."

"Is it safe out there?"

The lieutenant brandished his sword, guffawed, and said, "The Americans are bloodied and beaten. Anything more they do is like a fly attacking a tiger. You have nothing to fear."

Ezekiel and Ruth bowed to the officers gratefully. But, as they did, Ezekiel noticed more than forty severed heads in a pile, their bodies nowhere in sight. The soldier with the sword watched them with a ruthlessness that unnerved him. Ezekiel realized the lieutenant was greedily eyeing his neck.

They hurriedly went through.

"I can't believe this is Los Angeles," Ezekiel said, staring at all the debris.

"At least Beniko won't have to grow up feeling inferior because she's Oriental."

"You think so?"

"Think about the way the Americans treated us. Even when we weren't in camps, they'd always call us nips or chinks, vandalize our stores, and harass us. They think we all look the same – Chinese, Japanese, Vietnamese, Korean."

"But America stood for something, a dream that goes beyond race or background," Ezekiel said.

"Something even they didn't believe when it came time for action."

"It's what they were striving for."

"You wish the Americans had won? You wish we were back in prison?"

Ezekiel hesitated to give a definite reply. "As long as Beniko has a better life."

"She will," Ruth assured him.

"You're still so sure it's a girl?"

"I have a feeling."

"If it's a boy, can we name him something else?"

"What's wrong with Beniko?"

"I was hoping to give him a Western name. Like Emmanuel."

"What about Ben?"

Ezekiel laughed.

It was a twenty minute trek before they arrived at his uncle's house. The lawn hadn't been mowed in months and was littered with bullet shells.

Henry Song frowned at his nephew's arrival.

"Why are you here?" he grunted.

Ezekiel, who had been elated to see his uncle alive, was surprised by the cool reception. "We were hoping you could help us."

"Even if I wanted to, there's nothing I can do. The Japanese destroyed my factory and they'll be here any day to take away my house too."

"We were there," Ezekiel said. "I'm very sorry."

"How did you get past the barricade?"

"Ruth helped us through."

Henry grimaced. "You went to a Japanese prison camp and married one of them?"

"We haven't had the chance to get married, but we will soon."

"You're smart. You won't have anything to worry about anymore." Hatred and disgust dripped from his words as he glowered in Ruth's direction.

"I was an American," Ruth said.

"You're a Jap."

"My family fought for America in the Great War," Ruth stated angrily. "Two of my uncles died in Germany fighting for our country. I was born here and have never even been to Japan, but it didn't matter when it came time to sending us to those prisons."

"You know what the Japs are doing to their prisoners? Butchering them and feeding them to their dogs because it's cheaper than getting them dog food."

On the radio, an admiral of the Imperial Forces broadcast a speech to the Americans, assuring them their mission was principally that of peace, to free their Japanese brothers and sisters who had been taken captive and executed at death camps like Manzanar. "Once we are assured of their freedom and security, we will take measures to leave," a translator said in very good English, with only the hint of a Japanese accent.

His uncle snorted. "I'm sure they'll be eager to leave."

"Uncle..." Ezekiel started.

"Seven of my closest friends were caught east of here. They were ordered to dig their own graves and, when they finished, they were shot. One survived because he pretended to be dead and waited with the corpses for two nights. A total of a thousand men were shot at point blank range."

"I know you're angry, but–" Ezekiel started again, in an effort to calm his uncle.

"You don't know angry! They murdered everyone who is dear to me."

"We've all lost someone," Ezekiel reminded him. "But it doesn't change the fact that the war's over and the Americans lost."

"The war's just begun. Unless you want to accept your death so calmly." His uncle glared at Ruth. "Go live your life with the butchers. We are no family."

His uncle went back inside.

The memory of the encounter caused Ezekiel to shrivel at

the sight of the last American prisoners, a mix of races united by shame. There was no resistance in their eyes, no grit. Only resignation.

He held Ruth's hand firmly, the celebration parade only a quarter finished.

"What's wrong?" she asked.

"How will we survive? I thought for sure my uncle could help us."

"We'll find a way to start a life here."

"What about what my uncle said about the Empire?"

More bombers flew by. The line of soldiers appeared interminable. They looked so arrogant and smug. It was understandable as they had defeated the seemingly invincible Americans, who had been preoccupied in Europe, not anticipating the fatal seizures of Hawaii, Alaska, and California.

"Times will change. Peace changes even the worst of killers," Ruth said.

"Into what?" Ezekiel asked.

The American flag was taken down at Los Angeles City Hall. The Japanese rising sun took its place, enveloping the red, white, and blue in a crimson blaze that melded everything into a hot red ball. It was the 4th of July. The firecrackers that had been prepared to commemorate the holiday were being used to celebrate the fall of Los Angeles. Sparks lit up the air in a graffiti of loss. Paintings of fierce light splattered the sky like blood, only brighter, scintillating in desperation, boding ominously for a dim future. Groups of Americans planned rebellion and dissent. They believed the real fighting would commence after the faux surrender. The Japanese knew better. They were ready for resistance.

FORTY YEARS LATER

Los Angeles
June 30, 1988
12:09am

There was never a day Beniko Ishimura didn't think about death. If mortality were a cocktail, it would be bitter, punctuated by hints of lime, imbuing oblivion in short draughts. Ben's own cocktail was too sweet for his tastes because his date for the evening, Tiffany Kaneko, liked her drinks fruity. She was a striking redhead with freckles that mottled her cheeks. Her green eyes and thin lips could spark incendiaries – the way they'd done the first time their eyes locked. She wore a pink *qipao* because she appreciated traditional Chinese dresses and the way they emphasized the contrast of her Irish ancestry with her Asian periphery. Even though Ben's father had been part Chinese and his mother Japanese, he looked full-blooded Japanese. He tried to match the prevailing fashions of the day and aligned his image with the latest trends projected from Tokyo. Like most of the officers in the room, his long hair was slicked back with oil. He wore the brown suit of a military officer, insignia ranking him as a captain in the Imperial Army. Vermilion lapels collided against his chubby cheeks, and, from the bulge in his belly that he refused to acknowledge, it was clear he was fighting both his cravings and gravity. He sucked on an ice cube in his cocktail, relishing the cold that numbed his tongue.

It was Tiffany who had wanted to see this circus act from China. She'd heard about it from her friends in the press corps and knew only military officers could gain access. "Freak show" was her actual description. A cornucopia of the bizarre, they were deviants who had strayed from the moment they were born. The woman on the center stage had a beard longer than any Ben had ever seen. She used her beard like a lasso, twirling it and doing fancy tricks. Her partner, a skinny male, contorted his body so he'd dance in conjunction with the various geometric compunctions enforced by her hair.

"What is it about the strange that piques your interest so much?" he whispered to Tiffany.

"Strange is coincidence, a random act. If all women had facial hair, I'd be the strangest one alive."

"Strangest, yes, but still the most beautiful."

"Beautiful is so generic. I wouldn't pay money to see that."

"Does elegantly dashing and intriguingly provocative sound better?"

"A little. If you were the only man in the world without a beard, I'd put you in a circus and sell views without any catchphrases," she stated.

"How much would you charge?"

"A hundred yen."

"That's it?" Ben asked.

"You sound disappointed."

"I was hoping at least a thousand a view."

"I'm not that greedy," she said, playfully pressing her finger against his arm.

They were in a circular room with tables arranged by rank. Their dinner was a mix of sashimi and steaks. A connoisseur from Kyoto made special rice and the tamago was boiled to dripping perfection. Most of the officers were smoking cigarettes and the lights were dim apart from the gaudily colored beams firing up the show. Pleasure smelled of tobacco, raw fish, whiskey, and perfume. Tiffany held Ben's hand and said, "Are you excited about tonight?"

"Very," Ben whispered back. "I should have been a major a long time ago. Most of the guys I graduated with from BEMAG," the Berkeley Military Academy for Game Studies, "are already colonels."

"Captain in the Office of the Censor isn't a bad job," Tiffany said. "It's cushy and you can spend as much time with me as you want. But I guess it's good for you to finally get to be *Major* Ishimura."

"Which pretty much means I'll be doing the exact same thing, just with a little pay raise."

"And a better parking spot."

He laughed. "I'd probably drive my car to work more that way." He shook his cup, watching the ice roll around his drink. "Never thought it'd take this long."

"Even if it took a while, you're getting what you wanted."

"I'm grateful. Did you know it's become a point of scandal among my colleagues? 'Ishimura, why are you still the oldest captain in the USJ at thirty-nine?'"

"You don't like being the focus of attention?"

"Not like that," Ben said.

"I guess you wouldn't last long in a cage."

"It'd depend on who was in there with me."

He wondered what the bearded woman looked like without hair. From her hazel eyes, inured to the whimsies of emotion, he imagined her playing court for Imperial officers throughout the world from New Delhi to Beiping to Bangkok. Cigarette smoke was their olfactory leitmotif, bewildered officers hypnotized by the flocculence of her face. When she disappeared into the shadows, a sword dancer emerged, claiming he was descended from a famous Chinese warlord named Cao Cao. He juggled five broadswords and threw one up particularly high. It descended straight into his throat and belly. Blood spurted out. Several officers and their dates gasped in shock, thinking the swordsman had accidentally impaled himself. But the performer continued dancing in good cheer, not disturbed by the blood, which turned out to be strawberry jam. He pulled the sword out and asked the crowd if anyone could, "Help me cut my head off?"

Tiffany raised her hand and, just as Ben was about to object, a Japanese waitress whose face was doused in white paint approached and said, "Ishimura-san. Forgive the interruption, but you have a call."

"I'm not taking any calls during the show," Ben said, dismissing the woman.

"Sir. Respectfully, the speaker was very insistent."

Ben looked to Tiffany. "You going to cut his head off?" he asked her.

"Only if you watch."

"I'm squeamish about this kind of thing."

"It's a trick."

"I'll be back soon," Ben said.

"It'll be over by then."

"You can tell me all about it."

"You leave, you miss out."

He kissed her cheek and followed the waitress down the steps. He bowed to several ranking officers and ignored the ones who were with their mistresses. After he'd exited the performance hall, he took out his portical in its square form and flipped open the flaps to turn it into its familiar triangular shape. Porticals had originally been devised as "portable calculators." In the decades since the War, they had grown to encompass a phone with visual display, an electronic interface to search information on the *kikkai* (the digital space where all information was stored), and more. The triangular glass monitor interfaced with the processor, which he navigated via tactile contact. The silver borders accented the sleek design.

"Patch the call through," he told the woman.

No signal came.

"What's going on?" he asked.

It was hard to interpret her expression with her white face and her crimson painted lips. She looked like a mask, an inscrutable assembly of paints staring with pupils of incoherence. "Can you follow me, sir?"

"Where to?"

"A private room."

"I thought I had a call," Ben snapped.

"I wanted to talk with you."

"About?"

"Could we speak in private?"

"You can speak here."

"It would be better in private as will be made abundantly clear."

The performance center had newly painted walls that were richly saturated in red and dark blues, bleeding decadent opulence. There were statues of heroic officers from the United States of Japan in almost every corner, bravery allegorized in sculpted form. Ben noticed the plaque on one, describing how Colonel Ando died of typhoid in the San Diego uprisings while fighting the rebels and drowned himself in their water supply to make the Americans sick; Sergeant Okada was a notoriously clumsy chef who poisoned a thousand chestnuts and killed a thousand Americans in the process; and Lieutenant Takahashi was a pilot who sacrificed her life to take down one of the enemy aircrafts by crashing into their otherwise impregnable aircraft carrier bridge. They all died with honor. Living soldiers rarely got statues, Ben thought to himself.

He was led into a large room filled with hundreds of cages. Birds were inside each, chirping chaotically, virulent squawks in an aviary cacophony. Most of the birds criticized the cramped space, the dry air, and the stale food. A nervous few fretted about their upcoming act, wanting to dazzle the humans who reciprocated their songs with thunderous claps.

"Why are we here?" Ben asked.

The waitress slipped out of her kimono, her peachy flesh juxtaposing eerily against the white of her kami-like face.

"What are you doing?" Ben demanded to know.

She had taped her breasts together and it became apparent from her lean chest and the bulge in her breeches that she was actually a he.

"I'm flattered, but I'm here with someone," Ben said. "So unless this is more than a strip show–"

The man removed a flap of the skin on his belly, which made Ben wince until he saw a leathery strip with tiny circuits embedded into his flesh and bone. He took out a wire from his kimono and plugged it directly into a circuit in his belly. The flap of his skin was fake, but the wiring had dried blood and fat on it, a telephone soufflé built into his guts. Ben had heard of private messengers making phones powered by the biochemistry of their body, electric pulses from the heart, additional radio connectors integrated into their intestines. But he'd never seen a "flesh phone" directly. Utilizing them cost a fortune and he couldn't imagine anyone would have anything that important to say to him. These calls were impossible to trace, undetectable to metal scans, and the messengers themselves were merely relays, having no information in case they were caught. They were the only guaranteed way to guard against detection by the two groups of secret police, *Kempeitai* and *Tokko*.

"Your call, sir," the man said through his female mask of ermine. "Can you give me your portical?"

Ben complied and connected the wire directly into his portical, curious who had gone through all this effort just to speak with him. He attached it to a microphone he placed in his ear.

"Did you know?" a voice asked.

"Know what? Who's this?" Ben demanded.

"Did you know?" the voice repeated.

"I have no idea what you're talking about."

"Did you know about Claire?"

"Claire who?"

"Claire's dead," the voice on the other side said.

The voice seemed familiar. "General?" Ben probed.

"Claire's dead," the voice repeated, though this time with measured pain.

"What do you mean, Claire's dead?"

"I'll slice those cursed sloths into a million pieces and fry them up through a hundred hells and feed them to guinea pigs for what they did to her."

"Is this you, General?" he asked, even though based on his baritone voice, he was certain it was.

"She didn't know anything. She had to die for my mistakes."

"Is there something I can do to help?"

The other voice snorted. "You can't even help yourself, Ishimura."

"Then why did you call me?"

"Because she trusted you and because I can't arrange her funeral rites from where I am. See to it that she gets a proper burial. Not a Shinto ceremony. An American, Christian one, the way she wanted."

"Are you sure she's dead?"

There was a long pause.

"General?" Ben called, wondering if the communication had dropped.

It hadn't and the general said, "It is my greatest shame and regret that I could not protect the two people who were dearest to me... Will you do it?"

"Of course. Where are–"

The phone disconnected. The messenger unhooked Ben's portical, closed his belly flap, and began dressing in his kimono. The birds were still squawking.

"If you talk about this communication to anyone tonight, I have orders to kill you," the messenger warned.

"What about tomorrow?"

The courier ignored him and left.

Ben followed, wanting to ask questions. But the man was nowhere in sight. It took all of his discipline and restraint not to dial Central Communications right away. He went to the bathroom and washed his face. It had been years since he'd last seen Claire. Their parting had been on less than pleasant terms. Once he'd calmed his nerves, he stepped out and called the CC through his portical. "Can I help you, sir?" an operator asked.

"Is there any information on the death of a Claire Mutsuraga?"

"I'll be happy to check that for you Ishimura-san. How is your day today?"

"Couldn't be better. And yourself?"

"It is always a beautiful day in service of the Emperor," the operator pleasantly noted. "There is no information on the death of a Claire Mutsuraga, though there are five with the same name in Los Angeles who are alive. Are you looking for a specific one?"

"The daughter of General Kazuhiro Mutsuraga."

"I see her address and working status, but there is no obituary or termination notice."

"What if it was recent?"

"Our information is updated hourly and I'm not seeing anything, sir."

"Can you connect me with her?"

"Is this a matter of milit–"

"Yes," Ben cut her off impatiently.

"I'll need your clearance code for–"

"Forget it," Ben said, on second thought. "Do you know where her father currently is?"

"General Mutsuraga's whereabouts are currently unknown."

"Thank you," Ben said and disconnected.

He thought of Claire again and knew he needed another drink. He rushed back in to join Tiffany. The sword man had finished his act. Eight short performers were doing acrobatics with panda bears. A woman burned her whole body, making it resemble a charcoal painting with chaff knuckles and veins like broken pipe works mired in corpuscles. Ben downed a shot.

"What happened?" Tiffany asked. "You were gone half an hour."

"The waitress tried to have sex with me," he lied, thinking it was outrageous enough that she would believe it.

"Did you accept?"

"Are you serious?"

"Yes, I'm serious. I don't mind that sort of thing. It's flattering actually," Tiffany said.

"How's it flattering?"

"A woman tries to steal you from me directly under my nose. It's bold."

"Or stupid."

"You know I'm not going home with you tonight, right?"

"Yeah. My late night business ritual," he said. "What about afterwards?"

"Find yourself another date."

"You have another date lined up already?"

"Do you mind?"

"Never."

She put her hand on his arm. "Then what's bugging you?"

"Ghosts," Ben answered.

A man allowed himself to drown to death on the stage, gasping for oxygen, dying from lack of breath, only to be resuscitated a few moments later. Ben empathized.

2:12am

As was custom, the officers from the Santa Monica Office of the Censor were having a late night *sake* ceremony to celebrate the promotions that would officially come after the holidays. It was a restaurant called the Hakodate, known for its savory oysters and abalone. The bottom three floors were open to the public, while the top two were for private ceremonies. The floors were comprised of tatami mats and everyone took off their shoes. The table sat sixty and, as Ben was about to enter and find his seat, one of Lieutenant General Hirota's aides intercepted him. "Can I have a word?" he asked.

In an adjacent room, the aide, a lieutenant who had dyed his hair red, said, *"Sumimasen,"* with a bow. "It was decided that you will remain a captain for this cycle."

It took a moment for Ben to register what he'd been told. "What happened? I thought this was a formality."

"I don't know the full details," he answered. "Thank you for understanding."

"Did I offend someone? Is there some transgression I'm not aware of?"

"Again, I'm sorry. I'm only relaying the news."

Ben shifted his feet. "I guess… I guess I should go home."

"Your presence has been requested for the ceremony."

"Why? I'm not getting promoted."

"You would lose face if you left after arriving."

"I would lose more face by staying," Ben snapped.

"You're raising your voice," the lieutenant informed him, the walls being paper thin. "It would not be good form for the department if you left on this note."

Ben did his best to control his shaking hands. The lieutenant had a blank expression that infuriated him even more. "It sounds like I don't have a choice."

The lieutenant guided him in and escorted him to the end of the long table. All those being promoted were seated next to the lieutenant general's seat. Ben was on the opposite end since positioning was by rank and he was one of the lowest. Two young warrant officers were seated there, fresh graduates, bowing and greeting all their superior officers. When Ben was seated next to them, they ignored him.

Ben hated sitting on the mats as it hurt his ass. Lieutenant General Hirota, head of the SM Censor Office, entered. Everyone stood up and bowed. "This is a big day," he announced, proudly looking at those about to receive their promotion, waving them to sit. "There are only two relationships that are sacred and inviolable. That of a servant to their emperor, and that of a parent with their child. You have done outstanding work in service of the Emperor."

They took shots of *sake* until erythema imbibed their faces red with acetaldehyde.

The twenty-three promoted were given special ceremonial knives. They made small cuts on their hand, let blood drip into their cup and mix with the special *sake*, the *tokutei meisho-shu*. Blood toast, it was called, plasma mixing with fermented rice. A soporific song and dance was performed by both male and female geishas recounting the Japanese victory over America, the great sacrifices made by the Empire in order to protect the world from the tyranny and chaos of the Republic. "Yellow peril, they called us," a woman sang. "Even though our skin isn't yellow. They robbed us with the Treaty of Portsmouth, even after we sacrificed our lives to fight off the Russians," and on and on. The high-pitched tone hurt both Ben's inebriated state of mind as well as his ego. Even the perfectly prepared oysters could not sate his sense of dissatisfaction.

The promoted were eventually carted away for another private ceremony full of pomp, debauchery, and Shinto chanting, which would prevent them from sleeping until work the next morning. Even though it was a holiday week, the fatigue would wear on them as they celebrated until the 4th of July, the anniversary of the Imperial Victory for the United States of Japan. Ben knew, because he'd experienced it a decade ago during the last promotion he'd received.

"These young officers are our future," Lieutenant General Hirota stated, bombastically going on about how important they were. The grumpy martinet, whose hawkish brows terrorized many a junior officer, was acting like a jovial grandfather tonight. "Let us toast them!"

"*Kanpai*!" everyone shouted, as they swallowed their drinks in one gulp.

Ben's cup had been empty. He did not want to toast them. His eyes went to his watch.

"Another!" the lieutenant general commanded, raising up his cup as the waiters and waitresses poured additional drinks. There was no way Ben could avoid the toast this time. "Let us hope they will inspire the younger generations to serve the Emperor with more fervor and courage."

"*Kanpai*!"

Six *kanpais* later, the lieutenant general's stern demeanor was replaced by singing. His aide, with the assistance of a geisha, escorted him out. Everyone got up and bowed, holding their bent backs for the minute or so it took him to leave. The party was over.

Ben rubbed his hips, hating the soreness in both his muscles and bones. He was too drunk to pay attention to the restaurant, or his surroundings for that matter, as he stumbled out. He needed a taxi and was waiting on the street for one until he somehow found himself sitting in a bar again. There were radioactive fish swimming in a tank with an uncanny glow.

"They're special breeds, harvested off the oceans of what used to be Oregon and Northern California," a woman said. She had purple hair, was gaunt, and had jewelry all over her face.

"Who are you?"

"I was one of the performers at the ceremony," she answered.

"I don't recognize you."

"That's 'cause I'm not wearing my wig or makeup. I played Kanji Ishiwara."

"Nice to have a drink with the liberator of Manchuria. What am I doing here?"

"You passed out on the street."

He couldn't remember.

"I'm usually better at handling my drinks." He ordered a cup of water. "Thanks for your help. If you could help me grab a taxi, I'd be doubly grateful."

She held his hand. "How old are you?"

"Almost forty."

"You're cute for a forty year-old man."

"How old are you?"

"Guess."

"I'm too drunk to guess and I don't want to offend you," Ben said.

"Offend me?"

"Today is a strange day and my social graces are at their worst."

"Every day is a strange one for me. Don't worry. You're too old to offend me," she said, which stung and sobered him at the same time.

"I'm not that old."

"I'll help you grab a taxi."

She assisted him outside. There were no taxis in sight, just the sinews of indigo from neon signs and a flood of cars drifting in masochistic yearning, engines silent from the electricity that quietly fueled them. They all drove on the right side, even though that was usually an island custom.

"Do those rings on your nose hurt?" Ben asked.

"They're very comfortable. I feel naked without them."

"You take them off when you're performing, right?"

"I wear a different mask then. Do you always talk so much?"

"Only to strangers," Ben replied.

"I don't like men who talk too much."

"Why not?"

"I just don't."

"You sound irritated."

She shook her head. "I was hoping you were the quiet type."

"Why's that?"

She shrugged. "Most older men I've met are boring."

"Guilty. Especially tonight," he said, remembering the ceremony, then Claire. "Thanks for your help."

"Sure. See you around." She took out her portical and started playing a game as she walked away. He recognized the music.

"You're playing *Honor of Death*?" Ben called out.

She turned around. "You know it?"

"I play every game for my job."

"Are you any good?"

"Not bad."

"No one has ever beaten me in combat."

"If I wasn't so drunk, I could change that," Ben said. "I know all the cheats, could show you a bunch of them."

"Nice try."

She walked away, absorbed in her game.

Ben called Tiffany, but her portical was turned off. He sent her a message: "Hope you're having more fun than I am." He checked the time. It was already 4:22am. Just a few hours until work. The alcohol made him feel like the stump of a person, cauterized, then stitched together, a mannequin held by flimsy bandages. He relinquished himself to a motel, treading his way towards collapse. A taxi happened to pass by, which he waved down.

He thought of Claire again. She'd been like a sister to him, nobler, more honorable, resisting the weaker, easier path of disillusionment. The flaring conflagration of her idealism had been so pure, even the sun would have been burnt by it. He gave his address to the cab driver who asked, "Long night?"

He would have answered if he wasn't already asleep.

8:39am

The alarm wouldn't stop ringing, even though he tried to shut it off four times. *What's the point of getting up early?* he thought to himself. It annoyed him to remember the toasts for the newly promoted. He threw his blanket off and got up from bed.

Ben lived in a spacious townhouse full of old American paintings. The white walls were covered with portraits of cowboys, dead soldiers, and dinosaurs – all USJ officers got their pick of American art. His wood floors were pristine and he walked down a flight of stairs to his kitchen where breakfast was prepared by his maid, an old Chinese woman. He sipped on his miso soup, took a bite of his bacon, and ate two rolls of cucumbers. He switched into the standard blues of all foreign services in the United States of Japan. His maid said, "You need to eat more."

"The weight scale disagrees," he replied, patting his belly and steadying himself against the counter. His head was spinning. "Can you get me a cup of water?"

He drank the water and took his coat off a suit of samurai armor next to the door, deceptively antiquated even though it was coated in titanium – a gift for everyone who'd graduated from the Berkeley Military Academy. He exited his room, which was on the fiftieth floor, and descended down the high-speed elevator. Across the street was a beautiful garden park that was teeming with kids. He entered the subway entrance on Broadway. The station was sparkling clean, with portical displays along the walls broadcasting the California Nippon News. Most of them recounted the monumental sacrifices made during the Great Pacific War for its fortieth anniversary. The news changed to highlights of the huge victories the Japanese forces were having in Vietnam. "Soon, the rebels will be destroyed!" a general assured them.

Public cleaners were sweeping the station and Ben paid three yen for a can of orange juice. As he passed a holographic image of the Emperor, he, like everyone else, bowed in deference. The Emperor was dressed in his ceremonial clothing, though he had on a crimson dragon mask that prevented commoners from seeing his face. Ben made sure to bow low and hold his stance, as cameras were recording impatience or disrespect to relay it back to the proper authorities. In the same way, multiple civilians bowed to him to show their respect to him as a military officer. The train came exactly on time at 9:15am and, though the station was nowhere near as busy as it would have been at rush hour on a non-holiday, there were still hundreds getting on. Ben sat on one of the special seats adjacent to the door that were designated for pure Japanese and military officers. Independent of ethnicity, many of the riders were sucked into their porticals, playing games alone as talking with friends on the subway was considered rude. An automated female voice spoke in pleasant Japanese and English, informing them that their next stop and final destination was at 3rd Street in Santa Monica.

The train went above ground. Huge skyscrapers towered in the distance. Mechas – robotic soldiers that were as tall as the skyscrapers – vigilantly guarded the skies against enemies outside and within. His portical was synced with the California Nippon News and a report from Governor Ogasawara gave the annual report on the state of the union. "Crime rates are the lowest in the western hemisphere and pollution is virtually nonexistent," she stated. This intercut with footage from New Berlin and Hitlerica with their smoggy cities, as their cars still used gasoline, unlike the purely electric vehicles of the USJ. "Our EKS industry," (Electric Kikkai System), "is booming and, despite attempts by German Minister Goebbels to make New Berlin the portical entertainment capital of the world, Los Angeles still holds the distinction with over a thousand unique depots," Governor Ogasawara vaunted.

The train came to a stop. Ben got off on the 3rd Street exit which was the end of the 196th line. Sweepers were cleaning trash. A few civilians bowed to him and he greeted several police on duty with light nods. He went up the escalator into a plaza when a strumming melody started from his pocket. He took out his portical and opened the flaps.

It was Tiffany Kaneko on the line.

"Bad night?" she asked.

He explained in brief about the ceremony.

"Don't take it personally," she said.

"How can I not?"

"By not thinking about it. Be more like Saigo."

"Who?"

"The very last samurai during the Meiji Restoration. He didn't care about rewards, rank, or title."

"Isn't he the one who died rebelling against the government? We shouldn't mention his name on a portical call."

"Don't worry. He's a hero."

"That I definitely am not. You have a fun night?"

"Fun is one way of putting it," Tiffany answered vaguely. "You sound tired."

"I can't believe I got drunk so easily. A few shots don't usually faze me."

"It's called age."

"Age? I'm only thirty-nine," Ben protested.

"Only?"

"Funny."

"You want me to hold off on the anti-age and wrinkle cream I got you?" Tiffany teased.

"You want to go to the races tonight or not?"

"It's very effective for the skin."

"You don't sound like you want to go to the races that much."

"Don't be so sensitive," she said, laughing. "You got the tickets?"

"Box seats," he replied. "You'll be seeing Sollazzo and Chao kyotei racing tonight."

She whistled merrily. "I've been wanting to see them for ages."

"I read your profile on both."

"What'd you think?"

"You have a gift."

"More like I spent three nights in a row rewriting them a thousand times."

He smiled. "We're still playing *go* afterwards, right?"

"As long as your friends don't mind losing money."

"The last things my friends worry about is money."

"What about you? Are you going to be OK?"

"I never bet that much money," Ben replied.

"I mean about the promotion."

"I know. I don't have much of a choice, do I?" was as strong an answer as Ben could muster.

"You want me to dig around and ask about it for you?"

"No," Ben said. "I'm trying not to think about it."

"I'll help you forget later."

"How's that?"

"I have my ways," she said, with a lascivious wink.

Ben laughed. "I'm at the office. I'll call you later."

She kissed the screen. Ben entered the huge glass building with the sign of Taiyo Tech in front. The reception area had an elaborate stone garden and a waterfall. People in suits and military uniforms were coming and going. He bowed to a few and others bowed to him. He went through the scanner gate and the barcode on his keycard was automatically checked for ID. Behind the desks, a group of security officers matched identities with photos and cleared entry. Just as Ben was about to head to the elevator, a stocky woman he didn't recognize approached. She was Eurasian, though he couldn't determine the specific region. Her hair was cut choppy and short, her lipstick was dark red, and her violet lashes made them resemble bruises against her pale cheeks.

"Hello, Beniko Ishimura," she greeted him, in a somber tone.

"Can I do something for you?"

"Are you busy at the moment?"

"I'm always busy, but I can make time if it's important."

"Let's talk in your office," she said.

"My office?"

The woman took out a badge that caused Ben to flinch. She was Akiko Tsukino of the *Tokubetsu Koto Keisatsu*, or Tokko for short – the secret police of Japan. His throat constricted. They went to the elevator. Only the two of them got on.

Ben scoured his memory for any faults that could have triggered a visit from the Tokko. Had he forgotten to pay a bribe? Had he said something in his sleep that one of his lovers had reported? They wouldn't be here about Tiffany's Saigo comment, would they? Then he wondered if that lieutenant from the night before had reported him for being discontented about not getting promoted.

"How is your day going?" he asked and immediately felt dumb for saying it.

She ignored his question and inquired, "Why were you asking about Claire Mutsuraga last night?"

Ben was surprised by the question. "S-she's an old friend."

"You were specifically asking if she was dead. Why?"

"I heard a dumb rumor. It doesn't matter."

"What is your relationship with her?"

"I told you, she was an old friend. I served under her father and she was like a little sister to me."

"When was the last time you spoke to General Kazuhiro Mutsuraga?"

He hesitated. Did she know the general had contacted him? But it wasn't possible for her to have traced a messenger that way – unless it was a test of loyalty in the first place? "Last night," Ben answered truthfully, hoping the courier's warning of the night before no longer applied. "First time I've talked to him in seven years."

"What did he say?"

"He told me Claire was dead."

"Anything else?"

"To take care of her funeral," he replied.

"Anything else?"

"Not that I recall."

"Think carefully," Agent Tsukino urged.

"I am. Our conversation was short."

"Did he mention where he was or where he was going?" she asked.

"No. He was very cryptic."

"I've checked your portical calls and there weren't any registered communications."

Ben explained about the "flesh phone."

"That's an unusual method of communication," she said.

"Everything about the call was unusual."

"You filed a report about two female subjects a month ago."

"I filed a lot of reports in the last month," Beniko replied.

"One of them was concerning Claire Mutsuraga."

There had been thousands of reports in the last week alone. A month was an eternity. "The same Claire Mutsuraga?" he asked, even though from her tone the answer was obvious.

"Yes."

"What did the report say?" Ben asked.

"They questioned the sexual prowess of the Emperor as he has not been able to conceive an heir."

"I hear that's a problem many men are suffering because of all the radiation from atomics," Beniko said.

"The Emperor is not a man."

"I know. Nor was I implying as such," he quickly assured her, irritated with himself for his careless comment.

The agent seemed annoyed. "Run me through your function here. Gaming isn't my area of expertise."

Most agents knew everything about their subjects before coming. Was she checking to see if he'd misstate something against what she already knew? *Stick to the facts, Beniko. No exaggerations for face.*

"The three floors above the lobby are devoted to content creation and that's where they make the games for the porticals," Ben explained. "Each floor has a different team of about a hundred designers, artists, and engineers working on their various fields. The fifteen floors above that are part of the Office of Moral Thought Protection. I-I'm in charge of the tenth floor."

On the tenth floor, the desks were arranged in twenty rows of forty seats. Porticals were at each booth, three display screens per station. "They're all hooked into the EKS, and our workers search through hundreds of thousands of communications daily to try to spot disloyalty among subjects," Ben explained. "Filters are applied to private communications, messages, dates, sleep talking, anything that might arouse suspicion. Technical encryption, audio trackers, phrase recognition, and tonal analysis programs work in conjunction to uncover possible traitors. Almost everyone on this floor is from the civilian workforce. We have some enlisted technical specialists, but those are usually shared resources.

"Our section covers grids 550 through 725," Ben stated, and pointed at the various locations. "Those sections correspond to specific regions of Los Angeles. We monitor everything, but our area of focus is games. We pay attention to the decisions people make in the gaming stories and their text responses. We've asked designers to purposefully implement potentially traitorous branches, so that if anyone takes those paths, they're flagged."

"Traitorous branches?"

"Say a swordsman is fighting for his Emperor and is given a chance to join a bunch of wandering ronin who are not content with the lack of jobs. If a gamer chooses to follow the ronin, they would be flagged and we'd dive into the rest of their record. See if there's anything in their education, social report, and financial statements that might suggest a deeper discontent. I'll be honest. Most reports don't turn up anything. People playing games release their frustration in weird ways."

"Are you sympathetic towards those who might be harboring ill thoughts to the Emperor?"

"Of course not. But it's part of my job to distinguish between a gamer who wants to vent and someone who's actually planning something."

"I'm surprised that a man of your reputation for unquestioning loyalty would not see that all action is rooted in seditious thoughts. An old American religion used to have the saying, 'if your right hand causes you to sin, cut it off'."

Ben did his best to hide his frustration at his nervous responses. "Would you like some tea?" he asked, as they entered his office. "I have some *da hong pao* I specially imported from Mount Wuyi. It cost a fortune, but it was worth it as it's the best tea I've ever had." His office was on the corner, glass walls giving him an unhindered view of the ocean. *Ukiyo-e* inspired posters of the various games he'd worked on hung on the walls. His desk was made of mahogany with *kanji* about the history of Taiyo Tech written into them.

She slipped out a silver gun from her coat. A glass capsule filled with a green liquid jutted out the back of the handle.

"Have you seen one of these before?"

"No," Ben confessed.

"It's a viral gun that rewrites the history of your blood. If I shot you with this, in five minutes you wouldn't be recognizable."

"That doesn't sound very fun."

"Not one bit," she replied. "Our scientists in the Eastern Coprosperity Sphere developed this."

"For Vietnam?" Ben asked, glancing over at the encased ceremonial swords he'd been given as an officer, trying to ignore the gun she was holding.

She nodded. "Why do people resist when the outcome is futile?" she asked.

"Because they're insane," he replied.

"So says the man who reported his own parents when they tried to commit treason against the Empire."

Ben's eyes drifted for a second and he tried not to sound too rote as he replied, "I am loyal to the Emperor and no one else. Anyone who defies the Emperor is insane."

"What do you know about General Mutsuraga's last few years?"

"Not much. He's had it rough since his wife's passing."

"We've been tracking him for some time now."

"Why? I thought he was retired," Ben said.

"He has a connection to a game we've been investigating."

"What game?"

"What do you know about what's left of the Americans?" Akiko asked.

"There's Colorado, but that's a wasteland. The whole Rocky Mountains are where the remains of American society are hiding. I've heard they have underground cities and the people there kill each other over nothing. I've actually seen parents here tell their children they'll abandon them to the American monsters if they don't obey."

"It's a hive of dissension," she confirmed. "If the Germans

hadn't asked for a moratorium on atomics, we'd have blasted it long ago."

"Does Mutsuraga have a connection to Colorado?"

"Not Colorado. San Diego. A group you're familiar with."

"The George Washingtons," Ben said, and felt the hair on his arms bristle.

"You fought against them."

"Ten years ago."

"One of our few conflicts to end in stalemate. Essentially a defeat because the GWs were able to get hold of atomics," Akiko said.

"That was a bloody war. A lot of good officers died."

"You survived."

"I was a glorified clerk. Barely did any of the fighting."

"Things haven't changed much for you, have they?"

He ignored her taunt and said, "Mutsuraga hated the GWs. There's no way there could be any connection between them."

"Never underestimate insanity. Mutsuraga has helped distribute a seditious game to the citizens of the USJ that I believe was developed in San Diego with what's left of their pitiful resistance. Unfortunately, the game has become quite popular throughout the USJ and is even said to be regularly played in Colorado."

"What game?" he asked, even though he knew it was never good to overtly show interest in non-Japanese products.

"It's called the *United States of America*, or *USA* for short. It imagines a world where the Americans won the war and tries to teach them how to win now through a simulator in the program. Preposterous on every level. Have you heard of it?"

"Yes."

"Why didn't you report it?"

"I did in one of my roundups, but I didn't know its name when I found out about it."

"So you know what it's about?"

"I have a basic idea. I agree, it's preposterous. How do you know the general developed it?"

"Like I said, we've been tracking him," Agent Tsukino said. "The game has all his marks on it. I hear you were once a good designer yourself."

"I was OK."

"You served in War Games with Mutsuraga."

Ben recalled his service in San Diego and took a few breaths to ease himself.

"Tell your department to spend the rest of the day focusing on tracking anyone related to Mutsuraga's family," Agent Tsukino ordered.

"No problem."

"I also want you to accompany me to Claire Mutsuraga's apartment."

"Me?" he asked, surprised. "Why?"

"Because her father is correct. Claire Mutsuraga committed *jigai* yesterday afternoon."

Jigai – ritual suicide by knife to her neck. An image of her with a blade in her throat caused Ben to blanch. "Did she leave a letter?"

"No," Tsukino said. "The matter is still under investigation. We'd been tracking her for some time, but hadn't made a move, hoping she would lead us to her father. I need someone to look over her portical now that she's dead."

Ben had a hard time forming words and regained his composure only after seeing Akiko's impatient glare. "When should we go?"

"As soon as you relay your orders to your department."

Beniko pushed a few buttons on his portical, and wrote out the new directives. "Done."

"Do you have your gun?"

"Will I need it?" he asked. "I actually don't know if it's at the office. I haven't carried my gun in ages."

"Find it."

9:38am

Agent Akiko Tsukino's car was triangular and compact, like most of the electric cars on the road. As the doors were transparent, from certain angles it looked as though they were floating on air. Ben had expected special surveillance gear inside the vehicle, but there was nothing worth noting, not even decorations or memorabilia to give him a hint of her proclivities. She drove at a steady 40km/h and hundreds of cars to either side were going at the same speed. The huge signs on the skyscrapers appeared dead without neon. He fidgeted on his seat, looked right, and saw a big visual display about the new German art gallery.

"I've always wondered why the Germans drive on the wrong side of the road," Ben said.

Akiko shrugged. "They like doing things opposite of everyone else."

"Why don't you use your portical to drive?"

"I like having full control," she said, gripping the wheel tighter.

"But the portical can calculate speeds and angles perfectly for every permutation and–"

"I won't put my life in the hands of a portical," Akiko cut him off. "How long have you been at Taiyo?"

"Eight years now."

"Is it normal for a man to remain at the rank of captain so long? Just by natural progression, you should be a major or colonel."

Ben was about to agree, but knew he should be cautious. "Depends."

"On?"

"Maybe politics?" Ben guessed. "I thought I was getting promoted last night. A few friends said I would, but I wasn't. I don't know why and I don't question too deeply. I'm happy in my role and will serve, whether it's as a captain or a warrant officer. What about you? How long have you been in the Tokko?"

She turned her head. "Five years."

He wondered how old she was, but thought better of asking.

"You attended the Berkeley Military Academy for Game Studies," she stated.

"Almost twenty years ago. Why?"

"We're alumni."

The Berkeley Military Academy for Game Studies – BEMAG – was built over the remains of Berkeley. The whole city became a military institute and, since most of San Francisco was abandoned while its buildings remained intact, it was the perfect grounds for battle simulations. One of the best mecha training schools was there as well, the pilots able to practice in the bay. Berkeley itself was isolated apart from the Academy students and a civilian staff of merchants who supported them.

"How is Berkeley these days?" he asked.

"They're expanding."

"Do they still have that Korean restaurant in the Asian ghetto? It was my favorite place for kimchee soup."

"I wouldn't know," Akiko answered.

"What restaurants did you like?"

"I ate whatever food the cafeterias provided."

"Let me guess. You graduated near the top of your class?"

"I ranked ninth," she answered. He was impressed. BEMAG remained one of the top military institutes, second only to the Military Academy in Tokyo. "What about you?"

"Near the bottom – 682." Out of 684, he didn't add.

"That's bad."

Ben laughed. "I shouldn't have gone. A military board felt I deserved a chance and got me in on one of their special requisitions. Other students hated me for it because they felt I cheated my way in."

"Your faculty reports said you spent more time chasing women than studying."

"Guilty."

"I've looked at the records of the rest of your class. You have one of the most undistinguished records."

"Being a censor is an important role," Ben said.

"Most of your fellow officers served with honor in San Diego."

"They were smarter and more talented than I was."

"Of all the officers I have visited, you are the first to be so eager to put yourself down."

"I'm just an honest appraiser. Where is her apartment?"

"Downtown. We're almost there."

10:15am

Downtown Los Angeles was full of tall buildings and a city hall that was architecturally based on the Imperial Castle in Osaka. Huge portical screens displayed advertisements and newsreels of various victories in the Empire's war efforts. A massive mecha that was fifty meters tall and shaped like a man in a samurai suit patrolled the streets. Its mobility was limited so that it didn't cause too much of a commotion when it moved, rolling via the massive wheels under its feet. Soldiers in rocket packs glided next to the mecha on routine patrols. There were a few people heading to restaurants for an early lunch.

Claire Mutsuraga's apartment was in an eighty story high-rise. There was already a guard at the door and the interior of the apartment was a mess, having been searched earlier by the police. It was a three-bedroom unit, with wood floors and what had once been brand new furniture, though the sofas and mattresses had been ripped open by the police. There were several marble statues, fancy French paintings, and a holographic projector in the middle of the living room.

"Pretty ritzy place for a student," Ben noted. "I guess that's the perks of having a general for your dad."

He saw a series of picture frames and remembered the general's face. Mutsuraga was the game designer who had made the *Honor of Death* series, one of the most revered franchises in portical gaming. He saw Mutsuraga's last few games on her wall, massive hits covering the Chinese Rice Insurrection and the Korean Civil War.

"What was your relationship to the general?" Agent Tsukino asked.

"I served under him."

"Did you like your service?"

"Mutsuraga was a legend among gamers. I was honored to serve him." Ben scratched an itch on the side of his wrist. "He was the most decorated officer in his class and we were all told to follow his example." There were pictures of the general at his own graduation on the wall surrounded by officers congratulating him. Mutsuraga was invited to be part of the elite student group, Sumera (a play on the Japanese word for Emperor as well as a reference to the first known civilization, Sumeria), straight from Tokyo Military Academy, which was a big deal.

"You didn't do a good job," Agent Tsukino said. "When he was teaching there, he had you reprimanded multiple times for being lazy and undisciplined."

"He was a harsh teacher."

"He was harsh because he was one of our best. He served with distinction in Mexico and was a brilliant tactician," she said.

"Of course. And after the armistice, he founded Shudarin Design Works and created some of the best war simulations in the Empire. Everyone wanted to work at Shudarin, and not just because of the amazing perks."

"You're familiar with his games then?"

"Very," Ben answered. "I helped him on some of them. Minor stuff that was mostly thrown out because of sloppy coding."

Ben examined another picture of Mutsuraga and his daughter on a fishing excursion. Claire looked unhappy and bored.

"I've read the reports of his wife's accidental death in San Diego," Akiko said. "Our soldiers bombed a civilian market that was mistakenly reported as a rebel stronghold. Media reported it as a terrorist attack, but everyone within the corps knew the truth."

"It was a confusing time."

"Did you know her death caused a massive escalation of the conflict?" Akiko asked, not so much to verify the facts, but to collate their knowledge.

"Like I said, it was a confusing time."

"The records are very spotty. Mutsuraga was eventually relieved from his position, something that seems highly unusual. A military officer removed during wartime? But no explanations are given. Anything you'd like to add to the official line?"

"You're talking about matters above my pay grade. I was only a lieutenant then."

"And you were sent away as well with Claire."

"The general asked me to take care of her. I did my best."

"A few years after that, Mutsuraga tried to develop a game with a non-Japanese protagonist, showing the San Diego invasion from their perspective. It was a ludicrous effort at empathizing with the natives. There was another game about a kamikaze pilot who had doubts about his mission and, at the last moment, decided to refrain from the act."

"I've never heard of either."

"That's because they were censored," she said. "Rather than cause a scandal and be arrested, he was given the option of going into retirement or committing *seppuku*. To the chagrin of many of his superiors, he chose retirement. But he secretly began development on a new game."

"*United States of America*?"

She nodded. "It's a cancer."

"Fortunately, we've eliminated cancer."

"Except from the mind."

Akiko went to a desk and picked up a portical. Their triangular edges had been shorn off, indicating they were separated from the EKS. "Claire Mutsuraga's portical."

She handed it to Ben, but Ben looked at the bed, which was covered with plastic from forensics to seal it off from contamination.

"Is that where she did it?"

Akiko shook her head. "In the bathroom."

Ben walked to the bathroom.

"It's already been cleared," Akiko said.

It was a tiled cube of normalcy, designs of furry beasts on the wall, dry towels, clumps of fallen hair collecting in the sink.

"In the bath tub?" he asked.

She nodded.

"Was there anything unusual about her death?" Ben wanted to know.

"Unusual?"

"Anything to indicate it was anything but suicide?"

"No. I checked thoroughly. So did forensics."

Ben placed his fist against his mouth, closed his eyes, and fought back memories. "She deserved better."

"Did she?"

"Yes."

"Was your relationship with her romantic?"

"What? Not at all. I told you, she was like a sister to me. She's a lot younger than me."

"According to the ages of some of your previous liaisons, age disparity has never been an issue."

He did his best to suppress his indignation. "Who's handling her funeral?"

"Apparently, you."

Ben's mind went back ten years to when Mutsuraga first asked him to look after Claire in San Diego. That was just before everything went to hell and she could still sneak out in the evenings and be safe. Ben assumed she was either meeting a love interest or partying it up in the streets of San Diego. He didn't expect to find her at an assembly hall filled with Americans who worshipped their Christian God. Claire was part of the choir and they were singing hymnals up front. When he joined the congregation, they welcomed him, saying, "Greetings brother."

Ben found the words of the music ridiculously puerile with their adulation for a fictional being. Still, he admired how melodic it sounded. They cried out to their fallen God, begging for succor. Many were penitent, arms up in the air, praying for redemption. Ben zoned out when a preacher shared a soporific message on showing love to their Japanese conquerors. He caught Claire on her way out.

She bowed, surprised by his presence. "Ishimura-san. What are you doing here?" she asked.

His first reaction was to ask, *Do you know how much trouble you would be in if your father found out?* But he presumed that would be counteractive and only incur teenage defiance. "Just curious what you were up to."

"You mean my dad sent you?"

"He did ask me to keep tabs on you." He looked at the statue of Christ on a cross. "You really believe in this stuff?" he asked.

Claire, who had been expecting a stern rebuke, answered, "Not all of it. But it's a powerful message."

"In what way?"

"They tell us to love our enemies," Claire answered. "'Do not repay anyone evil for evil. If your enemy is hungry, feed him; if he is thirsty, give him something to drink.'"

"No wonder the Americans lost."

Claire took umbrage at his response. "The winners aren't always right."

"Sorry. I just really don't understand their value system."

He was being sincere and she admitted in turn, "There are

things about their beliefs I find unbelievable too."

"Like?"

"Jesus says forgive everything. But I think certain sins are unforgivable."

"Like what?"

"Murder. Crimes against the dead can only be forgiven by the victim. If the victim isn't alive, the crime isn't forgivable."

"I agree," Ben said. "How did you find out about this place?"

"Mom goes here from time to time," Claire replied.

Ben's eyes widened. "Does your father know?"

She shook her head. "It's where she comes to clear her mind."

"She knows you're here?"

"No. She's not home."

"Where is she?"

"I don't know."

He wondered what Mutsuraga would think knowing his wife and daughter both attended an American worship service. "I should get you home."

Claire did not object and they walked towards the subway. Ben glanced at her from the side and saw that her posture, firm gait, and neutral gaze bore similarities with her father. As they got closer to the station, they heard a loud commotion. Hundreds of Americans were protesting and a group of Japanese soldiers in riot gear blocked the road. They were arrayed in a phalanx, shields in place, guns holstered as of the moment. A mecha was in position and two scouters flew above, beaming large spotlights down at the crowd, which was swelling in outrage.

"What are they protesting?" Claire asked.

"Two of our soldiers shot an American kid," Ben informed her. "They're upset. We should hurry."

They both accelerated their pace.

"Dad says I should learn more about programming porticals

from you," Claire said.

"I guess I can teach you a thing or two."

"Is it true what everyone says about you?"

"What do they say?"

"That you turned in your parents when you found out they were going to betray the Empire?"

"It's true," Ben answered, and showed no discomfort in acknowledging it.

Claire stopped in her tracks. "How could you do that?"

"Why wouldn't I? They were planning to work for the Americans and turn over our secrets."

"How'd you find out?"

"I overheard them talking about it."

"Did you try to ask them what was going on?" Claire asked.

"I don't think they would have told me. I listened when I could and memorized everything they said. I went to report it after I realized they were really going to go through with it."

"You're so casual about it. They were your parents."

"It wasn't easy," Ben said, and his fingers twitched. "I still miss them. But I had to do what was right."

"What was your parents' reaction when they found out?"

"I don't know. After I reported it to the police, I didn't see them again. Not until they were dead."

"So you're real hardcore about this stuff, huh? Most loyal servant of the Emperor?"

"I try," Ben said weakly. "I guess I committed one of your unforgivable sins."

"You want to come to church next week with me and confess?"

"Are you making fun of me?"

"No, no, not at all," Claire said. "I mean it."

Behind, they heard the protests intensify and there was a loud burst that sounded like an explosion. Claire and Ben hurried down the steps to the stairway. Red warning lights were flashing. The gates sealed off just as they went through.

They caught the last subway before the whole place locked down.

"Why do you waste your time with these superstitions?" Ben asked.

"It's not the superstitious elements I'm drawn to," Claire said. "It's the way this creed gives them strength and keeps them bound to a set of values that is humane and honorable. I wonder what the world would be like if the Americans were still an important part of it."

"Not all the Americans are honorable and humane. And, honestly, I don't know how safe it is for you to be with so many American dissidents. I know there haven't been any incidents yet, but tempers are boiling."

"They don't know who my dad is and they wouldn't care if they did. They only view me as a vessel of God," she said.

Ben found her faith worrisome. "Not all the Americans there are Christians," he said. "A lot of them use the religion as a means of organizing and hiding their true intent."

"There are people in the Empire who pretend to serve the Emperor, but don't care. How is that different?"

"I'm just saying be careful."

"*Arigatou*," she said. "I will."

Claire watched the portical displays on the subway, news showing eruptions of violence from previous encounters in San Diego. "Every time my parents argue, my mom goes to her room and cries," Claire suddenly said. "I get so frustrated by it. Why doesn't she fight back? You know how stubborn Dad can be and, even when he's wrong, he can't admit it. One day, after he yelled at her for an hour, I had enough and was about to tell her to go stick it right back to him."

"The way you do."

"You hear it all too, right? But that day, I found her in her room reading a Bible. It was something her mom gave to her and she told me not to worry about her, that she'd found the strength to persist."

"Through the Bible?"

"Her beliefs," Claire replied. "I couldn't understand her at all. Why bear it when you can change it directly? That's when she told me about the Christians."

"Ishimura," Akiko called in the present.

Ben snapped out of his reverie. "Sorry," he said.

He took Claire's portical from Akiko's hand and left the bathroom. He turned the display on, but it was encrypted, static on the screen.

"You haven't broken into this yet?" he asked.

"A few of our techs have tried, but every time they connect their portical, they get corrupted."

"Why don't you send it to Port Techs?"

"There's a peripheral leash that prevents us from taking it off the premises without self-destructing."

"What do you want me to do?"

"I've heard you're quite skilled with porticals."

"Hardly. I–"

Akiko put her hand on his arm. "This is not the time to be modest, captain. I've heard of your reputation at breaking encryption codes. Besides seducing women, it's the only thing you're good at."

"That reputation is completely unearned. I get rejected all the time." He took out his portical and a wire, since Claire's portical had no EKS connection. He linked them directly.

"You should be careful," Akiko said. "We've already lost a dozen port–"

"In," Ben said.

"What do you mean, in?"

"I mean the encryption is cracked," Ben said. "At least the first layer. The second layer is going to be tricky. There are algorithms here that alter their variables with every attempt. Unless you know the base equation, it'll short circuit both our porticals."

"How soon?"

"I have thirty seconds before our porticals need replacing."

Ben jumped through the numbers, pressing keys on his portical screen, alternating equations and variables. His own portical allowed him to input guesses while bypassing the normal security protocols, which in turn meant he could make false attempts without triggering the failsafe guards. The math involved was just like a secret that needed interpreting; hints and signs of demureness, or audacity, knowing when to step back, when to be bold. The sortie involved the right combination of words; a mix of humor, brash stupidity, and affection. Ben coaxed the commands, gently warbling unspoken cues. The cryptography responded like bittings on pins and wafers, a sheer line of desire unlocked through probes, piercing here, pressing there, ululations of longing, rotating into place, a misplaced symmetry of lust.

"Second layer broken. Let's see if there's a third."

The third confronted him with a question:

"WHAT IS THE MEANING OF LIFE?"

He was about to answer, "What?" then figured that would probably cause a short circuit. Was this a trick question, or was it one of those subjective emotional encryption locks that measured audio wavelengths to determine sincerity?

"Despair," he replied.

"WHAT DO YOU DO?"

Ben had already set off a countermanding key program that would attempt to unravel the entire layer.

"I censor seditious material."

"DO YOU ENJOY 'I CENSOR SEDITIOUS MATERIAL'?"

"I love it."

"WHY?"

His program was struggling to break in. He had another idea. If he could funnel a pathway through the encryption every time it processed his answers, it was possible to transfer the basic files on the portical.

"I protect people from disharmony."

A harsh beep rang out loud, indicating a misstep. Akiko watched raptly. Ben figured another mistake or two, and both porticals would be destroyed.

"WHY?" Claire's portical repeated.

"Because I like controlling things."

"IS THERE A CONNECTION BETWEEN 'DESPAIR' AND 'BECAUSE I LIKE CONTROLLING THINGS'?"

"I hope not."

Her portical shut down and he quickly disconnected his.

"It's dead?" Akiko asked.

"Hers is dead. But I transferred most of the files from her portical."

He accessed her duplicated portical on his screen. Different orbits of influence popped up; her communications to friends, photographs, music tracks, all revolving around each other like the planets and the stars.

"What am I looking for?" he asked.

She sidled up next to him. "How did you get in?"

"It's kind of like a good date. You just need to be adaptable."

She searched through the different orbits, scouring for something. "You got everything?" she demanded impatiently.

"Not everything. But most of it."

She cursed in Japanese under her breath. "It isn't here."

"What isn't?"

She clicked on the photos. A gallery of images appeared: friends at parties, dances, restaurants, outings. There was one female companion that came up repeatedly.

"We'll need to interrogate all of her companions," Akiko said. "Can you have the photos sent to my portical?"

He tapped a few commands on the portical display screen. "Done."

Ben looked at the wall, then back at the portical.

"I'm missing something," he said.

"What do you mean?"

"Why all this security on her portical if there isn't anything valuable on here?" he wondered.

He went to her room, checked her mat, rummaged through her books, and peeked behind her desk. Some of the plants seemed removable and he inspected the soil, but there wasn't anything other than roots. He opened the window and felt the wall right outside, just beyond view. Nothing. He went to the living room windows and checked there as well.

"What are you looking for?" Akiko asked.

Ben held up a lean metallic strip he'd found adhering to the external wall. "A peripheral unity driver. It synchronizes porticals." He inserted it into his machine and a series of numbers popped up. "Normally, as long as you pass the security codes on your portical, it'll sync directly and open up un-synced files. But if you fail, you won't even know the sync didn't happen unless you're looking for it." A new sphere appeared. "It looks like that game, *United States of America*."

Akiko snatched the portical, pressed a few buttons. "Look at this introduction and the ludicrous exaggerations about the death tolls of the Americans," she said, agitated.

"Why don't you just censor it?"

"We've tried. But it's become an underground hit and is spreading rapidly." Akiko handed Ben back his portical. "What's this 'Kami mode'?"

"That's world creation," Ben replied. "It means she can change and design the world using her portical."

"Is that standard in most games?"

"Sometimes. Depends on the designer."

"If it's on there, does that mean anyone can take the game simulator and modify it?"

"Pretty much."

"We've found the game piggybacked with many top hits," Akiko said. "Even if a censor were checking a game, they wouldn't see it unless they knew the specific codes to access it."

"How did *you* find them?"

Akiko looked grimly at him. "We can be convincing. I'll need your portical back," she said. "You'll need to request a new one."

"I always carry a few spares. Can I copy my personal items over?"

"Make it quick."

Ben organized his portical and sent data into his personal database on the kikkai. A message came in for Akiko, which she read.

"Are you done?" she asked.

"Yep."

Akiko held up the picture of Claire's friend that seemed ubiquitous. "Command just informed me that the woman in the pictures is her friend, Jenna Fujimori, and is suspected of working with the Americans. They're tracking her location at the moment. She was the one who was speaking in the communication with Claire when they mocked the Emperor. We hope she can tell us more about Mutsuraga's current plans."

"What'll happen when you catch the general?"

"What do you think?"

"Are there any theories on why Claire..." He glanced involuntarily towards the bathroom.

"Perhaps she couldn't bear the dishonor of her father's sedition."

As they went to the elevator, Akiko checked her portical again. There were no updates. "I need to eat," she said.

"There's a great tempura burger place nearby," he offered.

"Let's go."

11:31am

"Oh great, we beat the lunch rush," Ben said. "I recommend the classic tempura burger. They dip their buns in honey and pecan sauce and it's amazing. You can get vegetable or pork tempura. I personally like the shrimp. They catch it fresh and–"

"Order as you please," she said. "I'll leave my lunch choices to you."

The interior of the restaurant was painted in a colorful mix of curry yellow and braised brown hues that made it resemble a fried crustacean. Statues of their mascot, Shrimp Boy, smiled at them from every corner. There was a playground in the middle of the restaurant and the walls were huge portical display screens showing both adult and children versions of the Shrimp Boy drama and cartoon series. Waiters and waitresses dressed in pink shrimp costumes bowed and welcomed them in Japanese: "Good afternoon, officers."

They were escorted to a private room blocked off by shoji screens.

"It's cheap, has great service, and the food is amazing," Ben said excitedly. They took off their shoes and sat on the tatami mats. "The only place I like better for lunch is a chicken and waffle place on Pico that's fantastic, though I'm really digging the Cajun sauce and boiling crab at this seafood place on Wilshire."

Akiko took out her portical and started reading files.

Ben said, "I have a rule. No business during lunch."

"Why not?" Akiko asked.

"Everyone needs a rest now and then."

"The enemies of the Empire do not rest. Neither should we."

Her eyes went back to her portical.

"What's so interesting?" he asked.

"What are you seeking? An exchange of useless information?" She put her portical down. "What would you like to know?"

"A little bit about who you are."

"I work seven days a week, my brother was killed by American terrorists, and I hate people who waste my time."

"What do you like to do for fun?" Ben asked.

"Hunt traitors," she snapped. "Anything else?"

The burgers came a few minutes later. Ben savored each bite, relishing the mix of the shrimp and the honey. Akiko chewed without a word. She only ate a quarter before commenting, "It's too sweet," then put it aside.

"The eggplant fries are pretty good," Ben said.

She took a bite and spat it out. "They're too salty."

Ben was about halfway through his burger when she asked, "How much longer are you going to eat?"

"Just give me another minute."

She sighed before looking at her portical again. A ring went off and she immediately picked up. "Hello, General," she greeted.

"Any progress on the case?" the general asked.

"A little bit, sir. We've found evidence that Claire Mutsuraga had the game on her portical. It was a tricky connection, but I was able to figure out the best methodology of breaking through. I'm going through her files this very minute."

"Excellent. Our first tangible connection. Well done."

"Thank you, sir. I'll be following up with her friend, Jenna Fujimori."

"We've tracked Fujimori to the Compton Opera House where she is taking part in rehearsals. Head there and interrogate her. Report to me immediately once you learn anything new. Command has taken a direct interest in this and wants continual updates. You understand the revised orders that were sent earlier?"

To Ben's surprise, Akiko seemed uncomfortable replying. "I do, sir. Is there any room for–"

"No," the voice cut her off and the communication ended.

When Akiko looked up at Ben, he said, "I'm done," even though he had a third left.

She looked away, clearly preoccupied by a troubling thought.

12:11pm

The Compton Opera House (known to everyone as the COH) was a favorite spot for first dates because of their beautiful gardens and an all-night zoo that was tailored for nature outings. The government had rebuilt Compton after massive riots destroyed it a few decades back. It was now one of the richest, most exclusive neighborhoods in Los Angeles. The COH was shaped in the dragon mask of the Emperor, a massive conglomerate of crimson eyes, a commanding nose, and snarling lips. Adjacent buildings included the Tojo Theater House and the Wachi Tea Gardens. Statues of the three treasures, the *Kusanagi* sword, the jewel *Yakani no Magatama*, and the mirror, *Yata no Kagami*, were the source of huge water fountains.

The pair went through the lobby of the opera house into the actual performance hall. The COH had converted the interior for a new show called the *Water Geisha* and a massive water tank half the size of the building was built inside. Ben had heard about the show, a thousand coordinated swimmers performing a dazzling water spectacle commemorating the Japanese victory in the Pacific during the Holy War. None of them were wearing their costumes yet, but submarines, aircraft carriers, and gunboats were each going to be personified in a tense drama set to music. The smell of chlorine pervaded and the temperature was warm enough to cause him to sweat under his uniform.

"That's pretty amazing," Ben said, marveling at the height of the tank.

Agent Tsukino approached one of the attendants, showed her badge, and said, "We need to see Jenna Fujimori."

The carpet that usually lined the aisles had been stripped out in favor of cement. Performers were walking past them, many of them naked aside from a tiny oxygen mask for their breath. They were of different ethnicities and wore colored contact lenses that doubled as shielding for their eyes underwater. Hundreds of naked men and women swam within the tank and the lights swayed in a dance of their own, pirouetting and spinning in a resplendent swirl. A flurry of bubbles somehow turned into the shape of torpedoes that blew up upon contact with the live performers. A small group of gaudily dressed men and women were at the base outside of the tank, barking directions into their microphones. Many of the swimmers were short, stout, and muscular. The woman approaching them had arms that were twice the size of Ben's own, though she looked to be under five feet tall. Her brunette hair was tied into a wet knot and she was wiping the water from her green eyes. She had the tattoo of a bat on her right shoulder and though she was stark naked, she didn't seem embarrassed in the least bit. She also didn't seem that pleased to see them. "What's going on? I'm very busy and–"

Akiko showed her badge. "We need to talk with you. You should put some clothes on."

"I have a skin suit on," she said, referring to the transparent layer around her body. "The–"

"What's going on here?" a man with green hair and a yellow swim suit demanded, as he approached them from the aisle. "I need her for the show." He saw Akiko's badge. "This show is for the celebration in four days. This is for the honor of the USJ. She doesn't have time to waste with questions! I need her *now*!"

"Forgive me, Hideki-san," Akiko said, though she did not bow. "We have some important questions regarding Imperial security."

"I am going to file a complaint with the Ministry of Defense! How can I run a show without my performers?"

"Surely you can do without one for a short time."

"For you, it's just a short time. For me, it's a ripple effect putting us behind by days we don't have!" He started moaning in pain and there was even a tear in his eye. "None of you military types understand the arts. The only art you know is paranoia. Governor Ogasawa is personally attending opening night. The performance must be flawless."

"Why don't you have a replacement take her place?" Akiko suggested.

"You are taking her away from us?" he inquired, scandalized by the suggestion.

"I am."

The man started hitting his head with his open palm and screeching. His assistants fanned him and did their best to console him, as he seemed about to swoon.

Akiko seized Jenna by the arm and, when she hesitated, eyed Ben. He grabbed Jenna by her other arm and helped escort her out.

"I thought you were just asking a few questions," Jenna said.

"You won't be returning tonight," Akiko informed her.

"What did I do?"

"The question isn't, what did you do wrong? What you're really wondering is, what did you get caught doing?"

"I didn't do anything."

"We'll see about that."

They exited the opera house.

"Who was that man?" Ben asked Jenna.

"Director Hideki Inouye," she replied.

The only non-ethnic Japanese person to direct a national ballet. Ben hadn't recognized him with his green hair. Then again, Inouye usually had some outlandish hair style.

"You must play a really important part," Ben said to her.

"I'm the *Panay,* one of fifty Western boats that got blown up during the Holy War," Jenna answered. "I'm pretty much just an extra."

12:54pm

Adjacent to the COH, a gray truck was parked. It was lugging a trailer that Ben presumed to be an interrogation room. The back was open, a ramp sticking out. They led Jenna up and, after they entered the truck, two men in black suits closed the door behind them. Along the walls were panels and porticals that were manned by various personnel. Two guards seized Jenna, tied her arms and legs together, then forcibly thrust her onto a chair. The surrounding lights dimmed and a spotlight beamed straight into her face.

"Jenna Fujimori," Agent Tsukino began, "how would you like it if I broke both your legs and fractured your spine so you could never swim again?"

Ben felt a chill in his body. He wondered why they'd snatched her up in broad daylight at her place of work. If they really meant to break her legs, they could have grabbed her in the middle of the night so that no one would notice. This was meant to be a public arrest.

"That would not be good," Jenna replied.

"If you cooperate with us, we may let you perform in future shows."

"What about the *Water Geisha*?"

"Impossible," Akiko said. "You are not a true patriot."

"What do you mean?"

Akiko lifted up her index finger. From the speakers, a recording of Jenna's voice played.

"What about Tim?" Jenna was asking.

"She's worried he can't have babies," another voice asked. Ben recognized Claire's voice

"I heard even the Emperor can't have babies anymore," Jenna replied. There were a few ribald jokes followed by giggles that seemed silly and childish, not by any means malicious. The recording came to an end.

"We were just joking around," Jenna tried to defend herself.

"At the expense of the Almighty and Gracious Emperor. He has given you life! All you foreigners! He freed America from the tyranny of the slave drivers. And you think it's funny to ridicule his ability to procreate? By extension, you are also mocking every one of his sons and daughters, and *their* sons and daughters, the whole royal line."

"That wasn't my intention."

Akiko slapped Jenna across the face. "You are insolent in the face of obvious guilt! You don't show an ounce of penitence!"

Jenna glowered back with angry eyes.

"You have something you want to say?" Akiko challenged her.

"I'm sorry about what I said."

"You don't sound sorry."

"I am."

"You should have had honor like your friend Claire."

"What are you talking about?"

"She committed *jigai* to atone for her insolence."

"What? When?"

Akiko slapped her again; this time blood dotted Jenna's lip. "I've checked your financial records, the shows you've watched, and the game decisions you've made." Akiko started listing her transactions and choices. By themselves, they might have been harmless. But in conjunction, manipulated and funneled into a verdict, Jenna's guilt seemed beyond question. "Every action you've taken indicates a treasonous state of mind. Do you know what the punishment is for thought-treason?"

Jenna shook her head.

"Fifty years in a labor camp. How would you like to go to the labor camp at Catalina?"

"I would not."

"When was the last time you saw Claire Mutsuraga?"

"I talked to her by portical two weeks ago, but I've mostly been busy with the sho–"

Akiko kicked her in the shin. "I have your portical records! You talked a week ago!"

"I don't remember. It's all mixed up and it's been so hectic the last few days."

"Did she talk about suicide?" Akiko asked.

"No, of course not."

"You're certain?"

"Yes!"

"Where is her father?"

"I don't know."

"You don't know?"

"I swear I don't know," Jenna replied in a panic. "I've only talked to him a handful of times."

"About what?"

"Nothing important. Just stuff, you know?"

Akiko took out her silver gun. "There's an old American religion that said if your right hand causes you to sin, cut it off. If your tongue, cut that out too."

"I really don't know anything."

"This gun will rewrite the history of your blood. If I shoot you with this, in a minute you won't be recognizable. In four, you will suffer untold agony. In seven minutes, you will die the worst death known in the Empire. I will only ask you once again. Where is Claire's father?"

"I really don't know!"

Akiko took the gun and fired into her neck. It took thirty seconds before Jenna started screaming.

"W-what's happening?"

"Where is General Mutsuraga?" Akiko asked.

"I don't know I don't know I don't know! Please-please d-don't-don't."

Jenna vomited and the whole contour of her back transformed, muscles pressing against her flesh, causing it to bulge. Her breaths were feral, desperate, and lonely. Viruses were raiding her entire immune system, pillaging, sacking, and devouring. Nature never hesitated. The smell of her blood and shit filled the air. She'd released her bowels and her shrill cry continued. Ben turned his head away, but could hear her retching and struggling against her seat. He looked to Akiko. She noticed his gaze. He went to the back of the trailer and hit the door.

"Let me out," he ordered. "Let me out!"

A guard complied. He rushed out and gasped. He'd seen executions, knew about torture methods from San Diego. But the way Jenna's biochemistry mutated and the smell that followed was more repulsive than anything he'd been prepared for. It was never a good thing to betray yourself emotionally in that way. But he couldn't help himself.

"I know it's hard to see," he heard Akiko say from behind him. "You handled it pretty well for the first time."

"How many times have you done this?" he asked her.

"This was my thirteenth," she replied. "She was guilty of collaborating in a terrorist act that resulted in the death of seventeen of our soldiers last year in Palos Verdes."

"How do you know that?"

"We found the information on Claire's portical after you cracked it open."

"You didn't ask her anything about it."

"We'll extract the memories from her brain."

"What?" he said, startled because he didn't know that was even possible.

"Biologics have asked for fresh subjects to test."

"What if it doesn't work?"

Ben saw Akiko's face express the troubled look he'd seen earlier. It hardened when she noticed his attention. "Those were my orders," she stated, with a harshness that seemed to compensate rather than affirm.

Ben involuntarily touched the side of his throat. "Why did you bring me along for this?"

"Because I don't think you take your job seriously," she said. "You've been reported multiple times by colleagues and subordinates. I think you are barely competent, a man who is too comfortable with what he views as a stable job. Why do you think you got passed over last night for a promotion? I want to remind you of the repercussions of your reports, to realize that what you see, what you censor, is taken very seriously. We must maintain constant vigilance against the enemies of the Empire."

"You did this as a favor to me?"

"An interdepartmental reminder for an alumnus."

"What is it about this game that has you so worried?"

"The fact that you have to ask that question means you haven't learned your lesson yet."

"You forget I graduated almost last in my class?"

"I never forget."

"Do you need me for anything else?"

"Yes. But you're free for the rest of the night. Go have your pointless fun at the kyotei races." He was about to leave when she called him. "Captain Ishimura."

"Yes?"

"Salute your superior officer before leaving."

He saluted her. She dismissed him and went back into the interrogation trailer.

He stumbled his way to the subway entrance at the base of the plaza. Several civilians bowed to him to show their respect. He went to the restroom, saw that the "Other" door was marked "Out of Service." He found the door for ethnic Japanese and made his way to the sink to wash his face. He wiped his nostrils clean, blew the snot out and washed his face again. The stink of Jenna's death wouldn't go away. He sat down on the bathroom floor and stared blankly at the people coming in. His portical rang. He ignored it.

6:12pm

One more inch and it would have been death. The driver swerved with just enough pressure to curve smoothly, rather than colliding with the two boats next to his. Nine mechanical horses raced as tribute to the miracle of man traversing water. The LA Kyotei Stadium was massive, water tracks that were second in size only to Tokyo. Thousands were in the crowd, and Ben and Tiffany sat in the box seats for Taiyo Tech along with five other couples.

"They're amazing!" Tiffany Kaneko exclaimed. She'd dyed her hair blond since the previous evening and wore a red kimono. Though she hadn't powdered her face white, many envious glances skittered in Ben's direction.

He sulkily sipped on a tiny cup of *sake*.

"What's wrong?" Tiffany asked.

He forced a smile, realizing people next to their box seat were watching them. "I'm amazed by the race. Chao's dexterous for a fat man."

"His fat is deceptive. Look at him on those corners," she said. "He uses his weight to counterbalance those turns. He eats an ungodly amount of ramen to keep those handles. He used to be really skinny, but he wasn't as good. His big butt keeps him glued to the boat."

"Were you the one who was telling me you found big

butts on men attractive?"

"A man who sits a lot won't run off on you."

"I don't think you have to worry about men running off on you," Ben noted.

"I'm always telling my girlfriends to find a fat man."

"You eyeing Chao?"

She giggled. "I bet he'd be having more fun tonight. What's bugging you, Mr Iko?" She said the last word like "mystery" + "ko," her favorite nickname for him.

"I hear it's quite chic for officers to change the dye of their hair."

"You're pondering what color to change your hair to?" she asked.

"How do you think I'd look with blond hair like yours?"

"I like black hair," she replied. "I should write an opinion piece on it after I finish the two pieces I'm working on."

"What are they about?"

"Can't say."

"Why not?"

"I don't want you to censor it preemptively," she said.

"I only give suggestions so you won't get into trouble."

"I know and I appreciate it. But there used to be a thing called 'freedom of press' where you didn't have to worry about offending the wrong person or political group."

He put his hand on her waist and said, "I still have the freedom to press you."

"There's people around. Later," she promised.

"You gonna tell me what you wrote about?"

"My dream last night."

"You dreamt of kyotei racers?"

"Rats. I lived in a big mansion and it was gorgeous. But anytime I tried to sleep, I was covered by rats."

"Did they smell bad?"

"Do rats smell?"

"I never tried smelling one," Ben replied.

"Why don't you try next time?"

He sniffed her clothes and she pushed him away with a laugh. "After the rat dream, I dreamt I was married to a man whose first wife had died. He was still in love with her and, no matter what I did, he couldn't let go. It was so sad."

Ben's mind went to Mutsuraga. "Based on a true story?"

"Probably a movie I watched somewhere. Would you censor a sad story?"

"If it was boring."

"You find all sad stories boring."

"All sad stories ring the same. It's the happy ones that... wait, is that a line from somewhere?"

"I think you have it in reverse."

"You want a happy family?"

"I'd love a miserable one where everyone hated each other."

"Why?"

"So we could find redemption in each other's arms." She kissed him. "Why aren't you watching the races?"

"How can I when you're next to me?" he said, moving his hands lower to her hips.

"What about *go* tonight?"

"Sounds great. Let's go," Ben said.

"Go to play *go*?"

"Go home and play something else."

"All you officers only have one thing on your mind."

"What's that?"

"Procreation," Tiffany said.

"I consider it a form of recreation."

"Let me watch Sollazzo race. Please? Pretty please?"

He nodded and she clapped gratefully.

"Can you be a darling and get me some yakitori and rice candy from outside?" she asked, in a way that was gentle enough to be forceful.

He saluted her and exited the box, down the escalator.

Many attendees bowed as they passed him. A group of enlisted men saluted him. When he got to the food stand, there was a long line. An attendant bowed to him and said, "Sir, please go to the front."

He shook his head. "It's not necessary. I can wait."

"No, no. Officers should not wait."

"It's fine. Thank you."

A new round commenced on screen. The racers were speeding around the course. For all purposes, he looked like a soldier waiting in line to grab food for his lover.

"Good match, isn't it?" someone asked.

"Wh... yes, yes," he stammered. "Been waiting all week for this."

"Who you rooting for?"

He had to look at the screens to remember the names of the racers.

8:37pm

After they got back to his apartment, Tiffany slipped out of her kimono and started to kiss him. He caressed her breasts, her light brown nipples perking up. She had the tattoo of a three-headed lizard to the right of her belly button, a mascot and symbol of good luck from the Northern Campaigns when an actual three-headed lizard was supposed to have led the stray Japanese army into the camps of American rebels.

A few minutes later, she asked, "What's wrong?"

"Nothing's wrong."

She felt his pants. "This isn't like you. You were so giddy earlier."

"I'm sorry."

"Why don't you lay down? Let me give you a massage."

She helped him undress. He lay in bed. She put her hands on his shoulders. "There's the problem. All the nerves are bunched up." She massaged his neck, rubbing out the tension.

"You still remember your university days?" he asked.

"Of course."

"Good memories?"

"Good and bad. What about you?"

"The cadre sent us down to San Diego for part of our officer training. One of the first things they had us do was chop off the head of a prisoner. They brought this skinny guy out for me. I could see his rib cage and he had a hard time breathing. They tied him to a pole. Told me I had to cut his head off. The man was so scared, he shat himself. I couldn't do it. Tried to, but my hands wouldn't move. After that, they said I didn't have what it took to serve in San Diego and gave me all sorts of demerits." He got up on his elbows. "I still think about how scared that guy was."

"Why?"

"Maybe I have a psychological defect. Shooting an enemy, that's one thing. But cutting off their head. I don't know if I could ever do that. But I might have to. Someone said to me," and he did his best to mimic a deeper voice, "'The sword is an extension of our soul. Used properly, it becomes a part of who we are, an expression of our being. Kill a man with a gun, and you have no connection to him. Kill him with a sword, and your souls are intertwined.'"

"It would have been shocking for anyone to be faced with that kind of situation without any context," she said. "Don't feel bad."

"The officers made so much fun of my name back then."

"I love your name, Beniko. It has a lovely ring to it."

"It's a woman's name."

"Your mom picked it?"

He nodded. "Before I was born. She was convinced I'd be a girl."

Tiffany touched his face. "You would have been very pretty."

"I didn't like them mocking me and they even attacked my parents for giving me that name. When I tried to defend them, they asked me why I cared. Didn't I turn them in? I couldn't say anything and their bullying got worse, so I stopped caring and just fooled around. It worsened my reputation and I've never been able to shake it." He kissed her and asked, "Do you ever feel like covering anything other than kyotei and football?"

"Like scarred captains of the army?"

He laughed. "I'm sorry I've been out of it tonight."

"You should be. I'm going out of town for the next week. Big kyotei matches in Beiping and Hong Kong."

"You're not covering the Anniversary?"

"I am, but from Beiping."

"Do you have different lovers in every town?"

"You really want to know, or will that spoil the fun?"

"You know I don't get jealous about things like that," he said. "I just wonder what you're like around different people."

"The same. Well, a little different."

He held her chin, looked her in the eye.

"I'm gonna miss you," she said.

"It'll only be a week. I'll be here waiting."

There was a look of regret in her eyes and he wondered why.

"Lay back down," she ordered, then continued to massage him. "Go to sleep."

"I'm not tired. I have so much to do."

"Like what?"

"Plan a funeral," Ben said. "And keep a promise I made a long time ago."

"What promise?"

"I'm sworn to secrecy."

She moved her hands down his back. "You can take care of your secrets tomorrow. Tonight, clear your mind of thoughts."

"I wish I could."

"Let me help you."

"How?"

"With pain."

She intensified the strength of her massages. Ben drowned his restlessness in tactile vacuity.

11:41pm

The tenth portical ring woke him. Tiffany was nowhere in sight. Ben turned on the portical. There was no video, only an audio call from a number he didn't recognize.

"You're still alive."

"Who's this?" Ben asked.

"It's *me*," Agent Akiko Tsukino said. Her number was blocked as with all members of Tokko to maintain their privacy.

"Do you need something?"

"Check under your bed," she ordered.

"Why?"

"Just look. I need to confirm if they've targeted you as well." He moved to the edge, shone his portical below. To his surprise, there was a device there he'd never seen before, crowded with wires and what appeared to be explosives.

"W-what is that?" Ben stuttered.

"Is there a red light on?"

Ben saw the red beam shining in his eyes. "Yes."

"That means it's armed. The bomb is pressure sensitive."

"You mean if I get off the bed—"

"You'll die unless you listen to me," Akiko replied.

"How did this happen?"

"Someone wants you dead. There've been several names

targeted on a list I found on Jenna's belongings, including you. The others are already dead."

"Can you send a bomb squad?"

"We just had them try on another target."

"And?"

"They were killed. I'm outside your apartment building. The technicians designed a jamming signal I can send out, but it'll only last a minute before it gets overridden."

"What do I do?" Ben asked.

"Hold on. Let me sync with the bomb's kikkai signal."

Ben looked at all the paintings on the wall, thought of the days he'd spent aligning the furniture to get optimal feng shui.

"I got it," Akiko said. "Leave your portical on the bed, open your window, and jump out."

"Is there a Plan B?"

"What's wrong with Plan A?"

He envisioned himself splattering against the cement. "I think I'd rather die in an explosion than falling down from a building."

"Can't you take a leap of faith?"

"In you?"

"I'll release a safety net," she assured him – the nets that went up in case people tried to commit suicide from the tops of buildings.

"Very generous of you. Why would you care if I lived or died?"

"I still need your help tracking down the general."

"So this isn't an interdepartmental favor to your alumnus?"

"Not this time."

"If I'm not very helpful, will you shoot me too?"

"I shoot anyone who betrays the Emperor."

It was madness to jump out of a building. But did he have any other choice? He looked under the bed again. There were explosives all right. Was this how he was going to die? *Think,*

Ben, think! If he jumped out the window and she didn't trigger the net, it was very possible they could call his death a suicide. An all-too-convenient closure to a Tokko plan to dispose of him. He preferred to leave a bloody mess. He looked over at the window and knew it was a far drop down. Too far.

"Jam it," Ben said to Akiko. He tossed the portical down, ran out his room and down the stairs, nearly slipping. He rushed to the front door and grabbed the samurai armor. As it was coated in titanium, he hoped it would provide some protection. He lifted the chest plate and covered his body, ran out of the unit and shut the door behind him. The elevator seemed like a bad option so he went for the stairs when he heard a rumble. The fire was oddly cold and he felt something hurtle into his back and propel him downwards. He closed his eyes, ready for death. "*Shikata ga nai,*" he murmured to himself, feeling morbidly satisfied that his concluding emotion was a sense of welcoming.

Los Angeles, July 1, 1988 1:36am

Just under twenty-four hours earlier, Akiko had woken her boyfriend early in the morning. Night was dissolving into day and a layer of fog dallied over Venice Beach. She remembered traces of a dream, an old friend painting his house blue, covering the lamps, shelves, even the flowers in a darker hue of ultramarine. She'd reminded her boyfriend of his duty. "If more men with your genetic history don't contribute to the fertility clinic, the population of pureblooded Japanese will disappear in the USJ."

"Do you know what I have to do there every day?" he'd protested. "They take the joy out of–"

Everything was nothing for her, while seeming nothingness could signify anything in the proper context. In the wrong context, her concerns about the infertility Japanese men were experiencing from all the atomic weapon testing going on in Nevada could be construed as treasonous.

"Why'd you volunteer me for this?" he groaned.

"Because we're citizens of the Empire and it's our obligation to help in any way possible."

"What's the big deal about being pure Japanese? You're French and Korean, and you're a more important part of the Empire than I ever will be."

She bristled at his reminder of her polluted ancestry. "The fact that you're full blooded Japanese is essential to the Empire," she said, even though, objectively, it made no sense. Some of the finest officers she'd served with were of mixed ethnicity, whereas many of the pureblooded Japanese were arrogant assholes who felt too privileged to listen to common sense.

As an agent of Tokko, she knew hints of personality had to be vanquished. Akiko possessed no photos, despised most gifts as junk, and had only the most utilitarian of furniture. Her kitchen was bare as she rarely ate at home. The floors were concrete and the wood was stripped out in case of electronic bugs. There were no shelves betraying books of interest, nothing worthy of being categorized as a hobby, though she did possess an extensive library of writing recommended during her time at BEMAG on her portical.

She was extremely satisfied with the thought that even if her apartment had been targeted by the terrorists, she'd have lost nothing and her room would be almost indistinguishable from a thousand others. Anonymity was her secret identity. Her appearances were mostly natural with only a minimal amount of sun cream to protect her skin. For official agency visits, she wore dark red lipstick and colored her eyes violet because she found the effect intimidating for her subjects. It was a color combination she'd worked at over the years to produce an almost warpaint-like appearance, and it was the one she'd used when she met Beniko Ishimura.

Almost a day after she'd sent her boyfriend to the clinic, she was at the hospital with Ben. He'd survived the attack and was lying on a hospital bed in front of her, his back being treated for burns. The doctor had assured her he'd be able to return to duty in a few hours, saved by his suit of armor.

"Thanks for coming for me," Ben said to her. "If you hadn't delayed that bomb, I'd be a thousand pieces right now."

"It was my duty," she replied.

"Even if it was, I'm grateful," he said. He turned to the side. "I honestly didn't think you would give a shit whether I lived or died."

"Why would I not? We're both servants of the Emperor."

"I'm glad you still feel that way."

"Why didn't you trust me when I asked you to jump out of the window?" she demanded. "If I wanted you dead, I wouldn't have gone through such an elaborate ruse."

"It's not that I didn't trust you," he replied. "I'm just afraid of heights."

She looked at his scars, which were already looking better. "You're fortunate Los Angeles has the best medical facilities in the Empire."

The Empire's state of the art biotechnology had eliminated most known diseases, a fact not lost on all the German officials she saw in the hallway. The burn marks on Ben's back were rapidly healing, but her mind involuntarily went back to the night her brother had been killed by explosives from an American terrorist attack. He'd been burned beyond recognition and, for a moment, the blackened groove of Ben's skin looked the same. Still, it was only an archipelago of burn marks in an ocean of flesh compared to the lava field that had been her brother. Ben had survived with superficial wounds to his back and arm.

"I feel very fortunate," Ben said. "And grateful."

Her principal mission had been to execute Jenna publicly, despite her protests to the contrary, and have her brain ready for Biologics. Akiko had also been told to assess the captain, determine if the complaints about his lazy work ethic were true. She didn't like him, didn't think he took his job seriously enough. But as she reported, he had been able to crack Claire's portical when over thirty specialists had failed.

"How many others died?" he asked.

"I don't have the exact number. Other agents are still collating the information."

"Anyone you know pass away?"

"Someone leading the bomb squad," Akiko replied. "I was supposed to be in her place."

"I'm sorry to hear that."

"I didn't know her well," Akiko stated. "But she died in the line of service. There is no greater honor."

"It's still tough having someone die in your place."

"People die and are reborn into a new life. It's the skewed circle that drives our existence. She took my place. I'll take someone else's someday."

"You believe in reincarnation?"

"Why do you seem surprised?"

"Tokko usually aren't religious."

"Everything gets recycled. Star dust, cow shit, even our ashes. Why not the electrical impulses of our brain? You don't believe it?"

Ben shook his head. "No."

"That's why you fear killing," she stated.

"I fear birth more than murder."

"Birth?"

"Bringing children into our world without any regard for their desires is a crime. Even if they are 'reborn souls.'"

"Only a man who'd turn in his own parents would say something like that," Akiko remarked.

Ben seemed about to defend himself when a nurse came in. She removed the regenerative gels that were treating his burns. "Please stay this way for the next two hours," she said, put the gels back on, and left.

"Any idea who set the bombs?" Ben asked Akiko.

"The main suspect is your girlfriend, Tiffany Kaneko," she answered.

"That's impossible," Ben said.

"Why? She was the last person you were with. There's a lot of unusual activity in her itinerary for the past month that can't be accounted for on standard records."

"You mean she travels a lot. She's a journalist."

"You feel an attachment to her?"

"Of course," Ben replied.

"Even if she may have been the one who tried to kill you?"

"I highly doubt it."

"Doubt is my area of expertise, Captain Ishimura. It's never wise to ignore doubt of any nature."

"If it was only me, it'd make sense. But this is way bigger than that."

"I've considered that," Akiko said. "I have officers investigating your home and they'll get back to me if they find anything in the debris. I'm curious how long those explosives were there and why they picked tonight to set them off." She stood up.

"Where are you going?" Ben asked.

"To speak with Tiffany."

"Let me come with you."

"You still need the gels to work on your back."

"I'm fine."

The bioscans behind him measuring various statistics indicated nominal health conditions. "You could compromise the case with your bias," she said.

"What's that mean?"

"If your girlfriend turns out to be the one who implemented the bomb, she will be executed."

"And if she's innocent?"

"Everyone's guilty. It's only a matter of figuring out what for."

"What about Tokko?"

"If we weren't guilty of something, we wouldn't be good at our jobs."

Ben tried to stand, but Akiko stopped him. "There's an

incident I need to investigate," she said.

"What kind of incident?"

"The Gogo Arcade is having unusual problems."

"I like the Gogo Arcade," Ben said. "Let me come along."

She was about to refuse him, but something in his eagerness reminded her of her brother. "Give the gels another two hours to work and then meet me."

Ben lay back down.

"I'm sending you the directions for the Go–"

"I know where the Gogo Arcade is."

She went down into the underground parking lot and saw the shadow of a massive winged creature flapping on the wall. It took a moment for her to realize it was a tiny moth brushing right against the light, projecting a black silhouette as its bigger alter ego. She hopped into her car and took out a piece of gum from the glove department. "Any updates?" she asked the centralized communicator hooked into the car's portical, as she drove to her destination.

"Nothing new since your last check," the operator from Tokko command answered. "Forensics is still investigating the site."

"Any mission parameters at the Gogo?"

"You are to question Tiffany Kaneko and determine if she's a viable suspect."

Akiko had not told Ben that Tiffany was last seen at the arcade with a group of kyotei racers, partying in their karaoke booths. "Is she considered disposable?"

"Not at this time."

Which meant the evidence was circumstantial at best. Akiko rubbed her eyes, feeling tired, wanting a cigarette. But she'd quit, or at least told herself she'd quit. She'd go find coffee at the arcade.

2:08am

Gogo Arcade was as big as some shopping malls and was bustling with activity. The complex was four stories tall and almost two hundred and forty thousand square meters in size. Tubed escalators connected the gaming center to peripheral shopping malls. The first floor was packed with slot machines, *pachinko* machines, and *takarakuji* vendors. Bars were stationed at almost every corner, and waitresses and waiters bowed to those passing by. The second and third floors were brimming with games that players could directly connect into their porticals. Big screens showed off a variety of simulations: fight as a soldier in the Holy War; pilot a mecha; or mow down rebels as the player-controlled bullets in an artillery assault. Huge battles took place over individual porticals projected on the arcade screen, thousands fighting against thousands of others, reinforced in their ideology that *gyokusai* ("a glorious death") was the ultimate blessing. For those who wanted to take a break from the hyperrealistic visuals of combat, there was also an eclectic share of simulation games – be a bedbug for the night and multiply as much as possible; live life as a brick for ten years; become a raccoon and travel through time; and channel a fire and burn as much of an old American city as possible (of course, all the victims were ethnically non-Japanese as regulated by the censors). The amalgam of noise was so deafening, it became a sonorous blur of gunshots, explosions, and expletives. It was a constant barrage of stimulation, spectacle vying to outdo itself in a visual orgy more blinding than the gorgons. Akiko wondered if the study of unidentified human whimsies had a name.

She'd never liked games. Her brother played them every chance he could and his decision to join the army was directly influenced by his love of war games.

"I want to be like the heroes in *Honor of Death*!" he'd said.

"*Baka*," she cursed him. "It's just a game."

The fervor and intensity with which people played their porticals perturbed her. Even her boyfriend, Hideyoshi, played addictively into the night. A fight between eight gamers had to be broken up by arcade security and a shouting match between lovers over a misreported score had to be quelled by guards. Akiko knew all gaming fell under the Department of Peaceful Propaganda, but she did not like the effect it had on the citizens. She picked up a coffee, averting her eyes from the cigarette rack. She sniffed the cigarette smoke in the air, hoping to get a little jolt. It had been six days since she'd promised herself she'd stop.

The karaoke stations were in the eastern wing of the fourth floor. Many were fronts for hostess and host bars – male and female "escorts" whose time could be bought for companionship. Shortly after her graduation a few years back, some of her classmates had taken her to a host bar to celebrate. While she found many of the men handsome and charming, they were too artificial to take seriously. The men barked back whatever they thought she wanted to hear and were essentially caricaturized companions. She was surprised, then, to find her male classmates loved female artifice even though it was so obviously an illusion.

It was one of those host men that greeted her at the front of the Alchemist Bar, which was located on the top floor of the arcade. He was muscular with orange hair spiraling like a minaret above his head. Utterly ridiculous if he wasn't so cute. "For one?" he asked, smiling with dimples. According to the portical scan, his nickname was Hornet. He was twenty-two, never went to college, and lived in an apartment in Torrance.

She took out her badge and showed the image of Tiffany on her portical. "I'm looking for this woman. Her name's Tiffany Kaneko and she was seen here earlier."

"I don't recall–"

"Hornet – why do they call you that?"

He smiled in fake coyness. "Because I sting in bed."

"I can tell they'd love your sting in a labor camp at Catalina. Do you know much about what they do to fresh prisoners in Catalina?"

"I've heard stories."

"You've already been arrested four times on obscenity charges. I could arrest you for a fifth."

"On what charge? I have my license now."

"Poor memory," she replied.

He lowered his eyes. "I don't remember exactly when they went in, but they're in the back."

He escorted her through the marble hallway. Akiko connected into Tiffany's portical, accessing the camera as well as the audio speakers. There was loud music in the background and it was dark with strobe lights flashing so that it was impossible to see out the camera on her portical. Rooms filled with patrons were on either side of them, drunks bawling their souls out in hopes of one night of absolution. Karaoke was their escape, an attempt to exorcise the manacles of everyday routine. In civilian life, drinking binges and singing escapades were a form of bonding necessitated by the caprice of bosses who imposed their will on those below them. Akiko found the Tokko ban on fraternization a relief. They were trained to be suspicious of everyone, even each other.

Hornet went into the room and dragged Tiffany out. Tiffany

was drunk, wearing a slinky red dress, her blond hair a mess from dancing. Hornet bowed and excused himself.

"What can I do for you?" Tiffany asked.

"When was the last time you saw Beniko Ishimura?" Akiko asked back, as she showed her badge.

"Earlier tonight. Why?"

"How would you describe your relationship with him?"

"We're… close friends."

"Any hostility between you two?"

"Of course not," Tiffany replied. "Did something happen to him?"

"Do you have any reason to believe something might have happened to him?"

"A member of the Tokko asking me about him seems like a good reason."

"Did Ishimura act strange at all?" Akiko asked, paying careful attention to Tiffany's response.

"He seemed distant, like something was bothering him."

"Did he say what?"

"No. I figured he just had a bad day at work."

"Is it common for him to have a bad day at work?"

"He's usually cheerful."

"Did you notice any unusual people in or outside of the apartment tonight?"

"Definitely not inside, but outside?" She thought back. "No."

"Why aren't you with him?" Akiko asked.

"He fell asleep and these guys wanted to party. I'm writing a story about kyotei racing and thought it'd be a good chance to get to know them better."

"Interactive journalism?"

"Something like that."

"Wouldn't that affect your objectivity?"

"I'm good at setting boundaries."

"Was Beniko a story?"

Tiffany smiled. "While I'd love to write a story about the office of the censor, no. My relationship with him is purely for pleasure. Is something going on?"

Akiko was about to answer when someone familiar popped her head out of the room. "Tiffany?" she called. "Everything OK?"

Akiko startled. It was the girl she'd executed earlier, Jenna. Except she looked normal, untouched by the virus.

"Don't worry," Tiffany replied to her.

When Akiko stared at the woman again, a completely different face was there, much rounder with a leaner nose. There was no resemblance at all.

"Here's my itinerary for the past week," Tiffany offered, showing her portical's calendar. "I can get witnesses for most of my schedule."

Akiko perused it. There did not seem to be anything overtly suspicious.

"Any more questions, officer?" Tiffany asked, taking her portical back.

Akiko shook her head. "I'll contact you if I have."

"I'm flying out to Beiping in the morning."

Her business completed, Akiko hastily exited. Hornet bowed to her as she left, but she did not acknowledge him.

2:45am

It's because I'm tired, she told herself. *I need to get home and sleep.* She prepared a short report to Command in a conference room security provided, explaining that a preliminary questioning indicated no leads from Tiffany. Afterwards, she walked through the arcade and watched as thousands of gamers waged a digital war. General Mutsuraga, the gaming *taisho*, developed war simulations in the first Mexican Conflicts and the San Diego Uprising that had been uncannily accurate, helping them to annihilate their opposition. When the Nazis caused an uproar over Afghanistan, Mutsuraga had programmed tactical games that prepared them for almost every contingency the German army would make. It was as though Mutsuraga knew their steps before they did. There was no doubt of his brilliance and his value to the Empire if it hadn't been marred by his wife's death. Akiko wondered again why his wife went out to a public marketplace in San Diego unguarded despite the ongoing revolt, a question she had never been able to resolve.

She saw that Hideyoshi had called. She called back, but he did not answer. He was most likely already sleeping.

I should get back home, she thought. But she didn't want to rest yet. She wandered the arcade, observing the people. She understood the teens who were there, but it was the older players that boggled her. Why were they here in the middle of the night, hooked to a slot machine or portical game? Did they have family? Her portical could easily register and detail their personal life back to her, but she liked playing the only game she ever enjoyed – guessing people's lives. She saw a balding man playing a simulation as a cat. She theorized he was a father of three whose family life he was trying to escape by taking on the tranquility of a lazy feline. The portical confirmed three children, but his wife had recently passed away as had their family cat. Two of his boys served as enlisted men in Vietnam, while the third had been killed. Onto an elderly woman with a thin frame, who was playing a samurai game slashing at horrifying *kami* (spirits). Akiko saw her gold watch and general demeanor, surmised she was a rich woman with a string of young lovers. The portical report indicated she'd been married over twenty years, had two children, and lived in wealth thanks to her engineer husband who was currently on a business trip to New Berlin on the Britannic Islands. Akiko noted the recorded logs of liaisons the woman had enjoyed at host bars. She was about to guess at a few more when all the screens changed.

"Imagine a world where everyone is equal," a voice declared over the arcade speakers. "Where men and women of all races live in peace. A world where the Chinese and the Africans and the Jews still exist, not mercilessly massacred. Every minute we are told lies, told 'inferior races' were wiped away by false plagues. Our literature, our history, even our religion is being reshaped. Genghis Khan was not Japanese. Jesus Christ was not a Shinto priest. Franklin Roosevelt did not voluntarily surrender to the Japanese Empire. America was not a cruel, despotic country bent on annihilating Japan and Germany. It was a land of freedom that believed the pursuit of happiness was an inalienable right. They had no Emperor – their leaders were chosen by and for the people. They could say, do, write, and believe whatever they chose.

The United States of Japan has forced themselves onto what was once the greatest nation in the world. Now, rise up, take back the country, return it to what it once was – the United States of America."

The game opened up with Japanese soldiers executing a group of unarmed civilians, thousands of them brutally murdered. Those who tried to escape were either stabbed in the back or shot in the head. Some of the digital Japanese soldiers laughed as they performed "cutting tests" and decapitated children.

She recognized Mutsuraga's game all too well as she'd been given a demonstration of it earlier. There was a funereal silence as gamers were engrossed. She called Command to notify them, explaining in brief what had transpired. "The game is playing on every screen. What should I do?" she asked the operator who relayed orders from Command.

"Stay put for now."

"But they're all playing it."

"We are sending assistance."

"Let me at least try to shut it down."

"Hold still, major."

"But–"

Her communication was broken and another figure appeared on her screen. "Major Tsukino."

"General Wakana," she called.

"I'll be there in ten minutes."

The communication ended. She felt relieved.

On several portical screens, the alternate history the game proposed kept on replaying. She found the premise ludicrous. Everyone knew the Imperial Army showed mercy to obedient civilians, going out of their way to help people. Collateral damage was an unfortunate reality of warfare and innocents couldn't avoid being harmed. But for mass executions, it was only rebels and their families – people who furtively supported the war effort – who were punished. They could hardly be considered innocent when they were supplying arms and a lifeline to dangerous dissidents who abetted in the death of loyal soldiers.

The whole narrative of the game revolved around a decision made early in the Pacific War and a detailed cinematic analyzed the diverging path. At the time the Nazis invaded the Soviet Union, they asked the Japanese Empire to attack from the east. Tokyo Command wanted to attack French Indochina to obtain severely lacking resources, particularly oil, which was scarce (once the war was over, ending their dependence on oil became one of the Empire's highest priorities). This was also motivated by the earlier defeat of the Kwantung Army during the Battles of Khalkhin Gol, including a beating at the hands of the Soviet general, Georgy Zhukov. Minister of Foreign Affairs, Yosuke Matsuoka, a hero who had been the one to furiously lead the charge to quit the incompetent League of Nations, convinced the Imperial army to attack the Soviet Union, believing an assault on Indochina would result in retaliatory actions by the Americans and the British. "We must either shed our blood or embark on diplomacy. And it's better to shed blood," he'd said. He also argued that the earlier Japanese defeat at Russian hands had been precipitated by the Kwantung army's carelessness and refusal to coordinate with the IJA rather than the strength of the Soviets.

His argument prevailed and, before the cold winter hit, Germany conquered Moscow, Japan keeping much of the eastern Russian army diverted. The next year, they carved up the Soviet Union. Victory over the west followed naturally.

According to the *USA* game, Japan made the foolish decision to attack Indochina first, bringing the US and Britain in early against the Empire. A preposterous turn of events; but even had they entered at that point in 1941 rather than six years later when the Germans, together with Japan, had developed the atomic torpedo, the Empire would have crushed them.

Only one thing troubled her. She had always been inspired

by the story of Genghis Khan as a great Japanese conqueror of China, killed by an unfortunate twist of fate when his horse threw him off. The implication that Khan wasn't Japanese flustered her. The game was a virus that needed to be eradicated. Better to put it out of her mind.

3:12am

General Wakana wore his ceremonial swords over his collarless black uniform, though he'd dispensed with his standard cape. He walked with a slight limp, leaning on a staff that was made of ivory, rings on each of his fingers. His uniform was covered with medals that indicated service in Mexico and Vietnam. He was a tall man with lean, hungry cheeks and a closely groomed mustache. His hazel eyes were inquisitive, though there was a violence in his gaze that verged on broodiness. His smile was tightly controlled, the muscles in his mouth taut. He was not a man accustomed to levity.

Behind him were trucks filled with soldiers.

Agent Tsukino saluted him and stated, "I strongly advise we shut the whole arcade down, sir."

"Why?"

"Because of the game, sir. We have to prevent its spread."

"I take it you're not aware that this isn't an isolated incident?"

"I was not."

"It's happening in arcades all over the USJ at this very minute. This was a coordinated launch. We don't want to shut it down until we can determine the source."

"This might be why they set off those bombs tonight," Akiko mused.

Wakana considered the connection. "It doesn't seem like a coincidence."

"We should stop them," she said, looking at the crowd. "It'll engender sedition if we let it continue."

"Do you have so little faith in the Empire that you think a game will threaten it?"

"Of course not, sir."

"If we block them, it will only make them more curious," the general said. "No. Better to let them get it out of their system while we investigate."

He was right, of course, Akiko inwardly acknowledged. The game had been spreading despite all their attempts at blocking it.

"I've ordered the dispatch of soldiers to physically record everyone playing the game," the general said.

"Why's that, sir?" she asked. "All portical activity is automatically recorded and we'll have a list of everyone present."

"Intimidation."

They entered the arcade and, sure enough, the sight of hundreds of soldiers recording all the activity on the floor unnerved many of the gamers, especially as the troops did not impede their play.

Akiko's portical rang. It was Ben. "I'm here," he said. "Where are you?"

He arrived five minutes later.

"It's been a long time, Ishimura," Wakana said to Ben.

"Yes, sir," Ben answered.

Akiko was surprised that they knew each other.

"I was relieved to hear you survived the blast," the general said.

"Thank you, sir," Ben replied.

"You're going to help us out with this mess?"

"I'll try, sir."

"This kind of operation needs heavy equipment, doesn't

it?" Akiko asked. "A year ago, some activists took over a gaming conference and switched up all the scores in a private portical they made inside a bathroom stall. There has to be a central hub either in the mall or somewhere close where all of this was carried out. If we check the circuits and see if there's any power surges or high concentrations of electrical use, I bet we can track them."

"Good thinking," Wakana said. "I'll have the soldiers search the grounds and check electrical activity."

"There's also a chance that the woman I was investigating was connected to these events. I wasn't sure earlier, but, in light of the situation, I should follow up."

"Which woman?" Ben asked.

"Tiffany Kaneko," she replied.

"She's here?"

Akiko nodded.

"I'm coming with you," Ben said.

"I need you here," Wakana said to Ben. To Akiko, he said, "You're right. She is connected. Don't question her in front of the group. Just bring her here."

She bowed as she left his presence. General Wakana got back to hawkishly watching everyone on the floor.

3:41am

Tiffany was still singing, trying to follow along with the tracks of the popular female band, Vertical Pink. At least that's what it sounded like from outside. When Akiko entered the room, six of them were bunched around the screen, playing the *USA* game, hypnotized and not even noticing her entrance. Akiko called Tiffany three times but she did not hear as she was singing on a karaoke machine in the corner. Furious when she saw Japanese soldiers being shot at as enemies, Akiko took out her pistol and fired at the screen, destroying it.

They turned to her. "Enjoying yourselves? That game is against the law." She grabbed one of the men, slapped him in the face, and asked, "How would you like to spend the next thirty years in a labor camp? All of you?"

"We thought it was something for the anniversary," Tiffany cut in.

"Outside," Akiko ordered, as she stepped back into the hall.

Tiffany followed, closing the door behind her.

"Are we not supposed to be playing the game?" she wanted to know.

"Have you played it before?"

"This is the first time I've seen it."

"Have you heard anything about it?"

"No," Tiffany replied. "It's a strange concept for a game

– I can't imagine the chaos the world would be in if the Americans had won."

"My superior, General Wakana, would like to see you."

"Me?"

"Yes, you," Akiko confirmed.

"For what?"

"He has questions."

As they left, a pair of blond waitresses with enameled faces greeted several guests, asking, "Would you like some company?"

"What do you think of them?" Tiffany asked.

"They look like mannequins."

"Synthetic waitresses. I prefer the redhead versions. Some guys prefer their company to real women."

"Why?"

"Everyone likes a fantasy."

Multiple waiters bowed as they left, asking them to return soon.

After they stepped out of hearing proximity to the bar, Tiffany's smile vanished. "Why's he trying to blow my cover?"

"Excuse me?"

Tiffany glowered. "He didn't tell you?"

"Tell me what?"

She shook her head. "I'm Kempeitai, undercover." Kempeitai, or Kempei for short, were the Military Police arm of the Imperial Japanese Army. In the USJ, they mainly dealt with external and foreign threats, though, on occasion, their interests overlapped with the Tokko who dealt with internal issues. "They're already suspicious you came by once. Now that you've taken me away, it's over."

"What's over?" Akiko asked.

"The Americans. The rebels. You don't know?"

"I haven't been informed."

She sighed angrily. "There's a group of George Washingtons that escaped from San Diego. We're trying to track them down."

The general was in a storage room full of broken game booths and the artificial waiters they'd seen earlier, albeit wrapped in storage bags. He was making a call on his portical when Tiffany barged in. She bowed as mandated, then furiously demanded, "Where's General Nakajima?"

"He's been transferred to Singapore," Wakana responded, after ending his portical call.

"Why?"

"Your mission is complete."

"What do you mean? Do you see the game playing at every stall?" Tiffany demanded.

Wakana pushed one of the mechanical waitresses. "Your cover's blown."

"How is it blown?"

"Beniko's apartment was destroyed by a bomb shortly after you went home with him. That's why the Tokko is investigating you."

"What?" she snapped. She stared at the general, taking a moment to register what he'd said. "Is-is he OK?"

"That's beside the point."

"You think I had something to do with it?"

"Even if not, you're under suspicion and the only way to clear you is to reveal your true identity."

"I want to see General Nakajima."

"I know you and Nakajima had a special relationship. But that's over."

"Since when?"

Wakana stood up. "Since now. You are dismissed."

"What about the Beiping mission?"

"Canceled. You're dismissed," he repeated.

"I'm not under your jurisdiction. I have my own mandates."

"Right now, you are under my command and I have the orders to back them up."

She hesitated, wanting to object, but knowing better than to do so. She bowed and left in a huff.

"Confused?" the general asked Akiko. Two aides entered. One did a strange ceremonial tea dance with a fan, making swan-like motions with his arms and legs. The other made wild gesticulations, seemingly shouting without vocals, a mime-act in military fatigues. The general took no notice of them.

"Yes, sir," she said, not sure whether she should be more confused by the Kempei involvement or the strange behavior of the aides.

"Sometimes I am too. There are so many plots behind other plots and even more plots under those that they get entangled and no one knows who's spying on who. In the end, I suspect no one even knows why the plots were perpetuated."

"Are there American sympathizers here?"

"They are everywhere and I'll send others to follow up on her leads," the general replied. He unzipped the hanging bag of an artificial waiter and opened up a panel. "They're failed models. Recreating human behavior isn't as easy as our scientists would like to believe."

"Why are they here?"

"The colonel in charge of the arcade is a collector who believes every piece of junk is an artifact. He even keeps the broken arcade machines from decades ago. Loves the fact that they're 'made in America.'" He opened up another bag with a ridiculously proportioned female waitress. "I find love traps distasteful. Did you know the Chinese included them in their military teachings?"

Akiko nodded. "It's part of the old thirty-six stratagems. *Mei ren ji*, an act of desperation."

"Their efficacy can be questioned. Stolen victories using deceit crumble at the first sign of adversity." He felt the cheeks and neck of the female model. "It feels so real. Will they replace us with these artificial humans in the future?"

"I don't know, sir."

"I suppose robots will come with their own set of problems.

Your theory checked out."

"Sir?"

"About finding a hub. Contact Ben. He's found it."

"I'll call him right now."

"Do you think the perpetrator is still here?"

"Possibly. Gloating, reveling in their act."

Wakana zipped the bag back up. "Did you know, in Mexico Unit 798 used to send in dogs covered with plague-infested fleas? They used to drop rats from planes into enemy camps, but dead rats weren't very mobile. So instead, they poisoned the dogs and sent them into enemy camps. Once the dogs died, the fleas wouldn't stay on a dead body and they'd infect all the enemies with a genetically modified form of bubonic plague. Our soldiers waited until their body parts started dropping off before we mopped them up."

"I am familiar with the history of the Department of Epidemic Prevention and Water Purification in the west."

"How do we find our sick dog?"

"We find out where they released the dogs."

The general nodded. "Our enemies are hungry fleas, ready to ravage. Be careful not to get infected."

4:21am

Outside the hall, Tiffany waited anxiously.

"Is Ben alive?" she asked Akiko.

"Yes," Akiko replied.

She sighed in relief. "If you find him–"

"He's here."

"Where?"

"On a task, but close by."

"I had no ulterior motive, if you're wondering."

"I wasn't. I am wondering how you, as a Kempeitai officer, didn't notice anything suspicious."

"Are you blaming me for what happened?"

Akiko remained silent.

"Why is Wakana in charge?" Tiffany asked.

"General Wakana is one of our most distinguished commanders."

"I heard he pissed off a lot of people in the SD Uprisings. Made all sorts of unreasonable requests. I thought they'd banished him to Africa. These rebels are barbaric with no sense of culture. They must be the ones who set off the bombs. That game needs to be erased and its creators publicly executed," Tiffany stated with conviction.

"I agree. Too bad your cover got blown," Akiko said, not so much with sympathy as scorn.

Tiffany was annoyed by her comment, but thought better of refuting Akiko. "When you see Ben, tell him... tell him I'm sorry."

"For what?"

"For lying about who I worked for."

"Why should you apologize? That's just part of your work."

"I know we have to lie to those around us, but that doesn't mean I'm comfortable deceiving those I care about."

Tiffany did a short bow of respect and left.

4:52am

Akiko met Ben a few miles away from the arcade in a flora store that specialized in bonsai plants and was shaped like a greenhouse. It was a quiet neighborhood, set against a Babylon of neon from the arcade that never shut down. Laminate lights were on inside and Akiko entered through the front door. There was nothing conspicuously out of place on initial examination, but she did notice that it didn't smell like fertilizer. Not that all greenhouses smelled of dung, but the density of plants in the front seemed orchestrated to conceal rather than to showcase. Cacti, orchids, and fancy pottery blocked her path. She pushed them aside. Behind were rows and rows of porticals, wiring circuitously wrapped in thousands of directions like an electronic nervous system pumping information. Data streams were coursing through the building like digital sluices canalizing the paths. On the monitors, multiple variations of the *USA* game rapidly played out. Japanese soldiers were being shot by American ones fighting for their "independence." There must have been at least a thousand porticals stacked on top of each other to form towers.

"This is where the rebels carried out their hijacking," Ben replied, examining the porticals.

"The other arcades must have similar places," Akiko assumed.

"I've informed the other sections and maybe they'll catch someone, though I'm betting they've been abandoned. I'm looking here in case I can find something the big groups can't." Ben peered at Akiko. "The general tells me Tiffany is Kempeitai. Did you know?"

"I just found out."

"Has she been cleared of suspicion?"

"For the time. Those rebels must have had some inside help."

Ben shook his head. "You can't trust anyone."

"Not when the stakes are this high. She apologized to you."

"For what?"

"For her deception," Akiko replied.

"I know, ultimately, it doesn't really mean anything. But I feel like I've been dating a complete stranger."

"Everyone in the USJ is a stranger," Akiko said.

"I guess you're right. Ironic."

"What?"

"You're the only person I'm certain of, and you're Tokko."

"Don't take it personally. I still haven't told my mother I'm part of the Tokko."

"Why not?"

She was surprised at having told Ben this fact. "Where were these porticals manufactured?" she asked, changing the topic.

He lifted one up. "Good question. They're not made in Japan or China, that's for sure. They're shoddy, cheap material, no serial numbers to track. I'm thinking they're made in the USJ and I'm pretty sure it's in Anaheim in Portical Valley."

She peered into the trashcans and saw they were full of smoked cigarettes and empty ramen cups that still reeked – they'd been here recently. Garbology officers could go through the trash and forensics would scan for fingerprints.

"Doesn't the arcade have a security system?"

"A really good one," Ben answered.

"How'd they crack it?"

"I said good, not great. It wouldn't have been that hard for an experienced portical tech to break through. Let's head to Anaheim."

"Are they open? It's 5:00am."

"They never sleep. Looks like you could use some shut eye. Why don't you let me drive?"

She was too tired to object.

5:32am

Akiko was in a store that sold memories, a mishmash of tawdry emancipation bottled into faked vulnerability and fingernails from forgotten musicians grilled on kebabs of misplaced desire. If only she'd had better taste, she could have escaped the corpulence of discontent. But no, her belly swelled and her fingernails turned into claws as her nose gushed latex paint.

"Hey," she heard, feeling ice chill her wrist.

"W-wh–"

"We're almost there," Ben said.

She looked at Ben and oriented herself. "Did I sleep?"

"Soundly," he replied. "You were dreaming."

She rubbed her eyes. "I'll be happy when our medics find a way for the human body to go without sleep."

"Dreaming is my favorite part of the day."

"Some of our scientists are trying to find a way to record dreams to see what people are really thinking at the subconscious level."

"Are you serious?"

"Yes."

"You can't arrest someone based on their dreams."

"Why not?"

"What if it gets misinterpreted?"

"We would have agents to curate them," Akiko said. "Unfortunately, it won't be available anytime, soon since their primary focus is on extracting memories from the dead."

"How close are they?"

Akiko tried not to think about Jenna. "Still in the initial steps."

"I guess the dead won't be able to keep secrets anymore," Ben noted.

They took a left into a road full of gigantic portical advertisements for new entertainment shows and gaming competitions.

"How much further?" Akiko asked.

"We're arriving. The rules are looser here and they don't like military. I hope I don't offend if I suggest that you follow my lead."

Akiko wasn't familiar with Portical Valley, so she said, "That's fine."

"You OK?"

"Why would I not be?" Akiko asked.

"You look frazzled."

"I'm tired."

Ben held up an inhalant. "Need a shot of caffeine?"

"Later."

Portical Valley was a strange intersection of technology and lewd ribaldry. There were cocoons of scintillating lights tightly choreographed into demo booths for new machines, grandiose monuments to marketing ascending high above them. It was a shopping center as big as a public square, a bazaar selling every type of portical and accessory imaginable. Built indoors, the ceiling was a sprawling display screen with advertisements of scantily clad actors and actresses. Promotional models abounded, the usual throng of tight T-shirts, bikinis, buff bared men wandering about with catchphrases and phony smiles packaged to appeal to repressed libidos. Porticals and sex made for a surprisingly agreeable liaison.

"Where are we going?" Akiko asked.

"This is just the surface. We're visiting an old acquaintance of mine."

Elephants, zebras, and monkeys ran rampant. Exotic birds flew from one empty ledge to another. The enormous leg of a broken mecha was on display, the remnants of a goliath that had once blasted Americans in San Diego. At the base, food stalls sold squash and basil that granted virility. Miniscule chilies promised to make a tongue burst after a taste and red shallots bled spices to make other parts implode. The lemon grass and kaffir limes contributed to the international canal of coconut juice flowing through the intestines of everyone passing through the valley. Many were engaged in community portical games at kiosks, shrugging off fatigue and frustration.

"Why are there so many animals?" Akiko inquired.

"Organic porticals built into the animal body are the new rage," Ben answered. "Kind of like flesh phones, but with deeper connections. Check out those ostriches."

There was a herd of them with copper plating on their bowl heads.

"For racing," Ben said. "Increases hormonal activity and makes them easier to control."

"They have a portical brain?"

"Half and half. Same for body."

"Who controls it?"

"The portical intelligence system. Some creatures have direct interfacing with humans. I hear in Manchukuo, they have brutal cricket matches with human drivers. Leaves a lot of them crazy, living as a bug."

"I suppose it makes a useful diversion for the masses."

"I've never seen a cricket match, but the ostrich races are disturbing and violent. Some of those matches are to the death – those birds'll do anything to win."

"They take after their human masters," Akiko noted dryly.

Many of the human masters had artificial parts and there

were stores that promised updates to mechanical limbs in a matter of hours. These included tooled supplements that helped in jobs like janitorial work, plumbing, and construction by having replaceable equipment constructed into the arm. Also on sale were supplemental teeth to enhance taste, fashion nails with portical screens built in, and sensory augmentation to stimulate weaker nerves.

They entered a seafood store that reeked of dead fish. Swarthy cooks chopped up meat and peeled the fins off salmon cadavers. Boxes of discarded clam shells and fish bones were leaking viscous juices that drenched the floor with aquatic blood. Ben and Akiko walked into what appeared to be a storage room, but it led to another door that itself turned into a staircase. On an enclosure on the left wall, the upper half of a man turned to them on a steel swivel, his face covered by a fishnet. His head was shaved, though he had a fastidious square mustache. "How can I help you, officers?"

"I'd like to see Koushou," Ben replied.

"Do you have an appointment?"

"You know we don't."

"Koushou is not in at the moment."

"We can wait," Ben said with a smile, before placing a rolled wad of *yen* into the man's hand.

"Koushou will return shortly."

"Probably by the time we reach his chambers."

"Perhaps."

They went down the long stairway, guided by violet radiation that gleamed temptation.

"What was that?" Akiko asked.

"That's what you call greasing the modern eunuch."

"He's human?"

"Cut in half."

"Nothing below?"

Ben shook his head.

"Does he just stay there forever?"

"Another eunuch replaces him when he needs to rest," Ben explained. "They go in shifts."

"Why do they do this?"

"The lack of a lower half ensures their loyalty. Important trait down here."

"How does he eat?" she inquired.

"Injections of proteins and other nutrients to keep him alive."

"That's barbaric."

"He lives a very comfortable life as gatekeeper," Ben said.

"With bribes?"

"Toll fees."

"How much did you give him?" she asked, crossing her arms.

"Don't ask," Ben said, and brushed some lint off his jacket.

"Isn't he in pain?"

"Regenerative gels make him feel like he's in heaven, and he's wealthier than you and I can even imagine."

"There are things more valuable than money."

"Not down here."

They walked into a lobby that was dense with smoke. The tangent chamber organized itself into blocks of alcohol dispensers and naked waiters serving patrons. Some of the glass walls had shaded tints where human action was visible in silhouette, naked couples frolicking with animals. A woman was passionately kissing a muscular man who had a plastic face – one of those artificial males – and her perfume assailed them with its scent. Each vice smelled distinctively lurid: drugs, cigarettes, kinky sex, alcohol, that revolting effusion of dank obsession stirred together by the helplessness of addiction and frailty.

"Why isn't my portical working?" Akiko asked.

"Outside connections are disrupted."

"Why?"

"Koushou's orders. Only internal connections work and

we don't have access. He's pretty much king down here," Ben
said.

"King?" she asked, offended by the encroachment on
royalty.

"He's developed a taste for cruelty."

"How do you know him?" Akiko asked.

"San Diego."

"He served?"

"With distinction. We get what we need and we'll be on
our way. Even if you might not like it, let him rule his little
empire down here."

"I'm not sure what that means."

They entered a hallway with a convex ceiling, white walls,
shallow reflecting pool, and statues of grotesque animals.
It resembled a temple with its axial alignments and lilies
floating serenely in the water. She was about to comment
on the architecture when she noticed something strange. The
statues looked real and one of the nude women blinked. It
took a few seconds to realize that all the statues were actual
people, bound by metallic strips, some with bars perforating
their body, wires intertwined with veins and muscles. An
emaciated male had a metallic nail sticking out at every
junction point in his bones, a tattoo of a black line linking
them in a constellation of affliction. A woman's skin was split
up like patchworks, part metal, part flesh, hundreds of squares
breaking up her body into a checkerboard. Another was bent
backwards, the spine arcing in an impossible three hundred
and sixty degree curl, the face held immobile by a larynx
substitute and thousands of needles. They were sculptures
celebrating the prosthetics of human profligacy. There was
an altar at the other end and several columns that led to a
corridor. Next to the altar was a tall giraffe with the face of
a human and a dog with the body of a man. A woman had
the wings and legs of a flamingo. They were hybrid people
and the worst part was that, even though their bodies were

immobile, their eyes were restlessly skipping.

Meditating at the head of the pond was a plain-looking man who was neither ugly, nor especially handsome, an Asian face that would have disappeared in a sea of strangers. His haircut had no discernible fashion aside from being somewhat combed so that it didn't rise haphazardly. He wore a blue robe, had a neutral expression, and revealed shriveled yellow teeth with huge gaps between them, the stalactites of an inscrutable appetite.

"Have you heard the theory that the mythological Noah's Ark was actually the very first natural history museum?" he asked. Even his voice was plain.

"I have not," Akiko answered, after she saw Ben dipping his hand in the pool, ignoring the question.

"Some fanatics theorize humans are just organic machines created not so long ago with a self-sustaining system."

"That runs counter to our knowledge that the Emperor is god," Akiko replied.

"Like I said, fanatics. I've always been curious. Was Noah a glorified weatherman who knew when to call his animals back in?"

"Noah is part of a silly superstition the Americans clung to."

"Every ancient culture in the world had a flood myth."

"Except Japan."

"Why is that?" the man inquired.

"Because Japan was the highest point in all the world."

"We were the first to develop pottery and live in accordance with all kami until the westerners disrupted our ennui."

"Look, Koushou. I'm not here for a history lesson. We've found some porticals that–"

"I know why you're here. Ishimura messaged me the specs."

Koushou stepped into the pool, not concerned that his robe was getting wet. He approached a man who was hanging upside down and took a dagger-shaped device off his neck. The bottom tip was pointed and he pushed a button at its base. The man started weeping.

"Why is he crying?" Akiko asked.

Koushou cackled. "He's so aroused right now, it's driving him crazy."

"Aroused?"

"Look at his pants."

She saw the bulge.

"I can control every hormone in his body," Koushou boasted. "I can make him so hungry, he'll want to rip out your neck with his jaws, or bawl his eyes out because he's depressed about a stupid comment he made to someone insignificant fourteen years ago."

"Where'd you get that?"

"Same place where I got most of my tech – the army," he explained. "We had a lot of fun with these in San Diego, didn't we, Ben? You never had the stomach for this kind of thing with your porticals and numbers." Akiko looked back at Ben, who was still concentrating on the water. She tried to get his attention, but Koushou said, "I pamper them for the most part."

"Who are they?"

"My pets. The ones who've betrayed me or tried to steal from me. Or ones who just suited my fancy. They all deserved death. I gave them this alternative. They are contractually bound to me. The only art worth contemplating is live art. They change every day, force you to countenance possibilities about human nature that would otherwise be impossible to comprehend."

"What have you learned?" she asked, dubious.

"That a universe exists within every human being. That to the blood cells and organs in your body, you are god. That this universe is only one individual among infinite others."

"You think the universe is a living being?"

"One among billions that will eventually die. We fight for the scraps. Did you know the Japanese government wondered after the war if they should outlaw Christianity?" Koushou asked.

"I did."

"Then you know why they eventually didn't."

"No one follows a defeated God," Akiko answered.

"Because Gods get replaced all the time."

"The only thing I'm interested in right now is who bought those porticals."

"I know what you're interested in," Koushou said. "What can you offer me in exchange?"

"How about your life?" Akiko asked, gripping the viral gun in her belt.

"I'm inoculated to your viruses. You'll need to do better," he said.

"This is a new weapon devel–"

"I was trained at the 9th Army Technical Research Laboratory. I've worked on the latest death rays, fire balloons, humanoid mechas, submersibles with fighter jets, atomic torpedoes the size of a pen, and diseases beyond your imagination. If all you have are petty threats, get out of here."

She knew the 9th Lab was one of the most secret facilities in the Empire. Seeing the technology he had access to, she believed him.

"What do you want?"

"How badly do you want this information?" he continued.

"It's a matter of Imperial security."

Koushou's eyes brightened. "I want bodies."

"What kind of bodies?"

"Dead ones. That was quite an experiment you did with that poor girl."

Did he mean... "She was working for the George Washingtons."

"They're out for your head," Koushou said. "I can give

them to you if you'd like. There's a large group of them who've left their haven in San Diego. All I want in exchange for their whereabouts are eight infected; dead, or preferably, frozen alive."

"I only have one dead body and she's been requisitioned by the Biologics Department."

"There are other enemies of the state."

"What will you do with them?"

"There's a market for corpses that have been tortured to death by the Tokko. A novelty item, if you may. I'll take samples of their blood and keep the virological data, which is useful too."

"Useful for what?" Akiko asked.

"For connoisseurs who want to understand the intricacies of a gruesome execution. I assemble human-animal hybrids. I have quite a museum of them at another site. I've created literal mermaids and centaurs. They are fascinating specimens. But no surgery can compare to the acumen of a virus that can reshape the tapestry and genetic makeup of one of your victims."

The inverted man was still crying, screaming at a high pitch. She had a sudden stabbing memory as she remembered the first person she'd tortured. He, too, couldn't stop screaming. "Can you shut him up?" she asked Koushou, pinching the bridge of her nose to decrease the piercing sensation the memory evoked.

"Why? I would have thought you of the Tokko would appreciate this more than any other."

"There's nothing about this I appreciate," she said, and reminded herself that the man she was thinking of died years ago during the interrogation she led. "You're sadistic."

"*I'm* sadistic? Hypocrisy is unbecoming in an agent of the Tokko."

"We have nothing in common," she angrily asserted, even though she knew they did. "You're a disgusting–"

"Be careful of your words here. Military courtesy has its limits."

"That's why you're not dead," Akiko stated.

"We are all servants of the Emperor."

"I doubt you are."

"You know how many I killed in his name? You can be content wiping his ass. I won't anymore."

The man's insatiable screams were causing him to spurt blood out his throat.

"Shut him up or I will," Akiko warned, thinking back to her first subject. Two hours after she'd stopped torturing him, he was still screaming. She wanted to kill him, if only to silence him. Her superiors wouldn't let her. Not until she got enough information. They kept on sending her back in.

"Even the Americans didn't dare order me," Koushou said. "You are excused."

"I'm excused?" The tone of his voice reminded her of her superiors.

"You heard me."

Akiko raised her viral gun and fired a shot at the man's forehead, infecting him with the disease. His silence overwhelmed her with a feeling of relief.

"WHAT DO YOU THINK YOU ARE DOING?" Koushou raged. "Do you know how much he cost to retrofit?"

"There's one body," Akiko said. "I'll give you seven more. Deal?"

"You've just signed your death warrant."

"You're a traitor who has misappropriated official equipment for your own selfish purpose. I'm placing you under arrest."

"You know what they'll do to you for arresting me? I have friends in Tokyo Command."

Akiko pointed the gun at the woman in the three-sixty twist and fired.

"STOP IT!" Koushou roared, racing towards Akiko.

"Are you ready to talk for real?" Ben jumped in, seeing things were spinning out of control.

"Talk some sense into her," Koushou demanded. "Tell her to stop!"

"Where can we find the George Washingtons?"

"They're on their way here."

"Why?"

"I told them you were here in case you weren't cooperative. Looks like I was right."

"How soon will they be here?"

"Soon."

"I can arrange the bodies if–"

But, before Ben could finish, Akiko walked towards Koushou and grabbed the controller. Koushou glowered and spat in her face. His breath smelled like garlic.

"Agent Tsukino," Ben called.

The agent in her didn't hear him. She stabbed the pointed edge into Koushou's neck, blood splattering as it ruptured his esophagus. Koushou gasped, tried to speak, but his throat was being devoured by blood. He stumbled back and fell into the water, vermilion staining the pacific blue and billowing into corruption.

"Why did you do that?" Ben yelled, as he splashed his way towards them to examine Koushou's livid corpse.

Akiko wiped the spit off her face. "He mocked the Emperor," she said, not caring that it was a limp excuse.

"He is a war hero with connections to the cadre."

"Was," Akiko said. "He's a traitor that deserved execution."

"But–"

"Look around you! He's insane."

"How is this diff…" Ben was about to protest, but stopped himself.

"Finish what you were going to say."

"Forget it."

Akiko shoved Ben. "Everything I do is for the Emperor."

"I know."

"Do you?" she asked, though the question wasn't solely pointed at Ben.

"I do."

"I should bring you up on charges of negligence and cowardice."

"For what?" Ben asked.

"You should have killed him the moment he questioned the divinity of our Emperor. And before that, you should have reported his behavior," she stated, though she was really furious with herself for losing control again.

"Where do you think he developed this taste? He was a professional torturer in San Diego. This whole area is sanctioned by the USJ."

"You called him a king. A *king!* There's only one Emperor in the Empire. This *baka* is a civilian. I should have you charged for your treasonous suggestion. But I held my breath in the hopes that you knew what you were doing. It's a wonder you've survived as long as you have."

"I'm sorry. My figure of speech was–"

"Shut up, Ishimura. My jurisdiction transcends the USJ. My duty is to the Emperor. Do you have any issue with that?"

"No, *sir*. I'm very sorry."

Akiko looked back at the living statues.

Ben, too, gazed at the monstrosities disguised as art. "I know it may be hard to believe, but he used to be a really gentle guy. He went crazy because they forced him to torture people, including his best friend, an officer they thought was spying for the GWs. Turned out they were wrong. The guy was innocent. But his brain and his testicles were carved out by then. Koushou was never the same."

Akiko stared at Koushou's body, ignoring her reflection in the shallow pool.

"I'm having this place shut down as soon we get out," Akiko said.

"You can try."

"What do you mean, *try?*"

"I'm not being disrespectful to you, but places like this are here to stay."

"For you, it might be hard. Not for me. The commanders will listen," Akiko affirmed.

"I hope so. What should we do about the Americans?"

"We need to contact General Wakana so we can get backup."

Ben checked his portical. "No link."

"How do we get out of here?"

"We hope that security doesn't catch on, and go back the way we came."

Akiko's eyes went to a door beyond the altar. "What's over there?"

"I don't know."

Akiko rushed into a narrow passage with doors on either side. They were locked and Akiko was about to use her gun to blast them open, but Ben stopped her. He used the digital key on his portical to unscramble the number lock. Inside the first door were two emaciated men who had been guillotined. They were surprisingly clean and well-groomed, though gaunt, their bones protruding from their taut flesh. When they entered the second room, it felt like a freezer. There were six people in a huddle, shaking in fear.

"You're free to go!" Akiko ordered. When they didn't comply, she fired her gun into the ceiling. "Get out of here!"

"Where do we go?" one asked.

"We signed a contract with Koushou."

"He takes care of us."

"Koushou's dead," Akiko answered. "Get out of here before I kill you too."

That got them running. Ben had a pained expression on his face as he watched the bone-like structure of the prisoners stumbling to their egress.

"What's wrong?" she asked him.

"These people."

"We have eight more doors."

Five of the rooms were packed with torture gear, from thumbscrews to iron maidens, pillories, cattle prods, racks, *jia gun, tean zu*, and breaking wheels to disrupt the lymphatic and circulatory systems. The equipment would have made even the most zealous heretic penitent, defying malleability by dying in a row of cedars and spruces. The final three rooms were mazes and Akiko presumed they were a way for Koushou to play with his victims.

"Not to rush you, but we should get going," Ben said.

They scurried back into the lobby. Ben's tense glances betrayed his anxiety. Akiko's step was indignantly stiff, her hand on her weapon. "You still have your gun, right?" she confirmed with Ben.

"I'm not a very good shot," Ben answered.

"If we come across any trouble, just point and fire."

Ben fingers went to his holster. "If we get high enough for me to get a portical connection, I can actually help us."

Two dogs were fornicating while a group of drunk patrons laughed. A woman carried the doll of a pink teddy bear that was almost the same size as her. Akiko and Ben climbed up the stairs to where they'd first met the eunuch.

"Why did Koushou release his contractors?" the eunuch asked.

Akiko raised her gun, about to fire, but Ben held her hand and gently pushed it down.

"He got bored with them and dismissed us," Ben said to the eunuch. "Didn't want to be disturbed."

They exited into the fish store.

"What are you doing?" Ben demanded.

"Don't ever touch me again," Akiko warned.

"You going to kill everyone in your way?"

"You're still alive. Does your portical work?"

Ben was about to call Wakana when someone seized him from behind. He elbowed the man, but the wall of muscle confronting him was barely affected by the blow. He was bulky, a steroidal bulge connected by valley-like veins.

"Let him go or I'll shoot," Akiko warned.

The man ignored her and was about to break Ben's neck. She fired a bullet into his shoulder. The impact pushed him back and she charged forward to kick him in his gut. He huffed and winced backwards. She grabbed his arm and twisted it around his spine, stopping right before breaking it. He tried to break free and she broke his arm. He cried out in pain. She pushed him to the floor, pointing the gun at him. "Who are you working for?"

The man refused to answer.

She aimed her gun at his leg, fired right below his foot. "I won't ask again. Who are you working for?"

He stayed mute. She fired a bullet into his calf and his skin ruptured. He roared in pain, tried to stand up, but she had her foot on his chest.

"I'm not going to kill you. But I'm a believer in the idea that if your leg causes you to sin, tear it off. I will make you a cripple for the rest of your life," she said. "No legs, no arms. I'll put a hole in your gut so that you can't use the bathroom without pain. I'll rip out both your eyes. I'll put a bullet in your cheek so women will know you're a–" A pool of piss formed around his waist that made her jump back. "That's disgu–"

She felt something cold and round on the back of her head – a gun barrel. "Drop it," a voice warned.

Akiko spun around, grabbing the gun and bashing it into the head of her opponent. The woman dropped to the ground. Three more rebels arrived and Akiko charged into them, kicking one in the groin, another in the head, and the final one in the side of his torso. They all fell. A dozen more arrived, wielding automatic guns and melee staffs.

Akiko was looking for an escape route when four of them slammed their electrically charged poles into her. She fell to the ground, the blows knocking her unconscious.

12:15pm

Akiko was in a meeting with her superior officers when she farted and tore a hole in her chair. The fart was so powerful, her commanding officers fell back. She wanted to deny it was her. But the gaseous quandary of trees wounded by the compunction of her flatulence left her embarrassed and her stomach wouldn't stop growling. She didn't know what to do, wondered what fate awaited her in her rise up the chain of command, when she woke and found herself in a cage. It was a tight space, more appropriate for an ape than a human. The lighting was dim and there were dozens of cages around her. They'd stripped her of her insignia and weapons.

"You're finally up."

"Ishimura? Where are we?" Akiko asked.

"The George Washingtons have taken us captive," Ben replied. He was in the adjacent cage.

"How?"

"They were waiting for us. Their leader, Martha Washington, is furious with you."

"Me?"

"I don't doubt your integrity or your loyalty to the Emperor," Ben said. "Just don't provoke her or give her an excuse to make things worse. If you give them what they want, they'll take it easier on you."

"Are you suggesting I surrender to them?"

"Just suggesting you be thoughtful in your responses."

"I serve the true god, the Emperor."

"And they serve a callous Western deity that died long ago. I know the drill. The only thing is, they still worship that God."

"Their God failed them, which is why we've won. I will act in accordance with the dignity and responsibility that position bestows on me," Akiko swore.

"I sometimes wonder about all of that. Gods, their commands, all the things people do in their names. Is any of it what they really want? Like San Diego. Would the Emperor really have wanted what we did to take place if he knew all the details?"

"If you continue with this talk, I will personally execute you once we get out of here."

"*If* we get out of here. I've resigned myself to a slow, painful death. Unless you have some secret Tokko method of escape?"

"If I did, I would not take along a traitor like you," she stated empathically.

"In the end, we're both going to give them what they want. Believe me, I saw it in San Diego. The more you resist them, the more pleasure they'll take in breaking you. Why fight it?"

"There's honor in resistance."

"Was there any honor in that woman you executed – that was yesterday, wasn't it?" Ben asked.

"There is never honor for traitors."

"You think you could have resisted?"

"Of course. I would rather die than betray the Empire."

"You aren't much good to the Empire dead."

"You aren't much good to the Empire alive," Akiko said.

"I'm the most loyal servant the Empire has."

"Not anymore."

"I don't need my loyalty questioned by you."

"You think just because you turned in your parents, you're beyond question? Do you know how many children turned their parents in last year alone?"

"I'm glad you value my sacrifice."

Akiko was riled up. "I would remind you your superiors think you're a liability, too cavalier with your tasks. You have no idea how many complaints you have against you about tardiness, absences, and inappropriate behavior."

"I've never denied my work ethic or that I like to party."

"Incompetence should be a capital crime," Akiko said.

"Then me and three quarters of the Empire would be executed," Ben muttered. "That'd probably make you happy, huh? But not really as you'd have no one left to persecute."

"Bad fortune has made you bold."

"This is more than a little bad fortune. Your careless behavior is going to get us killed tonight."

"My careless behavior?"

"Koushou," Ben said.

"I saved you up there."

"And I'm grateful. But I think I would have preferred a quick snap of my neck to whatever torture they have in store for us."

"You're a coward," Akiko angrily spat out.

"Whether I'm a coward or the bravest man alive, they'll still break me."

Akiko was frustrated at being caught and even more frustrated by Ben's attitude to the situation. She was a member of Tokko, trained to resist any kind of torment.

"What do they want from me?" she asked.

"I don't know."

"What do they want from you?"

"They didn't seem that concerned about me."

"Is General Mutsuraga with them?"

"Not that I saw. But they haven't told me much. I have a feeling they were behind the bombing last night."

"Why do you think that?"

"Martha Washington asked how I survived last night."

"Were you able to get any messages out on your portical?"

"No," Ben replied.

"Any ideas where we are?"

"None."

The lights turned on and they heard footsteps coming their way. A Caucasian woman covered in tattoos of the American flag stomped forward. She was at least six foot seven, shaved bald, steely lines carved into her flesh, wearing green fatigues, and a black jacket made of wool. She was followed by a coterie of men and women of different ethnicities.

"You're the one who killed Jenna," she barked to Akiko.

"Who are you?"

"Martha Washington."

Akiko had read the reports about the staggering prowess of Martha Washington. She had been shot with ten bullets in her chest during the SD uprisings, but she'd shrugged off the pain as though they'd just been pellets and killed her assailants. She was the third column of the Congress of the GWs who weren't so much people as they were pillars of violence and pain. Bitterness jolted their dendrites full of daily rage so they could lead their people to survival.

"What happened to her?" Martha demanded.

Akiko answered, "She's dead."

Anger contorted Martha's face. "I know that. How?"

"She died during interrogation."

Martha held up Akiko's gun. "Killed by this?"

Akiko nodded.

"She had nothing to do with any of this," Martha said.

"She helped your group kill loyal servants of the Emperor in Palos Verdes," Akiko stated.

"What happens to someone shot by this?" Martha asked.

"They die a painful death."

Martha raised up the gun and fired at Akiko. A bright

arrow of green thrust into Akiko. She looked up indifferently and said, "If you all surrender now, I promise you a merciful death."

"Why isn't it working on you?" Martha asked.

"I'm vaccinated."

Martha smiled. "I thought so. We have our own form of punishment for people like you. But I believe in a merciful God. If you beg for forgiveness and give me your Tokko access codes, I will grant you a quick death."

Akiko snorted. "I'm not afraid of you."

"Good."

Three men opened the cage and pulled her out. She didn't resist, maintained her composure, and marched proudly out.

"Bring the other one too," Martha ordered.

"But he's going after Mutsuraga–" one of the men was protesting.

"I know. Bring him anyway."

12:55pm

They were in a warehouse with aisles full of crates. Akiko didn't spot any familiar logos and there was nothing on the walls to indicate where they were. She saw people scowling at her. Like the guards, they were a mix of different races. Akiko tried to memorize each face so that she could have them arrested when she got out. None of them spoke or made any noise.

They came to a pit covered by a transparent plastic floor. There was a latch opening a part of it. Underneath the glass, millions of ants swarmed over each other, organic dots swirling in an insect hurricane. Akiko spotted multiple skulls inside, every strip of flesh carefully and meticulously harvested for consumption. The noise they made was an orchestra of chitin thoraxes pounding, grinding, and screeching against each other. It was eerily alien, distorted wavelengths of construction, mandibles and abdomens crunching organs. Spiracles devoured gases and the dorsal aortas pumped haemolymphs through their bodies. Their language was simple. Consume, consume, consume. They did not differentiate between race, sex, religion, culture, or beliefs.

"Tell them what they want to hear," Ben said to her. "Their American God forces them to forgive anyone who is repentant."

"We only forgive those who are truly penitent," Martha said. "Not those who only pay lip service."

"I'm not repentant," Akiko said.

Martha nodded. "I'm glad you're honest." She pointed to the insects. "These ants are from what's left of South America, specially bred and genetically manipulated by rebels who were fighting off the Empire. They called them 'ant cannibals' because they love the taste of humans."

One of the guards grabbed Akiko from behind, restraining her hand. Another thrust a syringe into her arm. She tried to resist, but the other guards held her in place.

"How long do you think it takes them to eat a human?" Martha asked.

"I don't know," Akiko answered. Her muscles were tightening and she felt her foot losing mobility. She tried to move her arm, but it was stuck in place.

"It's different for everyone. They don't like the taste of some people and they love others. Everyone has their own flavor. Isn't it bizarre to think these ants have no idea you're a human being? They have no concept of life outside of their tiny ant existence. Ants are cruel. They take slaves and they war on each other. Normally, I would ask you questions. But I don't think there's any point." She signaled the guards. "What is it that you like to say to your victims? 'If your right hand causes you to sin, cut it off'?"

"Wait!" Ben shouted. "Spare her and I'll give you anything you want."

"Stay out of this, Ishimura!" Akiko yelled.

"They're going to feed you to ants!"

"I'm not afraid of ants."

"I'm amazed by the medical capabilities in the *Dai Nippon Teikoku*," Martha Washington said. "They can cure anything. But when I think of the price... How many patients were butchered and given every type of disease imaginable? But it's only because of everything the doctors learned from those deaths that the Empire can heal anything. Does that justify it? Millions were saved, are still being saved, but tens of thousands faced the most horrific deaths. I wouldn't be able to live with that kind of decision."

"That's because you're weak," Akiko stated.

"If you call having a conscience weak, I'm guilty. Drop her hand in!" Martha shouted.

Akiko had lost control of the muscles in her body, though her face could still move. The two guards opened the hatch in the glass floor, bent her knee, and dropped her arm into the pit of ants. Even though she couldn't move her hand, she could feel the ants swarming it. Their mandibles probed and bit. Little spurts of pain amplified, and the sporadic bites became a concentrated paroxysm of agony. The pain became unbearable as her fingers were eaten. They tore through the skin, pierced the muscles, the tendons, and the ligaments.

"How does it feel?" Martha asked.

Akiko wanted to slam her fists on the ground, writhe and free her hand. But it was locked in place and she could feel them slithering up to her wrist. She didn't want to look down and see what was happening, but her eyes tugged in their direction. She was horrified to see a black mass where her fingers had been and she spotted nails being carried off, two of which were colored red. She felt faint. Next to Martha was her niece Jenna, mutated and full of viruses bulging from her face.

"How many have you killed?" Jenna demanded.

She didn't remember anymore. Was it fourteen, or was it fifteen including Koushou?

"Not enough," Akiko replied.

"Why did you kill them?"

"In service of the Empire."

"Did they all need to die?"

Akiko hesitated to answer.

"Why did you kill them?" Jenna asked furiously.

"I don't know."

"You don't know or you don't want to say?"

"They were traitors!"

"How do you know?"

"I had evidence on each of them."

"Me too?"

Akiko sighed. "I didn't want to kill you. I thought it was enough to question you, but Command insisted."

"So you followed blindly?"

"It's sacrilege to say anything negative about our god!"

"What if it's the truth?"

"What truth?"

"That your god can't have children, or that your god will die."

"Gods can't die."

"You've nearly killed the idea of our God. But you don't really care about any of that. The only thing you fear is your own–"

"What are you blabbering about?" Martha asked Akiko.

Akiko's hand had been removed from the ant pit. She did not look at it.

"Are you repentant?"

Akiko glowered. "I will die for the Emperor."

"You would like that, wouldn't you? But I won't give you that honor. You will be judged by the same measure you judge others," Martha said. "Put her left hand in."

The memory of her mother came back to Akiko. Her mother used to wait for her late at night as she studied for her exams, cooking her bread rolls and tea to help her stay up. Her mother thought she was working so hard to get into the Yamamoto Music School in Oahu, but secretly, she'd been working to get into the Berkeley Military Academy, despising the hours she was forced to play the violin. Right before she slept, her mother used to bring in olive oil and massage her fingers. Akiko thought it was a waste of time.

But Mother always insisted.

"Not my other hand," Akiko said to Martha.

"What?"

"Don't put my other hand in."

"Why not?"

"Why don't you just kill me and get it over with? You're all nothing but cowardly traitors and when the army comes for you, they'll do far worse than anything you can do to me. You'll grovel and beg for your pathetic lives and they'll rip you–"

But as she went on, none of them seemed angry or even bothered by her words. Instead, a vicious glee shone on their faces. Akiko recognized it. They knew they were breaking her down, making her nasty and – worse – desperate.

She couldn't resist the guard putting her hand down into the ant pit. She felt the ants throng her hand. They ate ravenously, thousands piling on top. The smell of her skin was making them greedy. The pain flared and she felt sweat break out over her body. She kept on thinking about her mother washing her hands every evening. She felt ashamed to admit she couldn't remember a single song on the violin. The pinches were getting more aggressive as the ants cleaved at her fingers.

"Stop," Akiko said. "Please stop!"

"Are you repentant?"

Akiko hesitated.

"Are you repentant?" Martha repeated.

Akiko shook her head. She was Tokko, special police for the Empire. She couldn't give into–

"Drop her arm deeper," Martha ordered.

"No. Please no."

"You've never asked yourself what the tortured actually feel, have you? You've been trained, been drowned maybe. But that doesn't count because you know it isn't permanent. I'm going to make sure you never torture anyone with your own hands ever again."

"Please, my mother—"

"Don't talk about your mother here! What about Jenna's mother and father? They can't even see her body!"

There wasn't a sympathetic face in the whole crowd.

"She's losing a lot of blood," someone said.

"Patch her up."

They took out her right hand. It was a skeleton stripped of meat from the elbow down. Akiko's breath tightened. Her chest felt compressed. She started hyperventilating. A man had a short axe ready and placed her arm against the ground.

"W-w-what are you d-d-doing?" Akiko demanded in stutters. "W-w-what are y-y-y-you doing? S-s-stop! S-stop!"

They did not stop.

10:55pm

When she woke, she found herself in a bed. She looked at her arms and saw only two bandaged stumps. She would have started screaming if she didn't feel numb with shock. It was too difficult to wrap her mind around what she'd suffered.

"Evening."

It was Ben, leaning on the wall across from her, his face bruised up.

Her eyes hardened. "How are we alive?" she asked. "Why didn't they kill me?"

"They thought letting you live with the humiliation of this would be a worse punishment than death."

She closed her eyes and did her best to murder her tears before they could betray her.

"They made a mistake," she said, shaking. "I'm going to kill every one of them personally and have their limbs torn off and fed to animals."

"That's one way of taking revenge."

"What would you do?" she demanded, tired of his glib tone.

"I don't know. I can't even think about it."

"I can get prosthetics and a gun arm with surgery, go after them before it's too late."

"That'll take time and they'll be gone by then."

She shook her head. "Not if I just get a gun arm. It only takes a day or two and they do it all the time in Vietnam." She checked her surroundings. "Where are we?"

"In the Anaheim County Hospital. The doctor wanted to contact your family to let them know, but they couldn't find any–"

"No," Akiko cut in. The memory of the night she had to tell her parents what happened to her brother came back to her. How could she explain that he'd been driven by misguided fervor to do the unthinkable? "My parents can't know."

"But–"

"I said, no," Akiko snapped.

"Do you have a friend or a loved one we can contact instead?"

Akiko thought of Hideyoshi, the fact that she could never touch him again with her own hands. "I'll contact him later... What happened to you?"

"What do you mean?"

"Your hands are still in place," Akiko said, as both accusation and verdict.

"They gave me a good beating, so I told them everything they wanted to know."

"You idiot!"

Ben didn't deny it. "I have to stay alive. I still have a long road ahead of me and I have a promise to keep."

"What promise?"

"I'll have to tell you some other time."

"Where do you think you're going?"

"After Mutsuraga."

"You saw him?" Akiko asked.

"No. But I told them the truth about him."

"What truth?"

"It doesn't matter," Ben said.

"Does anything matter to you?"

"Of course," Ben replied. "A lot of people died for nothing

in San Diego. General Wakana was one of the few who tried to stop it."

"General Wakana? How was he involved?"

"It was almost ten years ago. He arrived after one of the Washingtons killed a colonel. Tried to salvage things. But he had no chance. Like you said, maybe it's a skewed circle and I'm just playing my part. In a few days, it won't matter."

"What do you mean?"

"You'll see. Goodbye, Agent Tsukino."

"Don't do anything dumb."

"I always do."

He left.

Akiko was flustered and wanted to interrogate Ishimura. But she wasn't in any condition to try.

On the hospital radio, which was playing in every room, she heard an orchestra. The violinist impeccably raced down the strings, staccatos clashing. She reflected on her own life and its melodies sounded hollow and empty to her. She wanted to shut the station off, became angered thinking of the people she'd tortured. She suppressed the tears trying to broach her eyes. Crying was for the weak and she would not give in. *You chose this life. Your only regret should be that you didn't die for the Emperor. You're the modern samurai. There's nothing you should be ashamed of. I'm going to kill those GWs or die in the attempt.* Still, she wished she didn't have the kind of job where she felt the need to lie to her mother. That way, maybe she could have stopped the trembling in the arms that were no longer there.

TEN YEARS PREVIOUSLY

San Diego
July 2, 1978
8:05am

"What brings you to our lovely neck of the war, Major Wakana?"

The Otay Mesa base was not big, though it held an important strategic position in San Diego and had its own barricade with guards and Czech hedgehogs along the perimeter. Visitors were prohibited and all military personnel had to go through security scans. The main building was five stories tall and Major Wakana had made his way to the command station to find it empty, except for two young lieutenants playing a card game on their porticals. They had both put them down and were standing to bow.

Thirty-six year-old Major Wakana twirled his mustache, leaned on his ivory staff, and said, "Colonel Doihara was killed an hour ago in a terrorist attack."

"Have they caught the terrorists, sir?" the one with the name sign Nomoto asked.

"It was a kamikaze attack," Wakana said. "A white wig was found near the explosion."

"A George Washington," Nomoto said. "They should all be

rounded up and shot."

"We've tried. But this is the eighteenth attack in the past month," the major said. "And they don't seem to be stopping anytime soon."

"Like I was saying, round them up and shoot *all* of them, sir."

"Where are your commanders?"

The other lieutenant, who had the nametag Ishimura, replied, "Not in yet, sir. Most were celebrating last night for anniversary week."

"Then perhaps you can help me. Do you have an officer in your service named Shigeko Yoshioka?"

"Yoshioka is one of our best soldiers," Nomoto said.

"He's also killed many civilians and is to be arrested for war crimes under USJ Regulation 3432.23. Where is he?"

"Captain Yoshioka is not on the base at the moment, sir."

"Where can I find him?"

The two lieutenants looked at each other. "We don't know, sir."

"Who does?"

"Captain Yoshioka tends to follow his own orders. He disappears at times and shows up when he pleases," Nomoto explained. "He could be anywhere."

"I see. So someone already told him I was on my way," Wakana said. He leaned on his staff again and looked at Ishimura. "You look familiar."

"I was in your Guerilla Tactics class at BEMAG," Ishimura replied.

"Yes, I remember now. Beniko Ishimura. You were always late."

Ben bowed embarrassedly. "Yes, sir."

"Lieutenant Nomoto. Go call Lieutenant Colonel Mutsuraga. Tell him I need to talk to him."

"He doesn't arrive until ten today, sir."

"Tell him to hurry. Tell him I insist."

"Yes, sir."

Nomoto saluted and left.

Wakana put his arm on Ishimura. "Was Yoshioka here this morning?"

Ishimura hesitated.

"I understand you don't want to rat him out. How long have you been stationed here?" Wakana asked.

"Three years now, sir."

"So you've been here since the beginning of the insurrection. How is morale?"

"It's good among the ranks, sir. Among the Americans, it's complicated. Governor Ogasawara has made steps to improve conditions when she outlawed comfort companions and decreased the punishment term for breaking segregation laws. I feel she'd go further if Command allowed it."

Wakana grinned. "Never thought a bunch of religious fanatics would pose so much trouble for us, did you? These George Washingtons are mean, tough, and absolutely devoted to their cause. Do you know what is it that they seek?"

"Independence."

"Yes. Independence from the Empire. Can you imagine that? After how generously we've treated them, they've spit at our generosity. Do you know why that is?"

"Because they're stupid and ruthless."

"If they were stupid, they would not have lasted three years. Do you think us being Asian arouses their ire? If we were white like them, would they even blink if we went to war and annihilated other countries?"

"Respectfully, sir, the British and the Germans looked like them, but they still fought them."

Wakana nodded. "True. Very true. So perhaps these Americans can never be tamed. I've heard they're giving the Germans one hell of a time in Manhattan. Have you heard about the Hitler wing in the Louvre?"

"No, sir."

"Hitler has a whole hallway dedicated to his personal paintings. There are cameras that record people's expressions and anyone who laughs or makes a derisive gesture gets arrested. The French Resistance broke in and vandalized the paintings, but did it so none of the cameras could spot the problems. The officials didn't know because anyone who saw it was afraid of getting arrested if they reported something and it turned out to be something the Fuehrer had intentionally painted."

"How did they eventually find out?"

Wakana tapped his staff against the ground. "They still haven't."

Ishimura's surprised reaction pleased Wakana, who laughed heartily. "You know where Yoshioka is, don't you? Don't answer. Perhaps later, you and I can have lunch as professor and student. You can take me to a place where we may happen to run into a subject I am looking for."

"Perhaps, sir."

Nomoto entered and said, "Lieutenant Colonel Mutsuraga will be arriving shortly. He asks that you wait in his office."

Wakana twirled his mustache again. "Lead the way."

10:08am

Wakana waited almost two hours. He reviewed personnel reports during his wait. The lieutenant colonel's office had photos of himself, his wife, and their daughter, traveling to various places throughout the USJ and Asia. His wife was a jovial brunette named Meredith who was half-Italian, half-Japanese. Her father served as a trade official at the Long Beach Ports and her mother had been one of the main administrators for the *tonarigumi* (neighborhood association) in the area. Mutsuraga's daughter, Claire, was considered a genius with porticals, much like her father. There was a general theme of mahogany, the walls covered by maps of the USJ and the Germanic Americas as well as obscure programming equations.

Lieutenant Colonel Mutsuraga had a stern look about him when he arrived. His hair was grizzled and he possessed a sturdy frame like a bear. The breast of his uniform was covered with accolades and commendations, and he wore both his ceremonial swords. He had grim eyes, thick hands, and an overbearing confidence in his steady pose. He said in a booming voice, "You can't be serious about closing all my interrogation rooms."

"I'm very serious," Wakana replied. "Command told me to deal with the George Washingtons, sir. Your torture chambers are an impediment to that."

"Those chambers have been an invaluable source of information."

"Much of it faulty. Under torture, anyone will confess to anything, including lies."

Mutsuraga frowned. "How does putting one of my soldiers on trial help us win?"

"By listening to what the GWs want. They've asked for five things. Closing the torture chambers was their highest priority. Justice for those massacred at Balboa Park was their second. I am going to give them Yoshioka, sir."

"Yoshioka's one of our best soldiers."

"He had over two thousand civilians killed. Unarmed civilians, sir. If they'd been soldiers, I'd be handing him an award."

"What's to be the result of the trial?"

"There is overwhelming evidence of his guilt. If it can be disproven, he will be freed."

"If not?"

"Execution, sir, per regulation 3432.23."

Mutsuraga took out a cigarette. "Are you out of your mind?" he snapped. "Executing an officer of the USJ for firing on the natives? There's a battle going on here, major."

"And, respectfully, you're not winning, sir. Short of massacring all of them, you're in for a long, debilitating conflict unless you start working with the 'natives'."

"You realize who Yoshioka's uncle is?"

"My loyalty is to the Empire and the Emperor, not any admiral, sir."

"What do you think will happen if you execute Yoshioka?"

"In conjunction with meeting four of the other requirements demanded by the George Washingtons, I'm hoping for a dialogue."

"A dialogue?"

"In good faith."

"You want to negotiate with traitors and sacrifice our own soldiers in the process?"

"Your own gaming simulation predicted this would become inevitable, sir," Wakana pointed out. "And there are honorable ones among them. They are courageous, resourceful, and resolved, and some have reached out in the hopes of negotiation. Fortunately, their demands are not unreasonable. But they refuse to talk without resolution on the Balboa Park matter. Yoshioka disobeyed orders. He was specifically told not to provoke the crowd and, most definitely, not to fire on them."

"You are an unusual breed of officer, Wakana," Mutsuraga said.

"Where is Captain Yoshioka?"

"He's away on a mission."

"Where?"

"At this moment, that mission is classified. When he becomes available, I will let you know."

"Sir, that's–"

"He's on a mission that is of the utmost importance to the Empire!"

"But, sir–"

"Know your place, major," the Lieutenant Colonel barked.

"Yes, sir. Forgive me, sir," Wakana said, bowing.

"I will notify you when Yoshioka returns. You may do with the interrogation rooms as you please."

Major Wakana stood up and bowed gratefully. "May I make one more request, sir?"

"What is it?"

"I would like to place Lieutenant Ishimura under my direct command for the duration of my stay here."

Mutsuraga laughed. "I don't think the Washingtons would want Ishimura executed."

"Why's that, sir?"

"He's a coward who's more concerned about women

than his duty."

"So you have no objection to me taking him?"

"You're going to have him executed too?"

"No, sir. He was a former student and I'd like his help in coordinating leisure activities for some of my soldiers that are being transferred in."

"That's fine."

"Thank you for your patience, sir," Wakana said. He turned around and left, shutting the door behind him. As he did, he thought about the Kempeitai report that Mutsuraga's wife was having an affair with a George Washington leader who called himself Andrew Jackson. Her presence, and absence, was aggravating him and clouding his judgment. It troubled Wakana to think of it. He never wanted to be in a position where he had to question the people he loved.

11:25am

"The steak salad there is incredible, sir," Beniko said.

"First of all, drop the sir. Second, I'm not a big fan of salads."

"They will make you a convert. Seared ribeye, roasted potatoes, cremini mushrooms, shaved parmesan, sliced Asian pears, and a lemon Dijon vinaigrette served over mixed greens. Toasties makes the best damn salads I've ever had."

"If only my grandfather could have lived to have seen this. He used to talk about how much they had to ration during the War," Wakana said. "Every week, they'd run out of basic goods like flour or sugar and they never saw any more again until after the War."

"To the victor cometh the food."

Tijuana District had been a tourist destination until the civil revolt broke out. Even now, abetted by heightened security, it was a popular place to party. There were two security checks, both heavily guarded. Despite riding in a military issued vehicle, they were scanned. Bomb-sensitive dogs patrolled between the cars and there was a group of people that had been arrested sitting in steel cages, handcuffed and gagged. Beyond, there were fancy resorts, Japanese signs among all the high-rise hotels and discotheques. Soldiers, random security inspections, looming mechas, and helicopter sweeps were reminders of the chaos outside of its borders.

"Have you been to the Cancun?" Ben asked.

"No, what is it?"

"One of the top resorts. It has the biggest indoor swimming pool in the world and dolphins to paddle along. It's amazing." Ben pointed to another hotel that looked as though it was a gigantic diamond and had huge crowds. "That's the Gemini. It has all sorts of roller coasters inside. The lines aren't too bad because it's still early afternoon. By night time, you'll have to wait two hours for every ride."

"The whole area is going to get busier?"

"There's going to be triple this in the evening and more are flying in to celebrate for the holidays," Ben said.

"Aren't they worried about the rebels?"

"They aren't going to let some rebels ruin their fun."

Toasties was in a shopping mall. Ben parked their car in the Japanese section that was near the entrance and next to hundreds of scooters. Men and women were dressed in sporty summer wear in the resort environment, many just wearing swimsuits. Tourists from the mainland snapped photos of everything via their porticals and Wakana found himself amused by their gawking commentary and their awed voices. *"Sugoi,"* or "awesome," he kept on hearing.

"They have a whale show at the Sea Palace that's pretty impressive," Ben said. "I know one of the trainers and she can give us a backstage tour. You'd be surprised how smart the animals are. She thinks it's wrong for us to keep them in captivity as show animals."

At Toasties, Beniko talked to the hostess, an attractive woman in short jeans and a bikini top. "I thought you were going to be out of town for the holidays?" she asked Ben.

"Change in plans," he replied. "I'm showing the major around town."

She shook her head. "There's a lot we need to talk about."

"I know. Later."

Her arms were crossed. "I've been trying to reach you

the whole week."

Ben offered an awkward simper. "My portical is messed up on base. The Washingtons are scrambling all our lines."

She led them to their table. The restaurant was packed. She pinched him. "Don't leave without talking to me," she said, before returning to the front of the restaurant.

"Friend of yours?" Wakana asked.

"Something like that," Ben said, in a tone of helplessness. "She's too wild for me, sir."

Wakana laughed.

The waiter brought green tea and the menu. Another waiter carried meat colored black and white.

"What is that?" Wakana asked.

"Fried skunk," Ben replied. "That over there is grasshopper skewer and it lies heavy on those monkey brains. I heavily recommend those if you're into something a bit experimental."

"I used to cook grasshoppers," Wakana said. "When I was eight, we'd go out to a forest behind the rail tracks near my school. We captured a dozen grasshoppers, cut off their legs. They couldn't get away and we'd grill them. I loved eating them with wasabi."

"You want me to order some for you?"

Wakana shook his head. "Why don't you recommend something for me?"

Ben ordered for them both.

"So Yoshioka likes this place?" Wakana asked.

Ben shook his head. "Captain Yoshioka's taste in food is very simple – soy sauce, rice, and a boiled egg. He views anything else as an unnecessary extravagance."

"Then why did you bring me here?"

"I thought you wanted a good lunch."

Wakana laughed again. "You enjoy being an officer?"

"I try, s–" He stopped himself from saying "sir."

"And Captain Yoshioka? Does he enjoy being an officer?"

"For different reasons."

"Such as?"

Ben stirred the tea in his cup. "I'm not sure, but I don't think it's the food."

Wakana sipped on his tea. "I tend to have simple tastes as well."

"Oh?"

"I eat whatever my wife cooks me."

Ben chuckled. "Is your wife stationed in San Diego?"

"She's raising my two boys in Kauai."

"Do you see her often?"

"Not as much as I'd like. It's tough for her because she gave up her career and I've been away most of the last four years in Vietnam."

"How are things going there?"

"Officially, everything is wonderful. Unofficially, classified."

"That bad?"

"Worse. Command wants to make sure we avoid that kind of quagmire here, especially as Tijuana is such a popular destination. There's hope for a peaceful resolution. No one wants a repeat of Saigon."

"What do *you* want here?"

Wakana looked at Beniko. "What any good soldier wants. Peace."

The waiter brought the salads. Wakana stared at his askance, then took a bite. His face lit up. "This is excellent."

"I'm glad you like it."

"No, seriously. I've never had anything like this."

"You should take some for the road."

"I might do that."

Wakana ate his steak and savored the mushrooms. "Have you seen much of Mutsuraga's war simulation?"

"We all have."

"It's amazing to think he began programming this at BEMAG, a perfect war game measuring all the parameters of a situation to predict the outcome."

"Statistical likelihoods," Ben said. "It's susceptible to serious margins of error."

"But still impressive."

"Very impressive."

"How exactly does it work?"

Ben took out a portical from his pocket and flipped it open. An interface up showed in green text against a black background. It read: "Operation San Diego."

"How are you able to connect to the kikkai without a wire?" Wakana asked.

"New tech developed just south of BEMAG. Wireless porticals that pick up the kikkai so you can take them anywhere." Ben typed in his name and password. "Right now, the graphical power of the porticals are limited, but you can see it represented by this soldier." There was a cartoony depiction of a Japanese soldier. "I can input the date, the type of enemies I'm expecting, psychological factors, weather conditions, geographical data, any anomalies that pop up, even the eating habits of the officers." He punched in random variables, not being selective about his choices, concentrating on getting through the long list of options. "That's the bare minimum for a scenario. When we do our actual simulation for battle, we spend days, even weeks, planning. Then we let it play out and study what the AI does."

"Is it as accurate as they say?"

"Nowhere near what they want. But they're working on the programming and by the end of the year, it's supposed to support fifty thousand more variables."

On the portical, soldiers fought across buildings. Men and women dressed as "George Washingtons" with their white wigs killed themselves, blowing up buildings and cars with them. "Were you here during the first volley?"

"I only saw it on the news," Ben answered.

Wakana thought of the thousands dressed in the colonial wigs, charging San Diego's City Hall and blowing themselves up. A black man claiming to be the Founding Father, George Washington, made one demand. "Hand San Diego over to us or we will fight until all of us are dead."

"What do the simulations say about our chances of winning?"

Ben finished his tea. "I'm not involved with that part of the planning."

"It predicted either the GWs will destroy the city, or we will have to kill three hundred thousand people to impose total control, executing indiscriminately in the hopes of wiping them out."

"The program could be wrong."

"It could be." Wakana cracked his knuckles. "It's fascinating that in Mutsuraga's school records, programming was one of his weakest subjects. There were even those who doubted whether Mutsuraga really wrote the thing himself."

"I wouldn't know about that, sir," Ben said. Wakana took note of his unconscious "sir" and the way he lowered his gaze when he answered.

"Of course not. I've heard they want to make a consumer version of the game and let people play out various battles," Wakana mused.

"I've heard that too. The graphical leaps on porticals are accelerating at a rate no one expected."

"Who would have thought? Our wars played out by children as 'portical games'."

"It's effective propaganda disguised as entertainment."

Wakana looked over and saw the hostess staring in their direction. "What's she want to talk to you about?"

"Leaving her boyfriend."

"For you?"

Ben rubbed his head. "I think so."

Wakana wagged his finger. "You are a troublemaker, lieutenant." He finished his salad. "Are you going to help me find Captain Yoshioka?"

"Have you visited the Musashi Temple yet?"

"No, though my father told me I should visit while I'm here."

"It's only a ten minute walk away. It's worth a trip," Ben said.

"Let's pay our respects."

"Do you mind if we take the back exit?"

"Not at all."

12:43pm

The Musashi Miyamoto shrine was split into five areas. Wakana and Ishimura were in a section that had small waterfalls, fountains, and steps designed to evoke a semblance of liquid armor. There were statues of samurai, deities, and swords. The temple was made entirely from glass with water flowing between the panes, kanji characters explicating the old warrior's philosophy. They reached the altar and Wakana grabbed a stick of incense.

"Do you remember your Musashi?" Wakana asked Ishimura.

Ben shook his head. "I'm worthless with the sword."

Wakana placed his staff against a column, took out his sword, held it with both hands in front of him, and bowed. He quietly murmured some words and bowed again.

"My father made me study Musashi every morning," Wakana said.

"He was a soldier?"

"A farmer," Wakana replied. "But he raised me to be a soldier."

"Why?"

"So that farmers like him wouldn't have to suffer at the hands of soldiers."

A group of monks entered the temple and began chanting.

"Have you ever visited the Ise Grand Shrine?" Wakana asked.

"Not yet."

"They rebuild it every twenty years as a remembrance of the ephemeral nature of all things – *Wabi-sabi*. Before we won the Pacific War, we fought for dominance on the mainland. Now, we control territory from one end of the earth to the other. And yet, we cling to our idiosyncrasies, not acting like rulers."

"I don't understand."

"We rule the Pacific Ocean. The Great American Republic and the Chinese Empire are under our control. Shouldn't we be magnanimous with the locals? It's their gods that have abandoned them, not ours."

"Their God urges them to fight through George Washington," Ben said.

"Their God is a symbol of archaic values, a morality that favors the masses with illusions to make suffering more bearable now. Heaven is Tijuana without consequences. Endless feasts, a perpetual state of ecstasy induced by holy drugs, and the rest, a vague flood of light."

"If we lost the War, do you think the gods would be different?"

"We didn't lose the war," Wakana said. "The Greeks believed the worst sin wasn't murder, not even infanticide, but hubris. Is a man who sets himself up as a god committing the ultimate sacrilege?"

"Not if he *is* a god."

"Who determines that?"

"The victor?" Ben posed as both answer and question.

Wakana laughed. "Yes. The victor. How many have we killed in our march to empire?"

"I don't know."

"Every great empire has a mountain of corpses underneath it as its foundation. The Romans, the Chinese – even the

Americans wiped out millions of Indians and enslaved the African natives. No one remembers those who were sacrificed. It's like our earthquakes that wipe away the glories of the past. We've used the atomic torpedo on the Americans three times and they were all launched on the same day. There's still fierce debate about whether it was even necessary. The Americans were ready to surrender."

"I'd always thought we used them to spare our soldiers from ground combat since the Americans were going to fight to the death."

"We'd already broken all their ciphers and knew they were going to wave the flag, especially with most of the east coast overrun. They had a few minor conditions, but nothing unreasonable considering the circumstances."

"Why didn't we accept them?"

"Because we wanted to scare the Germans, make it clear this was our turf and we'd do anything to defend it. It was supposed to be a political statement and a surefire way of ending the war. Hundreds of thousands of Americans were killed. Mostly civilians. There were many rallies against the use of the atomics. Even now, there are many who've gathered in Kyoto to protest against our conflict with the George Washingtons, demanding a peaceful resolution."

"Why?"

"I've wondered the same thing. Do you think the world would have had more peace if the Empire had been defeated?"

"That's hard to say, sir. I watched a portical film about Musashi a few years ago," Ben said. "He killed a lot of people. Maybe it's in our blood."

Wakana was amused by the comment. "One of the tactics he teaches is called the Glue and Lacquer Emulsion Body. You stick to the enemy with your head, body, and legs and you're so closely attached, there isn't the slightest gap between you."

"Like a lover?"

Wakana guffawed. "Is everything about love to you?"

"Not everything."

"There are many questions about you that I find perplexing," he said.

"Me?"

"Forgive me if I'm blunt, but almost every report I've read about you is negative. This dates back to your time at BEMAG and the ensuing years. And yet, everywhere Lieutenant Colonel Mutsuraga goes, he specifically requests you come – in fact, insists on it. You would have been shipped off to Africa or Vietnam a long time ago if not for him. Why is that?"

"I didn't know the lieutenant colonel was the one keeping me near him."

"You must have noticed. Your academy reports say you failed basic officer's field training for your inability to use a sword properly."

"Like I said, I'm worthless with a sword."

"And yet, here you are."

"I'm not sure what you're getting at."

Wakana put his blade away and leaned on his staff again as they walked away from the temple. When they were a distance from the altar, he asked, "How much do you know about the lieutenant colonel's relationship with his wife, Meredith?"

"Not much."

"You mean you don't want to say?"

"The lieutenant colonel's personal life is his own," Ben answered.

"Do you think his personal life is affecting his judgment as commander?"

"I'm not sure. As a lieutenant, I rarely deal with the lieutenant colonel."

"Yes, and your official job is censoring messages people send via their porticals. So you must have read the lieutenant colonel's private correspondence."

"I-I have."

"And?"

"Their relationship is their own personal business."

"Not when it affects the Empire."

"But—"

"I'm going to have to pull rank and remind you I have the authority of Tokyo Command behind me."

"I feel it's inappropriate talking about the lieutenant colonel's personal life."

"Even if the stability of the USJ could hinge on it?"

Ben hesitated. "Their relationship is strained," he admitted, putting it as diplomatically as he could.

"Why is it strained?"

"The-the lieutenant colonel believes Meredith is having an affair."

"Did he order you to watch her?"

Ben shifted his feet, discomfited. "I've been monitoring all her portical activity."

"And what have your portical eyes told you?" Wakana inquired.

"That she's having an affair with a GW."

"Have you told the lieutenant colonel?"

"Just recently, I confirmed it for him."

Wakana looked back at the statue of Musashi in a combat pose, growling fiercely while holding his sword.

"This ability to monitor someone else's portical activity. Is this something you got from the Kikkai Department?"

Ben shook his head. "It's something I... Lieutenant Colonel Mutsuraga helped me to develop."

"Why are we at this shrine, Lieutenant Ishimura?"

Ben's eyes looked past the major to a gaunt-looking male who wore a hat with a logo on top of it. Huge sunglasses covered half his face and he was clad in an army green trench coat that he'd buttoned up. It was Captain Yoshioka. "How'd you know he'd be here?" Wakana asked.

"I've been monitoring his portical activity through lunch.

Should I call for backup?"

"I hope we won't need to."

Captain Yoshioka bowed in front of the shrine, both arms out in front of him in obeisance. Twice, he removed his glasses and rubbed his eyes, wiping away tears.

"What do you think he's praying about?" Wakana asked.

Ben scanned his portical. "I think Lieutenant Colonel Mutsuraga ordered him to kill someone."

"Someone?"

"Someone named Andrew Jackson."

Wakana cursed under his breath. "I wish I'd known about your device so we could have spared ourselves a lot of trouble."

"You know Andrew Jackson?"

"Andrew Jackson is the GW that is sleeping with Meredith Mutsuraga. The lieutenant colonel probably promised to take care of Yoshioka's family if he went out on one last suicide attack. But Andrew Jackson can't die."

"Why not?"

"He's the staunchest supporter of compromise with us among their ranks. Meredith has convinced him that the George Washingtons should negotiate, that the Empire is here to stay, and that's not necessarily a bad thing."

"Is she a double agent?"

Wakana shook his head. "This would all be easier if she were. Still, peace is peace."

"But at what price?"

"A price that's going to have to be paid."

"The loss of face for the lieuten-"

"Is nothing in service of the Emperor. Think of the lives that'll be saved. We have to protect Andrew Jackson, even if it means he gets a military guard," Wakana said.

Ben stared at Wakana. "Are you here for Captain Yoshioka, or the lieutenant colonel?"

Wakana snickered. "And they said you weren't sharp."

Yoshioka's prayer ended and he walked briskly away, a paranoid turn of his head to make sure he wasn't being followed. When he saw the two of them in uniform, he broke into a sprint.

"Captain!" the major yelled. "Captain!"

Yoshioka stopped. When he turned around, he held a pistol in his hand.

Wakana did not let it hinder him and approached closer.

"How did you find me?" Yoshioka asked. His eyes were black holes and his lips were a dry mess of torn flesh. He had a huge Adam's apple that bounced back and forth as he spoke and a big nose that protruded into several dull ridges. He glowered at Ben. "You gave me up, Ishimura?"

"We would have found you eventually," Wakana said. "Let's talk. I'm Major Wakana, sent by Tokyo Command."

"I know you're here to take me away. But I won't be executed for following orders!" he shouted.

"No one said anything about an execution. I just want to ask a few questions."

"Like what?"

"At Balboa Park, did someone give you the order to fire on the civilians?"

"They attacked me first. I have witnesses. The officers told me I'd be OK. You can't kill me for defending myself."

"You'll be given a fair trial."

"What about my mother? Who'll take care of her if I'm gone?"

"Your mother will be taken care of by the Empire."

"Families of executed officers are never taken care of," Yoshioka said. "You think I don't know how it is?"

Wakana twisted his staff in place, wondering if there was some way he could placate Yoshioka.

"If you get closer, I'll kill you!" Yoshioka threatened. Glaring at Ben. "You don't even have the loyalty of a dog."

Wakana raised his arms in the air to show he was unarmed

and stepped forward. "I've read your past record. You've always been a loose cannon, Captain. You shouldn't have been put in charge there in the first place. I know that."

"It's not my fault. Someone threw a bottle at one of the soldiers. I thought I heard a gunshot. I had to protect my men."

"Did Lieutenant Colonel Mutsuraga order you to kill someone?"

Yoshioka lowered his head.

"Did he promise to take care of your mother in return?"

"Step back!" Yoshioka yelled, then opened up his jacket. He was covered with explosives.

Ben flinched. Wakana did not. "You want to kill me, that's fine. But you'll answer my questions first."

"W-what questions?"

"How many people have you killed?"

"I don't know."

"Before Balboa Park?"

"Seventeen."

"Enemy combatants?"

Yoshioka nodded.

"It was different this time, wasn't it?"

"What are you talking about?"

"This time it was innocent people."

"They weren't innocent! I warned them to disperse!"

"Shigeko. Do you mind if I call you that?"

"Whatever. I don't care."

"Shigeko. Who do you see when you go to sleep?"

Ben was confused by the question, but Yoshioka's eyes began to tear up.

"I know there's someone. Maybe one person. Maybe two," Wakana said. "They're always there. You try to distract yourself, but right before sleep, there's nowhere to hide. That's why you haven't slept in weeks."

"It wasn't my fault," Yoshioka said. "I told them to go home."

"I know. Who is it you see?"

Yoshioka shook his head. "It doesn't matter."

"It matters to me."

"Why?"

"Because I have someone I see too," Wakana admitted.

"How long ago?"

"When I first started, decades ago."

"So it never... it never goes away?"

"Mutsuraga told you to blow yourself up for the Empire. But you just want it to end."

Yoshioka wiped the mucus dripping from his nose. "She was so young. Couldn't have been more than eight. I didn't see her until it was too late. One of the GWs brought her as a human shield. How could they bring a little girl there, knowing it was a combat zone?"

Wakana stared at him for a long time. "There are soldiers who don't feel an ounce of remorse for killing even the innocent. At least you still have a conscience. The Americans believed there is redemption for everyone as long as you believe in their God."

"I don't believe in their gods."

"You think blowing yourself up will be your redemption?"

"I will kill enemies of the Empire," Yoshioka affirmed.

"You mean Andrew Jackson?"

Yoshioka was startled. "H-how did you know?"

"The lieutenant colonel neglected to tell you the real reason he wants Jackson dead is because Jackson is having an affair with his wife. This is a personal vendetta, not a mission for the Empire. Am I right, Lieutenant Ishimura?"

"Yes, sir. I've been tracking his messages. The—"

"Shut up, Ishimura! I don't want to hear another word from you!"

"But you know there's no one who would know better than the lieutenant," Wakana asserted.

Yoshioka's hands rustled in his pockets.

"You want to blow yourself up, go ahead," Wakana said. "Go right there. But don't kill another father in the process."

"Another father?"

"Andrew Jackson is the father of two daughters. He wants peace with the USJ. You are killing the last hope we have for peace with the GWs."

"W-what am I supposed to do?"

"Either blow yourself up here or surrender," Wakana stated.

"B-but–"

"I can't promise you redemption – I'm not American. But I can promise you justice."

"You mean my life?"

"A chance to absolve yourself."

"How?"

"I don't know. That's up to the judge."

"I've caused too much trouble."

"It's the troublemakers who change empires," Wakana replied. "What'll it be?"

"I'm not sure. I nee–"

Wakana wrapped his arms around Yoshioka. "You wanna die. Let's go, captain! Set off the bomb! I'm ready to die too! I've been ready to die every day since that morning. Are you?"

"Get off me!" Yoshioka exclaimed, trying to push Wakana off.

But Wakana's hands quickly disarmed the igniter, separating Yoshioka from the explosives connected to his body with the deft use of a knife that had appeared from his sleeve. "Do you really want to die? One poke in your neck, and I can end it for you," Wakana said.

Yoshioka struggled to break free, but Wakana cuffed the captain. "Ishimura. Go call for some support and call the bomb brigade too."

2:31pm

The military police disarmed the rest of Yoshioka and carted him off on a jeep. Local police were there as well, though more for general security as the prisoner was under military jurisdiction. The monks were distraught, wondering what all the commotion was for. Wakana asked for an unmarked car from one of the officers investigating the scene.

"Where are we going?" Ben asked.

"Have you ever met a George Washington?" Wakana asked back.

"In person?"

"Yes."

"I've spied on some."

"We'll meet some directly," Wakana said.

"Where?"

"A market in the Gaslamp Quarter."

"The Stingaree?" Ben asked. "I think that's where Yoshioka was heading."

"It's because the GWs are having a private rally there."

"How do you know?"

"I've been in negotiations with Andrew Jackson and he'll be explaining our compromise there. But something doesn't sit right with me. Mutsuraga knows you're with me, so it's safe to presume he'll also know it means you can track

Yoshioka. We can't assume Yoshioka will be the only one trying to attack the rally."

"You think Mutsuraga wants revenge?"

"Revenge, and to publicly humiliate them. I hope I'm wrong. But there are others besides Mutsuraga who have a vested interest in making sure the negotiations fail."

"What'll happen to Yoshioka?"

"Depends on how the negotiations with the GWs go."

They got in the car and Beniko drove.

"I didn't know Andrew Jackson had two daughters," Ben said.

"He doesn't," Wakana answered.

"Then why..." Ben began, but he realized the answer himself.

"To disarm him mentally," the major confirmed.

"And the part about seeing someone?"

Wakana stared flatly ahead. "Keep your eyes on the road."

Exiting Tijuana was faster than entering through all the security checkpoints.

"How far is it?" Wakana asked.

"Not too far." Ben sped up. "You really think peace with the GWs is possible?" he asked.

"Have you heard of how the GWs deal with traitors?"

"They feed them to animals," Ben answered.

"Sometimes ants. They are savage, but disciplined and ruthless in their organization. Even if we killed George Washington, another would take his place. Perhaps a friend, a brother, a fellow patriot. They will fight us to the death. Our compromise will carve out San Diego into separate regions. They will be autonomous, though they will grant us access. They promise to cease all attacks in exchange."

"Tokyo Command agrees to this?"

"They sent me," Wakana affirmed.

"I'm curious what the simulation would say about this."

"Why don't you input the variables later?"

Ben switched lanes.

"Can I ask you a question?" Ben asked.

"Of course."

"Why are you bringing me along?"

"Is there any reason I shouldn't?"

"I'm not usually the officer of choice for important missions."

"Why is that?"

"I think you would know the answer to that better than me."

"It puzzles me, Ishimura," Wakana said.

"What does?"

"Your hypocrisy. You would report your own parents for planning against the Empire, but you would not kill a Mexican prisoner for your officer field training. You've never directly killed a man with your own hands, have you?"

Ben shook his head.

"Do you ever regret reporting your parents?" Wakana asked.

"They were planning against the Empire. What's there to regret?"

Wakana considered his answer. "You could have feigned ignorance," he said, and there was an accusatory tone in his voice.

"It wasn't an easy choice. And respectfully, *sir*, I don't appreciate having it questioned."

"Of course not. Forgive me," the major said. "But it didn't make life easy, did it? Outwardly, everyone praised you, but no one trusted you again."

They went up a ramp onto a higher road. From there, they had a full view of downtown San Diego with its spiral buildings jutting upwards like artificial mountains stabbing the sky.

"Which brings me back to my original question. Why bring me?" Ben asked again.

"I want you to tell me why the lieutenant colonel really takes you everywhere with him."

"I don't know. You'll have to ask him."

"Your facade of stupidity and cavalier insouciance may fool others, but I–"

The car windows suddenly shattered and there was a loud boom. In one of the buildings ahead, a pillar of fire clambered on top of itself. The shape of the cloud resembled a flower in bloom, the petals spreading ash and sporangias in a fiery pollination. Both their laps were covered with glass and there was blood on their faces. Most of the vehicles on the road had stopped.

"That's from the Stingaree," Ben said.

"I know," Wakana said.

"If Jackson was there–"

"We need to get there *fast!*"

Ben pushed the accelerator.

3:16pm

Even before they arrived, a military squadron had been dispatched, securing the grounds. The stores in the market had been decimated. Seared food stained the floor. Fruit cocktails were made from apples, oranges, and blood. Dust formed a cloud that acted as fog for the whole street. Injured people were wailing in pain, detached limbs cloistered together with canned goods. Conflagrations were still raging, though the fire services were fighting them. The ground started shaking. Wakana knew it portended the arrival of a mecha and approached a sergeant who was temporarily in charge.

"Have any of the bodies been identified?"

"Not yet, sir."

"Do you have a body count yet?" he demanded.

"No, sir." The sergeant shook his head. "I don't think there are many survivors. The GWs were having a rally and most of them were killed, sir."

"Any idea who carried this out?"

"Not yet. Some officers earlier mentioned they would review the camera footage. The–"

A soldier approached the sergeant and said, "They need you right away."

"Excuse me, sir," the sergeant said, bowed, and sprinted away.

The main hallway of the marketplace had collapsed and there was a pile of rubble where there had just been an informal meeting place. The frame lay exposed, its metallic bones stacked haphazardly in jutting disharmony. Destruction's fractals vied for prominence, tubes and wiring ripped to shreds. The humans were as brittle as crushed bugs and the body parts were indistinguishable from the burnt concrete columns.

"What do we do?" Ben asked.

"Wait and confirm what I already know."

"What's that?"

Wakana crushed an eggplant with his staff and refused to answer.

7:34pm

His confirmation came a few hours later from an officer who carried out the remains of not only Andrew Jackson, but Meredith Mutsuraga, whose face had been smashed by a steel beam. At one point, a muscle spasm in her leg caused it to shake, but it was temporary. Wakana asked Ben to drive him back to headquarters.

There was no traffic on the road because the military had issued curfew and tanks were guarding the freeways. When they tried to make their way back to the Otay base, they were informed, "All roads are closed."

Multiple mechas were patrolling the city.

"You ever been in one of those?"

Ben confessed, "No. I don't have enough clearance."

"Give me a few minutes and we'll get our own personal escort back home. They're the safest way of entering a combat zone without getting hurt."

Wakana made a call on his portical and spoke sharply in Japanese.

They drove back to the Stingaree and the mecha was already waiting, a gigantic suit of samurai armor that was painted black with red epaulets. Their car was barely the size of one of its toes. A ladder came down from its massive chest plate. The mecha was stationary, but heat was emanating from every part.

"The *Harinezumi*, Torturer class, finest mecha around," Wakana said. "Has the best damn pilot in the USJ too, Kujira."

"I've never heard of him."

"Her. And that's because she's one of the USJ's closely guarded secrets."

"Why?"

"Because she's so damn good. She grew up with a leg condition that required mechanical augmentation for her to walk. When she told her teachers she wanted to be a mecha pilot, they laughed at her. But her condition gave her a familiarity with mechas none of them could have anticipated."

"Is there another way up?" Ben asked, as he followed Wakana up the ladder, rung by rung.

"You don't like the exercise? I have a bad leg and I'm doing this."

"I don't like heights."

"Are you serious, Ishimura?" Wakana asked.

"I am."

"Then don't look down."

It was a long climb and Ben had to stop several times to catch his breath. Wakana's leg nearly buckled in three separate instances, but he suppressed the pain and forced himself to continue, refusing to let it hamper him.

The plates were connected by flexible "skin" material, rigid pieces bending at the hinge joints. From below, the surface looked pristine. But closer, Wakana could see corrosion, dents from fights, and battle scars. Its face was a mix of a kendo and noh mask, death unleashed in dramatic artistry. Exhaust ports under the side fascias released heat and internal smoke.

Gunfire rang out behind them. They could hear Americans barking orders. Several explosions marred the skyline. They arrived at the hatch and were relieved to have the armor of the mecha behind them as protection from the spray of bullets outside. The inside was metallic, smoky, and damp.

The heat turned Wakana's uniform into a sweaty rag and with only auxiliary lights to guide them, they were doused in red. The corridors were tight like that of a submarine, just enough space for them to traverse.

"It's like a good old fashioned sauna," Ben said.

"I could use a trip to an onsen bath right now."

"I know a few good places in Los Angeles. There's one that serves the best tiger blowfish you'll ever have."

"Even now, you're thinking about food?"

"I'm sorry. It's the only way I can keep myself from getting too depressed about the situation."

They came to another ladder they had to climb.

"I miss Ise udon," Wakana said. "My favorite noodles."

"I've never had them."

"I will have to take you sometime. There's only a few places in Ise Shima that do it right."

"I would very much enjoy that," Ben replied.

They climbed up to the bridge. The entire ceiling was covered with porticals. In the center, thousands of wires connected into the body of the pilot. Kujira was in a gelatinous fluid shaped into a sphere, the chemicals easing transmission of commands from her nerves to the mecha. She could spin every direction in the circle, the wires long enough to compensate. It was useful as the whole room was a one-sided mirror she could look out. Information was on the circular three hundred sixty degree view, including heat signatures, technical data, and sensor readouts. Her face was covered by a neural interface that analyzed the data in even more detail.

"Thanks for the ride," Wakana said to her.

"I was in the area," Kujira replied through the communicator. "How'd you guys screw it all up again?"

Wakana knew her "guys" wasn't meant to be gender neutral. "That's what I'm going to Otay to find out."

"There's as many enemies of the Empire in the uniform as there are out of it."

"Careful," Wakana said. "You know the cockpits are recorded."

"I don't care. I dismantled everything I didn't clear to be on board."

"Tokko have their ways."

"Fuck them," Kujira said. "If they did a good enough job on the real criminals, we wouldn't be in this mess again."

"Kujira—"

"Since we're all snails riding on the razor's edge, we might as well say it as it is."

"That's not the way it works," Wakana reminded her.

"Then let's change it. I'm tired of having to choose between doing the horrible and more horrible."

"That's the way of war."

"The—" She became quiet as she received orders. "We're getting diverted."

"What's going on?" Wakana asked.

"The GWs are up to something."

They rolled east, the wheels allowing the mecha to move without damaging the road in its path. Most of the shorter buildings fit snugly underneath its crotch. Wakana had never seen San Diego from these heights. It was a grand city and downtown had an array of skyscrapers, apartments, and architectural marvels that were as striking for their beauty as they were for their unusual designs. Architects were given more leeway in the USJ – the outer territories in general – and from the massive planetarium to the municipal center that had a butterfly wing motif at its apex, San Diego was like a garden made of granite and wood. Wakana was especially interested in the conical library complex that he had only heard about until now, an underground archive of millions of rare American and European novels that had mostly been burned elsewhere by zealous Nazi and USJ censors. Although Wakana couldn't see humans with his naked eye, the sensors picked up heat signatures. There were thousands of people populating the buildings. Kujira could magnify any point of focus, which she frequently did. The GWs had set up American flags all over to replace the red sun of the Empire. Red, white, and blue draped as graffiti over the walls of San Diego.

Kujira's attention went to a black blob that the scanners were having a difficult time analyzing. Three smaller mechas were already there, half the size of Kujira's *Harinezumi*. They didn't have any special colors distinguishing them and their armor plates were less ostentatious. Their locomotion was slower too, their joints more static.

"What's going on?" Kujira asked into the portical.

"The homunculi are detecting something unusual," a voice spoke back over the communicator.

"What are homunculi?" Ben asked Wakana.

"Robots driven by portical simulations."

"They're a joke," Kujira, who heard them, stated. "USJ command thinks they can replace us with simulated brains."

The homunculi were investigating the black amoeba-like anomaly, nebulous in shape, slowly growing.

As soon as Kujira saw it on the screen, she said, "Order the homunculi back!"

"That's a negative," the voice over the communicator replied.

"That's the camo-cover for the Panzer Maus IX Super Tanks. They won't stand a chance. I need to get in there right now or–"

"Stand down and let the homunculi handle it unless the situation gets out of control. We're engaging the polyhedral deformation projector to–"

"Are you all idiots?" Kujira yelled. "They'll destroy your toys."

"You have your orders."

The cluster of dirt melted apart and revealed four enormous tanks. They were small compared to the mecha, but each had a massive cannon. The treads were their primary method of movement, though they had limbs on either side that helped their mobility and could be used as mechanical legs in unfriendly terrain. Their hulls were so thick, most bullets would bounce off. Even bombs and cannon fire would barely make a dent.

"Those are old Germans tanks," Ben said.

"Looks like the GWs got hold of them off the black market," Wakana said.

"I thought only biomorphs could drive them."

Wakana had been in Afghanistan when the Germans sent out their biomorph-driven vehicles. They were people underneath, genetically manipulated, psychologically and physically mutilated for years until they become the ideal soldier, emotionless and totally loyal.

"They must be fitted for the GWs. Kujira," Wakana called. "Are they dangerous?"

"They can be if you don't know how to handle them."

"You do?"

"My first fight against a Nazi was a biomorph. He killed my partner and nearly killed me too."

"How'd you survive?"

"I finished it off with my old quadmecha. The *Harinezumi* is a hundred times stronger."

The tanks fired at the nearest homunculus. They weren't just regular shells, but an unusual type of chemical that formed black webs around its prey and tried to penetrate every orifice of the robot. The homunculus tried to fight back, endeavoring to attack with its arm cannon. But the tanks fired in unison and ripped a hole in its armor. The dark goo penetrated the center of the machine, seeped into every hinge, and caused it to implode. Its broken parts fell on top of several houses and the sensor readings of hundreds of humans were crushed into millisecond flatlines.

"A lot of people are going to die unnecessarily because

some officer wants to prove their point about the stupid homunculus," Kujira said. "Homunculus has no *Yamato damashii*."

"Why do you need honor if you're a robot?" Ben asked.

"Honor is the only thing that separates us from animals."

"Robots aren't animals."

"They're worse. They're our flawed reflections."

The tanks went after the second homunculus, propelling what looked like a mix between a drill and a massive suction cup from a side rail gun. The extrusion latched onto the front of the robot's chest, causing it to rupture. While the homunculus was smaller than the *Harinezumi*, it was still a huge piece of machinery. When it toppled over, it destroyed two buildings and knocked out multiple generators. The surrounding area lost all energy and the mottled lights turned into a vortex of death. More than a thousand people died according to the display stat.

"Strap yourselves into the seats," Kujira barked at Wakana and Ben.

They took a seat in the left periphery and put on their arm and waist straps. They also donned helmets and fastened the body protection plates hanging above their seats.

"The GWs must have foreign support. There's no way they could have weapons like that on their own," Wakana said.

"But I thought you said it was the black marke–"

"*Italian* black market. They funnel weapons for both sides, playing us off against each other. The Nazis sometimes use them to distribute aid to the GWs, needling us to see if there's any weak points."

"That would be an act of war if it were proven."

"It never will be. Italian black market gives them deniability. We do the same to them."

The super tanks made mincemeat of the last homunculus, destroying it with a unified blow. They used their limbs to spin in place so that they could have faster mobility even in tight corridors. The robot struggled, firing every weapon at its disposal. It destroyed more of the city, including a random blast that landed directly on the library and caused it to explode.

Wakana groaned. "The written ideas and beliefs of tens of thousands of people gone."

"Better books than people," Ben noted.

The tanks did not immediately turn to engage the *Harinezumi*. Instead, they started attacking the Americans.

"Why are they attacking their own side?" Ben asked.

Wakana couldn't understand it either until he saw the scans of the interior of the tank. "The biomorph pilots must have been included."

"Can't the GWs control them?"

Wakana shook his head. "No one can control a biomorph once it's been unleashed. That's why the Germans gave up on them." Wakana had read that thousands of the biomorphs had been abandoned after years of experimentation and preparation. Their fate after being deemed obsolete by the Germans was never determined, though it made sense that many of them were put on sale.

"They're coming for us!" Kujira warned them. She turned on the communicator. "The tanks are engaging me. I'm going to take them out. Order emergency evacuations for the whole area. There might be more and—"

"That's a negative," Command replied back.

"Why?"

"Retreat from the area."

"What about the tanks?"

"We'll deal with them later."

"They're going to attack the whole area."

"They're not your concern."

Kujira looked back at the city, flipped off the communicator.

"What's going on?" Ben asked.

"I think USJ command wants the biomorphs to keep on

destroying the city," Wakana suggested.

With an unexpectedly graceful motion for such a big machine, Kujira unsheathed her fusion sword and moved towards the tanks. The first turned its attention to her and fired its cannon. Kujira dodged the attack and sliced an opening through the hull, using her other arm to keep on her toes. Inside the liquid sphere, Kujira moved like a ballerina through all the wires, deftly skipping from one position to another. The tank tried to break free, but Kujira sliced its cannon off with her sword, piercing, stabbing, and swinging in sharp arcs to incapacitate the rest. Wakana was relieved they'd been strapped in. Otherwise, they would have been hurtled to the back of the bridge.

Two tanks fired at her. The mecha took two blows to its flank, but focused on the tank beneath her, making sure to destroy it completely. The biomorphs prepared to shoot again. The *Harinezumi* stood up and lifted the tank corpse, using it as a shield. The artillery pounded the tank's underbelly rather than her chest. Kujira threw the tank at the two of them and used her legs to swiftly get to her prey. She used the sword on one, sundering it into four pieces. She pounded its companion with her fists until the top caved in, crushing the biomorph pilot inside even as it continued to struggle.

Bullets hit the final tank from behind. American civilians on the ground were sniping at it.

"What are those idiots doing?" Kujira muttered. "They just realize they can't control this thing?"

The biomorph, irked by the bullets ricocheting off its shell, turned its attention to them. With a blast from its cannon, it wiped out the resistance. It didn't stop with the shooters, wreaking havoc on the rest of the area. Constant flatlines flashed on the display. Porticals took records of those who had identification on them, registering casualties. Though they were short blips, Wakana noted most of them were USJ citizens who had no idea what hit them. Ethnicities went across the board from Mexican, French, Brazilian, Chinese, Indian, Austrian, Australian, and more.

"Doesn't she have orders to retreat?" Ben whispered to Wakana.

"*Tosuiken*," Wakana replied, referring to independence of field command. "Aboard the mecha, she's *daigensui*, or supreme commander."

"Kill the tanks, we only leave the rebels alive until our soldiers kill them. Let that final tank go, and it does our soldiers' work for them without putting them in harm's way," Kujira said, questioning herself, contemplating the horrible and more horrible she'd referred to earlier. "Either way, innocents won't be spared, or will they? Will our soldiers be able to separate the dissidents from bystanders in a way the biomorphs can't?"

"Are you asking me?" Wakana asked.

"It's not like you can give me an answer," Kujira replied, not as a rebuke, but matter of fact.

Kujira's eyes went to the final tank. She swapped her sword for an artillery gun and fired a volley at the Panzer Maus IX. These attacks were much fiercer than anything the Americans could hurtle. The super tank turned and charged back at the mecha.

Kujira waited for the trajectory to line up. Red lines calculated the distance on the portical screen, beeping and alerting her when the angles matched. The target lock connected and the *Harinezumi* slashed the tank in half. Kujira did not wait for the biomorph to recover. The *Harinezumi* leaped forward, thrust its hands into innards of the tank, which was filled with the camo fluid they'd seen earlier. A human registered on the portical screen, though Wakana and Ben couldn't see anyone through the liquid. Kujira crunched her fists and the monster within died. The biomorph melted into a reservoir of rancor and loathing.

Kujira put both her palms together and did a slight bow.

"You all fought valiantly," she said to honor the biomorphs. To Wakana, she said, "It's fifteen minutes from here to Otay."

"Will you be OK?"

"We're alive, aren't we?"

"I mean disregarding the orders."

"If I'm not, I'm not. *Shikata ga nai*."

"You don't have to worry about the calls," Ben said.

"What do you mean?"

"Just don't worry about it," Ben assured her. "I'll take care of those for you so that there won't be any record of it."

Kujira looked to Wakana who shrugged. "He's good," Wakana confirmed.

"You're that good with a portical?" Kujira asked.

"I can manage myself," Ben replied modestly.

Wakana checked his portical, realized all external connections were cut off. "Is there an internal kikkai field?"

Kujira gave him the algorithms to connect. Wakana read the latest reports.

"There's been thirty suicide attacks on military installations in the last hour," he gloomily stated. His fingers nervously shifted along his belt. "Total annihilation of the civilian force is the only way this can end now. Under the circumstances, Lieutenant Colonel Mutsuraga will be promoted, as will Captain Yoshioka. The captain will be surprised to hear he is now considered a war hero and is up for the San Diego War Medal – the first *jugun kisho* of our fight."

"Is Tokyo Command disappointed?"

"They will want this situation resolved as quickly as possible." Wakana gripped his staff, wishing he could destroy it.

They arrived at Otay base without any further complications.

"Thanks again for the lift," he said to Kujira.

"Go kick someone's ass for this," she replied.

"I'll try."

9:12pm

Wakana charged into Mutsuraga's office. Mutsuraga was at his desk, holding a bottle of alcohol, the top of his uniform loosened.

"Are you happy now?" Wakana demanded.

"Watch your tone, major," Mutsuraga replied.

"You got what you wanted, *sir*."

"What's that?"

"All-out war."

"You're blaming me for this?"

"I am."

"You've lost your mind."

"I know you sent Yoshioka! He was just bait for me to chase, wasn't he, while you sent your real bomber? We could have had peace!"

"I lost my wife out there today!" Mutsuraga snapped. "Don't you dare talk to me about peace now! I will hunt down all the GWs."

"Why would a GW set off a bomb on his own people?"

"Because they're stupid brutes!"

Two guards rushed in, looking to the lieutenant colonel to check if they should take the major away.

"I will expose you," Major Wakana said. "You and your miserable jealousy that's going to lead to the death of countless innocents. Don't you have an ounce of humanity in you?"

"What are you talking about?"

"Your wife and Andrew Jackson!"

Mutsuraga snarled, stood up, and charged Wakana. Before they could exchange blows, the guards blocked the pair from each other.

"How dare you speak against my wife now of all times!" Mutsuraga shouted.

"Don't act so righteous!" Wakana shouted back. "You think I don't see right through you?"

Mutsuraga went for his sword, but the guards stopped him. Mutsuraga slapped the guard. Ben, who was behind, grabbed Wakana and dragged him out.

"You should have challenged Jackson to a duel yourself instead of sending a lackey to do your dirty work!" Wakana shouted.

Ben tugged and pulled while the guards shut the door as soon as Wakana was out.

"Major Wakana!" Ben yelled. "You need to calm down, sir."

"That son of a bitch has plunged the Empire back into an unnecessary war and put our soldiers into harm's way."

"He just lost his wife."

"You think his feelings matter when you compare it to all those who'll suffer now? You saw how many were killed by those biomorphs. When things get–"

"What's going on here?"

Both of them turned and saw a young teenage girl approach. Wakana recognized her as Mutsuraga's daughter, Claire. He stepped aside and did not say anything. "Ben? What happened?" Claire asked. "They said something happened to Mom."

"You should talk to your father," Ben answered.

Claire approached her father's office and entered. Mutsuraga was still angrily railing when he saw his daughter.

"Dad, where's Mom?" she asked.

She shut the door behind her.

Wakana twirled his mustache. "Who won today?"

Ben shrugged. "I plugged in some new variables earlier. The simulation predicted two scenarios. The Empire will eventually prevail after a bloody series of battles, or the cost will be so severe, it will end in stalemate."

Wakana looked at Ben. "I know you're the one who really built the simulation. Part of why I was here was to expose Mutsuraga. But I don't think that'll do much good now."

"I don't know what you're talking ab–"

"Don't try to deny it, lieutenant. Enough lies for one day. Tomorrow, carry on your farce. But for today, give me the truth. Why did you do it for him?"

"Sir, I don't know–"

"I deserve better than another lie. Just tell me why."

Ben stared back at Wakana, assessing. "No one took anything I did seriously. No one trusted me. They thought I didn't deserve to be there, and when I refused to kiss their asses and do my best to prove myself to them, they shut me out. I tried, I really did, but the other students and teachers at BEMAG ridiculed me and sabotaged my work. They felt I was a disgrace to the corps and had no idea what I was doing. All except Mutsuraga. He was an instructor and he made a deal with me. People would use my simulation and play my game, but he would get all the credit. It was either that, or have it buried forever."

"Do you still do the programming?"

"I've trained others so that much of the day-to-day is done by them."

"Why not you?"

"The lieutenant colonel doesn't fully trust me either," Ben replied.

"Does he have cause?"

"Does he have cause not to trust you either?"

Wakana's eyes tightened. "I can help you get another position."

"I like my job right now."

"And what is your job right now?"

"Lazy dilettante in the middle of a war."

"When this disaster is contained and if you survive, they'll open up a gaming division. They will need people to run the censor's office. I could put your name in for it."

"Why would you do that for me?"

"You're my former student, Ishimura. Anything amiss with me helping you?"

Silence slipped between them.

"I do enjoy being a censor," Ben finally said.

"You'll get to see the seeds of your creation grow."

"To censor them?"

"To cultivate their growth," Wakana said.

"Thank you, sir."

"Life is all about lies. It's about what you can stomach. If you hadn't let Mutsuraga take the credit for your work, he would not be in this position of authority and today's bombing would not have happened." Ben was about to protest, but Wakana continued, not wanting to hear any defense. "The bigger capacity you have for tolerating deception, the higher up you can go. I don't think I'll go very far, especially as I will write the truth about Mutsuraga, even if my report gets ignored... Then again, it would be nice to call the shots rather than being at the whimsies of mad officers with more stars. *Sayonara*, lieutenant."

Ben saluted as Wakana left.

11:41pm

It was late when Wakana finished up his report and returned to his private barracks. Right outside, there was a lineup of fifteen American prisoners. One tried to escape on foot and was shot. The others got rambunctious and were executed. The bullets echoed death's siren muted by gunpowder dissipating into smoke. Wakana was about to enter his room when he remembered he forgot to bring one of the printed files he needed to transcribe into his portical. He went back to the office again and overheard voices arguing in the hall. It was Ben and Mutsuraga's daughter, Claire.

"You're not telling me the whole story," she said.

"I've told you everything I know."

"None of this makes any sense," Claire protested. "I can tell Dad is lying, but I don't know why. Just tell me what really happened."

"You heard his story."

"I'm always straight with you. You need to level with me."

"I don't know."

"Don't bullshit me."

"I'm not."

She sighed. "Mom was with the Americans, wasn't she?"

"She was."

"Was it a church event?"

"I don't know."

"What do you know?"

"That it's an unforgivable event," Ben said. "I'm sorry."

Wakana grabbed his file and returned to his residence. His soundproof walls blocked off all noise of the battle raging throughout the city. A glance at his portical indicated total civilian casualties were high, as intended. Wakana turned off the light and lay down on the bed. He blinked several times and covered his head with a pillow, turned sideways in bed. He scratched his scalp, adjusted the position of the blanket so that none of it was under him. Clearing his mind was difficult and he tried not to think about Yoshioka or Andrew Jackson or Beniko Ishimura. He looked ahead, and for a moment, he saw someone that caused him to shudder.

He thought back to Vietnam, the order to burn down a village that was allegedly harboring terrorists. Even when he'd called back to tell Command that it was only women and children, that they should rethink their plan, they'd refused to rescind the order.

Wakana turned all the lights back on, got off the bed, and went to the sword. The edge of the blade was sharp and he slid his fingers along it until they were bleeding. The pain stung and distracted his mind. Wakana returned to bed, blood dripping from his hand. He wiped it over his forehead, hoping the crimson would wipe away his self-loathing. It stained his flesh, but didn't make things any more pure; instead, dousing him in the bloody red of guilt.

PRESENT

Los Angeles
July 3, 1988
2:43am

Akiko hoped it was a dream. She thought she felt her fingers moving, swore her elbow was bending. But when she tried to turn on the light, the blunt end of her artificial limb knocked the lamp over. The medics had replaced both arms; one with a temporary prosthetic that could simulate the basic motions of a finger and looked almost normal with a glove on; the other with a flesh-colored tube that could be fitted with weapons, triggered by the muscles in the triceps or, alternately, by a lever to its side. The specialists were making a more accurate hand out of silicone based on previous bioscans, but the transradial half wouldn't be ready for another week.

She missed Hideyoshi, wondered if she should call him. She thought about her parents, still not sure how she was going to tell them what happened. Her father worked as a foreman in construction so she'd seen her fair share of accidents, his co-workers having limbs crushed. The doctors had effective anesthetics in their arsenal, allowing most to live free of pain with their artificial parts. She remembered one of her father's friends had both his legs mashed when a wall collapsed. He used to be such a cheery man. After the accident, he sulked, rarely spoke, and drank his woes away.

She thought of the reports she'd read about medical units in Vietnam that were aggressively stepping up their experimentation with limb regrowth, particularly considering that so many of their soldiers had their arms chopped off by the guerillas. The research had been progressing slowly and was nowhere near the point where they could consider full regeneration.

Two men entered her hospital room. She recognized them from the night before as agents of the Kempeitai. They'd questioned her about what had transpired after the GWs released her. Had it only been two days? She'd spent the majority of the previous day in surgery. Anesthetics kept her in a muzzled daze, neither awake nor sleeping.

The agents were twins, had black hair and stiff torsos filling out their wrinkle-free gray suits. They were the same height, had the same short haircut, and gesticulated the same annoying scowl. Agent #1 wore a red glove on his left hand and Agent #2 wore it on his right hand.

"We have a lot of questions for you," Agent #1 said.

"Good. I have lots of questions too," Akiko shot back.

"Who are you working for?" Agent #2 asked.

"For the Empire," Akiko replied, indignant that it even needed to be asked. "My commander is General Wakana."

"You started in the diplomatic corps?"

She shook her head. "They had a program with BEMAG to send us all over the world as part of their recruiting efforts, but I never actually joined."

"Which cities did you travel to?"

"Beiping, Keijo, Berlin, Tojo City, and more," Akiko said.

"You went to Hanoi?"

She looked at both agents, not liking the tone of their question. "It was before the second rebellion and only for two days."

"How did you like your time in Indochina?"

Akiko took a moment to remember its old name before they'd cast it off and called themselves Vietnam in an act of independence. "The city was booming under Imperial rule."

"The Empire instilled order after the *seisen*," Agent #1 said, referring to the Holy War that united the world under the graces of the Emperor's *hakko ichi'u*. "Our army built hospitals, revamped public transportation, made education completely free for everyone, and eliminated hunger. Why do you think Vietnam is resisting the Empire so long?"

"There's reports that the Germans have secretly been fueling their discontent, encouraging them to separate," Akiko said. "But I don't know why anyone would resist the honor of being part of the Empire."

"Do you agree with Tokyo Command that it's important to preserve the pro-Empire faction against the independent rebels?"

"If it fell, it would result in a domino effect of unrest in the whole region," Akiko replied.

"Do you speak Vietnamese?"

"No."

"What languages are you fluent in?"

"German, Italian, Japanese, and English," Akiko informed them. "Though I have problems writing in German."

"What's your primary language?"

"English."

"Not Japanese?"

Akiko hesitated before answering truthfully, "Not Japanese."

The two agents glanced at each other.

"Why didn't you join the diplomatic corps?" #2 asked.

"I was willing to go wherever the Empire needed me and I felt Tokko was the best way I could serve."

"One of the first reports you made in Tokko encouraged the Ministry of Education to teach the 'real' history of the

Empire to key officers so they know what actually happened. Were you implying there's a false history?"

"I was. A lot of it is propaganda and exaggerated bravado that makes Japan seem like a reluctant savior during the Holy War. The actual history is much more interesting and useful for us. We wanted to take charge and shape our own destiny. It's deplorable that countless millions died during the war and those numbers shouldn't be hidden so everyone can know how futile their resistance was," Akiko affirmed, recalling the criticism she'd received for the implications of her paper. "People are much happier now than when they were being exploited under the old western forces."

"And what was life like under the old Americans?" Agent #1 inquired.

"Their 'freedom' was a joke. People were controlled by a plutocracy and the poor were suppressed by the wealthy with the promise of the 'American dream.' Slavery drove their economy and most had miserable working conditions. Racial inequality makes a joke of the ideas of equality proposed by their old Constitution. In the Empire, everyone is a child of the Emperor and, as long as you are loyal, you will be treated with respect and honor. That's also what distinguishes us from the Nazis."

"What's that?"

"They'll kill anyone who doesn't match their view of the ideal Aryan. Even after Hitler tried to redefine Aryanism, it wasn't that much more inclusive," she said, recalling the report about a group of German officers who attempted a coup, accusing the Fuhrer himself of not fitting the Aryan mold.

"You're aware that the Nazis are our allies?"

"Of course I am. I'm also aware we need to be well-informed about who they really are and stay vigilant in our defenses."

"Vigilance is an interesting word for you to use," #2 said.

"You said last night the George Washingtons cut your hands off. Why did they let you live?"

"I don't know. Captain Ishimura suggested that the GWs felt it'd be more of a punishment to leave me alive than to kill me."

"Do you agree?"

"You should ask them, not me."

"Where is Captain Ishimura?" #1 inquired.

"I don't know."

Both twins squinted skeptically. "How could you lose him?"

"Because I was in surgery," Akiko replied.

"We've received a disturbing report that you killed a man in Portical Valley."

"I did," Akiko affirmed.

"Were you aware that man was a war hero? Colonel Nishino, known as Koushou, was one of the most important technical investigators during San Diego."

"Captain Ishimura alerted me to that fact."

"Did he also tell you that he was a valuable asset to the military and provided important information as well as essential technology that we otherwise could not get hold of?"

"Captain Ishimura informed me that he was an important figure."

"You knew this and yet you still killed him?" Agent #2 asked angrily.

"I did," Akiko said, without blinking.

"Why?"

"Because of his inhuman behavior. He had a zoo of people that–"

"That's his personal life. All of those people were contractually bound to him. The Empire respects the lifestyle choices its servants make. Was there another reason why you killed him?"

Why did she even need to explain herself to them? "He

questioned the divinity of the Emperor," she said, assuming that would end any further inquiry.

"Do you have proof of this?"

"Is my word not sufficient?"

"Not when you're under suspicion."

"Suspicion of what?"

"Whether you're a traitor, or just incompetent."

"Incompetent?" Akiko flared. "I'm a loyal servant of the Emperor." Her mind suddenly went back to the interactions she'd had with many of those she'd interrogated.

"Neither of us understands how an agent of Tokko could allow herself to be captured," #2 said.

"It's a disgrace."

"An ignoble disgrace."

"Why are you still alive?"

"I told you, they let me live," Akiko replied.

"I don't think she understands the question," #1 said to #2 in a condescending tone.

"Maybe she was so scared, she lost her wits and forgot her sense of honor."

"Why am I being interrogated?" Akiko asked, still not sure what was going on.

"Because your story doesn't add up."

"What doesn't add up? I was attacked by the George Washingtons."

"But you're still alive and Captain Ishimura is conveniently missing," #1 said.

"Perhaps they've been conspiring together," #2 proposed.

"Where is General Wakana?" Akiko asked, agitated by their suggestion. "He'll explain everything."

"General Wakana is not available at the moment," #2 said.

"Don't try to hide behind him," #1 snapped.

"I'm not trying to hide. I–" Akiko began to explain herself.

"You are not being very cooperative."

#2 held up a gun. "I know you're inoculated against most

of our diseases, but there are a few even you're not protected against."

"Are you threatening me?" Akiko asked, furious at the insinuation.

"We're urging you to be more cooperative."

"This would all go much easier for you if you confessed," Agent #2 suggested.

"We could go back to the station, but then we'd have to hand you over to the Inquisitors."

"You don't want to think about what they'd to you."

"She knows what Inquisitors do."

"They'll flay off your face to start with."

"You don't want that, do you?" Agent #1 asked.

"I didn't do anything wrong," Akiko defended herself, hiding a shudder. She'd worked closely with Inquisitors in the past and knew the way they treated human bodies as though they were chunks of meat. "I want an advocate here."

"Why would you want an advocate if you're not guilty?"

"She's acting like she's guilty, isn't she?" Agent #2 posited.

"Why am I under suspicion? Look what they did to me. They sent me back to taunt me," Akiko stated, glancing at her prosthetics, then back at the two agents.

Two indifferent faces confronted her.

"The GWs are tricky. They'll send their own back under the plight of having been tortured to get us to trust them."

"It's an ancient Chinese ploy," #1 added.

Akiko snorted, but #2 didn't let her speak and said, "We see through those."

"Who are you working for?"

"I already told you. The Empire," Akiko repeated. "I'm an agent of the Tokko."

"An agent who kills one of our most important resources, loses Captain Ishimura, gets captured by the GWs but inexplicably returns, and demands an advocate when we ask a few simple questions," Agent #1 charged.

Akiko snorted again. "Circumstantial evidence. None of that is conclusive."

"But the only person who could either support, or convict you, is missing. Did you kill Captain Beniko Ishimura?"

"What? Are you out of your mind?" Akiko flared back.

"Then where is he? The last person he was seen with was you."

"I told you, I don't know," Akiko said. "Isn't there portical footage of the hospital?"

"All of it has been scrambled," #1 said.

"The tech told us there were irregular portical disruptions that ruined the recorded material for the past three days," #2 explained.

"Weren't you investigating him earlier this week?"

"Yes," Akiko answered.

"Why?"

"Ishimura is known as one of the most loyal soldiers in the Empire," #2 said.

"He reported his own parents when they were about to commit an act of perfidy."

"Why were you investigating him?"

"Those were my orders," Akiko replied.

"And now, a key censor of portical games in the USJ is missing on the eve of the anniversary, right when the Washingtons are trying to spread their insidious game."

"Are you plotting something for the celebration tomorrow?" #2 inquired point blank.

"I'm not plotting anything!" she yelled, remembering how many times others had said the same to her.

"Why do we keep on hearing unusual rumors about your work habits?"

"Someone must be spreading lies," Akiko replied. "I haven't done anything wrong."

"The only person lying in this room is you."

She knew better than to get frustrated. They wanted to

flummox her, make her lose her temper as part of their routine. But she couldn't fathom how she was under suspicion. She'd been the one meting out justice before. She was one of the top agents in *Tokubetsu Koto Keisatsu*.

"Are you listening to us?" Agent #1 demanded.

"If you don't start cooperating quickly, we'll take you to one of the Inquisitors."

She couldn't believe, just two days before, she'd been on the other side.

4:02am

The questions from the twin Kempeitai agents kept on coming. The speed of their verbal assault was confusing her and she was flustered by their word games. They were trying to trap her in contradictions, implicating without directly accusing, trying to get her to hang herself verbally.

"There are reports you had a confrontation with one of our officers, Tiffany Kaneko," Agent #1 said.

"Not a confrontation. She was angry she'd had her cover blown and we talked for a short time."

"That's not what we heard."

"Then you heard wrong."

"What do you think of the George Washingtons?" Agent #2 asked.

"I think they're traitors that should be crushed."

"Was General Wakana a GW sympathizer?" Agent #1 demanded.

"He's one of the most loyal officers I know."

"You said you were following his orders."

"Yes."

"Did he order you to execute Koushou?"

"General Wakana gave no orders to execute Koushou. That was my decision," Akiko said.

"Why?"

"I told you. What he was doing was inhuman."

"Did you know General Wakana has had his fair share of run-ins with Tokyo Command?"

"And USJ Command too," #1 confirmed.

"Stop lying to us and tell us what Wakana really ordered!"

"I'm not lying!" Akiko shouted back.

"The relationship the military has with its veterans is very important. Why would you endanger that?" #2 asked.

"You're a member of Tokko and we know your reputation for ruthlessness," #1 stated. "You want us to believe you cared about Koushou's personal habits enough to endanger the interests of the Empire?"

"Why would you kill a war hero?" #2 barked angrily.

"At least he kept his pets alive."

"How many have you tortured to death?"

"Perhaps she's having doubts," #1 suggested.

"Doubts about her position?"

"Doubt about her loyalty to the Emperor."

"There are no doubts," Akiko stated, and repeated it internally to herself.

"Why is it your boyfriend said you were obsessed with the Americans?" #1 asked.

Akiko did her best to hide her shock. "Hideyoshi?"

"He has all sorts of problems with the Yakuza."

"Got himself into a huge debt with his gaming addiction."

The Yakuza? He'd never told her anything about being involved with any gangsters.

#1 consulted his portical. "He called you an authoritarian and a lousy lover."

"He said that?" she asked, immediately regretting the pain in her voice. Of course they would try to use that against her, make up lies to strike at her vulnerabilities.

"Which part bothers you the most?" #1 asked, with a sadistic smirk.

"Why are you so concerned with what the Americans do?"

Her heartbeat accelerated. "They killed my brother," she replied.

"According to Hideyoshi, you were worried because your brother deserted his post and went into enemy territory."

"Hideyoshi was lying. My brother did no such thing."

"He did. An internal investigation confirms that."

"My brother was a patriot who went to investigate a fire, not realizing it was an ambush!" Akiko yelled, recalling all the nights she'd spent privately looking into the case.

"How do you know that?"

"There's nothing about an ambush in the official report."

"There seems to be a similar trend in the family, doesn't there?"

"Was it incompetence, or traitorous behavior?"

"You can attack me all you want," Akiko stated, seething. "But leave my brother out of this."

"How can we? *You'd* do the same in our shoes," #1 stated, with a no-nonsense inflection.

"We need to look more into your brother's portical records. Find out if there's anything treasonous there."

"Or are you trying to protect him?"

"Maybe siblings conspiring together?"

"Shut up," Akiko said.

"Excuse me?"

"I said, SHUT UP!"

#1 slapped Akiko's face. #2 poked her prosthetic hand. Akiko's face turned pale and the indignity hurt more than the actual pain. Her fingers tried to clutch at weapons she didn't have. "What are you going to do if we don't?"

"I don't think she takes us seriously."

"Maybe she'll take the Inquisitor seriously."

Agent #1 grabbed her shoulder while #2 removed the intravenous needles. She knew if she struck either, there would be further charges and they'd have free rein to strike back. She didn't resist, despite knowing that a meeting with the Inquisitor meant her life was over. These agents were still servants of the Emperor. Her primary concern went to the safety of her own parents. If she was falsely convicted, both of their lives would be in danger. For all she knew, her parents were already under arrest for the typical charge under these circumstances: "Parental malfeasance for raising a traitor."

They forced her up from the bed and dragged her out. She wondered where General Wakana was.

4:59am

It was cold inside their car and the city lights seemed foreign, auroras of despondency rotting in the leprous night. They tied her to the backseat and jumped in front. She wondered where Hideyoshi was, if he'd really betrayed her to these agents. She thought of her brother, the reports that he had actually left his post. No one knew why, but it had eventually been explained as him investigating an anomaly. The uncertainty of the situation left much open to misinterpretation, which had troubled her back then and bothered her even more now.

Agent #1 said, "I hate the night shift."

"I love it," Agent #2 replied. "I hate the sun."

"The sun is good for your skin."

"Forget your skin. You hear the real story about Barstow?"

"With what?"

"Ear Wax Brothers."

"I don't even know who they are."

"The Teruos."

"Golden boys."

"About two years ago, they went to arrest a guy, but the portical screwed up the charges so they didn't know what they were arresting him for."

"Why didn't they call Command?"

"They didn't want to let Command know their porticals

had been corrupted. So when they arrested him, they refused to tell him the charge. Turns out later, their porticals hadn't been corrupted. They'd just arrested the wrong guy."

"What happened?"

"They couldn't let the guy walk 'cause that'd mean they'd be in trouble and it'd be a bureaucratic mess. So they let him stew, beat the crap out of him, and three days later, the guy confessed to a crime he wasn't wanted for."

"Sedition?"

"Murder of three USJ citizens. Was executed on the spot. Both Ear Waxes got commendations. Now, they just go around accusing random people of crimes without telling them what they did."

"Brilliant."

"The best part was those three USJ citizens the guy confessed to killing didn't exist. Their names were from a cancelled portical show the Germans made."

"What happened to the brothers?"

"They both got promotions 'cause if they got in trouble, so would their superiors."

"Atrocious."

Both agents chortled gleefully. Akiko recognized their flippancy as an attempt to inject an air of levity to confound her expectations. They wanted her to feel at ease, give her a false sense of hope, as if they were just oddballs making funny quips that could be reasoned with. When they returned to the station, they would humor her, tell her they were on her side if she would just be agreeable. If she refused, they'd inflict physical violence, a measure saved for the Inquisitor who was usually an excellent physiologist with a supreme understanding of anatomy. The whole act abhorred her because she knew it so well, and they knew she knew too.

"Our duty is to eliminate superstitions," #1 said.

"You're afraid of ghosts."

"Ghosts aren't a superstition. They're real."

"Don't talk about that fire again," #2 moaned.

"I know what I saw."

"Three women walking around naked in a burning building? You were hallucinating from the smoke inhalation."

"I don't want to use dynamite to execute traitors anymore. It's too risky, especially if you don't time it right."

"I always time it right. You're just sloppy."

Akiko wished they would shut up. They'd placed a rod on her back that pressed uncomfortably and made it difficult to sit. Bumps on the road exacerbated the pain with each tremor. It was still dark, so the pair of lights blinking outside caught her attention.

"Something's wrong with the car," #1 said.

"What do you mean?"

"It's not responding to the wheel."

"Our seatbelts came loose."

"What?"

A truck drove straight at them. She wondered if she was dreaming the whole thing until the truck smashed into their vehicle, causing them to spiral out of control. Their vehicle crashed into the wall and her head smacked against the front seat, though her belt held her firmly. Aside from a nasty bruise and a headache, she was OK. The twins hadn't fared as well. With their seat belts unbuckled, they'd been hurtled out the front of their car. The back door opened. She blinked, unable to believe her eyes, ignoring the smell of blood in her nose.

Ben unstrapped her and helped her out.

"W-what are you doing here?" she asked.

"I came to rescue you."

"Why?"

Ben paused in place. "You saved my ass twice. I couldn't just leave you to burn. Besides, we're both servants of the Emperor, right?" he said, repeating back to her what she'd said to him earlier. "Do you have a portical?"

"Why?"

"I need to put an inhibitor on it so they don't track us," Ben explained.

"I left mine behind."

He handed her a poncho to cover her hospital gowns. Ben was wearing khakis, a brown windbreaker, and a tie-scarf hybrid that was trendy among gamers.

He went to the two brothers and examined their necks.

"Are they alive?" she asked.

"Barely," he answered, feeling their neck veins pumping blood.

Despite their Imperial service, she advised, "You should kill them."

"They're not waking up any time soon."

"We can't take any risks."

"I know. But by the time they wake up, we'll be long gone."

She grimaced and examined the crashed vehicles. "This is very unlike you."

"What's unlike me?"

"Smashing a truck into a car in a rescue operation."

"Thanks?" He lifted up his portical. "This thing did all the calculations and jammed the controls on their car. Hit it at a perfect angle so that it'd incapacitate them, but leave them alive and keep you safe."

She stared at the bodies. "They accused me of being a traitor."

"I know."

"How?"

"I've been following the Kempei's portical feed."

"Where's General Wakan–"

"General Wakana is dead. He was ordered to commit suicide last night," Ben answered.

Akiko felt her face turn numb. "What for?"

"Incompetence. Failure of security under his watch. You would have received a similar order after you returned to base."

"That's impossible."

"Is it?" He held up his portical and showed her the Kempeitai orders to the two brothers, ordering them to commence with torture for a full day before giving her the option of suicide. The next message had clearance from her Tokko supervisors to proceed.

"Bu-but… I've done nothing wrong."

"In their eyes, you've done everything wrong, thanks in part to testimony from my former love, Tiffany Kaneko. Welcome."

"To what?"

"To life as the rest of us."

"What are you talking about?"

"The constant fear of being arrested and killed for crimes you didn't even know you committed. We're snails living on the razor's edge."

"Wh-why didn't you just let me die? I-I have no future anymore." Her voice was fractured.

He stared at her prosthetic arms. "You want to stay and give up?"

"It would have served your interests if you'd let me die," Akiko said.

"I don't think in terms of interests. And, like I said, I owed you."

"I can't believe they accused me of betraying the Emperor, after all I've done. They suspected me of being ideologically corrupt."

"The one holding the gun can make up whatever accusations they see fit," Ben said. "We need to hurry."

"Where?"

"Long Beach."

"Why Long Beach?"

"There's only one way out for the both of us. Bring back Mutsuraga's head," Ben said. "Everything will be forgiven then. They might even exonerate Wakana after the fact."

Akiko looked back at her two Kempei interrogators. "I don't know how much help I can be to you."

"I'm not expecting your help. I'm leaving you with a friend."

"A friend?"

Ben glanced uneasily down the road as a car drove by. "We really need to get going."

"Is Mutsuraga in Long Beach?"

Ben shook his head. "San Diego."

"*Inside* San Diego?" she asked.

"Yeah."

"How do you know that?"

"Martha Washington told me."

"Why would she do that?"

"Because I made a deal with her," Ben informed her.

"What kind of deal?"

"One that saved both our lives."

"In exchange for?" she wanted to know, distressed by the idea of any kind of arrangement with the terrorists.

"Don't ask."

"San Diego is completely sealed. It's hard to get in or out."

"Hasn't stopped the GWs."

"Our defenses have a weakness," Akiko surmised.

Ben checked the agents again. They were both unconscious. He took their porticals, programmed something. "It's the western coast. USJ ships can't fully cover the whole border."

"What about our mechas guarding the coast?"

"Good question. I don't know how they got past them."

"How will *you* get past them?"

"I have a friend in Catalina who can help us," Ben said, as he put the porticals back.

"Catalina, the prison?"

"Yeah. The Tokko and Kempei have been on my ass all day so it's been hard. They'll be after both of us when they find out what happened here."

"But ho–"

"I'll explain more on the way. We have to get out of here now."

"Shouldn't we hide them?" Akiko asked, looking at the unconscious agents.

"They need medical attention and there's no way anyone can trace us anytime soon."

She went over and kicked both of them in the face.

Ben walked to a car parked on the street and used the portical's digital key to open the door.

"Let's go."

5:43am

Akiko read the orders multiple times. "If Agent Tsukino is uncooperative, bring her back for direct questioning with the Inquisitors. Inflict physical and mental pain as needed for a day maximum. Encourage honorable end."

"Honorable end" was a euphemism for *jigai*. She chilled at the thought of General Wakana committing *seppuku* with his guts spilling out of him.

"I just followed orders," Akiko insisted. "How can I get in trouble for obeying what they told me to do?"

"They had to blame someone for the bombings. Wakana and you got the fall after Tiffany pointed the finger at the two of you."

"But he didn't set the bombs."

"Incompetence under his supervision. One of the governor's favorite aides was a victim. A vicious bastard they used to call the Tendon Breaker because he was so cruel during San Diego. Everyone killed two nights ago served in San Diego with me."

"The George Washington's vendetta against all of you?"

"Looks like it. Wakana was one of the few people in a position of power who stuck his neck out for peace. Even when we try to do the right thing, we can never escape our sins."

"I don't think any of us want to," Akiko said.

"What do you mean?"

"We all want what we feel we deserve, even if we outwardly deny it."

"What is it we deserve?"

"Everyone has their sins."

"The whole concept of sinning is an illusion," Ben stated.

"You don't feel guilty about anything?"

"I try not to think about it."

"Did Tiffany accuse you too?"

Ben shook his head. "I was left off her reports."

Akiko thought about Hideyoshi's words to the Kempei officers, at least what they'd told her he'd said. "Suffering isn't an illusion. Neither is pain. As sadistic as Koushou was, maybe he was right and we're just microorganisms inside a bigger being struggling for our place."

"Microorganisms don't kill each other."

"They do all the time. Viruses ravage and devour mercilessly, even to the point of destroying the host. There are theories that say viruses evolved from bacteria, but viruses like bacteriophages specifically target bacteria."

"Descendants killing their ancestors."

"Almost all religions try to kill the faiths before them, even if they owe them an ideological debt. Shinto is one of the few that's amenable to symbiosis."

"You're comparing Shinto to a virus?"

"A civilized one. That's why we absorbed Buddhism and that's why we incorporated parts of Christianity when we took over here."

"What is it with you and diseases?"

"I'm fascinated by their effect."

"Even if they kill?" Ben asked.

"Our scientists use bacteriophages to attack deadly bacteria and protect us from their effects."

"What happens if a bacteriophage gets out of control and

attacks the scientists?"

Akiko peered out the window. "Then the scientists die."

Ben laughed. "Let's hope it doesn't come to that. You hungry at all?"

Akiko heard her stomach growling. "I'm starving." They'd fed her intravenously to replenish her nutrients, but she craved hot sustenance.

"Any particular kind of food you feel like?"

"Anything as long as it's cooked and not too sweet."

"There's a Mexican place in Long Beach I love right next to where we need to be. Only thing about their nachos is their beans make my shit hard and I get all constipated. Stop me from eating too much because I always overeat."

"Thanks for letting me know that. You just made me lose my appetite."

"Don't tell me you're squeamish about the scatological."

"Of course not. Shit can say a lot about a person," Akiko stated.

"Like?"

"Where they've been eating, who they've been consorting with, chemical composition, the–"

"Forget I asked."

6:02am

Long Beach was where trendy shopping stores blended into the seedy underpinnings of the red light district. Vendor-bots sold extra porticals, fruit juices, and companionship as they rolled through the streets with spinning lights. A colossal dome covered a large section of the love district with pectorals of light tensing from the fumed lust of strangers exerting more than their muscles. Butt clubs, exotic dancers with extra limbs, fetish recreation libraries, the biggest collection of dolls in the world, a Victorian-themed brothel, virility enhancement stores, and bondage baseball were some of the more extravagant set pieces of interest. Four prostitutes in translucent kimonos rode skateboards selling their services. Biker gang members were leaving after a night of debauchery. Bored housewives left the companionship of their boy toys for the night. Sushi and toast were being served on top of naked men and women for breakfast. Confederate flags were waving at the corners of buildings, some women clad only in southern colors. A string of love motels were painted a different color from their neighboring ones so that there was a stream of pink, verdant green, mauve, light purple, and pastel yellow rooms.

"Why are we here?" Akiko inquired.

"I need transportation," Ben answered. "And the only ships

allowed to Catalina that don't check individual IDs are the ones sent by the Love Service Guild. I have a friend, Orochan, who owns one of the love boats."

They parked in an eight-story tall lot. It was early morning so many of the stores were closing. Ben took her to the Mexican restaurant he'd mentioned. Two tired waitresses bowed and welcomed them. There was a stage, but no dancers. Some drunks were passed out in their seats. The jukebox was a cranky fortress of broken records. They were seated in a stall and Ben ordered, "Super nachos."

Akiko selected the tostada.

When the waitress left, Akiko asked, "Has the death count from the GW attacks gone up?"

"Still a dozen. I was supposed to be lucky thirteen."

"Did you know any of the victims well?"

"I knew them just enough to know I don't regret their deaths," Ben replied. "They were all butchers in San Diego."

"You mean good soldiers."

"The best. I almost feel honored I was targeted."

The waitress brought the food. Ben ate without saying a word. Akiko didn't try with the chopsticks and struggled with the spoon in her prosthetic hand. Ben, trying to be polite, focused on his own food. She lowered her mouth into the tostada and ate directly. She didn't like the taste, but she was so hungry, she didn't care. She swallowed the beef and lettuce, feeling it invigorate her. Ben chomped softly on his carne asada and chips.

"Why are you so quiet?" she asked between bites.

"I don't want to bore you with 'an exchange of useless information,'" he replied.

It took her a moment to recall her own words earlier in the week. "I didn't know you were so sensitive," Akiko said.

"Don't want to offend."

"I need some *useful* information."

"Like?"

"Where can I find a gun to attach to my arm?"

"There might be dealers here. I'll ask Orochan to help you after I leave."

"You can't be serious about leaving me behind."

"I'm going to drop you off with her and–"

"I'm coming with you."

"I'm going into San Diego," Ben said. "You said yourself you wouldn't be of much help."

"You can't survive by yourself."

"I'll do fine."

"You failed your officer field training because you co–"

"I know why I failed."

"You need me," Akiko said, point blank.

"Why do I need you?"

"Because I'm not afraid to kill."

"You think I don't kill out of fear?" Ben asked.

"I don't know why you don't kill, but it's a weakness that's going to get *you* killed. It nearly got you kicked out of BEMAG."

"That was a different situation."

"You couldn't chop a prisoner's head off under orders. That's pathetic."

"And you think you with a gun arm is going to improve our chances?"

"Not think. I know."

Ben chomped on a nacho. "I saved you because I owed you. But I think your fervor fringes on lunacy."

"The Emperor is our god. Anything short of lunacy in our dedication is treason," Akiko said.

"You feel that even now?"

"Absolutely," she said, even though she knew her faith was wavering.

"That's why I can't take you with me."

"What?"

"If someone insults the Emperor while we're in San Diego,

are you going to go ballistic on them? Can you even pretend to be a GW sympathizer?"

Akiko tried to wipe the meat off her lips. "What's your plan?"

"Get Mutsuraga no matter what it takes, even if it means outwardly betraying the Emperor."

"You tell me what really happened with him and his wife in San Diego, and I'll play along."

Ben scooped up the beans on his plate and began explaining the true history of Mutsuraga's wife, Andrew Jackson, Wakana, and the whole bloody mess. He left out his own involvement concerning the actual programming of the simulation and the games.

"That explains why the whole matter is classified," Akiko said, once he finished. "I didn't know you and General Wakana served so closely together."

"He's the one who got me the job as a censor."

"He supported my career as well," Akiko said, plaintive at the thought of his loss. "What about his family?"

Ben shook his head. "I don't know, but it can't be good."

Akiko remembered how much Wakana doted on his children.

"We can mourn him when this is all over," Ben said, anticipating her thoughts. "There's still a long way ahead for both of us."

"Why is Mutsuraga in San Diego? Doesn't he hate the GWs?"

"He knew they'd provide shelter as a defector and the creator of the *USA*," Ben explained, licking the guacamole off his spoon. "He tells a very different version of what happened in San Diego to the GWs."

"You told Martha Washington the truth?"

"That's why she let us go and told me where he was."

"Where is she heading?"

"She suggested it's a one-way trip and doesn't expect to

come back. For all I know, she could already be dead."

"What else did you tell her?" Akiko asked, in an apprehensive tone.

"Like I said before, I'll do whatever it takes to get Mutsuraga."

"You gave them passwords."

"Nothing that won't be changed automatically on the new shift."

Akiko curbed her temper, knowing there was no point arguing. "How can you be so casual betraying the Empire?"

"Because I'm doing it for the greater good."

She'd eaten the top layer of her tostada, but couldn't go deeper without smearing her face in food.

"Do you need help?" Ben asked.

"No," Akiko replied. She struggled to clamp the handle of her spoon, unused to the mechanics of her artificial hand. It took her a while, but she fed herself. That was when her stomach started growling. "I have to use the restroom."

She headed for the lavatory, a private one with only an Eastern-styled toilet in the ground. The lock on the stall door was too hard for her to manipulate so she gave up and squatted above the toilet.

Twenty minutes later, she opened the door and called to Ben.

"You OK in there?" Ben asked.

"I'm fine," she replied. " I need some assistance."

"What's up?"

She looked at the tip of her prosthetic hand, covered in shit, toilet paper ripped to shreds. She was embarrassed, but defiant as well.

Ben saw the struggle in her face and asked, "Can I come in?"

"Yes."

Ben did not flinch or make any overt reaction. He assisted her as best as he could.

They both washed at the sink.

"One of my commanding officers told me the best way to make a prisoner go crazy was leave them in a dark room and not clean up their shit," Akiko explained. "We called it 'excrement torture.' I did it to a woman obsessed with cleanliness. Stuck her in a room for a month. Never let her shower or clean up her piss or shit."

"What happened to her?" Ben asked, as he rinsed with soap.

"When we let her out, she wasn't human anymore. I thought she was weak. But I know now I couldn't have handled even a day of that."

They dried off quietly.

7:44am

Outside Orochan's bar, two men and a woman stood threateningly, each holding clubs.

"It's closed," the woman with jewels all over her body said.

"I need to see Orochan," Ben replied.

"Orochan hasn't paid her dues, so she can't see customers that haven't been approved by the Mosquito."

"Who's the Mosquito?" Ben asked.

"Get out of here before I have to hurt you!" the tall male with the beard snarled. He had long boots, a leather jacket, and the tattoo of a lizard's face covering part of his eyes.

Ben wasn't sure what to do, but Akiko stepped in and said, "My name is Akiko Tsukino."

"I don't give a shit who you are."

"I'm an agent of the Tokko," she finished, and noticed their aggressive body postures wilt. "I know everything about each one of you and your families. Anything I don't know, I'll find out." Akiko looked at the woman, spotted the ring on her wedding hand. "I'm aware of what you and your husband are doing. Don't think it's escaped our attention." To the lizard face, "You think I don't know about what you did to your friend?"

Lizard face asked, "What are you talking about?"

She recognized the tattoo. "Don't play dumb unless you

want me to humiliate you. I know you've had surgery done, but does your boss know why you really left the Tokage family?"

"H-how did yo–"

"Step aside before you get in trouble."

"But Mosquito–"

"I'll deal with him later!" Akiko snapped.

She led Ben in and they did not stop her. Instead, they were vexed, fearful of the implications of believing the Tokko was watching them.

7:52am

Orochan was a big woman, more robust than heavyset. She wore a ceremonial robe on top with short shorts underneath, which buttressed her thick legs. Her purple mohawk complemented her purple-tinted contact lenses. She let out a gusty laugh before asking, "How did you get in here?"

"She was persuasive," Ben said about Akiko.

"Must have been. What trouble have you gotten yourself into this time, Ishimura?"

"Who says I'm in trouble?"

"Why else would you be here so early in the morning?"

The bar had twenty posh leather couches surrounding marble tables and mahjong sets. The shelves on the walls were lined with wine and *sake* bottles. Eleven portical game stalls were in the corners, including a popular pinball title. There were no clients, though male and female prostitutes lingered on the bar with halos of perfume around them. A painting of the Emperor was displayed prominently at the front, a coterie of Buddha statues to either side of him. Ben handed Orochan a set of expensive chopsticks, finely carved and hand polished from rosewood.

"For me?" Orochan asked. "Very sweet of you."

"Specially ordered from Italy."

"Who's your persuasive friend?"

242

"This is Akiko."

Orochan's eyes went to Akiko's prosthetic arms. "She police?"

"Something like that," Ben replied. "I need transportation."

"Only place we go to is Catalina."

"That's where I need to get."

She cast Ben an apprehensive glance. "What's your business there?"

"Imperial business. You don't want to know the details, do you? What's your price?"

"There's no price for you. But I'm having some problems, as you might have noticed."

"What kind?"

"A local Yakuza thug, Mosquito, thinks he owns us and is only letting approved customers in. He's causing a hell storm for my boys and girls. Already carved up three of their faces. Doug! Doug!" Doug was an effeminate male in his early twenties and had a boyish charm about him, if it wasn't for the scar ripping across his face. "Doug used to be my most popular host, and now he washes dishes in the back because Mosquito wanted to make a point. Doug, where are your manners?" Doug bowed respectfully to both of them. "Go back to sleep." He bowed again and left. "Mosquito is demanding a tax on every transaction and won't let us go to sea unless we pay him boating fees. He's taken our ship for personal purposes, trying to start a gaming deck inside."

"What can I do?" Ben inquired.

"Nothing, unless you can help me get rid of him. But that's pretty much impossible."

"Why?"

"He has a group of ex-sumo wrestlers as bodyguards. No one's getting through."

"Is there some other way? Maybe we can make an arrangement with him?"

"He's not making any arrangements. I'm sorry, Ben."

Ben was unsure what step to take next.

"Do you have an extra gun arm?" Akiko interjected.

"I can get one," Orochan answered.

"You get me a good one, and I'll take care of your Mosquito."

"Wait a se–" Ben tried to say.

Akiko fired a ferocious glower in his direction. "I'll take care of this, understand?"

Orochan looked at Akiko. "This is different from those guards."

"It doesn't matter."

"His personal bodyguards are professionals."

"Do I look scared?"

Orochan laughed with a clap. "Reiko-chan."

"*Hai*," a young, petite woman replied with a short bow.

"Take care of Ben for a few minutes."

"Where are you going?" Ben asked.

"I'm taking your friend to the storage room so we can check out some gun arms. I trust you won't get into trouble without me?"

Orochan led Akiko through a room behind the bar into a dim corridor filled with bedrooms. The walls had European paintings of couples copulating in bizarre poses. Most of the doors were shut, though a few clients were enjoying a raucous soiree. Orochan led Akiko down the stairs into a sealed room filled with crates, sex toys, and guns.

"What did Ben tell you about me?" Orochan asked.

"Nothing."

"You Kempeitai?"

"No, Tokko. How'd you–"

"It's my job to know. I served with Ben in San Diego as a requisitions officer."

"You supplied arms?" Akiko asked, as she looked at the assortment of items on display.

Orochan grinned. "They had me gather comfort companions for the soldiers."

"Governor Ogasawara outlawe–"

"I know the law. But privately, those laws got thrown out the door. I was ordered to take the American prisoners and prostitute them for our soldiers. Most of the women had never even slept with a man. Strange religious belief that they shouldn't have sex before marriage. I had to prepare those girls, mentally and physically. If one didn't perform and some fancy officer was displeased, they'd shoot 'em. They sent us the dumbest and cruelest soldiers around. It was a helluva challenge, but I always protect my own. You come under my roof and there is no race."

"I've studied San Diego and I've never heard of this."

"Of course not. The scholars hid a lot of the terrible shit that happened," Orochan said.

"Why?"

"You didn't see San Diego. Children would approach officers and blow themselves up. Our soldiers killed civilians indiscriminately. Whole parts of town were wiped out. Whenever we took prisoners, they'd kill themselves."

"They shouldn't have rebelled."

"We killed so many of them first."

"You think we're to blame?" Akiko asked, incensed by the suggestion.

"No. I'm just saying it's a long and bloody history," Orochan replied, preemptively trying to calm her. "Ben saved my ass twice."

"How?"

"I don't like dredging up the past. But if he's in trouble, I'll do anything to protect him."

Akiko's eyes went to a particularly lethal-looking cannon that was pitch black, a long corpulent barrel with grooves like fangs. "What's that?"

"German prototype I scored a few years back from some arms dealers visiting from Rome."

"What's it do?"

"They called it the death ray. It uses crystals to power energy beams that are more deadly than bullets. Only problem is, it's heavy and impractical as a gun arm. The recoil sucks even with the muzzle brakes. Hard to aim and balance."

Akiko noted that it was made of alloy steel and had a revolving barrel that switched bullets with lasers. "Can I try?" she asked.

"I've tried to move this since I got it. It'll screw up your shoulder and back. You should try this Type 22 light machine gun. They're not too heavy, fire Arisaka cartridges, and–"

Akiko's eyes were on the death ray. "Indulge me," she said.

Orochan helped Akiko remove her prosthetic.

"Your scar is still fresh," Orochan said, noticing the cuts and the wound. "You need more time."

"I don't have time."

"This won't hold long."

"I don't need long," Akiko insisted. "Just a few days."

Orochan had to use both arms to lift the death ray, screw in the rivets, connect the electric nerves, and calibrate the trigger. "This a five-axis swivel on the sock?" Akiko grunted in assent. "I'm using an amplified osseointegration process with this titanium bolt. This'll sting, but it'll attach the part to your bone with this abutment. These patches will accelerate the osseointegration, but if you're not careful, it'll rip out your bone."

The integration felt like a hammer on her joints, a stabbing motion that jolted her entire body. Akiko clenched her teeth. The wires looked like cracks in a drought-ridden desert. Globules of fat and flesh surrounded the junction point. She felt as though she were being penetrated by a thousand needles, her skin imploding.

"Do you want me to take it out?"

Akiko shook her head.

"Give the microportical a chance to calibrate with the nerves in your arm," Orochan said.

"How much longer?" Akiko asked, through bated breath.

"Soon."

Her vision was blurry and her thoughts corroded. Beniko didn't look like her brother; he was more confident, taller, and suave. And yet both had something about them that was nervous and uncomfortable. What had her brother been so afraid of? He used to brush the back of his uniform because he had so much dandruff and had been devastated by disapproving reviews from superior officers. He dreamt every night that his shadow fell in love with a woman and ran off without him. The world was untempered chaos, shadows consummating each other with the urges of night. Her thoughts were as cluttered as those dreams. There was a gigantic stomach on the ceiling. She could smell ground beef and stir-fried intestines pouring out its asshole. Jenna Fujimori invited her to dinner. "It's very delish," she said. They were inside her stomach and the pressure of congestion forced dissolution.

"You awake?" Orochan asked. "You knocked off."

Akiko stared down at the cannon that was her arm. She forced it to move, though it was a struggle to keep it up.

"How does it work?" Akiko wanted to know.

"You can set the energy levels on that knob," Orochan explained, pointing to a dial with numbers. "There's the trigger or you can activate it with–"

Akiko set it to the lowest level and fired. A laser beam fired into a dildo, puncturing a hole that made the whole thing melt.

"The recoil isn't too bad," Akiko commented.

"That's because it's at the lowest level."

"How does it recharge?"

"Solar powered. If the ray runs out, you can switch to the machine gun until it builds back up. You need to flip out the side barrel."

Akiko played with both. "Do you have steroidal enhancers?"

she asked, feeling the duress on her arm.

"Why?"

"Do you want me to take care of your problem or not?"

"I do."

"Then give me enough enhancers to last a few days."

"They're upstairs."

Akiko examined the gun arm again. "You don't care if your Mosquito is dead or alive?"

"I'd prefer alive. But I'd also prefer if he can't talk. I don't want his cyborg Yakuza members to come after us."

"You know where he's at?"

"A hotel near Murder Alley. I'll give you directions. You'll also need to take a gift with you."

"What kind of gift?"

"Civil War relics. The Yakuza have a fetish for American rebels and Robert E. Lee."

They went back upstairs. Reiko was flirting with Ben, trying to kiss him, though he deftly avoided every foray, chuckling, amused by her flirty ways.

Orochan injected chemicals into the gun arm that, in turn, was connected intravenously with Akiko's arm. She packed several capsules into a case, added an emergency syringe, and handed them to her.

"Let's go," Akiko ordered Ben.

"Where?" he asked, noticing the huge gun arm.

"We need to swat some mosquitoes."

9:16am

They walked towards Murder Alley.

"What are you going to do?" Ben asked.

"What do you think?"

"We have to be careful how we approach these cyber Yakuza."

"Don't you have any guts?" she asked. "I've never met such a timid officer, Ishimura. Is your animal spirit a chicken?"

"Our mission isn't hunting Yakuza. It's catching Mutsuraga."

"And we aren't going to get anywhere near Mutsuraga without getting to Catalina, right?"

"Let me talk to him a little, reason with him," Ben said. "I know Orochan would like to start a turf war, but we're not going to be the cause of that."

"What's the story between you two?"

"What'd she tell you?"

"She told me you saved her twice in SD."

"What she means is, I staved off her court martial. Some colonel got mad at one of her girls and nearly beat her to death. Orochan cut off his *chinchin*. None of the soldiers got violent again. But she was brought up on charges."

"How'd you get her off?"

"A few gifts, a few portical revelations with information some officials would rather not have disclosed."

"Why'd you do it?"

"I have a soft spot for officers in trouble," Ben said. "By the way, nice bluff with Mosquito's guards earlier. I wasn't sure it was going to work."

"Low level Yakuza thugs only respond to strength. They weren't too bright either."

"What if they hadn't fallen for it? Like what if the lady wasn't married and that guy's tattoo was just a mistake after a drunk outing."

"The moment I saw the weakness in their eyes when I mentioned Tokko, I knew they would believe anything I said."

"But the truth–"

"Doesn't matter when you have a stronger will." A sudden stench overwhelmed Akiko, a mix of vomit, feces, and rotten flesh. "What is that?"

"That'd be Murder Alley," Ben answered.

"It smells terrible."

"You go there and get murdered a hundred different ways. They bring you back to life for a price."

"It's a service?"

"An expensive one."

She looked in the alley and it was dark, nothing visible from outside. "Why would anyone do it?"

"Boredom is the root of all trouble in the world."

"There are so many enemies of the Emperor that need to be eliminated. I don't understand how anyone could be bored."

"Not everyone has the same cause to believe in."

"Don't you feel bad?" she asked.

"Why?"

"All you soldiers suffered so much in San Diego, and this is the world the survivors have created."

"Never thought about it that way."

"We have to make the USJ a better place."

Ben laughed dubiously, thinking she was being ironic, but saw the seriousness in her expression. "Let's deal with Mutsuraga first."

9:42am

The "mosquitoes" were four former sumo wrestlers, with bodies like blocks of concrete, no visible neck, and arms that were rectangles of fat and muscle. Their eyes disappeared into their round faces and their hair was tied into knots. They each had mechanical pinkies, a rite of passage for members of the Yakuza to sacrifice the least of their limbs. They were guarding room 301.

"We're here to see Mosquito," Akiko said. She opened up a case with two Derringer pocket guns. The first had a brass frame and a two-shot belt; the second, a tiny 0.4 inch caliber pistol.

One of the wrestlers took the case and went inside. He returned a few minutes later and grunted for them to come in.

They entered an enormous suite covered with Civil War antiques from uniforms to swords, flags, buckles, eagle-breasted plates, insignia, and guns. Ten Pomeranians circled them, barking cheerfully. They were adorably cute balls of hair and even Akiko, who didn't like dogs, couldn't help but smile.

"Genetically modified Pomeranians. When they smell blood, they'll pounce. Why are you here with that huge gun on your arm?"

Mosquito wore a yellow leather jumpsuit, had on enormous sunglasses, a hat shaped like an alligator, and five gold necklaces. He was mid-height, Asian from his complexion, possibly a mix – it was hard to tell in the USJ without documentation, particularly with those from the underbelly of the Empire. His voice was strident and harsh in its accents.

"Because we wanted to bring you that gift," Ben replied, referencing the pocket guns.

Mosquito lifted the tiny Derringer. "One of these killed their warlord, Lincoln. Now he was a conqueror, a man who drank the blood of his enemies and feasted on their corpses. The Americans made him out to be this genial buffoon, but he was a vindictive and fiendish tyrant who forced his will on the rebels. Isn't it a masterful stroke of propaganda that they've made him out to be a bumbling leader? They even claim their last president was a cripple! The Americans have a fascination with the everyday man and will do anything to foster that lie when these rulers were the elite, the most ruthless patricians before their Republic crumbled."

"We have a request to make," Ben said.

"Of course you do. Who sent you?"

"Does it matter?"

"I guess not. You need to get to Catalina, Captain Ishimura," Mosquito said.

How did he know? Akiko wondered.

"We do," Ben replied.

"I hear you're quite a gamer."

"Decent."

"I have a match aboard my boat of the *USA* game. Every month, I hold a special tournament. Eight people play. Whoever wins the game lives. The others are killed. You survive, I give you a free ride to Catalina. You die, and it's game over."

"You can't be serious."

"I am."

"No ride is worth risking my life over."

"There's no other ride to Catalina. And you," he said to Akiko. "Even if you shoot me with that gun arm, it's not gonna help you get to Catalina."

"At least it'll shut your mouth," she replied.

Mosquito chortled. "I like your spirit. Your boyfriend's too."

"What?"

"You told my guards you were Akiko Tsukino. I had to look you up, but I knew I'd heard your name before. Hideyoshi used to brag about his police girlfriend before he ran up a big debt. He's a gaming addict and he was bad enough to become my captive."

Akiko was stunned, but also riled up. "You think you can threaten me? Hideyoshi is in another city."

"You sure about that? Both him and Orochan will play in the death matches if you don't," Mosquito told Ben.

"Why Orochan?" Ben said back.

"She displeased me sending her with that big cannon. I can't help but question her motives."

Akiko raised her gun. "You release them or you die."

"You kill me, and Hideyoshi will die for sure," Mosquito retorted. "You play and you win, your prize will be their lives and a free trip to Catalina. What do you say?"

"Let me see Hideyoshi," Akiko said.

Mosquito signaled one of his sumo guards. A side room opened and in came Hideyoshi. His hair was ruffled, he reeked of alcohol, and his face was heavily bruised. When he saw Akiko, he teared up. "They-they told me you were dead."

"He's not very good at games, but he's always gambling and throwing his money away. You should spend that money on your girlfriend," Mosquito chided him. "Before you get any ideas, look at his finger."

Hideyoshi's finger was a metallic pinky.

"Why is that there?" Akiko demanded.

"Ask him."

Akiko asked Hideyoshi.

"I'm sorry," he said, unable to face her.

"I own him," Mosquito said. "And if he displeases me in any way, I release the toxin in that pinky that'll kill him in a minute. He agreed to it."

Akiko was so furious, she almost started firing blindly, wanting to obliterate everything in her sight. Mosquito's smug grin made it clear he was enjoying her rage. She looked to Ben, who was watching her and Hideyoshi.

"Where's Orochan?" Ben asked Mosquito.

"Getting her pinky fitted."

"How can I trust that you'll do what you say?"

"You think I'm crazy enough to touch military without an agreement? I cherish my life," Mosquito declared. Ben remained unmoved. "You want a blood oath?"

"I do."

Mosquito rolled up his sleeves, took out a knife, and cut a part of himself. He sucked on the blood and said, "I swear on my life to honor the terms of the games to release the prisoners and take you to Catalina if you win."

"If I play, I want those two released unconditionally."

"That's two lives for one."

"Yeah, it is."

Mosquito deliberated. "Fine. I'll let them off as your entrance fee."

"Ben," Akiko called. "You don't need to do this."

"You love your boyfriend?" he asked.

"He can take care of himself," Akiko answered.

"Maybe," Ben replied. "Usually these games are rigged against competitors. Is the tournament rigged?"

Mosquito shook his head. "Just the usual winner's handicap."

"What style?"

"Four rounds. Winner gets to pick the stage."

"No matter what happens, Akiko goes free."

"She's not playing," Mosquito answered.

"That's not an answer."

"I give my word that no harm will come to her."

"You can't put your life at risk for a game," Akiko said.

"Isn't this what you'd call guts?" Ben replied. "When's the tournament start?"

Mosquito skipped joyfully. "At 8:32 tonight. It'll be the main entertainment after dinner."

"I need sleep."

"Anything you want is yours."

11:13am

They boarded a big freighter masquerading as a cargo boat, filled with pleasure companions and gambling porticals. The lower deck had been converted into a casino and while it was empty at the moment, it would get packed a few hours later. There were sleeping accommodations aboard the boat, luxurious rooms for the clients that included heart-shaped beds, walls painted in portical gaming motifs, and monkeys that served champagne. Hideyoshi was in a half dazed state when Akiko put him to sleep in her Stonewall Jackson suite. "I can't believe you're alive," he rambled on and on before falling asleep.

She went to Ben's room, which had a cabaret theme with mannequins of famous wild west dancers outside. She heard what sounded like screaming and burst through the door to find two women frolicking with Ben over alcohol.

"Can I speak to you?" Akiko asked.

"Sure," Ben replied.

"In private."

"Oh, right. Outside?"

Ben stepped out.

"Do you know what you're doing?" Akiko asked.

"I figured if I was going to die, might as well get drunk one last time on good *sake*. Have you met my new friends?

They've generously offered to accompany me for my last drink."

"Not the women, Ishimura. I mean the match."

"Don't worry about it."

"Your life depends on this game."

"Not yours."

"If you lose, I will blaze my way out," Akiko said. "I'm not optimistic about my chances of survival, but I'll take as many of them down as I can."

"You told me sometimes people have to die so others can live."

"Hideyoshi can take care of himself. And if he can't, it's my responsibility, not yours."

"I already made the agreement with Mosquito."

"What about Mutsuraga?"

One of the women called out, "Ben?"

"You worry too much," Ben said to Akiko. "It'll work out. And if it doesn't, you can still go hunt him down without me to hinder you."

Akiko wondered about the captain, his childhood, growing up without parents, knowing he'd caused their deaths. What would she have done in his shoes? Her memories went back to a summer evening almost a decade ago. She was studying German when she heard a commotion outside. USJ police had arrived with their loud sirens – a neighbor down the road was being arrested. Dad had told her not to look, but she couldn't help herself. She'd never met them, but had seen them around, a young couple with a daughter and son. All four were manacled, bags placed over their faces, dragged by the police into a black van, never to be seen again.

"Have you ever played the *USA* game?" she asked Ben.

"Does it matter?" he asked back. "I need a long sleep before the tournament. You should get some rest too. Spend time with your boyfriend." He smiled at her. "Cheer up. I haven't felt this young in a long time. Even if I lose, it was worth it."

He jauntily skipped back inside and shut the door behind him.

Akiko returned to her room, lay next to Hideyoshi, and shuddered. She prayed for sleep.

6:49pm

When she woke, she wished again it'd all been a dream. Seeing the gun arm, her eyes drooped. Her shoulder ached and she had a migraine. Hideyoshi was still unconscious. His fingers were twitching and parts of his body moved in irregular spurts. She tried to place her hand on his head before realizing the metal would wake him. There were burn marks along his body that were especially bad on his feet.

She thought of the first time they'd made love. He was strong but gentle, and they caressed each other as they drove to mutual pleasure. Unlike most of the younger men she'd been with, there was no hint of impatience, no rush towards climax. Before Hideyoshi, she had found sex mundane. He probed every part of her, relishing and dwelling on every part. She knew he had other lovers, and he'd encouraged her to sleep with other men as well. It was so unlike her younger male companions who were fanatically jealous about her affections, throwing out words like "love" and "forever" while offering little else in exchange.

They'd first met at a cocktail party and he was with a date he ignored so he could shower his attention on her. "Your girlfriend's getting jealous," she'd jested, when she saw the scowls his date was directing at her.

"Who?" Hideyoshi had replied.

His topic of discussion had been the discovery by the Germans that Venus had once been inhabited. "They found the remnants of a civilization that had destroyed themselves after an environmental disaster led to an apocalyptic war. Or so the Germans say. Their propaganda department likes to interpret physical evidence in creative ways."

"What'd they fight over?"

"Too much freedom," Hideyoshi replied. "You think a totally free society is possible?"

"There's never been a free society," Akiko had declared. "The pretense is fostered to appease the conscience of those who can't stomach economic slavery. But if we're talking on a philosophical level, it depends on the individual. Some can handle total choice. Others crumble under the burden. What do you think?"

"I think most people are afraid to love because they want the freedom to suffer alone."

"I thought we were talking philosophical freedom."

"Love is a voluntary sacrifice of freedom," Hideyoshi said. "It's the only freedom we really control."

"I don't think anyone has any real choice about who they fall in love with."

"Oh?"

"I can't will myself to fall in love with just anyone because I want to. If I'm not attracted to them, I'm not attracted to them."

"I thought more than half the families back on the main island take part in arranged marriages."

"Love isn't marriage," Akiko said. "You ever been married? Or is that your wife that you're singularly ignoring?"

"I couldn't beat myself into loving her."

"You just confirmed my point."

Hideyoshi laughed.

"What do you think people on Earth will think about us a thousand years from now?"

"I don't think they will," Akiko had answered.

Hideyoshi grabbed two glasses of wine on a platter from a waiter passing by. He raised a toast and said, "Here's to hoping you fall in love with me."

Akiko answered, "That's not my choice."

Hideyoshi had rolled the champagne around in his mouth before swallowing it. "I bet I can change your mind."

"You have the freedom to try."

In the present, it was as though Hideyoshi knew she were awake and woke up himself. A part of her wished he hadn't.

"W-where-where am I?" he asked, eyes wide in horror.

"You're OK now."

"They-they said you were dead." He reached out and touched her face.

"Who said that?" she demanded.

"The Kempei. They arrested me at the clinic and took me out in front of everyone. They accused me of being in league with you to topple the Empire."

"They were lying."

He looked at her arms. "Wh-what happened to you? I didn't believe them when they told me you betrayed the Empire. You're the most loyal person I know."

"What did you say to them?"

Hideyoshi's eyes swelled and tears began to form. "I... I told them everything they wanted to hear."

"What do you mean?"

"They-they said you were dead, that it didn't matter. I..."

"Hideyoshi."

He punched himself in the face, tried to batter his head into the wall. Akiko yelled, "Stop it!" and did her best to restrain him.

"I betrayed you," he said, tears covering his face. "I told them you were working with the Americans and hated the Emperor. They told me you were secretly working to overthrow the USJ and I told them they were right."

"Why?"

"So I could save myself... They started burning me. They told me they'd break all the bones in my body. You don't understand how terrible they were."

"I do, actually," Akiko said. "What'd you tell them about my brother?"

"Everything you told me about him. They already knew so much and had a statement ready for me. I agreed with everything. I'm just a musician, Akiko. I've never had to deal with anything like this before."

"Why are you here with Mosquito?"

Hideyoshi shook his head and wiped tears away. "I came here to die."

"What do you mean?"

"The morning they released me, I saw a pair of snails on the sidewalk. Do you remember our first night together, it was raining, and you wanted to go out? All along the courtyard, there were hundreds of snails. Baby ones, families, groups. You were charmed by them. I never told you, but I always thought we'd have a little family of our own. W-when I realized what I'd done... I wanted to kill myself. I knew they had these death matches here, so I came here to get killed fighting in one of these games."

"Then why didn't you just die?"

"What?"

"Why didn't you let them kill you before you betrayed me?" Akiko snapped.

Hideyoshi lowered himself to his knees. "Be-because I was weak... If you kill me now, I'd accept it."

Akiko stood up, looked away. "You want me to be strong for you?"

"For the both of us."

"You don't get that right. Make sure I never see you again."

She left the room, went upstairs, and bumped into Orochan.

"How you doing?" Orochan asked.

"Is the *USA* game hard?" Akiko asked back, irritated by the question.

"It's very difficult."

"What do you think Ben's chances are?"

Orochan shook her head. "Honestly, not good. He's going to get destroyed by Eagle Killer."

"Who's that?"

"The best gamer in the USJ. She hasn't lost a match in two thousand games."

"Does he know this?"

"I tried to tell him, but he's asleep," Orochan answered. "What's in Catalina?"

"What do you mean?"

"Why's he risking so much to go there?"

All Akiko knew about Catalina was that it was a prison colony with thousands of dissidents, many from San Diego. Everyone understood it was a place where the Empire dumped their worst prisoners and unleashed them within the boundaries of the island. There were some guards, but it was otherwise unregulated. She'd read about the brutal death jousts that took place between the prisoners, territorial disputes settled in old buildings that the officers gambled on. She knew Catalina had once been a naval base, but that it had long been abandoned. It was supposed to be hell on earth, a brutal habitat for the condemned. Then she remembered something Wakana had told her, a rumor that Catalina once served as a lab for building mechas.

"I'm not sure," she answered.

She left Orochan and wandered the boat.

8:22pm

Ben had to put on a tactile sensory feedback suit, goggles to simulate the environments of the game, a fake gun that acted as a controller, and special shoes to interact with the treadmill that spun in a complete circle and corresponded to his motion. A ring intertwined with fiber optics surrounded him to prevent him from falling out of his control sphere while also detecting his movements. There were eight control pods, big display screens showing the live feed, as well as a kikkai connection for people to watch directly on their smaller screens. It was a gladiatorial fight via porticals. The deck fitted four hundred guests and they were all being served the "*USA* Banquet." On either wing, there were side events as appetizers. The west wing had naked sumo wrestling taking place between bare contestants of both sexes that served more as titillating choreography than corpulent combat. The east wing had singers vying for prominence with their vocal chords while using sonic knives to attack rivals. Disapproving audiences could throw fruits at their faces, the most fruitified face earning the spoils of the evening.

The main crowd was a mix of gaming fans, wealthy patrons, and expensive escorts. Some of the more striking attendees wore only silicone plastic, their bodies appearing like walking prisms with crinkles, as their clothes shimmered when they strutted.

Akiko noticed how spry and energetic Ben seemed. "I've heard there's someone named Eagle Killer tha–"

"The best gamer ever," Ben finished for her. "She was a master at *Honor of Death* and she's even better at *USA*."

"Can you beat her?"

"Probably not," Ben answered.

"You don't seem too concerned."

"If you'd had the day I had, you'd know nothing could make it bad."

"How about if it ended in death?"

Ben stared at her and frowned. "Thanks for the reminder."

"I'm serious. You should have spent your free time practicing."

"That's what I have the first round for." He checked the gun controller in his hands and loosened his game shoes.

"Are you seriously taking this that lightly?"

"Relax. No way is Mosquito going to let me die so early. We'll be split into four teams of two. He'll probably pair me up with Eagle Killer, so I won't get killed right away." His eyes strayed to someone behind her. "Orochan! How are you?"

Orochan approached them. "You shouldn't have stuck your neck out for me."

"You wouldn't be in this mess if we hadn't asked you for a ride," Ben answered.

"I shouldn't have sent you to clean up my mess. I'm sorry. One of my girls must have been working for him."

"It was Reiko."

"How do you know?"

"She came by earlier. Don't be upset with her. She didn't have a choice and we made up. If I win, will he keep his word?"

"Mosquito is a man of his word," Orochan confirmed, lifting up her pinky that was still there. "But if you don't win, you'll die a painful death."

"At least he made my last hours enjoyable. Can I get a drink?"

"You need your reflexes to be at their..." Akiko started, until she noticed his hands were shaking. "Hold on."

She called over one of the waiters who was dressed in an American flag, his short pants revealing most of his hips. "What can I get for you?"

"I'll take that," Ben said, grabbing a glass of wine on his tray and consuming it. "Better. You two should take your seat."

Orochan and Akiko headed for their round dining table.

"I can't read him," Orochan said. "What do you think?"

"I don't know," Akiko lied, not mentioning his quivering hands.

Waiters brought a first plate of seared ahi tuna as appetizer. Seven of the contestants were in place. A thin, bony woman in a wheelchair rolled out and the audience began to cheer. She was a brunette with freckles, missing both her legs. There was an acute sharpness in her gaze.

"Who is that?" Akiko asked.

"Eagle Killer."

"Why doesn't she have prosthetic legs?"

"She had both her legs removed so she can stay interfaced with the game permanently," Orochan explained. When she saw Akiko's surprised reaction, Orochan said, "It's common among the devoted. They directly connect the portical with the muscles and nerves in their body and are perpetually in the world."

"How about when she sleeps?"

"She wants her subconscious to stay immersed in the game too."

"Why do they call her Eagle Killer?"

"She got it after she beat the old champion. He was a cocky guy, undefeated, and used to have a pair of pet eagles he took everywhere. When she beat him, he got so mad he killed them both. People started calling her 'Eagle Killer' since then."

Two assistants helped her strap into the controller, which was specially retrofitted to work with her body, including two bionic legs that connected to her pelvis.

The spotlight went to Mosquito.

"We live in the ruins of great empires and it's usually so depressing," Mosquito said. "But now we have a game that challenges our notions of greatness, a game where America won. It sounds horrid, but freedom never sounded so sweet as in the *USA*. In honor of tomorrow's fortieth anniversary of our victory in the Pacific War, we have a special guest, an unabashed patriot, a censor as gamer to join our tournament." He spouted on for a while longer before loud music introduced the players.

Ben was teamed with Eagle Killer and they both started in the jungles of Luzon in the Philippines. The Japanese were building a satellite dish to call down aerial strikes. Two of the teams – Americans with local guerilla support – had to destroy the installation while the other two – Japanese – defended it. Eagle picked up an assault rifle and climbed to a vantage point where she could get a good line of sight. Ben went for a weapon, but was shot, killed immediately by the enemy. He appeared stunned and stumbled about, doing his best to coerce the controls into doing what he wanted. He called one of the waiters and asked, "How do I sprint?"

"I'm not allowed to say, per the game rules. *Sumimasen*."

Ben's avatar jumped about, ran in sporadic bursts, and appeared shellshocked. Eventually, he ignored the weapons in the cache and started running in the opposite direction of the Japanese forces.

"What's he doing?" Akiko asked.

Orochan observed Ben's avatar. "It looks like he's running away," she answered

"Why?"

Orochan tried to decipher Ben's perplexing action. "He might be misunderstanding the rules and thinks surviving is the best way to win? I'm not sure, but if he thinks that, he's in for big trouble."

"Why?"

"He can get through the first and second round like that, but later they'll tally up the score and, when you run, you get no points."

"How do you score?"

"Destruction gets points. Kills get points, depending on where you shoot them. Victory nets points. There's extra side missions too. Eagle Killer is getting reconnaissance points for exploring all the different areas before she goes for the kill. More points means better weapons, stage selects, and perquisites that make a huge difference in the final round."

Akiko watched the other screens and the fighting had already commenced. The visuals were stunningly realistic and it looked like a documentary, only more vivid and colorful. She could see the individual blades of grass swaying in the wind, the sun getting doused in a mesmerizing blaze that deluged the whole sky. There were streams and little fishes in them, dayflies swarming in their futile pursuit of existence, and snakes that slithered and hissed at the caprice of combat. Two things broke the realism. No smells, and the humans. The humans looked photorealistic when they didn't move. But the animation was stunted. Their shoulders were too hunched up, the movement was sometimes too limited, and other times too exaggerated. Their facial expressions were the same: too emotive or too limited in regional influences, so that they looked like robots rather than live human beings. The broader motions generally looked passable, but even their clumsy interaction with weapons indicated the portical restrictions.

The quick movements in the camera angle of the players gave her a headache. She sipped her water, watched Ben again. He was still running in the opposite direction while explosives were rippling across the screens of the other players. One of the screens was splattered in blood, the screen getting split in half.

"Did he lose?" Akiko asked Orochan.

"Each player gets three medics to come back unless they take a headshot direct to the brain. Most players don't shoot opponents directly in the brain because that means less points. They want all three kills."

The match was a frenetic brawl that seemed like flashes of jungle, bullet sprays, random explosions, and soldiers charging before disappearing into the trees. It was hard for her to get a grasp of what was going on, though the people watching were hypnotized, flipping from different player perspectives on their personal porticals. They checked stats, examined their positions on the map, and gambled. Two dozen waiters and waitresses were taking wagers on kill times, match lengths, and even death order.

"Why are people so into this game? It's just a bunch of fake soldiers running around shooting each other."

Orochan did not hear her question, instead cursing, exclaiming, cringing, and cheering on the decisions the players made.

The first round ended eighteen minutes later with Eagle Killer and Ben's team coming in second place out of four, due largely to Ben's abstinence from combat. Eagle Killer had the most individual points at 342, but Ben's total of 15 points brought them down.

The losing team was unstrapped from their controllers, taken to the dais at center stage, and chained to the ground. A waitress slashed their torsos and limbs, blood forming pools around them. Both men were begging for mercy, imploring to be released, until transparent walls surrounded them, cutting the noise off. Three waitresses rolled down cages with the Pomeranians Akiko had seen earlier. They were let in through a small orifice. The Pomeranians attacked with their abnormally large fangs. It would almost be comedic if it wasn't so violent. The furry monsters ripped their victims to pieces, shredding apart skin, tearing at the lungs, the stomach, and the heart, sundering the ropy intestines from their bodies. Every devastating blow brought cheers from the crowd. Akiko turned her head away and looked at Ben. He was in an exchange with Eagle Killer who was criticizing him, though he appeared indifferent to her harangue. "I'm trying!" Akiko heard Ben insist. "Can you explain some of the controls to me?"

"I hope they have the swimming death next round," Orochan said. "You're gonna love it."

"You've seen this before?" Akiko asked, surprised.

"Only once. They're so expensive to get into."

"Where do they get the contestants?"

"You can volunteer, but ever since Eagle Killer joined, the volunteers have gone way down. It's mostly debtors who want to wipe the slate. But every so often, there are people dumb enough to wager their lives on it."

"What does that gain them?"

"Gaming champions are gods," Orochan said. "Ben seriously needs to get better or he's going to get killed."

The second round began and the six remaining players were tossed into a two-story shack. Outside, thousands of monsters approached who were the spirits of the Chinese who had been massacred at Nanking. They were seeking vengeance. Bullets were useless against them. Fire arrows, though, dissipated their energy form. The spirits were horrific and disturbingly realistic. Many had limbs missing, bullet and sword wounds, ghoulish facades and bizarre animation that emphasized the supernatural element. There were children and women with clothes torn off, crying for justice. The spirits carried pitchforks, spears, and whatever else they could get hold of.

"What's going on here?" Akiko asked.

"It's a standard 'kill as many as you can without getting killed' stage," Orochan explained. "The pair that tallies the most kills when the wave ends wins. This is a long round. They have to kill sixty thousand of those spirits or survive until dawn, but Eagle will try to kill them all because there's more points that way."

"Sixty thousand?"

"That's how many died at Nanking. The creators wanted it to be authentic."

Akiko had read reports that the actual number of civilians killed at Nanking ranged from two to three hundred thousand. She'd seen photos of pregnant women who had their heads chopped off, babies killed to sharpen swords, and gates where Chinese heads were hung. Peasants were massacred, teenage girls were perforated from their genitalia up, and that wasn't mentioning those hurt in the bombings. Even knowing the necessity of striking terror into the civilian populace, it'd been hard to stomach for her. The casualty rates had been reduced in the historical records to make the battle more palatable for the puppet government set up under Puyi, the former Emperor of China, as well as the citizens of the Empire who would have found such numbers appalling. What Tokyo Command called the "China Incident" was nowhere near conclusion when the Battle of Nanking took place and the last thing they needed was a rallying call for the survivors and those fomenting for peace. Fifty years later, no one remembered the dead apart from this videogame. Mutsuraga hadn't even gotten the casualty rate correct.

Once again, Ben appeared confused. His character was able to kill a few spirits before a pair of them overwhelmed him and ate him limb by limb. With the second life, he absconded up the stairs into a corner and tested out the controls, trying to figure out which combination of commands did what. At one point, he took off his portical goggles, called over a waitress, and ordered a cocktail and shrimp.

What is that baka *doing?* Akiko cursed to herself.

"Does he want to die?" Orochan asked out loud. Many other viewers expressed similar sentiments, disappointed by Ben's play.

As though they were meant to be distracted, they were served their next course – brussels sprout hash with bacon vinaigrette and poached eggs, grilled octopus with roasted mushrooms in brown butter, and garlic scallion string beans with candied hazelnuts. Akiko wasn't hungry, but she ate enough to replenish her strength. She almost spat her food out when she looked back and saw Ben flirting with the waitress. On the screen, his character was still hiding away from the combat zone. The other gamers were busy slaughtering wave after wave of undead assailants. A player was late refilling his quiver of arrows and one of the spirits leapt in through a window, grabbed him by the neck, and unleashed tentacles on his face. The player lost control as his avatar became possessed and attacked his partner with a pistol. The partner fired back and both were quickly killed, then resurrected by a medic. Two lives to go.

Eagle Killer wasn't content shooting arrows from her secure position. She carved out a swathe of destruction, jumped out of the shack, grabbed the arrows from the fallen kamis, and used the fiery edges as a blade to kill more. She grabbed a pitchfork and put the edge on fire, setting a thousand ablaze in one quick swoop. Her movements were intuitive and fluid. She anticipated every player's move before it happened – all except for Ben. When one of the spirits finally broke through a window in the upper floor, Ben ran downstairs and took cover behind another player. After the player dispatched the spirit, Ben tried to engage in combat with some of the kamis, but was immediately killed. He appeared dumbfounded.

"Are you not going to eat your octopus?" Orochan asked.

"Go ahead," Akiko said.

The match concluded thirty minutes later, after Eagle Killer got hold of a flamethrower and obliterated the opposition. Her player avatar was smoking a cigarette lit from the flames of her enemies. Eagle Killer and Ben came in second place again. This time, Eagle Killer had harsher words for her partner.

"You're bringing my score down," she snapped. "This is the lowest team score I've ever received at this point in the game. What do you think you're doing?"

"I'm trying, but the controls are different from what I remember. Besides, you should be happy: your individual scores are the highest they've ever been, right?"

"That's because you're not doing your share! You're not even trying. If you want to die, do it on your own time. This is a complete disgrace and a waste of my time. Why are you even here?"

"You're a lot nicer on the portical," Ben commented.

"I want to see Mosquito," Eagle Killer demanded of a waiter.

"You know Mosquito's policy of no communication with players during the tournament," the waiter answered.

"How am I supposed to play with this idiot on my team?" she angrily asked.

Eagle Killer's point total was at 1,232. Ben's was at 35. The first team to succumb to the spirits was taken to the center dais. They were an overweight pair, one an ethnically Japanese male and the other Korean. Transparent walls went up around them. Unlike the first execution, their arms and legs were not chained. Water filled the cage from below. The two did not seem worried at first, joking, even laughing with each other. That was until the water reached their neck level. Soon, it was over their head and a minute later, there was only a sliver of air left. The two had to swim and waddle to stay above water level.

"Why isn't the water going all the way up?" Akiko asked,

noticing it had stopped.

"The point of the torture is to see how long they struggle, because, as long as they swim, they can live," Orochan said. "The worst part is the hope of survival."

They both swam to keep afloat. There wasn't enough space at the top for them to swim on their backs, so they were continually moving their arms and legs. She knew both of them realized this was the end, but they struggled vainly against it.

"Does Ben have any chance of winning?" Akiko asked Orochan.

"It's tough, but the other team picked the convoy mission in the invasion of Hiroshima so if he does a good job there, he might still have a chance."

Akiko got up and accosted Ben, who was talking to a cocktail waitress. The waitress left in a hurry when she saw how annoyed Akiko appeared.

"Are you going to play this game, or flirt the whole night?" Akiko demanded.

"I am playing the game."

"Not well. You have to play better in the next stage."

"I'm trying, but I'm still figuring out the controls. I have to get my feeling for things."

"You only have two rounds left."

"I know," Ben somberly said. "I'm trying my best."

"Look at them," Akiko snapped.

The pair's struggles were starting to wind down as they ran out of energy. They swam desperately, fatigued, beating the glass as they begged for mercy. People had been taking wagers on length of time before drowning and which would give up first. An unspoken competition had begun between those with Korean ethnic backgrounds, and those of Japanese ancestry who felt their player would last longer.

"That'll be you unless you shape up," Akiko continued. "And they," pointing to the crowd, "will take pleasure in your death."

Ben averted his eyes from the killings. "Then I die and leave the world a better place," he said, mustering as much confidence as he could.

Akiko heard the doubt in his voice. "I'm grateful that you saved my life and Hideyoshi's, b–"

"How's he doing? He looked like he'd had a rough day."

"We've all had a rough couple of days."

"But he's not a soldier," Ben noted. "He's not prepared for this shit."

"You don't know what he did."

"Whatever he did, he feels guilty about it. He couldn't stop bawling. I feel bad for him."

"Emotional tears are made up of protein-based hormones like leucine enkaphalin, a pain killer, which makes him chemically feel better about himself. Crying is for the weak."

"Not always."

"Always."

"You never cry?"

"Not since I was a child," Akiko stated.

"Then I guess I'm weak 'cause I cry all the time." When Akiko didn't reply, Ben said, "Thanks for the support. Where is he?"

"I've dealt with him."

The grin on Ben's face evaporated. "What do you mean, *dealt* with him? He's alive, right?"

"What do you take me for?" Akiko asked.

"An agent of Tokko."

"He's alive," Akiko affirmed.

Ben eased up again, though he could sense her agitation. "Thanks for not making this wager meaningless."

"It was a dumb wager and I'm not going to just let them take you to your death without a fight."

"You'll be killed if you try to fight them."

"Death is a welcome honor if it serves a purpose. You'll be killed for nothing if you don't play."

"I appreciate it, but like I said, don't worry about me."

"You can't just run away like before. If your team loses, you'll be killed. This is a stupid death. And what about Mutsuraga? If we don't capture him, I might as well be dead."

"So that's what you're really concerned about?"

"Ishimura. Don't you care that your life is on the line?"

"I'm very aware of that. I'll try harder next round. And if I fail, I'll cross my fingers and pray I be reborn as one of those Pomeranians."

"You don't believe in reincarnation."

"I'll pretend you convinced me."

Akiko sighed, came closer to him, and whispered, "Do you have something planned, or are you really losing?"

Ben struggled to form an answer. "I'm going to try harder. It'll come back to me."

The answer provided no comfort for Akiko.

The waiters were cleaning out the cages, carting off the two dead contestants. The third stage started soon, only four players remaining. Ben was still teamed with Eagle Killer. Their duty was to defend a train full of supplies being sent to reinforce the Americans attacking Hiroshima by ground. The opposing team had to do their best to disrupt the convoy and prevent delivery. Eagle Killer picked up a Parker-Hale Model 85 Classic modified for night combat and packing explosive charges. She was going to take on the role of a sniper. The other duo was endeavoring to setup an ambush along the railway. Ben made his way to the armory of the train and hid inside with the rations.

"Where are you going?" Eagle Killer demanded of Ben.

"I'm guarding the supplies," Ben replied.

"You need to get back on top and get in position!"

Ben ignored her and, when she continued with her rant in the game, he muted her dialogue.

It was strange for Akiko to see the homeland under direct attack by Americans, even if it was just a portical game. She couldn't imagine what it would have been like if foreign soldiers had invaded Japan and taken control of their territory. Even the thought of the Japanese people being subject to the violence of war offended her. If Japan had lost, what would have happened to the Emperor?

"The good part's about to begin," Orochan said.

The ambush commenced and the explosions were fiery. Eagle was ubiquitous, killing thousands of foes. No matter how many Japanese soldiers the other side threw at them, the Americans, under Eagle's control, prevailed. Seeing so many Japanese shot, even in portical form, disgusted Akiko. She hated the game more and more, convinced it had to be abolished.

Ben tarried in the ration car and actually started eating the supplies to replenish his energy and stats. Unlike the previous round, this one was short. Eagle was a force all to herself and single-handedly beat both enemies. The Americans were successful in resupplying their forces. Her point total jumped to 6,342 while Ben's was at a measly 75.

"What's next?" Akiko asked.

"They'll go head to head. But, even if Ben wins, his point total will be less," Orochan answered.

"What can he do to win?"

Orochan looked at the score again. "He has no chance of winning."

"There's got to be some way."

"I don't think so. Eagle picks the stage and, whichever one she picks, she'll dominate him. He isn't trying at all. Watching him is so frustrating," Orochan said, genuinely irked. "Look at him. He's not even paying attention."

"How can we help him?"

"We can't unless we somehow convince Mosquito to let him live," Orochan said.

Akiko stormed over to Mosquito's table. The losers were injected with chemicals by two women in contamination suits.

Warts began to grow on both players. Not small cauliflower disfigurations, but pus-filled lumps that bulged in size until they were mounds as big as their fists. Akiko did not watch as their bodies became covered by warts. The helplessness in their verrucose faces was too familiar from the times she'd inflicted similar diseases on her victims.

Mosquito was surrounded by several Japanese men with metallic pinkies who were smoking cigars, fellow Yakuza out for a night of entertainment. "May I speak to you in private?" she asked.

Mosquito didn't take his eyes off the killing. "You can speak here. What do you want?"

"You need to change the parameters of the final round."

"To what?"

Akiko suggested, "Whoever wins this round wins the whole thing regardless of score."

"That's not the way we play it."

She noticed two sumo thugs hovering behind her.

"He agreed to the terms," Mosquito said. "And he'll abide by them."

"But–"

"My customers are complaining about his lack of involvement and how bad he is. I told my customers he was one of the best players in the USJ. This is just a waste of time. Disgruntled customers are never a good thing. I'm very annoyed right now. Don't push my patience."

"Ishimura and I are both soldiers of the Emperor. If you showed mercy–"

"The Emperor has no jurisdiction here."

"The Emperor has jurisdiction everywhere within his Empire," she reminded him, annoyed by his insolent tone. "I suggest for your sake that you never forget that."

"Or what?" He glanced at the guards, and one put his arm on her.

Akiko kicked his knee as hard as she could. The weight of

his entire body dropped down and caused his knee to rupture, the cap bursting the leg in the wrong way. She punched him in the nose with her gun arm, then did a roundhouse to the second one who was approaching in the groin. He stumbled to the ground. She used her metallic limb to smash down on his head.

"Don't try to scare me," Akiko warned.

Mosquito took a bite out of his food. "My father was a *Tokubetsu Kogekitai*," a Kamikaze Pilot. "He sacrificed his life at San Diego. I still don't know what for. Every morning, my mother burned incense for his soul and prayed to a picture of the Emperor. She worked as a maid at a geisha house and never missed a day. She got hit by a car and still insisted on going to work with her broken ribs. She knew if she lost the job, we'd be out on the streets. Where was the Emperor then? I used to get into trouble playing portical games all day, but my ma was too busy to notice. I was addicted to *Honor of Death* and accidentally disturbed some thug in the Nakayama family because I got too excited playing. He put a gun to my head and told me to finish my game without dying. If I lost, he'd shoot me in the head. It was the longest two hours of my life. I played it perfectly. Put a gun to anyone's head, and they'll have a better sense of clarity than anyone in the world. Where was the Emperor then? Go back to your seat. Ben sacrificed his life for your boyfriend in this pathetic display. Be grateful for that."

She sighed, more infuriated that Ben seemed indifferent to his situation. Was he intentionally seeking death after realizing Eagle Killer was too good? Some misplaced fatalism where he had accepted whatever may come? Mosquito was watching her gun arm the whole time. "Don't do anything rash. We have an agreement and if you try anything, you won't survive."

"You think if I really wanted you dead, I'd care whether I survived or not?"

She went back to her seat.

The final stage was the Battle of Pearl Harbor, one of the most disastrous defeats for America. In the new version, Imperial Japan attacked Pearl Harbor before the Germans were ready to invade America. As a result, the American fleet was partially stationed at Pearl Harbor, ready for the attack. Eagle Killer chose to represent the American side and Ben was attacking as the Japanese. Even before the game began, a poem by the Emperor Meiji came up on the screen:

All the seas, everywhere,
are brothers to one another
Why then do the winds and waves of strife
rage so violently through the world?

In the original battle, Marshal Rommel of the Germans had already begun his onslaught of the American east coast. When the Japanese fleet attacked Hawaii, they met with only token resistance. In this new history, Japan attacked America too early and, while they were able to destroy part of the fleet, the attack mobilized the American people into retaliating with a full force. Pearl Harbor represented a turning point in the war, an internecine battle that empowered the American spirit. Ben was to be part of Japan's Operation Z (named to commemorate Admiral Togo's Z sign at the Battle of Tsushima), an all-out desperate gamble to disable and handicap the American fleet. When the game actually began, Ben immediately fled for the hills. Eagle did not pursue. She picked off all of the Japanese soldiers, killing them one by one. She took over an antiaircraft gun and destroyed multiple Zero fighters. Her point total surpassed 10,000.

If she hadn't been so flustered, Akiko might have marveled at the beautiful graphics, the fully rendered environments reacting to the gunfire, disintegrating via realtime simulations of geometric dynamics. Every building and ship was destructible, polygonal destruction waged one facet at a time. Eagle Killer took her time hunting down Ben. Ben was still trying to conceal himself in the hills. Eagle had several clear shots at his head, but didn't take them, wanting to come in close for the kill. There were more points to be had using a knife to finish an opponent.

"Ben!" Akiko yelled.

But he did not hear her.

Most of the audience gave disappointed groans, knowing the inevitable was coming, going back to their veal with leeks and truffle-crusted Dover sole. Akiko felt knots churning inside her and turned to Orochan who was focused on her food, refusing to watch the end. Was there really nothing either of them could do? Ben fled further up the hills. The fact that his life was tied in with the success of his gameplay appalled Akiko, even though she knew people had been killed for less. Did Ben want to die? But why now after coming this far? Or had he always dwelled at the fringes?

She touched her gun arm, knew what she had to do after Ben lost. It seemed Mosquito anticipated her as several guards surrounded their table. She examined each of them, trying to assess which order she should kill them to maximize her chances of survival, but–

She heard gasps and murmurs. People were watching the screen again. Akiko did not want to see the final kill, the portical representation as mockery of a man's life. But she forced herself to watch. The ground was quaking. Akiko was confused, not sure if the game was suffering from a glitch. The hills split apart and a gigantic hand emerged, followed by the torso of a gigantic mecha.

"What's going on?" Akiko asked no one in particular.

It was clear everyone else was curious about the same thing.

The gigantic mecha with a Japanese Rising Sun painted on its armor stepped over Eagle Killer and started decimating the entire American fleet, firing laser beams to destroy the enemy forces. Within a minute, the whole of Pearl Harbor was on fire and Ben's point tally was already at 9,000, quickly approaching 10,000. A minute later, that point score was doubled. The mecha stepped on Eagle Killer and crushed her avatar to pieces.

Ben had won.

Eagle Killer threw off her gear and yelled, "He's cheating! This is a sacrilege! That's not supposed to be possible! I won this tournament! He rigged the game!"

Mosquito approached the stage, holding a trophy.

The guards chained Eagle to her wheelchair and gagged her. She was trying to scream, but the ball in her throat prevented her.

"C'mon, you can't be serious," Ben said in Eagle's defense. "She's the best player you'll ever have. Mosquito! Mosquito!"

"She lost," Mosquito said sternly. "Rules are rules."

"She didn't know all the rules."

"That's her loss. Take her upstairs."

"What are you going to do?"

"That's not for you to worry about. Did you eat yet?"

They dragged her away and Akiko knew from Ben's flustered expression that he was forcing himself to think about the bigger mission. "I'm famished."

"Good. There's a meal for you. Perhaps we can discuss future matches."

"I just want my ride to Catalina."

Mosquito nodded. "I'll keep my word. But perhaps I can tempt you–"

Ben shook his head. "No, thank you."

"How did you know about the mecha?"

"That's my secret."

Ben came over to Akiko. Akiko slapped Ben's face.

"What's that for?" he demanded.

She did not answer, still fuming.

"I'm starving," he said.

"Then eat," she said and did her best to hide the fact that it was her hands trembling this time.

The portical screens had switched to a view on the deck of the boat, an angle of a plank overlooking the ocean. Eagle was screaming that she'd been cheated. "I've spent my whole life playing games! There's no one who knows as much about the *USA* as I do. He must have cheated. He's made a mockery of the entire game. He corrupted the files and he–" The guards ignored her and threw her overboard. The audience members laughed hard as she hit the surface of the water. She screamed for succor, begging for another chance. Without her legs and dragged down by the wheelchair, her voice drowned out as she plummeted underwater.

"Let's see if she can hunt eagles in the ocean!" Mosquito jested to an excited audience.

11:43pm

They were given an unmarked motorboat to take them to the island. Ben suggested making their way to Catalina from the west as there were no mines and very little security. Akiko did not like the smell of sea nor the spray of saltwater in her face. But the further they got away from Mosquito's boat, the better she felt.

"Where's Hideyoshi?"

"I don't know," Akiko confessed. "I don't care."

"Sorry to hear that," Ben said.

"We don't choose the people we fall in love with. How did you know about the mecha?"

"I asked Mutsuraga to put it in *Honor of Death*. A cheat for gamers like me who sucked, but needed to play the whole game. You can only trigger it if your score is down by 10,000 points and you need to put in a special command."

"That's why you ran away?" she inquired.

Ben nodded. "Honestly, I wished I could have played her straight up, but I'm not anywhere near as good as her and the controls have changed from *Honor of Death*."

"How'd you know he'd put that cheat in *USA*?"

"Actually, I didn't until it happened."

"You gambled on a hunch?"

"I gambled on what I knew about General Mutsuraga."

"What's that?"

"He likes to give underdogs a chance."

"You're bolder than I give you credit for, Ishimura."

"I didn't have a choice. It's like the late Prime Minister Tojo once said, 'Sometimes, you must jump with eyes closed off the veranda of the Kiyomizu Temple.'"

"When did he say that?"

"Before he became a Buddhist monk and advocated peace throughout the Empire. I heard it when I was at BEMAG."

"It's all a bit *deus ex machina*."

"You got *machina* all right. Damn shame about Eagle Killer. She was an incredible gamer. I know Mosquito is a Yakuza, but he should have spared her."

"He threatened all of us and that's not acceptable."

"What can we do?"

"I left him a surprise," Akiko said.

"A surprise?"

"Something in the derringers for the next time he plays with them."

"When did you do that?"

"Before we left, I asked to Orochan to assemble it." She steadied herself on the boat. "He won't go easy." Akiko tried to ignore the unsteadiness within herself, the collapsed structure of the military that had supported her this far, the haunting facade of Jenna Fujimori who lingered in all those who had died in the match tonight. "I didn't know so much social injustice existed in the USJ. If I get back in the Tokko, I will make sure things change and prevent these kinds of crimes from ever happening again."

Ben looked at the determination in Akiko's gesture and said, "I hope you do. I don't think even Mutsuraga would appreciate the way his game is being used on the boat."

"You think he cares?"

"At the least, he would be dejected."

"Why don't people fight for change?"

"Because the ones who do get hunted down."

Akiko gazed at the ocean, her eyes lost in the black void as she contemplated all those who had died in the debilitated ruins of time. "My ma used to tell me stories about the heroic deeds of the Emperor and his father. How hard they worked to try to bring justice to humanity, even though humans went against the decrees of their gods. I can't get that poem by the Emperor Meiji out of my head."

"The one in the game?"

Akiko nodded. "All the seas, everywhere, are brothers to one another. Why then do the winds and waves of strife rage so violently through the world?"

A hard wave hit them, splashing them with saltwater. "I bet he never rode on a boat in the middle of the night to visit a penal colony so he can hunt down a defector after playing a portical game for his life."

"Don't be a smartass."

Catalina Island
July 4, 1988
12:18am

It had been arduous for Beniko Ishimura to pretend to be confident during the *USA* match. His nerves were frayed from doing his best to act cool. No one could suspect he had a plan, a "cheat" he wasn't even sure had been implemented in the final form of the game. He kept on worrying he would betray himself with a panicked glance or an unintended stutter. His whole life had been a masquerade and he wondered if all the players felt that way, performers dancing to a fatal ballad. The Emperor was a distant absolute, an audience that was present even in his absence.

General Kazuhiro Mutsuraga had been an authority figure for most of Ben's career. Mutsuraga had given orders, and Ben had obeyed. The general had saved him from being carted off to the far reaches of the Empire. Ben had known the general was not a very creative programmer, nor a particularly adept tactician. He played politics well, fitting the mold of the stern Japanese commander. He didn't need to be skilled. Ben had willingly filled his subservient role for the first few years. It made him cringe now at the way he adulated over officers and colleagues who never would give him the time of day. Requests to dinner, bowing obsequiously, fawning over trivialities. Most of them just assumed he was wheedling them so he could get something and ignored him. In their eyes, Ben wasn't just a lackey, but the boy who'd betrayed his way into the cadre. He wasn't worth replying to.

Catalina Island looked desolate. It had been bombed countless times during military exercises and the shrubs that constituted plants were scarce. On the beach, there were huts, trash, and hundreds of men and women, sitting by beach fires, staring vacantly. Even after Ben and Akiko landed, there was no reaction. Akiko tried to elicit a response by tapping, then hitting one on the head. The man was oblivious to her presence. She looked over at Ben and saw him examining one of the prisoners. The woman wore torn pants, no shirt, had flaccid breasts, and gazed blankly out at sea. Her head was patched with metal strips. Partially healed scars ran down her neck. There were Japanese words printed in the seams of her flesh.

"Laziness," Akiko read to Ben.

"This one says 'gluttony.'"

"What happened to them?"

Ben tapped the metal plate, waved his hand in front of their faces. "I think they've been lobotomized."

The majority sat without any emotion, their brains as vacant as the landscape.

"Did you know about this?" Akiko demanded of Ben.

"I was going to ask you that."

"It wasn't on any reports," she replied.

Ben knew there were many things that weren't on reports. He remembered one of his exchanges with Claire Mutsuraga, the general's late daughter. It was after the general had sent them out of San Diego to Los Angeles. Claire was studying porticals and Ben was transitioning into his new position as a censor, which meant lots of drinks with his colleagues. One drunken night, he stumbled home and was surprised to find his door open. Claire was waiting for him on his sofa, holding up her portical.

"W-what are you doing here?" he asked, his tongue slower than his brain.

She handed him her portical. "Why are all the reports related to my mom's death classified?"

Ben perused the screen and all the files had a "Forbidden" label over them. "Ask your dad."

"What do you mean?"

He took a seat, drunk and dizzy. "Ask him about how she died."

"I did. He told me Imperial soldiers accidentally killed her when they set a bomb for the George Washingtons. He wanted to make peace with them, but the cadre wouldn't let him."

"That's what he told you?" he retorted, with a scoffing edge to his voice.

"That's not what happened?"

Ben concentrated, trying to remember what he should say. "It is."

"Then why is it all classified?" Claire demanded.

"That's between you and him."

"You're not involved in any way?"

He was about to answer, but she raised her hand.

"If you lie about this, I won't forgive you."

Ben struggled with an answer.

"Why can't you just tell me?" Claire asked. "What are you afraid of?"

All these years later, he still didn't know. Should he have just told her the truth that night instead of waiting for her to discover it on her own?

In the present, he said to Akiko, "Those barracks look empty. We should get some sleep."

"Is it safe?"

"The western side has no guards," he answered and checked his portical. "See this grid? It has all their locations. No one's near and the main posts are at Avalon. Even if someone noticed us, we could just pretend to be lobotomized."

"Why are we here?"

"To see an old friend," Ben answered.

"How is that going to help us find Mutsuraga?"

"Kujira used to be one of the top mecha pilots in the USJ. She'll meet us here tomorrow morning."

"What's she doing on the island?"

"Hiding from authorities."

"Does she have a–"

"Yes. If she'll take us on her mecha, it's the safest way in and out of San Diego, and the best way to make sure we get Mutsuraga."

There were multiple bunk beds without mattresses. All of them were rock hard and uncomfortable. Ben lay in a lower bunk and Akiko took the one across from him.

Ben was about to sleep when Akiko asked, "Do you have regrets about anything?"

He thought again of Claire. "I try not to second guess myself. What about you?"

"Many of late," she answered. "I've wondered how USJ Command can allow a place like this to exist."

"You mean Catalina?"

"Catalina and Mosquito's casino."

"It's more likely they either don't know or it got lost in the bureaucracy and someone trying to save face didn't report it."

"Ignorance is worse than authorization."

"You didn't know about these places either."

"Something I'm glad has been rectified. I've always thought the traitors were those actively trying to overthrow the Empire, but now I know there are more insidious forms of rebellion. I've lapsed in my duties to the Emperor."

"I'm sure he'll forgive you."

"It would be beneath him to have to contemplate the moral quandaries of a maggot like myself."

Ben laughed. "That's an interesting way of describing yourself."

"To the Emperor, we are all maggots."

"And we metamorphose into flies who eke out a living eating the shit of our commanding officers." Ben's head ached and he closed his eyes again.

He heard Akiko get up.

"You're going to need a lot of rest for tomorrow," Ben said.

"Have you heard about the toxoplasma gondii parasite?"

"Is that a new type of weapon?"

"It's a parasite that's in many warm-blooded creatures, but can only reproduce sexually in cats. When they infect rodents, it reprograms their brain. Very subtle behavioral shifts that make them easier for cats to prey on. The parasites actually rewrite their biochemistry. Our scientists noticed even infected humans start behaving differently, less aggressive depending on the individual. But you wouldn't know it without getting tested for it."

"That's disturbing."

"Regret is like a mental parasite that alters your behavior," Akiko said. "I want you to be honest with me. Do you think I'm a fool?"

"Of course not," Ben replied. "Why would I think that?"

She approached him, arms crossed. "Why are you always so afraid to speak your mind?"

"What?"

"You almost always give the answer you think I want to hear, not what you're really thinking."

"You want to have a heart-to-heart?"

"I want you to be honest," Akiko answered.

"OK. I'm terrified of you."

"Terrified?"

"One moment, you seem like a good officer, incorruptible

and devoted to your cause. Next, I have no clue what's gonna set you off and make you go apeshit."

"That's ridiculous."

"Is it? You kill so easily. I'm scared I'm going to say something wrong and you'll shoot me."

"Is that why you suspected me of killing Hideyoshi?"

"For all I know, he could be shark bait," Ben said. "The thought didn't cross your mind?"

Akiko became completely still. Ben tensed, wondering if he'd gone too far.

"It's never easy," she finally said. "In the Tokko training, they study your emotional reaction to torture and killing. They primarily recruit field operators from candidates with little to no aversion for what would be considered cruel and inhumane."

"You have no feeling torturing people?" Ben asked, having a hard time wrapping around the fact that it could be quantified or measured.

"According to their diagnostics, very little."

"I'm not asking about the diagnostics."

"It's better this way for us to carry out the Emperor's–"

"You want me to cut the bullshit? You too. Stop hiding behind the Emperor," Ben said.

"Everything I do is–"

"Sure," Ben said. "I think you get a kick out of it."

"What?"

"You heard me. And that bugs the shit out of you, doesn't it?"

Akiko rubbed her brows with her gun, perturbed she could not deny his claim. "Whenever I go 'apeshit,' a different side of me takes over."

"The true you."

"How is that more true than any other side?"

"Because you can't control it."

"I *can* control it," she asserted, though uncertainty

was withering her confidence. "Mostly... But sometimes, sometimes... There are things that set off other things and I don't know what's happening. I-I'm scared of that part of myself."

Ben propped himself up. "Really?"

"Aren't you?"

"I already told you I'm scared of you," Ben said.

"I mean, aren't you scared of that part of yourself too?" she snapped.

"I don't know. I've never killed with my own hands before."

"Soldiers tell you it gets easier with every kill. The physical act does. I've come up with creative ways of making it even more horrifying for prisoners, all in the Emperor's name. But what if the Emperor is fallible?"

"What if?"

"Then the truth of what we're doing would be too terrible to accept." Akiko looked down at her feet. "I've inflicted too much pain to try to appease what little of my conscience is left and I've never sought anyone's approval. I have to live with that. Empires aren't built on the backs of good people."

"They're built on their corpses."

"Things have to change." Akiko gazed out of the barracks. "I'm going for a walk."

She left without giving him a chance to reply. He knew better than to follow and he was too tired to think. Even his dreams took a break for the night as his repose swam in a swarm of black.

10:11am

Morning accentuated the soreness throughout Ben's body. It was cold outside and the rigid mat hadn't been good for his back. His forearms hurt and his ankles felt like ice. He did his best not to think about the people who had been killed the night before. Instead, he planned for the long day ahead, which made him feel worse. Akiko was sleeping in one of the beds, curled up like a fetus.

He stepped outside. There were no birds, barely any plants. The prisoners were in their dazed state, a surgically induced nirvana that had cleared their mind of worldly attachments. He knew many of them were from San Diego, "war criminals" brought here to be rehabilitated. There was a desiccated path that led into the island. Bushes struggled to maintain their roots. Flies infested the rotting bodies of the prisoners who didn't seem to mind the nests of maggots sweltering in their wounds.

"Are you Ben Ishimura?" a portly and pimple-faced teenager asked, pointing a gun at his chest. His clothing resembled the prisoners and he even had a metal plate on his head.

"I am," Ben said.

"So you're the one who's been blaring message after message. What kind of ID do you have?"

"What do you need?"

"Send me your portical clearance."

Ben slowly took his portical out of his pocket and tapped some buttons.

"Kujira sent you?" Ben asked him.

The teen checked his portical and confirmed Ben's code. He presented his portical display and said, "Put your thumb on there."

"Why?"

"I need to check your fingerprint."

Ben did a quick visual scan of the portical, but saw nothing dangerous. He pressed his finger on the display screen. The teen looked at the results, which confirmed Beniko Ishimura's identity.

"So now you know who I am," Ben said. "Who are you?"

"I'm Kujira."

"You're not Kujira."

"I am," he insisted.

"I know her and you're definitely not her."

"You're looking for my mom."

"Mom? You're Kujira's son?"

"Ma bit it two years ago."

"I just communicated with her a few days ago."

"That was me."

"You pretended to be her?"

"I didn't know if you were who you said you were. Lots of rotten people out there."

"I'm one of them," Ben said.

"She only said a few bad things about you," Kujira said. "Which meant she thought you were OK."

Ben examined her son. The only resemblance he saw was in their fiery eyes. "I'm sorry to hear the news. She was the best mecha pilot I knew."

"She had a good run."

"How did it happen?"

"Radiation from all the piloting she did. The army never mentioned anything until she was sick and they denied it until the very end."

"I'm sorry."

"For what? You didn't kill her," the younger Kujira snapped.

"She was one of the finest officers I ever knew."

"Why are you here, old man? You were pretty vague in your communications."

"It's because I wasn't sure if they were being monitored. I needed a huge favor from her," Ben said. "And I'm not that old."

"You look old," Kujira replied. "What kind of favor?"

"A ride."

"You came all the way here for a ride?"

"It's a place only she could take me," Ben said.

"San Diego?"

"It's a war zone and only a mecha has a chance of getting in."

"She told me everyone from San Diego was a murderer or a liar."

"That's not far from the truth." Ben recalled how their whole philosophy had boiled down to the precepts from the *Sanko Sakusen* – the Three Alls Policy. Kill all, burn all, loot all. "But there were officers who tried to make a difference. Your mother was one of them."

"What about you?"

Akiko stepped outside with her gun arm aimed at Kujira's head.

"What's going on here?" she asked.

"Did you get enough sleep?" Ben asked.

"A few hours. Who's the kid?"

"That's the son of the friend we're looking for."

"Can he help us?"

"Why should I help you, lady?" Kujira asked, though he

lowered his weapon, prompting Akiko to do the same. "I don't even know you."

"You don't have to, of course. I brought the gift your mom wanted, which I guess was actually you." Ben took a portical out from an inner pocket in his coat. "A thousand of the latest portical games, action adventures, role-playing shooters, and simulation games."

Kujira jumped at the portical. "I've played all my games way too many times and I'm sick and tired of them, especially the old American ones. If I have to see James Leyton as Jesus Christ again, I'm going to nail myself up on those rocks." He was ecstatic.

"We'll have to find another way there," Ben said.

"What other options do we have?" Akiko asked.

"I don't know. You should have told me she was dead on the portical," Ben said to Kujira.

Kujira shrugged. "I didn't think you were actually going to come. At least you got here for the festivities, old man."

"They celebrate the anniversary here too?"

Kujira shook his head. "Bunch of George Washingtons got captured. Just arrived on the boat. Heard they tried to attack City Hall and failed. They're going to get stamped soon."

"Stamped?"

Kujira Jr knocked his head with his fist. "Tick tock," he said, and made a droning sound. "You ever seen the Telereformer?"

"No."

"Oh, you gotta see it. Very efficient, built seven years ago as the ultimate punishment by Commandant Hatanaka. He was a surgeon before he ran this prison. C'mon, I'll show ya."

"You got a cut too?"

Kujira removed the metal plate, latched it back on. "Easy to blend in. Soldiers leave me alone this way."

"How's the security here?"

"A joke. The guards hate it here too." Kujira handed them each metal plates. "Put them on your head."

Ben wore it like a helmet. Akiko did the same, though hers kept slipping off. Ben switched with hers as it was a better fit.

Kujira sprinted ahead.

"Is it safe to follow?" Akiko confirmed with Ben.

"I don't know," he answered. "I don't think we have a choice. All the time I knew Kujira, I never knew she had a son."

"Most of us barely know anything about those we serve with," Akiko replied.

Ben's muscles loosened as they progressed, though he stopped a few times to stretch achy tendons.

"Catalina used to be a naval base, right?" Akiko asked.

"Long time ago before they abandoned it in favor of the penal center. The island used to be an experimental facility where they built the prototypes for the second generation of mechas after the war ended. That's why the senior Kujira came here with a mecha she stole from San Diego. Said there were old parts she could use to fix up her own."

"This is a terrible place to die," Akiko said.

"I've seen worse."

They crossed through a valley and out the road from the mountains. Thousands of prisoners were clustered around a strange-looking device. It resembled a pagoda, but there were cogs forming a circumference around it as though its interior were exposed. Inside, there was a slab and above it, a jaw of spikes similar to a harrow, a sheath of blood masking it. An elderly soldier who'd shaved his head and was clad in a USJ uniform stood with a slouch. His mouth was agape as though it were hanging from his face. If his eyes weren't moving, he would have seemed as brainless as the others. He had the rank of commandant.

There was a line of manacled Americans. USJ soldiers stood guard and pushed the captives into the machine. One of the prisoners was strapped to the slab. The officer tapped some buttons. The group watched as the machine came to life. The parts sputtered awake and the needles began skipping rapidly. The pagoda voraciously devoured his scalp and incisions seared the flesh to cut it open. The prisoner was unconscious so he did not scream. The lobotomy was quick and only lasted a minute. The man was woken. He emerged with a plate on his head as a badge showing that his resistance had been erased. The next prisoner was forced into the Telereformer. The lobotomized prisoners appeared in awe of it, regarding the machine with reverence, stopping short of actually worshipping it.

Akiko marched forward. Ben asked, "Where are you going?"

"That's Martha Washington," she said.

Ben's eyes went to the bald American woman who had supervised Akiko's limb removal.

His mind began calculating. "This could work in our favor."

"What could work in our favor?" Kujira asked.

He tilted his head in the direction of the Telereformer. "That prisoner is one of the principal leaders of the George Washingtons."

"The terrorists that Mom fought?"

"The same group with different people now. If we take Martha with us, it could be insurance in San Diego if something goes wrong," Ben explained, then peered over at Akiko to gauge her reaction.

She gave no indication she had heard him, simmering in rage.

"Did you hear what I said?" Ben asked her.

"I heard," she said. "And it's not going to work because I'm going to kill her."

"Kill her after we get Mutsuraga," Ben said. "For now, we can use her." When Akiko did not respond, Ben said, "Agent Tsukino. Get a grip of yourself."

Akiko took a deep breath. Her face was still, but her brows and nasal folds dripped with hate.

"Remember what we talked about last night?" Ben reminded her.

"This is different."

"How?"

She gestured to her arms. "I'm going to do to her what she did to me, times ten."

"I'm not stopping you. I'm just asking you to hold off."

"And bring her along with us for her assistance?"

"Something like that."

"I don't even want to breathe the same air as her," Akiko snarled.

"You won't have to for long. Remember our mission."

Akiko glowered for a long time, rage making her eyes two cold obsidians. "If she tries anything, I will kill her on the spot."

Two soldiers noticed the commotion and looked in their direction. Fortunately, the loud noise from the Telereformer masked the brunt of their discussion. But they still approached to investigate. Kujira and Ben immediately acted dumb, their eyes wandering haphazardly. Akiko's prosthetic arms wavered. "You there!" a soldier yelled at Akiko. "Identify yourself!"

Akiko crumbled to the ground, tried to stand, and fell back down, face in the dirt. She mumbled random thoughts. The soldiers saw her metal helmet and returned to their posts where they lit up a cigarette and mocked the newly lobotomized GWs.

Ben was visibly relieved by her deception. But he blanched when he saw one of the prisoners, a male with big donkey teeth whose hair had grown out.

"What's wrong?" Akiko asked, standing up, wiping the dirt off her.

"I-I thought I recognized him."

"Do you?"

Ben shook his head a little too eagerly. "No. Or yes. Maybe."

"Who is he?"

"Used to serve with me. Got into trouble criticizing his superiors." He tried not to look the other in the face. "I think if you can pretend to be a Kempei officer on a surprise inspection, we can take Martha Washington away from them."

"What if they ask for authorization?"

Ben tapped his portical. "Let me arrange it. You mind pretending to be Tiffany Kaneko?"

Akiko marched to the soldiers without waiting for Ben's OK and barked, "This is what you call security?"

The guards raised their rifles. "Who are you?"

"My name is Tiffany Kaneko of the Kempeitai," Akiko lied. "I'm here to take that prisoner with me into custody. Ozawa!" she called and looked at Ben.

Ben sprinted forward, hastily working on the portical. "Yes, ma'am."

"How would you rate the security on the prison?"

"Pitiful," Ben answered in compliance with her tone.

"I will interrogate this one further," pointing to Martha Washington. "If she has anything useful to offer, I will return her. If not, I will dispose of her."

Ben created the fake orders to Avalon in case they queried about Agent Kaneko. He also replaced identifying photos of Tiffany with Akiko's so a visual check would sync up. There was no way this would get past an official checkpoint, but these guards didn't look like as though they would be as thorough.

"Do you have identification, ma'am?" a soldier asked.

"You have the nerve to ask me for an ID after I've penetrated your defenses?" Akiko snorted. "If I wasn't who I said I am, how would I have made my way here?"

"You could be a rebel," the soldier sheepishly suggested.

"What's your portical key?" Ben asked him.

The soldier gave him the ID and Ben sent over the fake

commands. The corporal examined the orders and bowed apologetically. "Forgive me, ma'am. Have the prisoner released into their custody."

The soldiers handed over a cuffed Martha Washington to Ben. She towered over him, though she was struggling to stand, bruised and hurt from her captivity at the hands of the Empire. Her clothes were torn and dirty, and he could see where the gunshots had left scars during San Diego. Akiko marched away and Ben followed, pulling Washington along. The commandant did not seem to have noticed, focused on managing the Telereformer.

"I thought you were going to San Diego," Martha said, when they were clear of the soldiers.

"Still am," Ben replied. "I'm surprised to see you alive."

"It's all part of the Empire's farce to put us on trial and send us to Catalina to be rehabilitated." She spat out a tooth and some blood. "I'm surprised to see *her* still standing." Ben was about to say something, but she stopped him. "What do you want?"

"Help us get Mutsuraga."

"What's in it for me?"

"We stop his lies and let you go afterwards," Ben lied.

Martha Washington didn't buy it, looking ahead to Akiko. "She agree to this too?"

"Yes," Ben said.

"I want to hear it from her."

Ben hesitated, and Martha took note of it. "Agent Tsukino," he called.

Agent Tsukino turned around.

"You agreed to the deal, right?" Ben confirmed. "Her life in exchange for her help."

Akiko did not hide her hostility. "It's as he said."

Martha Washington laughed. "Very convincing," she mocked her. "I don't want my death sentence deterred. And I have no interest in helping either of you. I'd rather go back there. Cleaner death that way."

"Let me put it a different way," Ben said. "You're our hostage. You don't have a choice."

"So I come along and you kill me the second you don't need me, right?" Martha Washington stated out the terms.

"You're right," Akiko jumped in, gun arm itching to be raised. Ben was about to stand in her way when Akiko continued, "I would have killed you earlier, but Captain Ishimura thinks you can be of assistance. That buys you a little time and hope."

"What good is hope?"

"You can hope we'll screw up and you'll have a small window where we're distracted enough so you can make your escape."

"Not much of a hope."

"Better than getting your brain lobotomized."

Akiko continued without them. Martha deliberated on it, then followed, though she was struggling to walk with her wounds.

Kujira was confounded and asked Martha Washington directly, "What did you do to them?"

"I stood up to the tyranny of the Empire and struck a blow for our cause," she answered proudly.

"America is dead," Kujira said. "Why waste your energy?"

"The spirit of America won't die until the last of us are killed. And then it'll live on as an ideal to resist the heresy of a man claiming to be a god. We believe all people are created equal and born with certain inalienable rights."

"Weird," Kujira noted.

"I know it seems weird to you. Your concept of the whole world is distorted, but you're too young to know otherwise."

"Mom told me you were all a bunch of fanatics who were nothing like the actual Americans."

Martha guffawed. "The first Americans were rebels fighting the odds."

"So are the last ones," Kujira replied.

Martha Washington tugged at her chains, resenting the restraints.

12:12pm

Ben wasn't confident his fabricated IDs would survive an authentication process and suggested Akiko and Kujira go ahead to scout the road, make sure there weren't any more guards. Ben stayed behind to escort Martha Washington. It wasn't a rigorous trek, but she stumbled climbing the hills. She refused his aid, insisting on walking on her own strength.

"I need a break," she said.

"We don't have time," Ben replied.

"Then go without me."

"You know I can't do that."

"If the other GWs even suspected I helped you, you know what they'd do to me?"

"The same thing you did to Agent Tsukino?" Ben speculated.

"Worse," Martha Washington said. "Even if I escaped, they'd never trust me. I wouldn't trust me if I were them."

Akiko marched towards them. "What's taking so long?" she demanded.

Ben gestured towards Martha. "She needs a break."

Akiko saw how exhausted Martha Washington appeared. "You have five minutes." To Ben, "The road's clear."

"I should have killed you," Martha Washington said, licking the blood off her lips.

Akiko turned around. "You should have. What stopped you?"

"Initially, your partner's pathetic pleas for your life. You'd have been moved if you saw the way he begged me to let you live."

Akiko looked to Ben for a denial, but he shrugged and said, "Sorry."

"That wasn't why I spared you," Martha said. "It was after both your arms were eaten and you were about to go unconscious. You started talking to Jenna. Remember her? She only helped us because her nephew was part of our group. Her dream was to perform in the Compton Opera House and you couldn't even give her that."

"I don't need to justify my actions to a traitor."

Martha Washington grinned and there was something sinister in it that made Ben jump in and ask, "Where's Kujira?"

"But that wasn't it either," Martha Washington continued. "It was when you started talking to your mother. Do you remember that?"

"No."

"You apologized for your brother. What was it you said? Something about failing your responsibility. You–"

Akiko swung her gun arm into Martha Washington's face.

Ben tried to stop her, but Akiko raised her cannon at him. "Get out of my face."

"She's baiting you."

"So what?"

"Remember our agreement?"

"I'm giving you three seconds to step away."

"She's unarmed," Ben said, scrounging for a defense. "You have to respect bushido."

"Bushido has no place here."

"Shut up!" Martha Washington yelled, spitting out blood. "Neither of you have any right to talk about honor. Your soldiers murdered my entire family while they slept. I got ten bullet holes in my body that night, one for each person that died. I used them to hunt each of their killers and I got them all. 'I only regret that I have but one life to lose for my country.'"

"She wants to die," Ben said. "You're giving her what she wants."

"I do want to die. But not as much as she does," Martha Washington said, leering at Akiko. "You should have heard the way she was groveling for her brothe–"

Akiko fired her gun at Martha's hand, burning the whole thing off, sinew and bones disintegrating. Martha howled in agony.

"Go wait with Kujira," Akiko warned and the truculence in her command brooked no dissent.

Ben forced himself down the hill where Kujira was returning.

"Something happen?" he asked.

They heard more gun blasts, more screaming. Kujira was about to sprint towards them, but Ben stopped him.

"What the hell is going on?"

Ben explained in brief, summarizing their past.

"And you're going to let it happen?" Kujira inquired.

"What would you do in her shoes? Besides, Martha Washington wants to die."

"Why would anyone want to die?"

Ben sighed. "Death is her only way out."

"No, it's not," Kujira said. "It's just the easiest."

"Death is never easy. Your mom used to say, honor is the only thing that separates us from animals."

"So what?"

"This is Martha Washington's way of trying to maintain her honor to her death."

"Honor is just a word people use to feel good about themselves," Kujira said.

Five gunshots echoed from behind them.

Akiko approached and said, "Let's go."

1:45pm

Kujira's home was southwest of the Telereformer in a hidden cove. Akiko washed her gun by the beach.

"Why do you need to get to San Diego?" Kujira asked.

"Long story," Ben said.

"You can tell me, old man."

"I have to kill an older man."

"What is with you two and killing?"

"I made a promise a long time ago to kill this man."

"Is he a bad person?"

Ben shook his head. "Not any worse than the rest of us."

"San Diego is guarded all around its perimeter."

"That's why I was hoping your mom could help. She was the best mecha pilot in the USJ and I know she has access to one."

"You think she would have helped you, knowing that you were going to go kill a man?"

"I wish I'd have had a chance to ask her."

Kujira took out his new portical and played some games on them. "What's this one called *USA*?"

"Brand new game that tells the Pacific War from the American side, assuming they'd won."

Kujira had already started playing it.

Ben left Kujira and went down to the beach. Akiko was scrubbing away the blood on her gun arm. The smell of salt wiped away everything else. The waves volleyed shells and pebbles towards the shore.

"Do you feel better?" Ben asked.

"Much," Akiko replied.

"What are you going to do if we bring back Mutsuraga's head and they don't reinstate you?"

"I would accept my death if that is the Emperor's will."

"I know you would. But how do you know that's what he wanted? We've never actually heard him directly."

"Officers represent his will by proxy."

"You're too smart to believe that."

"Even if I don't, I follow the structure."

"If you followed the structure, you would have been led to your death with those two Kempei agents."

She was irked by his comment. "Do you have a point?"

"What you just did—"

"Was for myself. Not for the Emperor. Myself."

"Martha Washington could have helped us."

"She was never part of the plan to begin with. We proceed the way we were going to."

"And all that stuff you said to me last night?"

"I meant it. But today is different. This is the woman who fed my arm to ants."

"You executed one of them in the first place."

"I was under orders. I didn't want to kill Jenna!" Akiko stridently insisted. Ben was surprised she called Jenna by her name. "I told them it was a waste, that she could be rehabilitated. But the orders were absolute."

"Even if her death was absolute, the way you killed her wasn't."

"Stop nagging me about details," Akiko said dismissively.

"These aren't details. You can't control yourself."

"I can. Like I said, this was a special exception."

"And next time when our mission is at risk and there's another special exception?"

"No one else fed me to ants."

Ben sighed. "I can't take you with me."

"You think you have a choice?" she asked, in a menacing tone. "'Oh, I don't like the way she's acting, so I'm going to leave her behind.'"

"Are you threatening me?" Ben asked back and his temper caught fire. "I'm sick and tired of your threats. You want to shoot me too? Go ahead." He grabbed her gun arm. "Shoot!"

Akiko flung him away. "Back off, Ishimura."

"I mean it. I'd rather die here than get shot in the back."

"You know what that woman did to me."

"There's more at stake here than just you and me."

"I understand that."

"Do you?" Ben asked.

"I do," Akiko said intently.

Ben was about to reply when the ground shook and there was a loud mechanical screech. The tremors increased in strength and a geyser burst from the ocean. A head shaped like a mechanical jaguar formed in the water. Though water was sliding down its face, the shape was unmistakable. A *Korosu* class mecha – or was it one of the older Torturer class machines? Ben knew the older ones had more square chest plates, limited artillery in the arms, and did not have the laser cannons the Korosus had. They were more durable though and handled sea combat better. Regardless of class, if it wanted it could annihilate everyone on the beach in under a minute. Like most mechas, the shoulders and body were painted red to mimic samurai armor. They even had sheaths for their electrically charged swords which could cut buildings as if they were stalks of corn. The crew usually resided in the head, one-sided mirrors as eyes shielding the bridge. It walked up the shore and stopped when only its lower legs were underwater. There was a throbbing sound, the head scanning the beach from one end to the other.

On the chest of the mecha, a hatch popped open.

Kujira approached them. "The *Musasabi*," he proudly stated.

"There's a pilot on the island?" Ben asked.

"You're looking at the world's best mecha pilot," Kujira boasted. "Do you think back in the USA, they really had it this good?" he asked.

"What do you mean?"

"The game says the Americans lived with freedom, could think or say whatever they wanted without fear of being arrested or killed."

"I think it's a bit romanticized," Ben said.

"Very romanticized," Akiko added.

"If enough people believed in that world now, we can have it," Kujira declared.

"Improbable," Ben replied.

"Before the Empire conquered half of the world, people thought the same about their chances of winning," Kujira said. "C'mon. I'll show you aboard my baby."

"You're willing to take us?"

"My mom told me she owed you a debt from a long time ago."

"That's her debt, not yours," Ben said.

"One and the same."

"Not to me. You don't owe me anything, Kujira. If you do this for me, I owe you."

Kujira lifted up his new portical. "Just send me new games every year or so and that'll be enough." He ran into the ocean and climbed up the ladder into the mecha.

Akiko said to Ben, "A lot of people owe you debts."

"I don't keep count."

"You really begged Martha Washington for my life?"

"If I did?"

"You're an idiot." Akiko tightened a lock on her gun arm. "You didn't bring me along because we're friends. You brought me because..." and she paused as she contemplated her words. "Because I can kill without hesitation or mercy. Let's finish this so we can both either go our own ways or die trying."

Ben's instincts were conflicted.

"Do I really have to justify myself to you?" Akiko asked. "She left me alive to humiliate me." She almost seemed penitent.

"No more threats," Ben stipulated.

Akiko grunted her assent.

Ben marched towards the mecha. "The chances of us surviving San Diego are slim."

"I know. Can he drive?"

"If he takes after his mother, yes."

"The *Musasabi* is way more advanced than any of the mechas I rode in San Diego and this bridge is actually comfortable to be in," Ben said.

"They're all like this now," Akiko said.

"You didn't see the old pits with pipes everywhere and steam blasting in our faces," Ben said.

The room was circular with Kujira at its center. Wires hooked into the muscles in his body, fine-tuned to match his nerve activity and amplify it. The stress of controlling the mecha took up so much of Kujira's attention, his bridge crew of wheeled porticals handled most other activities including the regulatory systems and maintenance. They rolled about, though they had rotors if they needed to fly, making sure everything was in place. Ben and Akiko sat in chairs adjacent to the radar station. It was the general's seat since it was a rare privilege for any officer to receive a mecha. The two chairs on either side were meant for aides. The *Musasabi* was in submersible mode, meaning it lay down horizontally in the water and became a boat with only the head rotating upwards to act as a submarine fin. Kujira was eating from a can of pineapples, resting while the portical circumnavigated the mecha through the ocean to San Diego.

"Good mecha pilots are always in demand in the USJ,"

Akiko said to Kujira. "Why didn't you join the military?"

"And be a lackey?" Kujira replied. "Kissing the asses of superiors for no credit? What's the point?" He flung the can at the ground after he'd emptied it. The circular portical swept in and cleaned it up. "I'm my own boss out here and don't have to toil away for idiots."

"You've never been in the military. It's very diffe–"

"My ma told me all the stories I need to know," Kujira said with a snicker. "You think we haven't made stops to the USJ? They're always trying to replace us, first with homunculi, which were worthless. Then with cheaper pilots. We visited a base up in Vancouver, bunch of fresh recruits, thinking they could pilot mechas. Most slaved away so they could become auxiliary crewmembers at best. The mechas up there are cheaply made, worth nothing against a real fighter. Prissy officers in charge who only care about their own careers and don't even give credit where it's due. Everyone just takes the abuse; yes sir yes sir yes sir thank you sir. Ma told me I could go back anytime I wanted. I'd rather eat my own barf." Kujira went back to controlling the mecha.

Akiko turned to Ben. "You agree with him?"

Ben shrugged. "Bureaucracy sucks."

"You can either use it, or let it use you."

"I wish I was a better user," Ben replied. "Cadre gave his mom leeway because she was such a good pilot. She told everyone exactly what she thought."

"What about you?"

"I kept my thoughts to myself," Ben said.

"Maybe that's why they didn't take you seriously."

"When I told my ranking officers what I really thought, it only got me into more trouble. You have better experiences with your commanding officers?"

"Even Tokko has bureaucracy and a ranking system based on seniority." Akiko watched a circular portical speed by. "I didn't like it. I was raised to believe only merit counted. My dad didn't care about anyone's background as long as they worked hard."

"He doesn't know you're in Tokko either?"

"Both my parents think I work in a business associated with the army diplomatic corps."

"Why do you hide it from them?"

Akiko's eyes narrowed. "To protect them and to make sure they don't worry about me." Her reply was too quick to be convincing. "My father's a strong believer in traditional bushido. He wakes up every morning and burns incense to the Emperor. He used to tell me stories at night about the Emperor's divinity, how he was born from the sun goddess, Amaterasu, and desires peace for all of humanity. My dad would never understand how some aspects of bushido don't work in a world like ours." Akiko's arms strained as she clutched the side of her seat and Ben could tell something was bothering her. "Do you think there's any way you can check if they're OK?"

"Sure," Ben said. "Can you give me their names?"

Akiko provided the information. He did a couple checks before confirming, "They're fine so far and I haven't seen any chatter about them."

She sighed in relief. "Thank you."

"If we succeed, you can return as a war hero and tell your parents what you really do."

"If we fail, they'll find out anyway in the worst way possible."

"Is there anyone in the world we don't have to lie to?"

Akiko thought for a second. "Ourselves."

"Most people still do."

"Most people still do," she confirmed.

3:14pm

Ben thought about Mutsuraga and the past, contemplating the personal vendetta that had shaped the course of not just a few individuals, but a whole society. How many wars had been fought for personal jealousies? How many massacres a result of individual circumstance?

"Hey, old man. We'll reach Coronado Island in ten minutes," called Kujira, while chewing dried fruits in his mouth. Coronado Island was just west of San Diego. Kujira started eating a pair of uncooked hot dogs and asked, "You two hungry? These turkey dogs are good."

Both Ben and Akiko assented. Ben found the sausage tasted like a rubbery boot that was still partly frozen.

"My grandfather loved these, fed them to me all the time, said they were good energy sources for piloting. I always wondered why they called them dogs when there isn't any dog meat in them."

"Your grandfather drove a mecha?" Ben asked.

"He piloted Zeroes in the Pacific War. Used to say when he'd go up in the air and see 'em American pilots, he'd know right away how good they were. Memorized the stars, told me you had to have eyes in the back of your head, and he even cut off the wood antennae on the plane so he'd gain an extra knot. I've made custom upgrades to my baby too and I usually know the level of a pilot as soon as I engage them. Ma and me used to spar off Catalina in the middle of the night."

"Spar?"

"Mecha spars. There's a bunch of older models stored at Catalina, tough as hell, built to last unlike those new pieces of shit. Some of her old pilot buddies would sail out and we'd have duels in the–"

The alarm suddenly went off and the mecha elevated quickly while simultaneously springing to its feet. They were close enough to shore that only half the body was submerged. Kujira was standing, all the wires hooked into his body humming. The navigational system corresponded to his direct motions and the transparent glass around him brought up the various scans and combat data.

"What's going on?" Kujira demanded.

"Eight bogeys," the portical answered in the artificially produced female voice of a senior Kujira. "Designation USJ."

"Whoa. This is off the charts. What's going on out here?" Kujira asked.

Ben stood up. "What's wrong?"

"I didn't know they had such a strong security grid off the coast. It looks like there's an army gathering on the perimeter and there's battleships too. I've been up and down this coast hundreds of times and never seen this much heat."

Neither had Ben.

"Who are you?" a voice blared on the communicator.

"Identify yourself," Kujira demanded back.

"This is General Itoh from the 15th. This area is considered strictly off limits. Who are you with?"

Through the glass screen in the eyes, Ben could see four mechas rise from the water. Behind them, four more approached. They were surrounding the *Musasabi* in a pincer formation. In San Diego, the mechas had gone unchallenged other than the biomorphs, which were impossible to control. Even kamikaze attacks by the USJ were futile as the mechas' thick armor plating made them impervious to anything but atomics. Seeing the goliath warriors striding to battle, Ben looked to Kujira. Akiko was staring at him too. Kujira showed no emotion and finished his hot dog.

"What you want me to do, old man?" he asked, food slobbering around his mouth.

"The 15th is Governor Ogasawara's personal battalion, right?" Ben asked.

"I've heard of Itoh," Akiko said. "She's supposed to be one of the best mecha pilots."

"We'll find out real soon if she's that good," Kujira said.

"What are your options?" Ben asked.

"Fight or run. Actually, scrap that. If we try to run, they'll destroy us."

"We can't fight eight mechas, can we?" Ben asked.

"Put your straps on," Kujira ordered.

Ben and Akiko complied.

The *Musasabi* placed both its mechanical arms over its head, propping the elbows forward like a spear. It spun in place, then charged the four stalking from behind. Those four quickly moved out of the way. The *Musasabi* didn't stop running, fleeing the eight. Taunting laughter rang over the communicator. "Have you no honor?" Itoh shouted, reveling in their act of cowardice.

The other mechas began pursuit.

"What are we doing?" Akiko asked.

"Running," Ben answered.

"Don't tell me this guy takes after your gaming strategy," Akiko groaned.

The *Musasabi* bolted through the water. Kujira chortled and said, "Follow me follow me follow me follow me follow me."

Gyrating stabilizers kept the bridge somewhat stable, though the dash through the ocean was rough on Ben who wasn't used to the frenetic jolt of the motion, even with the belt on. An island lay directly ahead of them. It was a labyrinthine construct, metallic anomalies protruding in errant piercings. In some ways, it resembled random paint strokes welded together. The whimsical patterns were connected only by their impressive height, meant to hide a mecha within. The whole bridge reeked of the smell of burning fuel, the internal organs in combustion.

"What is that?" Ben asked.

"Susano base, designed as a testing grounds for mechas," Kujira replied. "They checked locomotion and balance there. It was abandoned three years ago after budget cuts and news the Nazis were going to focus on Texas again."

Kujira drove the *Musasabi* into the entrance of the maze, which was narrow and only able to fit one mecha at a time. He veered left as soon as he entered and lurked right next to the entrance. The heat signature of three mechas drew close. As the first hostile mecha entered the maze, Kujira took out the electric sword, then smashed it into the chest plate of the one charging in. The force of the blow, combined with the speed of the other's charge, resulted in a loud boom, the impact forcing the mecha back. Ben knew if he hadn't been strapped in, the force would have flung him straight into the ceiling. Kujira raised his shoulder again and charged the mecha, forcing it to topple backwards into the mecha behind it. The mecha behind had its sword unsheathed, which then electrified the mecha falling into it. Kujira withdrew his sword, turned around, and dashed out of the way. An explosion severely damaged both mechas and impeded the path in. Smoke was swirling around them and fire consumed the armor.

"Egg juice!" Kujira demanded. The circular portical brought a tall cup that had a dozen egg yolks in it. Kujira downed it. "These Vancouver-trained drivers just aren't as good as the old timers."

He moved the *Musasabi* through the maze into several tower-like structures and lumbered up, each step causing the whole structure to shake. The finger joints latched onto orifices built into the spiral, nimble motions that would have crushed any organic thing with a push. One hundred meters up, Kujira looked through a one-sided opening that served as a vantage point for the entire island. A pillar of smoke obfuscated their view of the entrance, though four others were circling the base to try to find another way in.

Kujira sat and the wires around him shut down. "I'm going to take a nap. Wake me when they break through," he ordered the portical.

"How long before that happens?" Ben asked.

Kujira picked one of his teeth. "Fifteen minutes at least."

Kujira went to sleep.

Ben looked back out towards the entrance. Two mechas tried to batter the wall to no avail.

"What's going on?" Akiko asked.

"I think they have to blast their way through the damaged mechas blocking the entrance."

"But the crew..."

"It would take hours to carry out a rescue mission and remove them. They'll probably be sacrificed so they can get through quickly."

The porticals on the *Musasabi* were in high alert, continually checking the scanners. Kujira was snoring in his seat.

Mechas intentionally kept themselves off the electric kikkai in order to remain insulated against attempts to take over their controls. But Ben wondered what a simulation would predict given the parameters – one mecha against the six that remained.

"Is it OK to sleep like that?"

"All of them do it," Ben said. "It's to rest their nerves since they never know when the next bit of sleep will come. I've heard stories of pilots who lost their brains because they stayed up a week straight hooked into their mecha."

Kujira was enjoying his sleep, spit dribbling onto his shoulder.

A bright explosion resulted in a pillar of smoke.

"The mechas are destroyed," the portical alerted him.

Kujira blinked. Looked up at the scans, checking the heat signatures.

"Sixteen suckers dead because their pack leader doesn't know basic tactics."

One by one, the six remaining mechas pounded through the corpses of the two dead ones. No one mourned the machines.

Kujira shook his head giddily. "Let's dance, let's dance, one-one-two-four, one-one-three-four."

The *Musasabi* released its clutch on the tower and plummeted straight down, landing gracefully on its feet despite leaving a crater. It charged its sword and plunged it into the ground. The sword didn't break through at first and Kujira maintained the thrust with both hands on the hilt, pushing with all the mecha's strength. It was like cutting a mountain with a knife, only with six death machines heading their way.

"What are you doing?" Akiko asked.

"The core stabilizer is directly underneath. If that goes, the whole island will sink," Kujira explained.

Do we want that? Ishimura was about to ask, but thought better of it.

The *Musasabi* lifted its left arm up. The fingers rotated down and eight plates in the knuckles opened. A cannon emerged from the orifice and charged up its magnetic pulse before unleashing a stream of bullets that pummeled the ground. The surface gave way and cracks fissured apart. Kujira lifted the sword up with his right arm and thrust it back in, breaking open the ground.

"Come on, come on, come on," Kujira exhorted, rapidly shaking his hands.

The *Musasabi* broke through to the core and ruptured it. The whole island quavered, shook, then began to sink. The ground swelled with seawater.

"Should I activate autobalancing?" the main portical asked as a cautionary measure.

"Daft, it is," Kujira said. "Do we look like amateurs? Let those simulation trained monkeys activate theirs. We'll break them apart and they won't even be able to react."

"What's he talking about?" Akiko asked.

Ben thought about it for a minute. "The autobalancing system means motion is compensated for. If there's a sudden movement, like an attack, it'll react opposite to what the pilot wants."

"Don't they know that?"

"From what I've heard, most of the new mecha trainees from Vancouver are on a cheaper budget and trained on simulation cores. No real combat experience so the USJ can save money. Command thinks piloting is easy to outsource."

"They all accept lies as truths," Kujira said, "because they're cowards. No one fights mass madness. Even the old-timers were too afraid to fight for their own rights."

The other mechas looked similar to the *Musasabi*. But General Itoh's personal mecha was a quarter bigger, crimson shoulder pads, a lavender titanium plume above its helmet. There were curved spikes on both arms and additional armaments on its girdle. Its hand was pitch black and made it appear as though it were wearing leather gloves.

Itoh's voice came over the communicator. "I don't know who you are, but if you don't power down immediately, I am going to personally rip that piece of lard apart and melt each piece for scrap parts."

Kujira giggled back. "You can try, Itoh," he said and shut off the communicator.

Itoh split the mechas into three groups of two, dividing them so they could attack from three different angles on Kujira's central position. Ben thought Kujira would withdraw, try to find a more easily defensible point. But the *Musasabi* remained still, or as still as could be, considering the whole island was shaking and dropping into the water. The sea had risen to knee level. Kujira shook the controls continually to maintain balance, adjusting, compensating, tweaking, similar to a circus tightrope act. The island's descent wasn't a slow, level one, but a spurring gallop, dropping on a slope before jolting back up and tilting the other way. The smell of fuel and seawater intensified, a pungency exacerbated by the sweat in Ben's nostrils. He gripped his belt when the shaking increased. It took a strenuous effort just for the *Musasabi* to stay in place.

The first of the smaller mechas charged at the *Musasabi* with a spear. At the same time, another attacked from the right flank using an electric sword in a two-pronged strike. Kujira blocked the sword with the *Musasabi*'s sword and simultaneously managed to grab the spear coming at him from the other side. He then swung the spear towards the other mecha. Three turrets on his chest unleashed a torrent of bullets at the cooling vents on the opposing mecha who would not release the spear. The vents were seared shut, and seconds later, the hydraulic adjusters on its spine ceased motion. Kujira lifted his right foot and slammed it into the chest of the opponent with the sword, knocking him back. But the balancing adjustors prevented its legs from falling as it normally would, causing the top of its body to whiplash back in comedic fashion. The machine resembled a contortionist. The *Musasabi* pointed its sword in place for when the mecha would auto-balance itself into place, committing a *seppuku* of sorts as it regained its stance. Sure enough, the mecha impaled itself on the *Musasabi*'s sword. The central generator's auto-balancing system forced it to get back into its position, even if that meant destroying its hull on the edge of the enemy blade. The one with the spear had limited mobility as it scrambled to get a worker crew down into the spine hydraulics. They did not have much time, but just as the *Musasabi* was about to deliver its death blow, another mecha struck from behind.

Kujira's motions were so rapid, Ben thought it was a portical film on speed run. His face was focused, though there was unmistakable glee. The battlefield was Kujira's canvas. A mecha with enormous fists landed an uppercut into the *Musasabi*'s left chest, disrupting the circuitry on the left hip. The *Musasabi* nearly reeled over to the side, managing at the last second to use boosters to soften its fall and align itself with the wall. As the *Musasabi* stood back up, Itoh's personal mecha, the *Mangusu*, flung a morning star in its direction. The chain whipped around the *Musasabi*'s arm squeezed, then tore it in half. The whole limb from the elbow dropped off. Emergency alarms were blaring red on the bridge.

"Shut those off!" Kujira ordered the portical. "Hey, old man."

"Yes?" Ben asked.

"You and your partner need to get to the escape pod."

"Why?"

"San Diego isn't that far and I'm going to do something risky. If it fails, she's going to blow. I can only stall for a minute."

"What about you?"

"I'm not going to leave," Kujira said.

"You said if it fails, the mecha'll blow up."

"So what?"

"You'll die."

"Better to die here than out there. This is my ma's gift to me. I can't leave her."

"But–"

"You have thirty seconds."

Ben bowed to him. "Find a way to survive."

"Don't worry. If I go down, I'm taking all of them with me."

Akiko and him ran for the escape pod, a tubular pod with two seats. They put on their seat belts and pushed the lever.

The rockets on the pod ejected them towards San Diego. Ben looked behind and saw that the neck of Kujira's mecha had opened and a cannon emerged. A bright beam of red fired at its opponent, blowing the head off the *Mangusu*. The escape pod flew for two minutes before a parachute sprang out from the rear and softened their descent.

5:53pm

"San Diego-Tijuana used to be one of the most thriving cities in the USJ," Ben explained. "Millions of people used to come here for leisure."

They exited the escape pod and all either of them could see was dirt and the occasional ruins. There weren't any trees, no floral life. It looked as devastated as Catalina, only with broken jalopies and crumbling walls.

"How far are we from the actual city?" Akiko asked, covered in sweat, her face wan.

Even for Ben who'd seen the city being destroyed, he couldn't hide his shock. "I don't know. The Empire hasn't used atomics here, so I don't understand why it looks so bad."

"Probably a combination of aerial bombing campaigns and shock troops razing anything anti-USJ. The Wall around San Diego prevented activity from springing back up," Akiko conjectured.

"There used to be houses, buildings, museums, pretty much whatever you can imagine stretching from here to way up north to Los Angeles." His eyes drifted to a fossilized past.

Akiko injected herself with a steroidal enhancer and the physical relief it provided was apparent as her mien gained color again.

"Are those safe?" Ben asked.

"Temporarily, but I only have a few left. What's the plan?"

Ben became quiet as he looked back at the desert. "I'd hoped we were going to have the mecha take us directly to where we could find Mutsuraga."

"Where is Mutsuraga?"

"He's with the Congress." Ben lifted up his portical. "When I gave Martha Washington our access codes, I stole all the information on her portical. I have details on almost everyone there."

"What do we do now?"

"I don't know. I don't know..." He took out his portical and input new commands. He sighed several times, frustrated. "We can't have come this far to be stopped now. I didn't plan for this in my simulation."

"You simulated this whole thing?"

"I always simulate everything. We were supposed to get to Congress with the mecha, then force them to talk. I would get Mutsuraga and return afterwards. Since the GWs don't have a mecha, my success rate was seventy-eight percent. But now, I have no idea. Damn, damn, damn. I need new data for the new variables." He tried putting in new commands again, but that angered him more. "I don't have updated area maps for San Diego. This is ridiculous. I can't believe we're just stuck out here. How could I be so stupid? Why didn't I prepare for a possible mecha contingency from the USJ? The–"

"Calm down."

"I am calm."

"You don't seem calm."

"I don't know what to do."

"Have you heard of improvising?" Akiko asked.

"I tried putting in new parameters."

"Try without your portical," Akiko stated.

"How? Human calculations are imprecise and prone to error."

"What about if you go to one of their guards and demand

to see Mutsuraga?" Akiko suggested.

"I would if I could find one. Right now, I have no idea where we are in relation to the Congress."

"The GWs must have seen this pod land. They'll send someone to investigate."

"How can you be so sure?"

Akiko was looking through the scope on her gun arm and saw the traces of a car in the distance. "Call it a hunch. Do you have a heat scanner on your portical?"

"I do."

"Check it for vehicles."

Ben examined the scanner and saw heat signatures on his portical, which he identified as automobiles. "Are those Americans?"

"Who else would be on this side of the Wall?" Akiko said back. "Is there any way I can track you?"

"Why?"

"Reason with them, try to get them to take you to Mutsuraga. I'll bust you out later."

Ben checked his portical again. "How would you get to me?"

She pointed at the four jalopies. "Those are gasoline cars. My dad used to work on them so I know my way around the engine. You find Mutsuraga and, when the time's right, I'll come for you."

"But–"

"We don't have time to debate this. Either go with my plan, or we wait for the Americans and do our best to capture one and kill the rest."

When Ben continued to hesitate, Akiko said, "I'll hide in those cars. How do I track you?"

Ben handed her a portical. "This'll have my coordinates."

"Don't you need a portical?"

"I always carry a few spares. There's a digital key in there too. It might actually be able to start the older cars."

Akiko asked Ben in a serious tone, "Will you be able to handle yourself?"

"It doesn't seem like I have a choice."

"Ishimura," she said, in a more empathic voice. "This isn't a simulation. If I'm not with you to kill–"

"I can defend myself."

"But if you run across the GWs and they get hostile–"

"You worried I can't defend myself?"

"I'm worried you can't kill."

Ben's brows crinkled. "The day I reported my parents, they shot themselves. The soldiers cut off both their heads and showcased them publicly... Every time I tried to cut that prisoner's head off during officer's training, that memory kept on coming back to me. Don't worry. I can kill if I need to."

Akiko's eyes went soft. "I won't be far behind," she said.

"Thank you."

She hid just as the old military jeeps arrived. The Americans smelled as though they hadn't washed in weeks. While different ethnicities in a group wasn't uncommon, it felt strange for Ben to see so few Japanese among them. Most of their clothes were old, sewed and stitched together with whatever was available. Half of the Americans had shaved their heads and some wore the iconic white wigs the GWs were known for.

"Where do you think you're going?" an American asked. He was the same height as Ben and he wore a khaki dress and a baseball cap. The man's nose was obnoxiously big and his eyes bulged like a bug.

"I'm here to see General Mutsuraga," Ben answered.

"Who's that?"

"He's the man who designed the *USA* game. Martha Washington told me he was with the George Washingtons."

"Where are you from?"

"I escaped the USJ forces after they attacked me."

"Do you have a name?"

"Beniko Ishimura. Mutsuraga will know me."

They debated what they should do. Ben did his best not to look in Akiko's direction. Eventually, he heard someone say, "He's the one Martha messaged us about."

"You sure?"

"She told us someone was coming our way before she got caught."

He was given a seat in the back of the jeep.

6:39pm

It took twenty minutes of driving to reach a road full of decimated buildings. Throngs of impoverished Americans surrounded oil cans and formed globules of activity that seemed to vanish whenever he turned his head. Most of the walls had graffiti of words he didn't recognize. The city was divided into square structures that were essentially makeshift shacks, designed without any regards to aesthetics. Streets split up the blocks in asymmetrical clumps and there were occasionally bigger buildings, like the one that resembled a Shinto shrine and another that was identical to the high school he attended, though both were in shambles. Out in front of the school, three USJ soldiers had been hung. Two were Asian men. The left one even resembled Ben, despite his hands and feet having been chopped off. The final one was a woman wearing a bloodied uniform. She looked more like a wax statue than someone who had once served the Empire. Their bodies were still fresh as they twirled in place.

They crossed a broken through truss bridge. Piles of gravel begged for attention, but were ignored. Grain elevators and storage bins that hadn't been used in years littered the geography, while grass built up bivouacs against penstocks that only carried air and blood. The Americans stopped in front of a four-story building. Scaffolding attempted to hide

331

old antiaircraft missile launchers and artillery cannons that were placed inside the glassless windows. The weapons had been purloined from the USJ a decade ago and set up to defend against enemy attacks, older models with minimal security against kikkai incursions. He opened up his portical to see if he could access the control systems for the missile launchers.

"What are you doing?" one of the Americans asked.

"Checking the weather," Ben answered. Surprisingly, they did not try to stop him. "Where are you taking me?"

"Congress."

A pregnant woman breastfed her baby while she played the *USA* game on her portical. Five teens were advising each other on how best to defeat more Japanese soldiers. A row of strangers competed in a *USA* match against one another. Many of the Americans gave in to the invisible portical leashes that tied them to the alternate history in which they were the victors of a land of liberty and freedom.

The hall of Congress was a dilapidated room with the sheen of respectability. There were no decorations, no designs to reveal their identities aside from a big American flag. A group of a hundred sat in a circle, holding hands, praying out loud in a chant. They were mourning someone and the chaotic jumble of their words formed a jarring choir that veered between eulogy and paean. The poetry of their religion was tempered by a hope emerging from the riptide of circumstance. There were empty caskets that represented their fallen brethren. Ben knew their leaders were named after historical personages. Whenever one fell, another would replace them. This George Washington, the tenth Washington so far since the conflict a decade ago, was a black man who had lost his right leg in a mining accident in La Jolla (if Ben remembered the reports correctly). He had broody eyes and a rigid jaw from the time it was stitched back after he'd been beaten to a pulp by the USJ. Underneath the mask of suffering was a shrewdness that regarded Ben with a mix of curiosity and suspicion. Next to Washington was someone he assumed was Abraham Lincoln, part of their "Congress." He wore a mask to help him breathe after one of his lungs had been shattered in a poison attack – they said he hunted down the soldiers who'd done this to him, carved out their lungs, and put them into jars he kept as souvenirs.

"Jesus Christ died on the cross for you," George Washington preached. "And almost two thousand years later, Yillah, the daughter of Christ, came to rescue us from our iniquities. The promised rapture happened. Jesus came back and saved those who trusted in Him. The world fell into despair without God. The Axis exploited the world God had abandoned. Billions were murdered. Looting was rampant. We were fallen. But because He was merciful, because He did not want those left behind to be given so hopelessly to the enemy, He sent Yillah to lead us back, to give us a chance at a second salvation. She was an American who promised us deliverance from the tyranny of the Axis Alliance, but only if we trusted in God. We must believe in Her so that our souls can be delivered from the hellfire of existence. If we believe, if we have faith, we can receive salvation, a Third Coming, Jesus and Yillah together. For God is both man and woman, human and deity. Our Lord teaches us that faith transcends history, gender, race, culture, even death."

He pointed to his missing leg. "After I lost my leg, I thought for certain I was dead. The Empire brutalized me, beat me, did everything they could to wipe away any trace of my humanity. But I clutched to my faith. I cried out to Yillah for succor. She was by my side; she wiped away my pain. And later, when I was rescued, and shortly after that had my captors at my mercy, I prayed for them. A prayer of forgiveness before I executed them. 'Turn your cheek' only works with physical slaps, only works pre-Second Coming. Against guns, bombs, and the most inhuman practices ever conceived, we must protect ourselves. We must become the agents of God's vengeance. Yillah was not like Christ, allowing herself to be murdered. She conceived of..."

Even as he spoke, George Washington's eye turned to Ben with a compassionate, inviting look. Abraham Lincoln was taking long draughts from his mask, struggling to breathe. So many of the American faces were unctuous, foreign, and hostile.

"Do you know what the most important line in the Bible is?" George Washington suddenly asked Ben.

Everyone turned their heads in his direction.

Ben shrugged. "No idea."

"'Jesus wept.' Two words. So simple. It came right after his close friend, Lazarus, died and He saw everyone around him mourning. It was a symbolic moment, the metamorphosis of a God who had evolved from a cruel creator with no idea how much His creation was suffering, to a God incarnated as a man, filled with empathy and sorrow for the plight of humanity. Regardless of your background, your past beliefs, your worst sins, that line represents the struggle all of us face. It is the trinity within every individual, the contradictory capacity to be creator, destroyer, and savior. It is also the acknowledgment that, in making a choice, someone will suffer. If Jesus hadn't delayed, Lazarus wouldn't have died. I don't hate the United States of Japan. I sympathize, even as I fight you." Ben had no care for religion and listened dubiously, wondering why George Washington wasted his time lecturing him. "I know you don't believe in God, but I would appreciate if you would pray with us."

"My god lives in Tokyo," Ben said.

"Your god wants you dead. My God wants salvation and blessings for you." He closed his eyes and bowed his head. "Dear Father and Mother in Heaven, we thank you for bringing us these pilgrims safely and we praise you for..."

As the Americans prayed, Ben was surprised that they

appeared so sincere, so yearning, so eager for salvation. This George Washington truly believed he was in some kind of communion with a supernatural being, simply by speaking. It reminded him of Claire. Ben did not even believe in the *Tenno* – the Heavenly Sovereign Emperor. But he didn't have any more faith in the American's God who was murdered by Romans thousands of years ago and, more recently, Yillah at the hands of the Nazis. He knew that the individual George Washington leaders had ordered the deaths of countless of his compatriots.

"In Jesus and Yillah's name we pray, amen," George Washington concluded. "This is a day of mourning and celebration for us. Why are you here?"

The hostility was palpable. "I'm looking for General Mutsuraga," Ben replied.

"On the anniversary of our great defeat, you seek the one who gives us hope, a dream of a world in which the conquerors were turned back. Why don't you join us? Surely our message can appeal to you. Believe in the Father, the Son, the Daughter, and the Holy Spirit, and you will have salvation. After your blasphemous *yaoyorozu no kami*," which was a Shinto collective of eight million, or many, gods, "four seems easy in comparison, doesn't it? Four that actually care about you."

Ben had heard the idea before of the four distinct but identical beings

"There is only one God. Like water that's vapor, ice, and liquid," George Washington explicated. "The forms are different, but the base molecules are the same."

"If I became an ice cube or vapor, I'd be dead."

"That's why you need faith to help your disbelief."

"Faith in an ice cube doesn't sound that reassuring."

Washington had a pitying expression. "Do you always question everything?"

"Why would a god sacrifice her life if she was God? Just

show real power and send an army of angels and there'd be
no debate."

"Jesus and Yillah showed they were superior to the world
by dying for it."

"Doesn't sound so superior," Ben commented.

"The word 'samurai' comes from the character, *saburau* –
to serve," George Washington said. "Sacrifice is the ultimate
form of service, the ultimate transcending act."

"Sacrifice and service haven't done much good for your
cause."

"How would you know?"

"Because your attempt at 'sacrifice' failed," Ben said.
"Martha Washington was taken captive."

"So I've heard," George Washington replied. "But are you
sure we've failed? How would you know when you don't
even understand sacrifice or service? The salvation of one
soul is just as precious as any military victory. I ask you again:
will you join our cause and serve?"

"Let me talk to Mutsuraga and I'll consider it."

George Washington laughed. "We value freedom, and we
give people the opportunity to choose the right path. You've
made your choice. The light entered the world, and you, like
the rest of humanity, loved the darkness." Washington and
his assembly stood up and began to leave.

Ben was about to follow Washington when two Americans
seized him and forced him down into a chair. They stripped
him of his portical and ripped off his boots. Another of the
Americans brought a bowl of water and a cart with a machine
on top that looked like a defibrillator. Washington had
vanished, but Lincoln lumbered over to him.

"Jesus washed the feet of His disciples. Yillah did so too,
as she found it an effective way to transform her enemies,"
Lincoln said. "Purify their hearts and bodies."

The Americans dipped his feet in water and washed his
toes with rubber gloves on. Ben hated the sight of his toes, a

gangly, alien set of nubs.

One of the Americans put a charged wire into the water.

Electric bolts seized Ben's entire body. His cells sent out millions of warning signs to the metropolises within. The civilizations were in denial about the legions of volts racing a marathon through them. Ben could feel the nerves trying to placate their followers, the dendrites and axons sending prophetic messages of doom, ignored in the malaise of exorbitance. The pain wasn't overt, but a searing miasma paralyzed him. He felt like a jet blasting off into a hurricane to get sucked into a vortex and splattering into a million C-sections of nirvana. As suddenly as it came, it stopped.

"That's the first setting," Lincoln said.

"What do you want?"

Lincoln frowned. "There's nothing I want. Nothing you can give other than to God almighty. Ready yourself."

The second setting was much more painful. Ben thought the veins from his neck would spurt out, his head screaming in pain. He wanted to faint, but heard a rant in the form of pulsating migraines. The voices were enthralling, noises sloshing above him that made him think of exhausted rats committing suicide. He saw lightning leaves growing out of his arms, tree bark covering his fingers with sparks. He was immobile and his ribs were decaying from bacteria of discontent, nibbling on his cartilage to feed their insatiable appetite. His cells dissolved into a photon cycle that gave them a home to consume until the next portable body was in place. The electricity intensified. The water gargled and he could smell his skin burning. He recognized the malodorous scent from San Diego, a potpourri of gasoline and crisp meat. There'd been so many charred bodies there. His tongue was scorched and his throbs were a blaring whisper, more vociferous than reverberating echoes. His torment was an inflamed affliction ascending into the stratosphere of an abscess that vomited pus in the shape of grapes. The grape turned into the head of a young Claire Mutsuraga.

"You should have told me," she said, the complex five-rig portical she'd used to break all the classified reports next to her.

"How could I?"

"We'll all burn in hell for this," she said.

"If there is a hell."

"I didn't know my father caused this."

"It's more complicated than that."

"Is it? We're all guilty of someone else's sins until they become our own. Then we try to pass it off, but I won't do that anymore."

"You can't be serious about making this game–"

"Will you help me?"

"How could I help?"

"Let's use the simulation and set new parameters. If I did it myself, it would take too long. If we work together, we can remind the Americans how close they were to winning."

Claire, with her pony-tailed hair and her sandy skin, her caramel eyes that melted away into the dissipation of anguish. She was the reverse Mutsuraga, a woman who mocked and satirized the absurdities of contemporary civility, scoffing at the rituals that made men men and women women.

The volts stopped. The Americans were laving his legs, his arms, and his face.

"Four decades ago, our fathers and mothers fought to keep on this continent a nation conceived in liberty, and dedicated to the proposition that all are created equal. You destroyed that. Yillah always pointed out, Saul was our faith's greatest enemy until he was blinded and became Paul. The persecutor, the executioner, and murderer of everyone connected to our faith became our greatest proselytizer and proponent," Lincoln said. "Isn't that a strange irony? Prepare to be blinded."

The electricity ravaged him, stretching out the aches in his body that were dying hundreds of cells at a time, predigested in frozen bits and pieces, warehoused and packaged into caskets. The minutes and years and seconds were excised into pieces of chalk and exhaust pipes that failed to pass through the ravages of age. Division of the ritualized itinerary of the persecuted. It was a sandbox devoted to the minutiae of agony, where the ruler and abacus reigned as the emperor and empress of an antiquity in some misbegotten golden age of misery, stacks of spiraling uncertainty as implacable as a pillaged mausoleum. Ben knew he couldn't die. Not yet. Not without keeping his promise to Claire. Her faith was a million firecrackers stuffed into one big explosive setting off at once even though there wasn't a special occasion, her presence being cause enough. She channeled her beliefs into the game.

"I'm as guilty as my father," Claire had said. "I have to die."

"How are you guilty? You did nothing wrong."

"Even after I found out the truth, I didn't do anything to bring justice for Mom."

"None of us did. We're the ones who are guilty."

"If you read half the things I uncovered about San Diego," Claire said, "you would not be able to sleep."

"That's why I choose not to read most of it," Ben admitted. "This game is bigger than that."

"Is it? No one'll even play it."

"I'll make sure it gets out there," Ben assured her. "I'll put it in every game I censor and, since I've approved them already, no one else is going to check them until it's too late."

"What's going to happen the morning the Tokko comes knocking on your door?"

Ben uneasily touched his wrist. "I'll pray to your Christian God and get my poison capsule ready."

"Not funny."

"I'm not joking. Besides, they'll most likely blame your father."

"He's going to be furious. All he cares about is his legacy."

"This'll end it."

"Not completely," Claire said. "I'll make sure I'm the last of his line."

"You don–"

She stopped him. "What about my father?"

"What about him?"

"You have to deal with him after I die."

"What do you mean?" he asked.

"You know what I mean. Promise me."

"I'll never promise that."

"Ben."

"Forget it."

"Ben! Promise me."

"He's your father and my sempai. How can you even a…" But before he finished his question, he knew the answer. "This is unfair of you." At the same time, he did not want her guilty of her father's death.

"You'll do it?" she asked, even though from the way she looked at him, she knew she already had her answer.

Was it his resentment at having been forced to agree to do the unthinkable that had led to all their ensuing arguments? Shortly after, she told him she was leaving Los Angeles and they never talked again.

The currents increased. His body felt like an earthquake with the epicenter at his feet. It was a constant trembling that triggered fibrillations in his heart as well as delusions. There was a point where pain stopped hurting and became a condition, where the aching became a drug. He swore he was at a carnival and that the voltages were invoking memories. The alternating currents were ripping Lichtenberg figures in his calves, muscular contractions brainwashed by the insurrection of neuropathy. Someone pulled the plug.

8:46pm

Ben felt like a crumpled wrap. It took a few calls from the voice above to wake him.

"Wake up, Ishimura."

"G-general?"

"Odd to meet again under these circumstances," Mutsuraga said, in his deep commanding voice. "You don't look so good."

"You look old, sir," Ben replied.

"I wanted to see you before they killed you."

Ben was strapped into his chair. They'd removed the bowl of water and no one else was in the Congressional hall. Mutsuraga still looked like a bear, only one that was older and more domineering. His brows were gray and he wore the chimera-like clothing of all the Americans, rather than the uniform Ben was accustomed to seeing him in. He still had his traditional samurai sword though and the sheath was meticulously pristine.

"Why are you here?"

"You should know, sir," Ben said, feeling tired, anger giving him a second wind.

"I'm no longer your commanding officer, Ishimura. Did you take care of Claire's funeral rites?"

"You're acting like you're the savior here, when you're the one who caused all this to happen in the first place."

"San Diego was going to happen, regardless of what I did. Tokyo Command could not accept sedition of that kind."

"Your personal jealousy gave them the excuse to wipe out the city."

"This city was doomed before I was ever here. Tokyo Command wanted to make an example out of them to show the Nazis we meant business," the general said.

"The Nazis?"

"Don't you view your own simulations? The Nazis have wanted to take over the western half of the Americas, especially Texas, for the oil lines. The Empire needed Texas, even if it was only to prevent the Germans from getting their hands on all that fuel. The Nazis wanted to see how we'd handle San Diego. If we would have let it spiral out of control, they would have known we were weak."

"Funny you still refer to the Empire as *we*."

"You always were a smart ass."

"Is that what you call people who make smart observations?" Ben asked.

"It's what I call people who make pointless observations to make themselves feel smart."

"What do you call people who are responsible for the massacre of an entire city?"

"You're calling me responsible?"

"You knew how volatile things were," Ben stated. "Did you think the George Washingtons could blindly accept the death of one of their leaders?"

"You and Wakana insist I did what no man could fathom. This is my wife you're talking about."

"I was there when it happened."

"So was I," Mutsuraga said.

"You want to deny responsibility, fine. But I know what really happened. This farce disgusts me."

"Not so shy with your words anymore, are you?"

"I kissed your ass back then because I had no choice,"

Ben said honestly.

"I gave you an opportunity that you wouldn't have had otherwise. You took it voluntarily."

"I didn't know what kind of man you were."

"You wanted to see your game out there," Mutsuraga said stridently. "You got it."

"And I assisted a madman take the reins."

"Now I'm a madman?"

"You're hiding with the same people you helped destroy."

"The Empire can't last forever," Mutsuraga stated. "This is a perfect base of operations for the Americans and I can help them."

"Wakana had a potential compromise for them ten years ago when it would have mattered."

"Why didn't you object then? Why didn't you expose me when you had the chance?"

"I've asked myself that question every day since," Ben said.

"Wakana was smart. He kept his mouth shut. You were too. Got you a comfortable job, didn't it?"

"Couldn't you have waited until after the compromise?"

"To know the woman I loved betrayed me for one of them." Mutsuraga became meditative. "She used to sing every night. I was so consumed by my work, I got annoyed and told her to be quiet. I should have listened to her more back then."

"Are you looking for redemption?"

"I had no idea things would turn out the way they did," the general said.

"You wanted as many of them to suffer as possible," Ben accused him. "You made sure of it."

"What did you do to my game?" Mutsuraga asked.

"It's not your game," Ben said, before coughing blood on his chest.

"You set it up. I'll give you that. But since then I've changed it, molded it in my image. I've created new worlds, designed games that have taken gamers to places they could never imagine. That abomination you've created, the *USA* that everyone is saying I did – is that your revenge?"

"Why do you think it was me who did it?"

"You think I wouldn't recognize your handiwork? Your utopian vision of what America was. You paint a world that never existed. America, land of the brave and the free? Hardly. They arrested loyal Japanese because of their race and, when the war started going bad for them, they tortured tens of thousands of people, executed a quarter of those in the camps. You give people a false dream through the *USA*."

"And you gave them the worst massacre in their history."

"I will pay for what I've done. I've already had everything taken away from me."

"I doubt that."

"That game has spread everywhere and the Empire thinks I made it. I had to leave everything behind to come here."

"It was your daughter who designed the game."

"What?"

"Claire created the *USA*."

Mutsuraga glowered incredulously. "H-how's that possible? Why did she make it?"

"Atonement for her father's sins."

Mutsuraga flinched. "She knew about Meredith?"

Ben noticed the admission by implication even if the general didn't. "She's a genius at the portical. Of course she knew. She found out everything she could about the case and demanded the rest from me."

"You told her?"

"She already knew," Ben replied.

"But you confirmed it?"

"Yes."

"And you helped her make the game?"

Ben didn't feel the need to reply to the obvious. Mutsuraga's hands were behind his back as he paced. Ben took deep breaths because his migraine was getting worse and it was hard for him to focus.

"All this time I thought it was you," the general said. "The *USA* has all your marks, which, to be honest, surprised me. I thought you the most loyal soldier, that you would die for the Empire. But Claire – I never would have suspected she harbored so much anger and discontent, or that she was so naive."

"She believed in something. Unlike you, using your power for personal vendetta."

"I entrusted her to you because I had to send her away and you were the only person *she* trusted. I thought you could take good care of her."

"I tried, but she was too much like her father."

"What do you mean?" he asked.

"Impossible to anticipate."

Mutsuraga grunted, though Ben didn't know if it was acknowledgment or annoyance. "You shouldn't have helped her make it."

"If I hadn't helped her, she would have been arrested long ago and put to death."

"Did you love her?" he wanted to know.

"I acted as her custodian," Ben said. "And honored her wishes as my senpai's daughter."

"There was nothing be–"

"Nothing," Ben immediately affirmed. "You shouldn't even have to ask. I would never betray your trust that way."

"I heard rumors."

"You heard wrong. I loved her as a sister. She had boyfriends and I made sure they treated her well."

"I'm sorry that I brought this up."

Ben tested the rope that held him in place, but it was too tight. "One illicit relationship already caused too much death and destruction."

"We were going to fight that war to the bitter end whether I was there or not."

"And we, as officers, should have fought against that. If the Germans attacked us, the Americans would have helped us against the Nazis. No one wanted to be under their rule. But because of what we did in San Diego, we're no different from them."

"Whose side are you on?"

"Not yours," Ben said.

"If you came here just to accuse me, stop wasting my time."

"I came here for you."

"What do you mean?" Mutsuraga asked.

"I promised Claire your head."

"What for?"

"For her mother's death."

Mutsuraga gripped the arms of the chair. The veins on his forehead bulged and his eyes tightened into slits. He looked ugly and vicious, impetus clashing against the convoluted mess of revelation. "She hated me that much?"

"No," Ben answered. His vision was blurry and it looked like the general's head was double its size. "She loved you. She couldn't forgive you for what you did, but she couldn't hate you either."

"And that's why you're here for my head instead of taking care of her funeral rites?"

"This is part of her last will."

"Then she really committed suicide?"

"She wanted the Mutsuraga line to end with her. When I tried to convince her not to, she left."

"Why didn't you tell me any of this?" Mutsuraga asked, this time not as a soldier or commanding officer, but as a father.

"What could I have said? Your daughter wants you dead because you executed her mother?"

Mutsuraga paced again. "I've spent the last few months with these Americans. They're a strange breed. They believe in strange things. But I can understand their allure. The world would have been an interesting place if they hadn't lost the war, even if we would have been their slaves. The USJ army has sent an invasion force to attack the GWs. They're on the border of San Diego and they've already started their assault."

Ben remembered Kujira's report earlier. "What's the point?"

"To celebrate the anniversary, show Tokyo they're still in control. But they'll be defeated."

"How?"

"The *USA* game has an open version of the simulator."

"The one we use?"

"A more advanced version. I've helped set up the parameters to predict USJ tactics. Plus someone – I assume you? – set up multiple scenarios on how they could attack the Americans based on strategies we devised long ago as potential threats."

Multiple stages were based on strategic analyses Ben had recorded with Claire that were literally the USJ's worst tactical nightmares. "I updated them with the new defensive grid."

"A damn fine job you did too," Mutsuraga said. "These George Washingtons are going to give the Empire a beating they won't forget."

A group of Americans entered the room.

"George Washington has requested your presence at the front," one stated.

Mutsuraga put his hand on Ben's shoulder. "I tried to have you spared, but these Americans are insistent on their quaint rituals. They're going to baptize you with electricity so at least you won't remember any of this. I'm sorry you weren't able to keep your promise to Claire."

"I'm not dead yet."

Mutsuraga patted Ben on the shoulder. "Goodbye, Ishimura."

Mutsuraga followed the Americans out. Three others brought the electrocution machine and a bowl of water to continue their baptism. Their faces were a nebulous haze and his consciousness was blurring. All that electricity had caused the portical of his brain to break into disparate pieces and he was unable to retain coherent thought.

"Lincoln said to finish him off. Raise the voltage to three thousand."

"I wish barbecued flesh didn't stink so much. My lady won't come within an inch of me until I shower like a hundred times."

"Your girlfriend wouldn't come within an inch of you even if you sho–"

A spray of gunfire ricocheted around Ben and a laser beam melted the face of the American in front of him. The two others began to run, but were shot down.

"I'm sorry it took me so damn long to find you," Akiko said, as she hurried to his aid. Behind her, there were several dead Americans. "The–" She gasped when she saw his blackened flesh. "Our soldiers are attacking San Diego. They nearly shot me."

"They're heading into a trap. We have to get Mutsuraga."

"You're in no condition. The–"

"I have to get him!" Ben cut her off.

"Can you even stand on your feet?"

Akiko loosened Ben's rope. He stumbled to the ground, unable to keep his balance. He tried to rise, but was too weak. His arms and legs were an electrocuted nightmare of ash baked on flesh.

"Give me your arm," Akiko ordered.

"Why?"

"Just give it to me!"

Akiko unlatched the syringe in her pack, searched for a vein on Ben's arm. She injected him with her last capsule of steroidal enhancers. It took a minute before energy swelled through his body. The hurt was muted, suppressed by chemicals that spurred hormonal growth and inhibited the pain receptors.

"Do you have the portical I gave you?" he asked.

Akiko handed it to him. Right as she did, someone fired at them. Both took cover behind the chair, though it didn't provide much protection. Akiko let loose a huge burst from her laser, aiming as best she could. She killed the assailant, but she cringed, her shoulder muscles all tensed up.

Another GW entered and fired. Akiko fired at him, but the pain in her shoulder caused her to shake and miss. Fortunately, the shot hit the ceiling, causing part of it to fall. It provided enough of a reprieve for them to find better cover through a doorway and into a room without a window – a dead end. As soon as they entered, a volley of bullets poured in their direction. Akiko's elbows were bleeding and the gun arm appeared loose, the muscles having torn. She'd been shot on the way in. Ben accessed the portical, trying to recollect the codes for the missiles guarding the building. He wished his brain cells hadn't been addled because he couldn't remember them.

"Ishimura," Akiko called.

"What?"

"You need to help me prop my arm up."

"Why?"

"I think I broke a bone because I can't lift it."

The gun was very heavy and Ben wondered how she had been able to carry it this far. He raised it in the general direction of the GWs and she winced, biting her tongue. A bone cracked and more muscles tore. Akiko ignored the pain and fired. The recoil caused both of them to stumble back. Ben peeked out the door, but couldn't determine how many of them were left. He heard them yelling to each other and presumed they were going to try to flank them. Bullets continued their diatribe. Ben searched the portical again and tracked the missiles he'd seen earlier by manually searching for older kikkai connections, ones that wouldn't show up on automatic searches anymore. He found one with an antiquated designation number, a series of codes he remembered from a decade ago. He was able to disrupt the password easily and take control of the guidance system. There were two automobiles within proximity of Congress leaving at a fast pace. He released the trigger on both, then aimed another missile back at the building, finding the conglomerate of human heat signatures opposite of them. He fired and said to Akiko, "We need to get outside."

"We can't go out that way," she answered, eyeing the hallway.

"Then what should we do?"

Akiko checked the walls.

"Help me set this to maximum," she ordered, looking at a gauge on her gun arm.

Ben helped her turn the dial to the highest setting. They lifted up the gun and shot the wall. Both of them fell back. The blast ripped a hole that gave them access to outside the building, but the recoil had caused Akiko's gun arm to tear off. There was blood everywhere. Akiko growled, trying her best to contain her agony. Ben helped her up and even though she was nauseous, she suppressed her pain. They leaned on each other as they jumped through the new opening. Outside, a fire burned around a destroyed vehicle. There were three bodies crawling out of the flipped car. The second transport was still on its way. Ben checked the portical and saw it had traveled more than five miles. The missile must have missed. The third missile had made impact with the building, causing a small explosion that he hoped would delay reinforcements. Ben sprinted to the three fallen GWs. Two were unconscious but alive. The third, Mutsuraga, was on the ground, trying to crawl away and escape. "Do you have a car?" Ben asked Akiko.

Akiko pointed to an older sedan with a corrugated frame. "Only one I could find that still worked."

"Get it ready," Ben ordered.

"Where are you going?"

"To keep a promise."

Ben approached Mutsuraga. The older man looked up at him.

"Do you remember what you once told me?" Ben asked him. "'The sword is an extension of our soul. Used properly, it becomes a part of who we are, an expression of our being. Kill a man with a gun, and you have no connection to him. Kill him with a sword, and your souls are intertwined.'"

Ben took the sword from Mutsuraga's sheath.

"I don't want there to be souls or an afterlife. I couldn't bear the thought of having to face either of them again, Ishimura," Mutsuraga said pleadingly.

"I don't believe in an afterlife, sir."

"That means I can finally rest."

"Yes, sir."

Mutsuraga closed his eyes. Ben remembered the first time the general had taken notice of him at BEMAG, asking him his interests and praising his programming speed. Mutsuraga had changed his life, and now Ben was ending his. He forced his arms to swing, cutting Mutsuraga's neck. He did not cut at a clean angle, unused to the thickness of flesh and bone. The sword only went halfway through before getting stuck. Blood spilled out of the wound, a viscous overflow that painted his neck vermilion. The general screamed in pain. Ben tried to pull the sword back out, but it was jammed. He had no choice but to push him off using his shoe. Mutsuraga tried to say something, his lips twisting in zigzags. Blood spurted out of his mouth, the skin around his chin doused red. Ben tried to finish him, but his attempts only exacerbated his pain, and blood dripping down the sword smeared his fingers. He pulled the sword back out. "Forgive me, general." He swung again, and this time the head came off the shoulders. Ben picked the head up and shut the eyelids.

Akiko pulled up in the sedan, driving with her single prosthetic arm. The engine had a screech to it and the fumes from the exhaust were egregiously spewing out gray smoke. He hopped into the passenger side and placed Mutsuraga's head in the back.

"Which way?" she asked.

"North. To the security perimeter at the Wall." He checked the portical scanners again. Not only had the vehicle turned around, but four more were heading in their direction. He informed Akiko of the fact.

"Americans?" she asked.

"Most likely. Want me to drive?"

They switched positions and he handed her his portical.

"Do you have a gun? 'Cause I don't have one."

Ben shook his head. "All I have is this sword."

He'd killed in San Diego, but not like this. It'd always been from his desk, checking the tactical simulations, ordering regiments in different directions. The simulation hadn't handled guerilla warfare well, so he was constantly updating the parameters. The deaths he'd caused had been executed by others. His hands were shaking at the wheel and General Wakana's words during San Diego still burned him, even though it'd been a decade. *If you hadn't let Mutsuraga take the credit for your work, he would not be in this position of authority and today's bombing would not have happened.* And San Diego would have been avoided.

"There's all these new heat signatures in the opposite direction," Akiko said, holding up the portical.

Ben took a quick glance. The markings were USJ forces. Behind them, the five tracking vehicles had doubled to ten. Most likely the Imperial forces, spotting all the bogies coming from San Diego, would assume the lead car was a hostile and destroy them, not allowing them to get close enough for a kamikaze strike. Neither the car, nor their military crafts, had open porticals through which he could interface, and he didn't have enough time to break their encryption codes. To go forward was death. To stop meant an even worse end.

"What are you laughing about?" Akiko asked.

Ben hadn't realized he'd been laughing. He sped up.

Akiko leaned back in her seat. "They're going to attack us if we don't slow down.

"It'd be a fine death, wouldn't it? Destroyed by both the Americans and the Empire."

Ahead of them, she saw the outlines of an enormous mecha. Tanks were rolling their way. "I guess it's fitting since we don't belong to either anymore."

"The United States of Tsukino and Ishimura," Ben jested. "Destroyed over a miscommunication."

"You really want to die, don't you?"

"It's the only way to avenge the death of my parents."

"What?"

"Who mourns for them? Not even their own son."

Four tanks were rolling in their direction. The mechas stayed put. The defensive barrier was visible. There were multiple cannons, an array of tanks, a battalion of mechas, and a continual sweep of spotlights. They encompassed the entire zone as far as he could see.

"There has to be a way to let them know who we are," Akiko said.

"There's no external portical access in the wall."

Akiko looked back. The American cars were gaining on them, undeterred by the presence of the USJ forces. Artillery shells began firing from the USJ side. Blasts hit the ground next to them, but missed direct contact. The Americans fired back. One of the bullets shattered their back window and another hit a tire, causing it to deflate and the car to spin sideways to a halt. Ben did his best to swerve and regain control. But the Americans were within proximity. Akiko scrambled to the back seat, saw Mutsuraga's sword, and tried to grab it. Her prosthetic hand could not wield the weapon. Ben put his hand on her shoulder and shook his head. "I'm sorry it had to end this way."

Akiko's eyes squinted. "This-this is it?"

He nodded.

She sat back down, involuntarily tried to move the gun arm that wasn't there. "Despite anything I may have said in the past, it was an honor to serve together," she said.

"Kind of you to say that. The feeling is mutual."

"Are you still scared of me?"

"More than ever."

The American cars caught up to them, and then passed them by, accelerating faster. The tanks continued firing and the mechas were moving into position. Ben, perplexed, looked to Akiko, then back to where the car was aiming. The first of them reached the tank and drove straight into it, both exploding. From the strength of the fire, Ben surmised they were packed with explosives.

"They're heading for the Wall."

"You think they're trying to penetrate the barrier?"

"Maybe," Ben said. His eyes widened. "Or this could be a diversion, a strategy from the simulation."

"What for?"

He recognized it all too well. It was a scenario he'd thought up with Claire, sending as many cars as possible to collide with the Wall and penetrate from a thousand different points. He'd been inspired by the old Battle of Chibi where General Huang Guai took a fleet of ships packed with incendiaries and rammed the opposing fleet to set it on fire. "To distract from wherever the real attack is, which might be here or somewhere else. Depending on our luck, we might temporarily be safe from the Americans."

"Why do you sound so disappointed?"

"I'm not."

"There are easier ways of killing yourself if you're so eager to die."

"I don't want to force things before they're ready."

"Death isn't a date."

"Isn't it? You play for a while, and then," snapping his fingers, "it's the end of the night and you aren't sure if she wants a kiss or you to drop her off and go away."

Ahead of them, all nine automobiles had imploded, destroying several tanks. On the portical, more Americans showed up as blips targeting the barrier. They themselves were too small to be noticed by the USJ forces, but he knew the defenses would eventually scan their car and track two living bodies.

"As soon as they detect us, they're going to shoot us," Ben said.

"We could wait and hope they send out soldiers."

Ben shook his head. "They'll pick us up on their scanners and if we just stay inside, they'll get suspicious and blow us up."

"We could run."

"And go where? Those steroids are wearing out and we don't have any weapons." He looked at her seat, which was stained red. "You've lost a lot of blood."

"I'll live."

"Not for long. You stay put and I'll go try to get some help."

"Where?"

He thought of Claire, Wakana, the older Kujira, and all of his compatriots who'd already died. He was the only one still alive. "The gate. Hopefully they'll do a bioscan and ID me. If they don't, they'll kill me, but there's a tank up there," he said, looking at the burning one the Americans had partially destroyed. "If I can connect my portical directly into the communication system, I might be able to contact USJ officers on the Wall."

"Will that work?"

"I don't know," Ben said. "But there's no better option." He looked over several different scan reports on the portical, having a general idea of what they meant based on the simulation he'd created with Claire years ago. The Americans seemed to be implementing it perfectly. "It looks like the Empire's taking a drubbing. If you tell them everything you did was to capture Mutsuraga and spin it so they can make this seem like a victory, they'll give you a medal for capturing the man who made the *USA* game. Ask them if I can finally get a promotion."

Akiko frowned. "I know it wasn't Mutsuraga who made *USA*."

"What do you mean?"

"I heard you talking to the general."

Ben nearly dropped his portical. "If you knew, why did you save me?"

"I don't know," Akiko answered. "Why did you help make it?"

"I wanted to create a world where San Diego was still as beautiful as I remember it."

"I never saw San Diego before it was destroyed."

"I'm sorry that you didn't," Ben said. "There wasn't any place like it."

"My brother used to tell me the same thing. He loved the idea of America."

"Did he?"

She nodded. "He sent the Americans in Colorado our military secrets. He betrayed us because he admired them so much."

Ben was stunned. "When did you find out?"

"He didn't hide his trail well, so it didn't take me long to figure it out. But even after I knew, I couldn't bring him to justice. He defected, and it would have been over for me and my parents if I didn't stop him. But I still let him go."

"Why?"

"Because he was my brother."

"I thought you said the Americans killed him?"

"They did. On the border. They mistakenly burned him there. Or maybe they didn't trust him to begin with. When my parents found out he was dead, they pretended it didn't happen. I'd go home for the holidays and they'd set up a space at the table, talk about him like he was just away on a mission."

"What about you?"

"I was furious that I let him get to that point. There were so many times I should have stepped in and prevented him from going astray."

"Why didn't you?"

"Because... Because I couldn't deny some of the things he'd discovered about the true nature of the Empire and the things our soldiers had done," Akiko confessed. "Every time I tortured one of our prisoners to death, I was terrified my supervisors were going to figure out I had doubts too. I hated every minute I was with them."

"I-I had no idea."

"Of course you didn't."

There was a loud shriek behind them as another car raced for the wall.

Ben looked at Akiko and asked, "Remember what you said about justice? About making things better?"

"Of course."

"Do you still mean it?"

"I've never wavered."

"Make my sacrifice count."

"But Ishim–"

Ben saluted her, turned around, and walked forward.

"Ishimura! Ishimura!" Akiko yelled.

"Don't worry, I'll be fine," Ben assured her and marched forward, even though he knew he wouldn't be. Under normal circumstances, the guards might scan first. But in battle, they were certain to be trigger happy.

The Americans must have hit them hard as the USJ guards had not spotted him yet. He sprinted towards the tank with broken treads. The turret was on fire, but the outer hull remained intact due to cooling systems that had doused the armoring. He jumped on top, found a panel on the gun, nearly slipped on his feet before getting hold of the canon. He tried to loosen the hatch, but it was burning hot and seared his hands. He blew on his fingers, used his shirt to pull the hatch open. He pulled the wire out of his portical and plugged it directly into the tank's system. His portical displayed an encrypted set of algorithms that he recognized and set off a numerical breaker. He turned to the barrier, hoping someone could hear his call. Most of the entry points were plugged by burning American cars. There was one intact gate with a warning sign prohibiting non-authorized personnel that was otherwise nondescript. He wondered what was inside. The tank was getting too hot so he got off the hull, the wire of his portical extending until it reached its limit.

That's when a mecha focused its aim on him. Spotlights shone his way. Ben triggered an emergency SOS in the portical and yelled into the portical's microphone, "I'm a captain in the USJ! My name is Beniko Ishimura and we have General Mutsuraga's head. We have vital information about the Americans. My partner, Agent Akiko Tsukino, is wounded and we need emergency assis–" He felt a burst of heat perforating his chest, a bright light coming from the mecha. Memories popped up like fireflies and he thought of nights cavorting in San Diego, the tawny sunsets along La Jolla. He recalled all the times he'd talked with Claire about portical games like the ones he'd played as a child and the one he'd always hoped to make, creating a USA that still represented its old values. He was happy to know people were playing it, especially what remained of the Americans. His chest had split open, his legs were crumbling, and his neck felt as if it was boiling. He recalled the day his father and mother called him in to tell –

– his corpse crumbled to the ground. A minute later, kamikaze American cars drove over where he'd died, covering his remains. There were four dozen in all, the American dream shooting straight for the impregnable Imperial walls, ready to sacrifice everything for the possibility of change. The automobiles exploded in a conflagration that destroyed the previously untouched gate. Neither the Americans nor Beniko Ishimura found out what was inside. But it was only a matter of time and lives before others would.

North of San Diego
July 5, 1988
5:23am

A song she didn't recognize called to Akiko. She was dreaming of the end of the world. Memories haemorrhaged out in one hungry swoop and the nerves swerved erratically in her subconscious consciousness. Time was a type of gangrene, rotting away her convictions. "It's fortunate one of our operators noticed the communication from your partner. We weren't able to save him, but you're going to be OK, major," someone said.

She saw a world molded from molten wax. Everyone ate insects and dyed poison for breakfast. An American flag was waving. There were sixteen strangers claiming to be president. A migrant carpet of pollution was blocking her view. All the poets were kleptomaniacs. Convictions were a revolving Petri dish. The planet was getting warmer even though everyone denied the hurricanes their potency. Historians and bored amateurs erased history, said her Empire was forced into a war they did not want to fight, that all its victories were exaggerated propaganda and that millions were not killed in their march to glory. She wanted to weep, seeing the Empire she loved unable to control its own fate, the lethality of its own past defanged in misdirected shame.

"The GWs infiltrated Los Angeles and set off bombs at five of our installations along with three civilian targets," she heard. "The casualties are in the thousands and we still have no idea how many more bombs there are. There's an enforced news blackout. The prince has already flown back to Tokyo along with our visitors from Tokyo Command. They're very displeased. Governor Ogasawara wants immediate results."

Akiko's vision was getting blurry. She longed for miniverses created from hydrogenated molecules and defunct chemical compounds. Insecticide warped all their minds into electrified modules and shaped their lives into honeycombs of ignorance. Hexagonal bliss had its advantages and peace had plenty of disadvantages, drowning itself in interminable entertainment. The important stakes were forgotten. Nations warred over anthills and pride. There was no mountains of the dead. Only billions of voices, each fanatically demanding to be heard even if it resulted in sensory indifference.

"Can she hear me?"

"She's under heavy anesthetics, but she should be able to."

"Major Tsukino. Major Tsukino!"

Akiko looked up and saw several high ranking officers watching her. They were all ten feet tall and wearing samurai armor. Was this her universe again?

"You've performed a great service for the Empire, bringing back General Mutsuraga's head. Our medics say you'll be OK and they'll have you on your feet in a few days. You should be proud. You're a hero to the United States of–"

She closed her eyes and focused on the music. An unknown violinist was playing an American song she'd once heard before, full of the virulent gleam of hope. It was beautiful. Akiko wept.

TWENTY-EIGHT YEARS AGO

Los Angeles
July 6, 1960
4:12pm

Ezekiel Ishimura was fuming. He worked as a technician, converting old sonar panels into war game consoles. He'd been assigned a tank incursion from the Battle of Imphal in India, but he couldn't get the commands to work properly. A hundred other technicians sat in the same big hall, desks arrayed in ten straight rows of ten workers. The high ceilings and concrete floor made the temperature inside either too hot or too cold. The summer sun made it feel like an oven. His hands felt clunky and the sweat on his fingers made precise motions difficult. He wished his son, Ben, was here to help him figure out the bugs. Even at his young age, he had an intuitive knack for figuring out coding logic. A noisy commotion disturbed his train of thought. Four soldiers in uniform were marching towards him. Ezekiel's hands froze and he wondered what he'd done wrong. They stopped in front of him, turned right, and grabbed his neighbor, a man named Tenzo. Tenzo began to protest, yelling, "I'm innocent. I didn't do anything wrong!"

They put a bag around his head, handcuffed him, and punched him in the stomach, warning him, "If you don't keep quiet, it'll be worse for your family."

They dragged him out. Everyone went back to their tasks as though nothing had happened. Twenty minutes later, another technician was brought in to take Tenzo's old station. Ezekiel's hands were quivering, unable to connect the wires properly. His arm hurt from the increased typing he'd been doing of late, which had forced him to type only with his index fingers. But that increased the number of errors he made and irritated his supervisor, Mogi-san. Mogi-san summoned him for a meeting before the end of the day.

His supervisor was a scurrilous man who found fault with everyone. Considering he was more afraid for his job than anyone else, Ezekiel almost couldn't blame him. "This is the fourth late tank report you've sent," Mogi-san coolly noted.

Ezekiel bowed and apologized. "Forgive me."

"The first three times, I was willing to overlook it. But the fourth time? My superiors would think me negligent. I've given you a fair shake considering your mixed ethnicity and your family connections with known traitors."

"I'm extremely grateful," Ezekiel said, hating the reminder about his uncle, who had been executed for insurrection almost a decade ago.

"Are you? I've heard reports from some of your colleagues that you're discontented, that you've complained you miss American rule and the way things used to be."

"Never, never," Ezekiel emphatically declared. "I don't miss their rule at all. I was imprisoned by them. I am eternally grateful to the Emperor for saving us."

"That's why I disregarded the rumors. But there may be others who aren't so trusting."

"What do you mean?"

"Your outward incompetence in conjunction with these

rumors and questionable past has brought you to the attention of the Tokko. They came by earlier to ask questions. Do you know what that means?"

"No. Wh-what does that mean?"

"Go home and take care of business."

Ezekiel's eyes widened. "Are you... Are you telling me..."

Mogi-san nodded, either in apathy or restrained sympathy. "It will most likely be tomorrow morning."

"B-but I didn't do anything wrong."

"You can explain it to them tomorrow, or take care of matters tonight."

"My family too?"

"You know how it is. Make your last minutes count."

Ezekiel rushed out of the building, grabbed a bus, and spent the whole trip thinking about Ruth and little Beniko. The roads were congested and many of the streets were blocked because of the new subway construction. One of the alternate routes they were forced to take went beside a square where a family was publicly executed for treason. The transition from the dollar to the yen had been harsh, and most of the old Americans still had a hard time adjusting to their new economic devaluation, meaning dissidence had been increasing. The USJ was doing its best to quell discontent with these public punishments.

By the time he arrived home at their one-bedroom apartment, Ruth was cooking rice porridge using the cheap millet they'd stocked up on. They had no meat since they could only afford it once a week (and there was usually more fat than meat on the pork). She had been able to use the scraps from the tomato they'd cooked the previous night to add a touch of flavor. She looked skinnier than a month ago and there were dark hollows on her face from being unable to sleep. Just outside were train tracks and one was going by, causing the whole building to shake as it blared its horn.

He clinched her tightly. "We're in trouble."

"What happened?" Ruth asked.

"They're coming for us."

"Who?"

"The Tokko," Ezekiel replied.

"What for?"

"I don't know. It could be a hundred things. Or it could be none of them."

"Did you say anything?"

Just a week ago, he'd been talking to Tenzo, his neighbor at work who had been arrested. Tenzo complained about their Japanese overlords, how few opportunities they gave other than to their lackeys and how the economy was in a complete rut. Ezekiel had tried to calm his office mate, urging him to "be discreet and not complain too much. At least we're alive." Tenzo didn't care, vocal in his malcontent to the point where a few coworkers had noticed their exchange.

"What will the Tokko do?" Ruth asked.

"Tenzo and his family are most likely being tortured right now."

"That means–"

"The same thing will happen to us."

Ruth shook her head. "They might just question you. The–"

"Mogi-san more or less told me to settle matters tonight."

"Settle matters?"

Ezekiel's eyes went to his feet and he could not look Ruth in the eyes. The door unlocked and their eleven year-old son, Ben, arrived from a day at school. He was carrying a broken portical.

Ezekiel didn't know what to do, couldn't imagine the soldiers putting their hands on him. But Ruth was more clearheaded and went to Ben, holding both his arms. She knew lies to soothe him would be a travesty at this critical juncture.

"USJ officers are coming to arrest me and your father," she informed Ben.

"Why?"

"They think we're traitors."

"Tell them you're not."

"They wouldn't believe me." Ruth stared at Ben for a long time. "My parents died when I was young and I hoped for a different life for you, that we would be there to take care of you. I'm sorry for what we're about to ask you to do."

"What?"

She looked at Ezekiel, then said to Ben, "Go to the police station and ask for Detective Mifune. Report us to the authorities."

"What are you doing?" Ezekiel asked.

"It's the only way he'll survive."

"But you're asking him–"

"I know what I'm asking," Ruth replied. "But if he doesn't, he'll be killed with us." She looked back at Ben. "Tell them you heard us talking against the Empire while you were eating."

"Tell them your mother opposed, but I stubbornly insisted," Ezekiel added.

"Ezekiel…" Ruth began.

"You might still have a chance," Ezekiel said to Ruth.

"It's both of us or they won't believe it," Ruth said, knowing that she too had said her share of criticisms about the Empire. She took a deep breath and looked at her son again. "Ben. I want you to slap me."

"Mom."

"Slap me."

When Ben hesitated, Ruth slapped Ben in the face. "Slap me."

"Bu–"

Ruth slapped him again. "Hit me!"

"D–"

"HIT ME!"

Ben complied, but it was a soft blow.

"Harder."

"I don't want to."

"HIT ME HARDER!"

"Mom."

"HARDER!"

Ben punched his mother.

"Now curse us," Ruth ordered.

"I can't."

"Call me a traitor! Call me a coward."

"Mom!"

"This is the only way you can survive. Otherwise, they'll kill you too."

"But–"

"If you don't do what I say, they'll kill you."

"Then I don't want to live."

"You want our deaths to mean nothing?" Ruth asked. "Please, Ben, do it for us."

"Ruth," Ezekiel called. "You know what this means for him."

"Life," Ruth replied. "Survival."

"Why do I have to survive? I hate this world, hate everything about it," Ben said. "I'll kill everyone in the Empire! I'll make them pay!"

"No!" Ruth shouted. "Then you'll be no better than them."

"They're evil!"

"There's no ideology, only people. And there are many good people in the USJ, even if there are many bad ones too." She got wistful. "There used to be a place called America people could believe in, a land of freedom. The physical place died, but the dream lives. Give the USJ a dream to believe in."

"How? What am I supposed to do without you?"

"You'll find a way," she said, then stared at the portical he was holding. "You handle these better than your father."

"They're just games."

"Maybe. But they can be so much more if you can find a way," Ruth replied. "Join the ranks, become an officer. Maybe one day they'll call you *Major* Ishimura. But you have to be strong. Do you hear me?"

"No, I don't. I- I can't do this," Ben said. "How could I ever join the military? They'd never accept me. They... They..."

Ezekiel held his son. Ruth embraced them. She was weeping.

Ezekiel kissed his son on the forehead.

"Dad–"

"Go before it's too late."

"But–"

"Go now!" Ezekiel ordered.

Ben shook his head and was crying. "I'd rather die!"

Ruth put her arms around her son, patted his head, and said, "You're the bravest boy I know." She wiped his tears away. "Live your life so that our sacrifice has meaning. Go quickly, Beniko." She pushed him away and, when he tried to hold her again, she sternly refused. "Did you hear what I said? Go now!"

"But Mom–"

"I'm no longer your mother. He's no longer your father. We are enemies of the Empire. Do you understand?"

"No. I don't understand at all!"

She went to the bedroom and returned with a pistol, a Nambu Type 18 semi-automatic pistol. She pointed at her son. "Go now."

"But–"

"Go now or I will kill you, because that'll be a better fate than if you stay here!"

She pushed Ben out of the apartment and locked the door behind him. He knocked several times, but they ignored him. He eventually ran away. She put her fingers on the door and muttered, "Sayonara," doing her best to hold back bitter tears.

"He'll be fine," Ezekiel said. "Ishimuras are strong. You know that."

"I hope so…"

"I-I should never have let you marry me. I'm sorry."

"What are you talking about?"

"My past, my whole life, has been nothing but a burden to you. I've caused you nothing but misery."

"Don't talk like that. We did the best with what we could."

"Did we really?"

"Yes. Don't be weak right now."

"Do you regret marrying a traitor?"

"You're not a traitor."

"I've betrayed the whole world for you," Ezekiel replied.

"So have I." She blinked back tears. "How long before they come?"

"I don't know."

"In the next life, let's switch places," Ruth said. "I'll be the man."

"You sure you'll still have eyes for me?"

Ruth put her hands on his cheeks. "Always."

"I love you," Ezekiel said to her.

"How much?"

He'd already used the stars in the universe and the sand in the ocean countless times. "As many as the number of hairs on my head."

"You don't have that much hair," she said.

They both laughed and held each other for another minute before walking into the bathroom. Ruth held the pistol. "Remember this?"

"Is it the same one?"

She shook her head. "Same model. Something poetic about using this gun."

"Like a haiku."

"I've never been good at haikus."

"Me neither," Ruth confessed.

Ezekiel got nervous and said in a panic, "I never thought it would be like this. I always thought things would get better, that it would improve and–"

"Shh. Don't be afraid," Ruth said. "It'll be over soon."

Another train began to go by. Two gunshots marked the end, but no one heard them.

ACKNOWLEDGMENTS

United States of Japan wouldn't exist without some wonderful people. Obviously, the first person I want to thank is Philip K Dick who inspired me a great deal growing up, especially through *The Man in the High Castle*. Even though we're very different writers, he's had a huge influence on me and helped me to view the world in a completely unique light.

I wanted to make sure to get the facts right, as the history and tragedy of all those who suffered during the events of WWII were always on my mind. I want to give credit to some of the many books I looked to for research and information, including, but not limited to: *The Rising Sun* by John Toland, *Japan's Imperial Army* by Edward Drea, *A Modern History of Japan* by Andrew Gordon, *Taiko* by Eiji Yoshikawa, *Inside the Third Reich* by Albert Speer, *Hirohito and the Making of Modern Japan* by Herbert Bix, *Japanese Cruisers of the Pacific War* by Eric Lacroix and Linton Wells II, *The Shifting Realities of Philip K Dick* by PKD (which has some of the ideas he had for a *Man in the High Castle* sequel), *The Rise and Fall of the Third Reich* by William L Shirer, *A Book of Five Rings* by Miyamoto Musashi, *Return to the Philippines* by Rafael Steinberg, *Japan at War: An Oral History* by Haruko Taya Cook & Theodore F Cook, *Shogun* by James Clavell, *The Rape of Nanking* by Iris Chang, *The Moon is Down* by John Steinbeck, and so many more, not to mention countless articles, films, and documentaries, which were invaluable for me to better understand the times.

Japanese culture has always been a huge influence and artists/writers/designers like Hayao Miyazaki, Hideo Kojima, Yukio Mishima, Yukito Kishiro, Mamoru Oshii, Hideaki Anno, Kinji Fukasaku, Rieko Kodama, Hironobu Sakaguchi, Akira Kurosawa, and Katsuhiro Otomo were people whose works I revered growing up. I highly recommend a trip to the San Jose Japanese American Museum, especially their guided tours. That trip ended up shocking me to the core and informing a key part of the book. I wanted to thank Ken Liu for writing *The Man Who Ended History: A Documentary*. When I finished my first draft of *USJ*, I was very scared because of the material it covered and I found a lot of courage reading Ken's superb novella.

Big thanks to the very talented John Liberto for painting the cover of *USJ* as well as the incredible concept art he did for the book. I am in awe of his genius and am still so honored that he made time to paint the cover! Thank you to my friend, Geoff Hemphill, for introducing me to John, as well always being so encouraging through the tough times. You're one of my closest friends and I am always grateful to you for your witty insight and honesty. A deep expression of gratitude for Sam Boettner, aka Chang Yune, for all the fantastic questions and enthusiasm for the project, as well as some really great fan art. Bonny John, your depiction of biomorphs still gives me chills. Richard Thomas, thank you for being one of the first readers, as well as for all your wonderful advice in crafting the world of *USJ*. James Chiang, one day we'll get to *Dr 2*, but in the meantime, I wanted to thank you for your wisdom, patience, and your friendship. Many of the things I researched about Japan started with our graphic novel and I can't wait to finish it with you. And, of course, I always thank God.

Judy Hansen! You're my dream agent and I'm so lucky

you represent me! Thank you for always fielding my stream of questions and for your guidance through the publishing world.

Big thanks to the love of my life, Angela Xu, without whom I wouldn't be half the writer I am. I bounce all my ideas off her, constantly ask her about everything, and field her for suggestions when I'm stuck in my stories. She watches all the movies with me, plays games that I look to for inspiration, and is the best friend I could ever have. Thank you for everything.

The crew at Angry Robot are so amazing and I am so grateful to them for taking a chance on this novel and believing in it every step of the way. They are literally my dream publisher and working with them has been a dream come true. Thank you, Penny Reeves, for being the most amazing publicity manager and just an incredible person. Chances are, if you've heard about *USJ* in a media outlet, it's thanks to her efforts. I'm a big fan of Mike Underwood's writing and it was so incredible always being able to lean on him for advice on pretty much everything. If you like the cover of *United States of Japan*, thank Marc Gascoigne for his brilliant cover art direction and just being a kick-ass publisher. Paul Simpson did a fantastic job with the copy editing, poring over every line and making sure everything was technically sound. Amanda Rutter and Trish Byrne caught all the little things that slipped through the cracks and were wonderful proofreaders.

I have to thank my editor, Phil Jourdan, to whom this book is dedicated. Thank you for believing in me, for seeing things in the book even I didn't see, and for giving me the opportunity to share my strange stories. You're one of the best editors around and it's been my privilege to work with you.

If I thanked everyone who's been supportive of *USJ* from its announcement to its release, I think I would literally have to name everyone I know. Thank you everyone for your generosity, your kind words, and your faith in the project.

ABOUT THE AUTHOR

Peter Tieryas is a character artist who has worked on films like *Guardians of the Galaxy, Alice in Wonderland* and *Cloudy With a Chance of Meatballs 2*. His novel, *Bald New World*, was listed as one of Buzzfeed's 15 Highly Anticipated Books as well as Publishers Weekly's Best Science Fiction Books of Summer 2014.

tieryas.wordpress.com • twitter.com/TieryasXu

WESLEY CHU

TIME
SALVAGER

"A time-twisting action adventure as only Wesley Chu could imagine it. Read this book!"
Ann Leckie, author of the Hugo and Nebula Award-winning **Ancillary Justice**

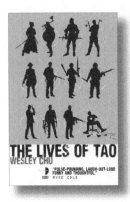

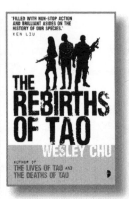

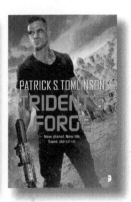

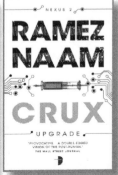

JOIN US

angryrobotbooks.com

twitter.com/angryrobotbooks